Natasha Cooper was Chairman of the Crime Writer's Association in 2000/2001. She reviews books in *The Times*, *The Times Literary Supplement* and the *New Law Journal*. She is the author of, among many others, *Creeping Ivy*, *Fault Lines* and *Prey To All*.

OUT OF THE DARK

An eight-year-old boy comes running out of the dark to find barrister Trish Maguire one wet Sunday night. Just before he can get to her, he's knocked over by a skidding car. Fighting to save his life, the casualty team find Trish's name and address sewn into his clothes. The police are convinced that he looks like her and must be her son. Only Trish knows he can't be. Her search for his identity takes her to a brutal inner-city housing estate, where she has to confront not only the reality of life for people whose Giros cannot be made to last the week, but also many of her own fears . . .

Books by Natasha Cooper
Published by The House of Ulverscroft:

NATASHA COOPER

OUT OF
THE DARK

Complete and Unabridged

ULVERSCROFT
Leicester

First published in Great Britain in 2002 by
Simon & Schuster UK Limited
London

First Large Print Edition
published 2003
by arrangement with
Simon & Schuster UK Limited
London

British Library CIP Data

Cooper, Natasha, *1951 –*
    Out of the dark.—Large print ed.—
    Ulverscroft large print series: adventure & suspense
    1. Maguire, Trish (Fictitious character)—Fiction
    2. Women lawyers—England—London—Fiction
    3. Detective and mystery stories
    4. Large type books I. Title
    823.9'14 [F]

    ISBN 0–7089–4840–5

Published by
F. A. Thorpe (Publishing)
Anstey, Leicestershire

Set by Words & Graphics Ltd.
Anstey, Leicestershire
Printed and bound in Great Britain by
T. J. International Ltd., Padstow, Cornwall

This book is printed on acid-free paper

For
Jonathan and Teresa Sumption

Acknowledgements

Any novelist moving into strange worlds (like the City or the Bar) needs a guide. I have been lucky enough to have had the help of many. Among them are Suzanne Baboneau, Mary Carter, Sally Field, Jane Gregory, Peter Krijgsman, Lisanne Radice, Jonathan Sumption and Sheila Turner. I am immensely grateful to them all. Matters of fact have sometimes had to yield to the demands of fiction, and none of my guides should be blamed for any of my diversions from strict accuracy. This is fiction and nothing in it should be taken as any reflection on any real people, institutions or financial products. There is no Mull Estate in Southwark, and I am assured that there is not enough 'European Junk' for the kind of bond I have imagined.

Natasha Cooper

He that wants money, means, and content is without three good friends.

Shakespeare *As You Like It*

Prologue

DC Martin Waylant pulled the door shut and let his head rest against the window. It wasn't a squad car, but his own 1966 Citroën DS. It smelled of the yielding leather seats and a faint hint of fuel, and it was the thing he loved most in the world. He let himself think about the hydraulic suspension and calculated how soon he'd have to top up the fluid.

He was having difficulty getting new side panels. Rust had begun to eat into the original ones like fire into a worm-eaten old plank and he'd have to replace them soon. There'd been a suggestion on his favourite website that some might be coming available. He'd go on the Net again next weekend and see if he couldn't track them down.

Opening his eyes, he could still see the light from her flat. He wasn't sure if he could really hear the achingly naggy music she liked or whether he was just imagining it. He stuffed a heavy metal cassette into the player and turned up the volume until the beat drowned out her dismal Elizabethan songs.

There were plenty of words for what was going on in his head and making him want to

1

puke or hit someone, but words were what *she* used and feelings were what *she* had and he wasn't having any of them now.

He'd once read a story about 'Red Indian squaws' in the seventeenth century, and he couldn't get it out of his mind now. The squaws had made needles out of thorns and sewn thin leather strips into the flesh of captured English explorers before ripping them out, leaving raw, bleeding patches in their prisoners' chests and arms and legs and worse. He rubbed his hand over his own chest, hating her.

The whole mess had started because he'd felt protective, and when he'd got to know her and the boy, he'd pitied her. Then, one Saturday afternoon when David was playing football with his mates, she'd taken him to bed and he'd discovered what a fantastic fuck she could be.

She might have been fifteen years older than him, but when she'd taken her kit off and let him rest between her soft lush breasts and shown him what sex could be like and let him do anything he wanted, he'd known what heaven was. He'd have done anything for her. Only then she'd let words in there, too, telling him her sad story and analysing everything, explaining all her feelings — and his — until he wanted to put a pillow over her head. He'd started to feel those needles digging into his chest when he'd tried to move away. She'd clung and wept and talked and talked. And she hadn't understood a thing. Then one day, when he'd flagged halfway through, she'd been kind and understanding. He might've been able to stomach that, if she hadn't talked on and sodding *on* about erectile dysfunction and how it didn't matter or make him less of a man.

With the beat in his ears and hate in his mouth, like sick after a night out drinking, he leaned forwards until his hot forehead rested against the steering wheel. He concentrated on its shape, the one spoke, the amazing curve, the way it moved under his hands as he drove the engine to its best performance on hard, twisting roads, until he'd forgotten the taste of hate and the feel of her breasts against his face.

Soon he'd have to decide what to do, how to get out of it all without anyone finding out he'd been bonking her. But not yet. Let him have the music and the feel of the car and no ideas or fucking words for a bit longer.

1

'I *didn't* kill him.'

This was the twelfth time Trish had said it that night, lying huddled under an old tartan rug on one of the sofas opposite her empty fireplace. Unlike everything else in the huge, sleek flat, the shabby rug had been part of her childhood. She hadn't used it for years, but tonight she'd hoped the familiar smell and reassuring roughness of the Shetland wool would take her back to a more innocent world.

She'd hardly known she was pregnant long enough for much more than one violent burst of impatience. Not now, for God's sake! I'm busy, she'd thought. But that had been enough. She'd miscarried the next day. The physical pain was over now, but her mind still felt raw.

Experienced advocate that she was, she could find all sorts of arguments in mitigation. The phone call confirming the result she'd already got from her pregnancy-testing kit had come to chambers at a particularly bad moment. All morning she'd been trying to concentrate on a fiendishly complicated piece of mathematical evidence in a fraud case. For years she'd specialised in family law, submerging herself in the agonising detail of brutalised childhoods and unhappy marriages, and now she wanted out. With this new brief she'd have a chance to prove that she could hack it in a wider, much less personal, world.

But the evidence was even more complicated than she'd expected, and that morning she'd begun to doubt that she would ever get to grips with it. Her head had been aching, her eyes dry and burning hot, and she'd felt sick and stupid. Already there had been six interruptions and each time she'd had to go back to the beginning of the file. Then had come the seventh interruption and the news that she was pregnant. The case was due to start in four weeks' time and was likely to last for months. She'd never be able to cope unless she were on top form throughout. Pregnancy would have screwed everything up completely.

'But I didn't kill him,' she said aloud to the empty spaces all round her.

If only she could pretend the whole miserable episode had been a medical mishap, nothing to do with a real child. But all she could think of now was the person the child might have become.

She and George hadn't been actively trying for a baby, although they'd agreed that she should come off the pill ages ago. In fact, it was so long ago that she'd almost forgotten about it. They were nearly always too tired to make love anyway. But there had been one night, soon after his father had died nine weeks ago, when tiredness hadn't seemed important any more. Trish still had no idea whether George had had some kind of subconscious urge to create a new life to compensate for the old; all she'd been thinking about was how to stop him hurting.

Now he was in San Francisco, unaware of the disaster as he tried to help his mother through her first weeks of loneliness by fulfilling her lifetime's dream of seeing the city. He'd been reluctant to leave London just then, but the trip had been the only thing either he or Trish had been able to think of that might help. His emails had already told her that he wasn't sure he was doing any good. In the last one he had written:

Talking seems very difficult for her and I've got no idea what she's thinking. That may be my fault or it may just be that we don't know each other very well. I realise I've hardly spent any time alone

with her since I was eight and went away
to school.

Would he have to know about the
miscarriage, too, Trish wondered. On top of
everything else? Should she tell him about the
one, never-to-be-forgotten moment when
fury had convulsed her whole body and their
child had died? Trying to decide whether to
confess adultery must be a bit like this. Only
not quite so hard.

The gibbous moon blurred against the
black sky outside her windows. There hadn't
been a single occasion since she'd met
George when she'd been even tempted by the
idea of infidelity. Not that they were married.
They didn't even live together, although they
had each other's keys and the freedom to let
themselves in whenever they wanted, but they
were absolutely committed to each other.

A shrieking squeal of rubber ripped into
Trish's thoughts. Then a bang, shocking as an
explosion, forced her to her feet. Showers of
broken glass rang against metal and concrete.
Running feet squelched in the rain.

'Oh, Christ! No. No!' cried a woman's
voice as Trish moved towards the windows.
'Can you hear me? Can you hear me? Oh,
help. Please help!'

Trish dragged open one of the five huge

windows. Despite her slenderness, she was wirily strong, but now all her joints ached with the effort of holding in her feelings and every movement was laborious.

'Can I do anything?' she called down, only just stopping herself from the silliness of asking if everything was all right. It obviously wasn't.

A woman was beating her fists on the crumpled bonnet of a long white hatchback. Yellow light from the streetlamps caught in the drops of rain falling from her dark hair. She turned to look up towards the sound of Trish's voice.

'There's a child. I didn't see him in time. I couldn't help it. But I think he's dead.'

Oh, God. 'I'll come down. Are you hurt, too?'

'No. But he's under the car. That's why I skidded. I saw him in the headlights. I can't get him to answer. He must be dead. But I wasn't going fast.'

'I'll phone for an ambulance. Hang on.'

Trish punched 999 into the mobile handset of her phone. She tucked it between her ear and shoulder while she grabbed a long coat to pull over the outsize T-shirt she'd put on after her shower, then picked up her keys in case the door blew shut behind her. She didn't want to be locked out on a night like this. Her narrow feet were bare, so she stuffed them into a pair of gumboots and clumped down the iron staircase to the street. Ambulance control answered as she reached the ground. She gave them the bare facts, relieved that she had a human being on the line and not an answering machine.

'We'll be there in about eight minutes,' the voice assured her. 'Don't touch the child.'

'Of course not,' she said, shoving the handset in her pocket with the keys and wading across the road in her loose boots. Her bare skin rubbed against the fabric lining and she kept stubbing her toes as her feet moved faster than the boots.

The driver's face was pale grey and her hair was draggled across her thin cheeks. Her mascara had run and she'd chewed off most of her lipstick. She was shaking.

'You poor thing,' Trish said in the professionally soothing voice she used for frightened clients. 'Are you hurt?'

'No. I told you. It's him. He's bleeding and hasn't moved. He won't answer me.' Retching, she grabbed Trish's arm, but she didn't throw up. 'I couldn't help it. He ran under the wheels. I couldn't help it.'

Trish freed herself to look, quickly straightening up again after one gut-punching glimpse of the small body.

10

'If he's bleeding that much he's not likely to be dead.'

They hadn't shown her the foetus in hospital, but her imagination had given her plenty of pictures to work on. She tried to think of something else.

'I'm a fool, I should have brought an umbrella. You'll be soaked. You haven't even got a coat.'

'It doesn't matter.' A train rattled over the railway bridge two streets away, and the woman flinched. 'Where's the ambulance? Even if he isn't dead yet, he will be soon if they don't come.'

'They're coming now,' Trish said, shocked to hear her own voice shaking. 'Listen.'

A siren was whooping in the wet air. The faint sound intensified until the familiar boxy white shape of the ambulance itself emerged from the gloom at the end of the road. Two minutes later the paramedics in green overalls jumped down, asking questions even before their feet had hit the ground.

Trish left the driver to answer them, and forced herself to squat down again to see whether there was any movement from the child. The surprisingly sharp edge of the gumboots cut into her bare calves, and her coat trailed in the wet road. She bunched the skirts up around her knees and bent down to

11

peer under the car. There wasn't much light, but she could see that the child was not pinned against the wall; he'd slipped into the road, and one of his legs was bent at an impossible angle. The pool of blood was spreading steadily.

She felt a hand on her shoulder and heard a voice urging her out of the way. Standing up, she swayed. Her hands reached out for something to hold her up and met the slippery, wet metal of the car's roof. Waves of dizziness intensified then gradually sank back. At last she could stand unsupported.

'Were you driving?' asked the second paramedic while the first lay prone on the wet road, shining a torch under the chassis.

'No. I wasn't even in the car.' Trish pointed to the open window at the top of her building. 'I live up there. I heard the crash, phoned you and came out to see what I could do. That's the driver. I think she's badly, shocked.'

'Probably. We'll get to her in a minute. How is he, Sean?'

'Alive. Broken leg. Multiple cuts and abrasions,' came a muffled voice from under the car. The paramedic inched back into the street and stood up. 'Can't see what else. We'll have to get this car moved.'

Another siren heralded the arrival of the

police. The first paramedic nodded to the two officers who emerged from their small white car. 'I think it's drivable. Shirl, you'd better reverse it. Not far, mind.'

'Hold on a minute,' said one of the uniformed police officers. 'What's going on here?'

A quick explanation had him taking the driver by one arm and moving her to the shelter of Trish's building, while Shirley clambered over the gear lever into the driver's seat of the crumpled car, fiddled with the mirror, then inched the car back from the blank wall opposite.

'Bit further,' called Sean, holding out his right hand, palm down. Then he whipped it up, yelling, 'OK. Stop. Stop!'

'Who are you?'

At the sound of the policeman's voice, Trish looked quickly away from the body, lying in a heap at the foot of the wall. With the car out of the way, there had been plenty of light to show her the astonishingly bright redness of the blood.

'My name's Maguire. I didn't see anything,' she said over her shoulder as she forced herself across the road to make sure no more harm was done to the child.

After a moment, the paramedic fetched a neck collar. He seemed careful — and skilful

— as he moved around the boy and fitted the collar, before dealing with the terrifying pumping injury in his leg. Trish relaxed a little as the bleeding turned sluggish and then stopped, but when she saw Sean open his medical kit again, she touched his shoulder.

'Dowting's Hospital is so close,' she said, fighting to keep all judgment out of her tense voice. 'Mightn't it be worth taking him straight there? In all this rain, I mean.'

She'd read about the damage that could be done to trauma victims by invasive treatment at the roadside. The paramedic didn't protest, but she thought he looked reluctant as he clicked down the lid of his rigid box of supplies. He called his colleague, who had been talking to the driver and her attendant police officer. Together they got the child on to a stretcher and into the ambulance.

'Now, I'd just like you to blow into this bag,' said a voice behind Trish. She turned at once, and saw the driver weeping in front of a burly police officer.

'Look,' Trish said, conscious of the driver's sweat and tears and the tremors that kept shaking her body, 'she's in shock and she may well have whiplash injuries. She should be taken to hospital, not interrogated in the road.'

She felt the woman's wet, icy hand

14

gripping her wrist.

'Don't leave me alone with them.'

'What's your connection with each other?' asked the big officer.

'We've never met,' Trish said brusquely. She did not want to get involved. 'But I live here and I heard the crash. I was the only person who even looked out.'

'I'm not surprised, in a neighbourhood like this.'

Trish was outraged. Parts of Southwark might be among the most deprived in the city, but lots of the old disused light-industrial buildings were being turned into lofts like hers or taken over by architects and designers. And just across Southwark Street, near Tate Modern and the river, there were flats that cost a fortune.

'After what I've seen at the nick every Saturday night, I wouldn't want to be out alone on the streets round here after dark,' he said.

Trish thought of all the evenings when she'd walked back from work over Blackfriars Bridge or picked her way home through the dark streets from the expensive parking space she rented under the furthest of the railway arches. She'd never been molested in all the years she'd lived here, and she'd never been afraid of the area or of anyone else who belonged in it. George didn't like it, of course. He much preferred the cosy, domesticated streets of Fulham, but they made Trish feel like an eagle crammed into a budgie's cage.

The thinner officer was demanding the driver's documents. She looked terrified now, as well as shivering and ill, and hardly seemed to understand what he wanted.

'Oh, come on,' Trish said, impatience adding a rasp to her voice. 'You know perfectly well that hardly anyone carries insurance details, or even a driving licence. The law requires a driver to present her documents to a police station within seven days of being asked to do so. She's got plenty of time. You have breathalysed her and found her clear of alcohol. She can't have been driving anywhere near the speed limit or there would have been a lot more damage to the car as well as the child. You haven't any reason to detain or bully her like this. And she should be in hospital.'

The officer's face looked as though all the life had been washed out of it. Trish knew she'd blown her cover and could have sworn in irritation. She'd been so careful to avoid telling these two that she was a barrister, knowing how much most of them loathed 'briefs' for the way they were assumed to use legal technicalities to protect the guilty.

'I wouldn't dream of trying to bully anyone, Ms . . . What's your name?'

'Maguire. I told you that before. Trish Maguire.'

'OK.' He turned back to the driver to give her instructions about taking her documents to the police station, before reminding her that they had her name and address and would be contacting her when a decision had been taken on whether to charge her. He hoped for her sake that the victim survived. Penalties for killing by means of dangerous driving were increasing with every case. Then he and his colleague exchanged glances and moved towards their car.

'Are you just going to leave her here?' Trish demanded, following them.

It appeared they were. They were not going to arrest her at this moment. Her smashed car was not causing an obstruction, and the wall had not been damaged. In due course, after their investigation was finished, she would be able to get the car towed to a garage. She wasn't injured. She wasn't their responsibility.

'But she needs medical care.'

'There's no sign of injury. If you think she should be in hospital, I'm sure you can make the arrangements for her.'

Trish wished she'd kept her mouth shut. This, she was sure, was punishment for her profession and her intervention on the driver's behalf. But she was too worried about the woman's condition to play games now. The rigors were shaking the driver so violently that Trish was afraid she might break her teeth.

The officers drove away. Trish felt panicky and powerless and quite unlike herself. All she could think of was the sight of the bloody, broken body that had been huddled at the foot of the wall. Hearing the sound of deep gulping sobs, she turned. The driver was bent double over the bonnet of her car, howling.

'He's going to die. I know he is.'

'Come on,' Trish said, trying not to join in. 'I'll drive you to hospital. Get you checked over. You'll be all right then. And don't worry too much about the child. He was still alive when they put him in the ambulance.'

'Oh, God!'

Trish was still conscious of her own lack of clothes and the clumsy great boots, but the need to get her protégée into someone else's hands was too urgent to waste time dressing. The T-shirt and coat would have to do. And she could probably drive such a short distance in the ridiculous boots. She helped the driver fetch her handbag from the car and lock the doors before they set off towards the car park that preserved Trish's soft-top Audi from the attentions of the local car thieves and graffiti artists.

She kept thinking about them as she urged the woman on towards the car park. It could have been no more than a reaction to the police officer's prejudice about her neighbourhood, but for the first time Trish felt uncomfortably aware of loitering figures at each road junction. Some were black, some white, but they were all youngish men. Most of them looked either shifty or aggressive. She kept her eyes down and walked as quickly as her boots and companion would let her.

Later, driving to the hospital, she thought the grim streets had never looked more desolate; high, flat-fronted buildings with blank windows made them seem like chasms. Under one of the railway bridges, splattered with pigeon shit and strewn with rubbish, she saw the sad lumps of two rough sleepers. They were guarded by a scrawny mongrel, whose eyes flashed as the headlights hit home.

By the time she was helping the driver through the puddles towards the Accident and Emergency entrance to the hospital, Trish could feel a huge blister on her right heel. She delivered her burden to the receptionist, who took the few details the driver could provide, including her name: Sarah Middlewich. The receptionist told her she'd be seen by the triage nurse as soon as possible. Trish couldn't stop herself asking for news of the boy.

'Are you a relative?'

Trish explained.

'Well, I can't tell you anything, but if you'd just wait there, next to your friend, I'll find someone who can.'

Sarah Middlewich clutched Trish's arm as she sat down, gasping that she'd left her mobile in her car.

'That's OK. You're not allowed to use them in hospitals anyway. There are payphones over there. Have you got any change?'

Tears poured out of the woman's eyes again. 'I need to ring Charles. He'll be worrying.'

'Your husband?'

'Yes. Look at the time. He'll be so worried.'

She looked so out of it that Trish tried to be gentle as she pointed to the bank of public phones about six feet away. When Sarah reached them, Trish let herself slump back in her chair, shutting her eyes.

'This is the lady who was asking about the boy,' said the receptionist, making Trish pay attention. There was yet another angry-looking police officer of her.

'I'm Constable Hill,' he said. 'And you are?'

'Trish Maguire.'

His eyes sparkled and his unsmiling lips stretched into a tight band across his teeth. She couldn't imagine what he was thinking to make him look so accusing, or why he was peering so beadily into her face. She leaned back. 'I think you'd better come along with me,' he told her.

'Why?'

'Just come. You wanted to know about the boy. I'll show you.'

Feeling as though she might be about to wake up in her chair with her mind buzzing after a nightmare, Trish accompanied Constable Hill to a large, dimly lit room full of machines, people in pale-blue scrubs, and an atmosphere of pumping excitement.

Between the blue backs, Trish saw the boy lying flat. His head was taped down and tubes sprouted from various parts of his body.

'Get her out of here,' said a tall man with a stethoscope around his neck.

'This is Trish Maguire,' said her policeman with an extraordinary mixture of satisfaction and portentousness in his voice.

They all stopped what they were doing for

21

a moment and there was absolute stillness. Then two of them turned to stare at Trish. They had blood down the front of their scrubs and on their gloved hands. She was conscious of a row of gaping faces before everyone went back to work.

'What?' she asked. A hand on her back pushed her towards the bed. Two nurses moved a little way apart to clear her view of the boy's face. She couldn't see anything to justify all this drama, so she glanced at the doctor, then at Constable Hill, then at each of the nurses. All those who caught her eye had the same expectant look on their faces.

'What?' Trish asked again.

'Don't you recognise him?' said the policeman.

Trish peered between the tapes and bandages and tubes. 'No. Who is he?'

'That's what we want you to tell us,' he said, pulling her back, out of the way of the medical team. His gripping hand hurt her.

Patiently Trish explained yet again about her role in the accident's aftermath.

'You're really telling us you've never seen him before in your life? That you don't know who he is?'

'How many more times? Yes, that *is* what I'm telling you.'

'Even though he was coming to find you?

And he looks just like you?'

'Don't be ridiculous. You can hardly see his face with all those scrapes and bruises, let alone the dressings. And what makes you think he was coming to me?'

'Well, he had your name and address sewn into the seam of his fleece, didn't he? What other explanation could there be?'

With the walls closing in on her and the floor bursting up to meet her face, Trish tried to protest. As she was losing consciousness, she heard the voice say:

'I bet you anything he's her son.'

2

'God, you look terrible, Trish!'

Her old friend, Anna Grayling, sounded so shocked that Trish hastily said she was fine. 'I didn't sleep much,' she added as she sat down at the wine-bar table.

If this lunch had been with anyone other than Anna she'd have cancelled, but the two of them were both so busy that they rarely managed to find a day when they could meet, and it had been months since their last encounter. Trish had hoped the coral T-shirt she was wearing with her black jeans and natural linen jacket would have given her some colour — and a disguise. She should have known better. Although Anna was an independent television producer these days, she'd started her career as an investigative journalist and she still saw far too much.

Trish put up a hand to make sure her spiky hair hadn't mysteriously flattened itself and was reassured. 'There was a car crash outside my flat last night, and I got embroiled with the police and the hospital. I fainted, too, and then they asked all sorts of questions. It took hours.'

'Poor you. But even so . . . ' Anna sounded genuinely sympathetic, but her eyes were full of the old professional curiosity.

Trish buried all thought of her miscarriage. 'When I eventually got home, I was too revved up to sleep, so I took a pill. And that's given me the mother of all hangovers.'

Anna pushed a menu towards her. 'Food's the thing for that. Without George to cook for you, you're probably malnourished, which will be why you fainted. Choose a lot. I'm paying.'

A smile fought through, as Trish thought of her perennially cash-strapped friend volunteering to buy lunch.

'Don't look so sceptical. I want to feed you up. In any case, I owe you.'

That was true enough, but Trish wasn't convinced. They'd been friends for years, but she'd learned to be wary of Anna's machinations.

'Then thank you. I . . . Oh, I'd like the fishcakes, I think, with some spinach instead of chips.'

'Great. And what about a bottle of Sancerre?'

'Only if you can manage five glasses. I've loads of work this afternoon, so I can't have more than one.'

'I thought barristers slacked off all summer.'

'Not these days — at least not at my level. All the big silks are off in their Tuscan palaces and French châteaux, but the rest of us are hard at it. I'm not in court at the moment, but that doesn't mean there's no work. I've got a big commercial case to prepare.'

Anna's face fattened in satisfaction. 'So I hear. You've got the fascinating Nick Gurles, haven't you?'

So this is why I'm getting a free lunch, Trish thought. Oh, well. It could be worse. 'You must know I don't talk about my cases or my clients.'

'Of course not.' Anna managed to attract the waiter's attention and ordered their lunch with two glasses of house white wine. 'But I did hear your head of chambers was acting for him and that you were to be the junior. Fraud's quite a change from all those damaged children, isn't it? Why did he pick you?'

I wish I knew, Trish thought, worried all over again. But she put on her most confident smile and said, 'I needed a break from family law — to let the aquifers refill and all that.'

'Yes. I can see how fifteen years of marital distress and child abuse could drain one's compassion.' Anna had always been able to

26

pick up Trish's allusions. It was one of the reasons why her occasional bouts of complete self-absorption had never irritated Trish quite as much as they did some of her other friends. 'But it must have been hard for you getting to grips with the City and people like Nick Gurles. I don't suppose there could be two more different worlds.'

'It's certainly been interesting.' And that's an understatement, Trish thought. She'd struggled for weeks with the evidence, jargon and personalities in the case — and the maths — longing for a *Ladybird Book of Finance* to guide her through.

The waiter brought their wine and Anna tasted hers. 'Not too bad. But Trish, I hope you're going to be OK. I mean, this case isn't your sort of thing at all, and Nick Gurles is said to be a nasty piece of work behind all that suave charm.'

Trish was far too experienced to rush into defending him. Instead, she raised an eyebrow and merely said, 'I didn't know you knew him.'

'I don't. But I was having lunch with my venture capitalists the other day, and they were full of the case, which is how I heard you were involved, and why I thought we ought to talk.'

Anna waited for Trish to add to her store of

27

knowledge — or gossip. Trish smiled, sipped her wine, and kept everything she knew about Nick Gurles to herself.

He'd started his professional life as an analyst in a merchant bank in the City and gone on to spectacular success in fund management there. Having a talent for PR, he'd also built up a reputation in the outside world and had become a bit of a hero to the personal finance journalists. Some years later, he'd been headhunted by one of the retail banks, the Domestic and Overseas.

The DOB, as it was nearly always known, had lost its pre-eminent position on the high street, and the directors had decided that the only way to regain it was to revamp their savings products. They'd had to pay way over the odds to lure Nick Gurles to do it for them, and to compensate him for the humiliation of moving so far downmarket, but it had been a dream appointment for them. Their shareholders, both institutional and private, were so excited that the share price boomed, the directors' share options began to look good again after years under water, and the atmosphere within the bank lightened at once.

He'd done well for them, bringing back a lot of their old customers and building up new loyalties. He'd been fêted and lushed up, given the biggest, lightest office and the best-looking of the leggy graduate secretaries. Then, just before the board had got round to offering him the directorship everyone knew he'd earned, he'd decided to return to the City. The DOB's share price dropped instantly, and the directors' share options looked more out of the money every day.

Things had got worse once it was discovered that he'd left a ticking timebomb behind. His last big project had been the launch of the MegaPerformance Bond Fund, which had guaranteed to pay savers 5 per cent more each year than Treasury bonds yielded. Unfortunately the fund had failed to generate the expected high returns and the investors' capital had diminished. Some of the disgruntled punters, who had assumed that they would get back all their original investment as well as the extra high yield, irrespective of what happened to the markets, had sued the bank and its directors for fraudulent misrepresentation. The directors had joined Nick Gurles into the action as a third party.

'How does it feel, Trish,' Anna asked gleefully, 'to be responsible for the man's future like this? You know that if you lose, Grunschwig's will kick Gurles out, and he'll never get another job in banking, don't you?

Serve him right, of course. Greedy slimeball.'

'I've been responsible for much more serious outcomes than anyone's career.' Trish thought of some of the children whose lives had probably been saved by care proceedings in the past, and of the others who'd died because neither social services nor the police had picked up danger signals or been able to protect them. But she didn't want to talk about any of them now.

'What were you doing lunching with your backers?' she said quickly. 'They're not being difficult again, are they?'

'God no. Business is fantastic,' Anna said, happy as ever to be diverted back to her own interests. 'We've got five new films in production and stacks of ideas.'

She tucked into her fishcakes, picking up the chips in her fingers and dipping them alternately into bowls of ketchup and tartare sauce, muddling the red and white into a sludgy mess. 'And it's all thanks to you, Trish. If we hadn't made the Deb Gibbert film, I'd probably be bankrupt by now. You've earned your fishcakes, even if you won't help me with City dirt.'

Trish smiled, although her memories of the unhappy woman who'd been the subject of Anna's campaigning television film were anything but amusing. 'How are the

Gibberts? It must be so tough for them both.'

'Tough? Being released from a life sentence after only four years? You must be joking, Trish. Deb ought to be radiantly happy as well as slavishly grateful to us. And that weedy husband of hers, too.'

'That doesn't sound as though you've seen them recently.'

'Oh, come on,' Anna said through a mouthful of sauce-dripping chips. 'You don't keep up with your old clients; I don't make friends with the subjects of my films. I did everything I could for Deb while we were in production, and we got her out of prison. I don't see how I could be expected to do more. I mean, *you* haven't seen her, have you?'

'No, but I'm in touch with her daughter. She wants to be a barrister.'

'That's different. She adored you from the word go.' Anna drank again. When she put down her glass, she looked different, less defensive. 'Actually, watching you with Kate made me see what a fantastic mother you'd make. You won't leave it too late to get pregnant, will you?'

The half-eaten fishcake suddenly looked fleshy and disgusting, and the pool of tomato salsa like blood. Saliva rushed into Trish's mouth. She hoped she wasn't going to be sick. Another sip of wine helped.

'I'm too busy to think of all that now.'

The nausea returned as Anna launched into a diatribe about the idiocy of high-flying women who cared so much about their own success that they forgot about having children, only to realise how much they'd sacrificed when they were too old to conceive, naturally or otherwise. Trish tried to concentrate on memories of all Anna's other diatribes about her own three children and how impossible they'd made her life for years.

'I mean, how are you going to feel, Trish, when you're on your deathbed and you realise you're leaving nothing behind you except reports of cases involving sleazebags like Nick Gurles?'

'Will you shut up?' The force of Trish's outburst shocked them both. 'Sorry. I'm a bit fragile just now, with the lack of sleep and everything. Anyway, from everything I've seen of mothers and children, I'm not sure giving birth is something everyone should do. Look, it's getting late. I can't wait for coffee. I have to get back.'

'Trish, just because some hopeless women abuse their children, that doesn't mean you will. You'll have to commit yourself to something one day. Join the human race before it's too late, for God's sake.'

'Anna, I can't deal with this now. I have to go. I'm sorry. Here.' Trish grabbed a twenty-pound note and handed it across the table.

'Don't be stupid, Trish. I told you, lunch is on me. There's no need to rush off. You haven't even finished your fishcakes. No wonder you're looking like death if you keep doing this sort of thing. Sit down.'

'Sorry. I'll phone you. Bye.'

Outside, Trish leaned against the wall of the wine bar, fighting dizziness. Only the thought that Anna might come after her and start the lecture all over again forced her to move.

The August sun was blazing in a clear blue sky. Within the gates of the Temple, all the buildings glowed as if they'd been washed clean and varnished by last night's storms. Trish felt calmer as soon as she was back among them. This was her place; she was safe here.

Passing the car park, she raised a hand to Jeremy Fairfield, who was getting out of his lusciously appointed top-of-the-range Jaguar. He stared disdainfully, as though he'd never seen her before, before turning away to pick something out of his car, so that he wouldn't have to speak to her. Trish walked quickly on to Plough Court, seething.

He might be one of the Princes of the Bar, earning well over a million pounds a year and consulted by governments, fraudsters and victims alike, but none of his success excused that sort of rudeness. They'd been fellow guests at a dinner only two weeks ago and had sat next to each other, so he must have recognised her. Antony Shelley, her head of chambers, was just as successful but, arrogant sod though he could sometimes be, he'd never have snubbed anyone like that, even the newest pupil in chambers.

With his air of a god stalking the earth and trying to avoid contamination by ordinary mortals, Fairfield represented everything Trish had most disliked about her profession from the beginning. She'd been a hurt, angry child then; all knees and elbows and scruffy clothes, driven by a longing to right wrongs and heal the victims of every kind of cruelty.

No longer hurt or scruffy, in spite of her deliberately aggressive hairstyle, she was still angry and still driven. Accepting Antony's invitation to act as his junior on the Nick Gurles case didn't mean she was selling out to join the fat cats. She was just taking a break. She could still do her bit to protect children at risk, even if she didn't devote quite so much time to them.

Remembering last night's crash victim and

the possible repercussions, she stopped in the doorway of her clerk's room.

'Dave?'

He looked up from his papers, spectacles sliding down his nose. Seeing Trish, his frosty expression thawed a little. In her early days his intimidatory tactics and Churchillian speechifying had first scared, then annoyed her, but now she was secure enough to be amused by most of them. Maybe that was why he'd dropped the portentous exhortations to fight them in the mags, and in the county court, and in the supreme court, and never surrender.

'Dave, the police may be round soon to ask questions about my past cases.'

'The police? Why? What *have* you been doing?'

'Nothing. A child was run over outside my flat . . . ' Trish began, then seeing his frown turning into a scowl, quickly explained that she hadn't been driving.

She gave him the whole story, adding that once she'd come round from the faint, she'd told the police she could only assume the child must have been either a client or in some way connected with one. Not wanting to get involved, she hoped Dave would field any enquiries they might make.

'But if he was a client,' Dave said at once,

'why was he running to your flat, not here to chambers?'

Trish felt her mouth slackening and clamped it shut. How could she have been so stupid? The miscarriage must have affected her brain as well as her psyche.

'God knows,' she said without much of a pause. 'But there isn't any other kind of child who'd be coming to find me.'

'Sure of that, are we?'

'Quite sure, if you mean what I think you mean. You're as bad as the police. They spent ages last night trying to get me to tell them the boy must be my son, running away from foster parents or something. But I can assure you, it's a biological impossibility.'

'I'm glad to hear it.'

'So *will* you deal with them for me, Dave?'

'Of course. You've got more than enough to do with the Gurles case. That's all that matters now, and it matters a lot. Going all right, is it?'

'Fine, thanks.'

'I certainly hope so. I told Mr Shelley you could do it, so don't let me down.'

'Have I ever?'

'Not yet,' Dave said. 'But there's always a first time. And this is right out of your field.'

Don't remind me, Trish thought as she retreated to her dingy room at the back of the building. There, staring at her, were the rows of lever-arch files in which she'd sorted the documents for the case. She had done a good job, she told herself, whatever Dave suggested.

All the papers were there, flagged with different-coloured mini Post-its: red for danger, or bits of evidence that might help the depositors or the DOB directors; green for the facts that showed Nick Gurles in the best possible light; and purple for deep background. She'd drafted all sorts of arguments the others might use against her client and prepared ways to counter them, citing all the relevant case law.

Today she was going to start to index and cross-check every single piece of paper evidence by hand, to make sure that it was all there and all correctly entered into the computer.

The case would turn on whether the judge believed the DOB had deliberately misled their customers in the marketing literature and the terms and conditions of the fund. Trish had been careful never to ask Nick Gurles directly, but he'd voluntarily assured her that there had been no intention to deceive on his part. All his financial modelling had told him that the fund would generate the advertised return, and so there would have been no point trying to pull the wool over anyone's eyes. Of course, he couldn't speak for the other defendants.

Trish knew that they would be explaining much the same to their counsel, the only difference being that they'd suggest it was Nick Gurles who might have had some nefarious intent that he'd successfully concealed.

The most difficult part of the preparation for her had been grappling with Nick's original calculations of the risk/reward ratio that had made him so confident of his MegaPerformance Bond Fund. She hadn't had to add up anything more complicated than her own VAT returns for years, and she still wasn't sure she'd completely understood Nick's sums. She hoped Antony Shelley would be able to absorb the principle on his own and not demand tutorials from her.

Now that she'd got to grips with most of the background and learned something of how the financial world operated, she was no longer surprised that so many of the most successful commercial barristers kept their money in straightforward interest-bearing accounts. She herself had been persuaded by various plausible 'financial advisers' to put her spare cash into all sorts of funds and bonds and now bitterly regretted the lot.

The completely legal rip-offs she'd discovered as she'd done her research, the hidden charges, the churning, the utterly useless investment performance of most of the fund managers she'd trusted with her money made her furious. Some had even pumped up their end-of-year figures by last-minute switches of investment in order to get a higher position in the league tables than their overall performance could possibly justify. Others endlessly set up new savings accounts with particularly good interest rates to entice customers, only to reduce the rates within a few months, trusting that inertia would keep the customers stuck in low-return accounts.

When Trish thought about the premiums she'd poured into her various pension funds, particularly in the years when she'd been earning very little and had had to make real sacrifices to ensure she kept up the payments, she was ready to march through the streets waving placards. She would have earned far more, even taking into account the tax relief, if she'd put the same amount of money into an ordinary building society (always providing that she had monitored its interest rate). The pension companies had waxed rich and fat on what they'd creamed off the top of her investment.

Some of the companies, of course, had

been challenged in court for their mistakes, but it was their with-profits savers who would be paying for those, not the individuals who had made the mistakes or the directors responsible for them — or the advisers who'd steered their clients towards the companies. Oh, it made her so angry she could have spat. But there was nothing she could do about it now except make her pensions 'paid-up' and put future spare cash into something more flexible and absolutely under her own control. Her fingers curled as she thought of the thousands she'd wasted.

'Hi, Trish!'

She looked up at the sound of the vigorous masculine voice and saw Robert Anstey, who'd been called to the Bar a couple of years earlier than she had. He'd been turned down for silk twice now and tended to take out his frustration on anyone within range. She occasionally wondered whether it was Robert's bitterness that had made her determined not to apply until she was sure she'd succeed.

'What can I do for you?'

'Boot's on the other foot, Trish. Knowing how unused you are to this kind of work, I thought I'd come and offer to be your guide, to stop you plunging into all the elephant traps everyone's been digging round you.

Antony's an absolute stickler, you know. In his book there's no such thing as an honest mistake, and he won't forgive you if you get even the tiniest detail wrong.'

'How sweet of you,' she said hypocritcally, 'but I'm fine.'

'Are you sure? I know how hard you find arithmetic.' He laughed. 'I must say, none of us can quite understand the game he's playing, putting a mathematical-illiterate on a case like this, but we're all ready and waiting to mop your tears and soothe your fevered brow when he lays into you. He can be quite terrifying when he gets into Genghis-Khan mode, you know. And manipulative, my God!'

'He's the most impressive man I've ever met. And I'm finding the whole case fascinating.'

'Do I detect just the faintest whiff of hero-worship, Trish?' Robert laughed again, the sound as rich and sickly as *foie gras*. 'Be careful. He eats earnest girls like you for breakfast.'

'You're very free with your clichés today, Robert. Have you been reading the tabloids again?'

'Ooh. Temper, temper. Caught you on the raw, did I, Trish? Well, as a penance, can I get you anything in Pret à Manger? I'm on

41

my way there now.'

'A quadruple espresso would be great. Thanks.' She kept the smile on her face for nearly two minutes in case Robert was playing some kind of Grandmother's Footsteps and planning to nip back to see whether she was showing any sign of weakness.

When she was sure he'd gone, she let her face relax. The trouble was that she hadn't a clue what Antony was playing at, either.

He'd never given her any explanation. All that had happened was that he'd erupted into her dark, shabby little room nearly a year ago, high on the adrenaline of a tough day in court. There had been colour in his face for once, and a glitter in his aquamarine eyes. Running his fingers luxuriously through his wild blond hair, he'd told her about Nick Gurles and what had happened to the MegaPerformance Bond Fund and offered her the chance of working with him. She leaped on it like a sea eagle splashing down on a particularly plump fish, and hadn't thought of the downside until later.

'Here, Trish.' Robert Anstey dumped a large cardboard cup of coffee on her desk. She swung round to reach for her handbag. 'No, no. Have this one on me. My practice has always been a lot more profitable than yours. And you're going to need your rainy-day fund soon.'

Trish added a soupçon of pity to her polite smile and was pleased to see how angry it made him. He should have known better. She'd had plenty of experience in dealing with patronising men. There were still an extraordinary number of those at the Bar, who considered that their anatomy automatically made them cleverer as well as more deserving than any woman.

Nick Gurles had shown signs of a similar aberration at first. Trish could see him now, about four years younger than she was, but absolutely confident and very smooth in his expensive clothes. He'd sat with one ankle balanced on the other knee, showing off his perfect shoe (beautifully polished under the instep, too) as he explained his creed during their first conference.

'No financial institution can be a charity, Ms Maguire. Banks are businesses, exactly like the little corner shop that sells you your newspapers and the odd pint of milk when you've run out. They have to take in more money than they pay out, in order to cover their overheads — that's rent, salaries and so on — and make a profit for themselves and for their shareholders. Are you with me?'

'Oh, I think I can just about keep up. Your problem must come, of course, in that banks — like corner shops — have to provide good enough value to make the customers come back,' Trish had said in the same tone he'd used, of an adult reading a story to a two year old. She wondered what Antony could have said to the solicitors to make their client assume she was that thick.

'Quite.'

She'd preferred the much-less smooth way he'd grinned at her then. 'So what exactly went wrong with this fund of yours?' she went on.

'All investments can go down as well as up. That warning was plastered all over the marketing literature, as it always has to be.'

'Come on, Nick,' she'd said, showing her teeth. 'This was a fund that guaranteed a certain percentage, to be paid annually. So what happened?'

'To put it simply, Trish . . . ' He broke off to smile matily as he used her Christian name for the first time. 'To put it simply, we were aiming to make the return for our customers by investing in European junk bonds. I mean, we didn't issue the bonds ourselves, obviously. Now, junk bonds are always risky, which is why the rewards are so high. But studies have shown that overall the risks are less than the rewards. Are you still with me?'

'So far.' She'd smiled sweetly and made a note.

'Great. The problem comes if too many of the bonds you've bought flop, as some always will, and you don't have enough that are booming.'

'Yes, I can see that you'd be stuffed in that case.'

'I couldn't have put it more clearly myself, though I might have striven for a tad more elegance.'

'So why the guarantee?'

'The guarantee referred, as was perfectly clear, to the annual percentage we were going to pay the investors; it had nothing to do with the capital they'd put in. We assumed that would be fine, but we weren't mad enough to guarantee it, for heaven's sake. The first hints of the problem came with the tremors in the junk-bond market, which made one of the financial journalists write a rather hysterical piece about our bond issuers, which made rather too many punters withdraw their investment, despite having to pay an early-withdrawal fee for that, which in turn exacerbated the whole problem. You see, once so many of them had taken out their money, the spread of bonds necessarily shrank, which meant that all my calculations of the risk/reward ratio no longer applied.'

'I can see that might have caused you problems.'

'Good. Now, had I still been with the DOB, I'd probably have been able to stuff my finger in the dyke and get the whole show back on the road.'

Talk about mixed metaphors, thought Trish.

'Unfortunately I wasn't there, and my replacement wasn't concerned enough to monitor things as I would have done. The directors panicked too soon, took counsel's opinion on the lack of a guarantee in respect of the capital, and closed the fund to new investors, which was the worst possible thing and ensured that a lot of punters lost money. They resented it and sued. The whole thing has been a complete fiasco. Are you still with me?'

'Yes. Although I can understand the punters, too. I've been looking at all the marketing bumf and I must say I'd have assumed I'd get back what I put in.'

'Would you? Why?'

'Because that's what bank accounts offer.'

'But, Trish, this *wasn't* a bank account. Surely you've grasped that much by now. It's the fundamental point. This was an investment — and they go down as well as up, as we correctly stated.'

Thinking about that conversation now, it occurred to Trish for the first time that it could have been her very inexperience of the City that had made her so attractive to Antony. If she could get her mind round everything in the case and reduce it to something she could follow easily, and sympathise with, they'd be well on the way to ensuring that they could convince anyone else. It was a reassuring thought. She hoped it was realistic.

Sipping her pile-drivingly strong coffee, she was glad she'd found a way to sympathise with Nick Gurles. In the past she'd often had to represent unattractive clients, but she'd always tried to find something to like, so that her advocacy would sound warm and therefore be effective. This time she'd found it in the DOB directors' attitude to Nick.

Their decision to join him to the action still surprised her. He'd been an employee, doing what he was paid to do. As far as she could see, they'd been motivated by a mixture of spite, because his departure had lowered their share price and therefore the value of their own options, and the need for PR damage control. If they lost the action, having someone as well-known as Nick Gurles to share the blame might mean that their shareholders wouldn't start demanding resignations.

Trish swigged some more coffee, hoping the caffeine would keep her awake as she went back to filling out index cards for the first of the lever-arch files. For once there were no interruptions and she was able to work steadily all afternoon. It was soothing stuff, needing absolute concentration but no mental energy. Her lack of sleep and the pill's hangover didn't impede her, as they might have done if she'd needed any creativity, and the constant physical movement and need to keep track of documents and facts meant that she couldn't think about her own problems. Or not too much.

★ ★ ★

Robert Anstey passed Trish's open door again soon after four o'clock on his way to the clerks' room. He was tempted to apply another goad, but she was concentrating so hard she didn't even know he was there. He hoped she'd make a cock-up of the case. If she did, Antony would come to him next time. Even so, he felt a faint stirring of sympathy when she suddenly shivered, in spite of the heat.

She was frowning over her papers and her

left hand was clamped down on the gelled spikes of her dark hair. Robert had always loathed the cut, considering it wholly inappropriate in these ancient chambers, but he had to admit it looked better under a wig than the straggly curls of some of the other women. And at least she was thin. Some of them positively wobbled under their gowns, the greedy cows.

Maybe he'd leave her be this afternoon. After all, she was no real competition. He looked away and saw Dave beckoning, with a fat-looking brief in his hand.

*   *   *

At one moment, needing to clear her brain of the overloading detail, Trish clicked on to her email and saw that there were several messages in her in-box. Most were of no consequence, but one was from George. She opened it, smiling as she read:

You can't imagine how much I miss you! But I'm pretty sure now that we were right about bringing Ma here. Getting away can't make her miss Dad any less, but it gives her other things to think about. Luckily she likes the place as much as I always have.

*And today talking seemed easier, too.
I'm beginning to think she could be very
funny, and she's got all sorts of
interesting ideas. I wish they hadn't
bunged me off to boarding school. I'd
have liked to know her better.*

He'd been eight, Trish remembered. The
same age as the boy last night. How could
anyone send a child of that age into
boarding-school exile?

She'd hardly ever thought of George as
vulnerable. He was always so sure of himself,
so calmly effective, that it was a shock to
imagine him as a homesick child. No wonder
he'd lost all touch with the person his mother
was. You'd have to shut yourself off to deal
with that kind of loneliness.

Shaken at the thought of what else his
strength might have been hiding, and angry
about what his parents had done to him, she
went back to his email.

*We're turning into the most unsophisti-
cated of tourists. I've only ever been here
to see clients before, so I've never done
the sights. But Ma and I are doing
everything, even eating seafood on
Fisherman's Wharf and gazing at the sea
lions.*

Bet you didn't know there's this great herd of wild sea lions, who live at the wharf. They smell fairly gross, but they're fun to watch as you eat your chowder in a sourdough-loaf bowl. Half of them look like moth-eaten old fur coats when they've dried in the sun, then they flop off the floats and turn into elegant sinuous swimmers.

We've eaten in a revolving rooftop restaurant — unfortunately the fog rolled in just as they were bringing our food so we revolved inside a damp grey blanket, but you can't have everything — we've ridden the cable cars and bought silk bits and bobs in Chinatown. Done everything, in fact. I've even bought you some black pearls.

I must stop. We're due for another walk up these demonic hills. My legs feel like stiff, sensationless rods already. It's lucky we're eating all the time or I'd be a wraith by now. See you in ten days, my love.

G

Refreshed by the thought of Gourmet George as a wraith, and by the reminder that there was more to life than clients, or damaged children, Trish went back to work,

51

only to be pulled up soon afterwards by the discovery that she was missing a document. It ought to have been impossible. But it was true. Cross-referring each statement as she entered it on her index cards, she'd found a gap in the chain of evidence.

There was a note Nick Gurles had sent to his head of department about the compliance officer's report that referred to something dated 13 March. Trish couldn't find any sign of it. In fact, there was nothing at all from 13 March. She checked in her old diary to make sure it hadn't been a Bank Holiday and found that it had been a perfectly ordinary weekday.

Every other piece of paper referred to anywhere had been provided by the solicitors, Sprindlers & Partners. Trish had numbered and filed them all. She needed this one, too.

Thanking God that she had embarked on this time-consuming process while Antony was still away, she reached for her phone and dialled Sprindlers' number. When she got through she asked for Peter Loyle, the partner in charge of the case.

'He's on holiday,' the receptionist said. 'Can someone else help at all?'

'Is there anyone in his office at the moment who's working on the Nicholas Gurles case?'

'I don't know, but Lucy Ranking might be able to help you. I'll put you through.'

52

Lucy Ranking was not very knowledgeable, but she obviously wanted to be helpful and she kept apologising for the missing note.

'I'll start looking for it at once. I'm sure I can find it, if it's here. I think I know where to start. And I'll bike it over as soon as I've got it. If I can't find it I'll give you a ring at once. Is that OK?'

'Great,' Trish said, 'but don't worry about the bike. I've had enough for today. Bung it in the post, would you? Thank you. Bye.'

Her phone rang as soon as she'd put down the receiver. It was Dave, telling her that a policeman had just left with as much information about her recent cases as he could be given without a breach of client-confidentiality.

'Thanks, Dave. Didn't he want to see me?'

'Of course he did, but you'd said you didn't want to be involved, so I refused to call you. He didn't press it, just asked for the list of cases and names of your clients. If you ask me, they're just going through the motions.'

'Then they must have a good idea who the boy is. Did they tell you anything about him?'

'Not a thing, and I didn't ask. You do not want to be involved. You've got too much to do on the Gurles case. Forget the boy. He's not your problem and there are plenty that are. Concentrate on them.'

Trish left chambers. Outside, the air was still and warm, and the soft light pink. She nearly always dawdled over Blackfriars Bridge, often stopping to look up at St Paul's, solid and beautiful between the flamboyant high-rises. But this evening the City held little allure for her, so she turned her back on it all, for once preferring the massed slabs of the National Theatre and the muddle beyond. As she let her gaze sweep round, past the London Eye, across the river towards the rooves of Whitehall, she thought of Dowting's Hospital, hidden by the theatre.

'You don't want to get involved,' Trish reminded herself in Dave's voice and then again in her own.

At the Southwark end of the bridge she hesitated, thinking of the boy, and of George aged eight and abandoned to boarding school. For a second she looked back towards the Temple, then knew she had to find out more. She turned right to walk to Dowting's.

3

The boy had been moved up to a ward on the tenth floor. The nurse Trish found there recognised her name at once.

'I'm so glad you've come. He can't tell us who he is, and he's frightened to death. God knows what kind of a mother he must have.'

Trish gripped her bag and told herself that she'd been mad to come. 'How is he? Physically, I mean.'

'He's got a broken leg, broken ribs, multiple bruising and concussion. He had an arterial bleed from a cut in his thigh, but that's been dealt with. He's recovered consciousness, but he's not talking much — which may be the concussion, or it may not.'

'Has he really not said anything about who he is?' Trish asked. 'Anything at all?'

'No. He says he can't remember, doesn't know why he was on his own in a Southwark street or why he had your name sewn into his clothes.'

'And he's in pain?'

'Yes. We're giving him analgesics, but they're never enough. He's a brave child, though. He doesn't make a fuss.'

'May I see him?' Oh, Trish, don't be a fool, she told herself.

'For a few minutes. But if he becomes distressed, you'll have to go.'

'Of course.'

'And see if you can get him to tell you anything.'

'I'll do my best.'

Trish didn't think the boy was asleep when she reached his bedside, but he was lying with his eyes closed. His injuries looked less terrifying now that he wasn't immobilised and tubed, but they were still bad enough. One of his legs was strung up in a cradle, both his eyes were black, and one side of his face was criss-crossed with dark-red cuts and grazes. A faint crease appeared between his brows.

Seeing that she was simply adding to his difficulties, she walked closer, saying, 'Hello. My name's Trish Maguire. Is it all right to sit down?'

The lids flickered and lifted. His eyes looked very dark and very frightened. Trish smiled.

'Hello,' she said again. 'I think you wanted to see me last night, didn't you?'

He shut his eyes again. Trish was relieved. This indifference might let her off the hook.

56

Then she saw that the black lashes were wet. Fat tears oozed out and spread over his bruised face. His breathing deepened, but he made no other sound. One almost flayed hand emerged from the bedclothes, palm upwards.

Trish took it. Her own eyes grew damp as she felt him relax at her touch. Still holding his hand as gently as she could, she manoeuvred the nearest chair so that she could sit down. When his tears had stopped, and he'd sniffed to clear his nose, he looked at her.

'Can I get you anything?' she asked quietly. He shook his head while his hand clung to hers. 'Can you tell me who you are?'

'David,' he whispered.

Trish bent closer. 'What's your surname?'

He shook his head again, which must have hurt because the crease deepened between his eyebrows. He lay very still, resting against the pillow and looking straight ahead.

'OK. Don't worry about it now, David.'

His eyes slid round towards her again.

'Your surname doesn't matter, but if I'm to help you I need to know why you wanted to see me. You did, didn't you?'

'She told me.' He was whispering again. 'She said: 'Go to Trish. She'll look after you till I can come to c'llect you'.'

57

'Who, David? Who told you?'

She felt a tug against her hand and let him go. He pulled up the sheet, covering himself up to his small, pointed chin.

'It's wicked, letting a poor little mite like that get lost in London in weather like last night's.' Trish looked up to see that the speaker was one of the other nurses. 'You're Trish Maguire, aren't you?'

'Yes. But I've no idea why he wanted me. I'm as lost as he is.'

'Give it time,' said the nurse. 'The police will find out, even if he doesn't remember. They're talking to all the missing-persons charities now. It won't take them long.'

David's frown was back and his mouth tightened, but he kept his eyes shut. The nurse nodded meaningfully at Trish and mouthed something she couldn't interpret. She smiled and waited until the nurse had walked away.

'It's all right, David,' Trish said quietly then. 'She's gone. You can open your eyes.'

Watching the cleft between his flying dark brows, Trish rubbed the space between her own with the middle fingers of her left hand. It was there that the headaches always began. 'That's because you frown so,' George often told her. 'It's not surprising it hurts. You're clenching all the muscles, pulling them down. Let go.'

Missing him even more than usual, she took her fingers away from her face and let them rest lightly on David's forehead.

'I'll do whatever I can to help. I hate answering questions, too. Have you had any food in here that you like, David, or would you like me to get you some chocolate or something?'

Trying to remember what she'd wanted as a child when she was ill or hurt, she came up with Lucozade. Her mother had always produced a bottle at the first hint of a temperature. The sticky sweetness and the strange taste of it, as well as the glamorous orange bubbles, had become part of remembered comfort.

'Do you like Lucozade?' David looked so surprised that she knew he'd never heard of it. 'Or Coke?'

'I'm not allowed Coke. I have juice. Apple juice.'

'That's a good idea. Shall I get you some?'

'Yes.' There was a pause, then two more fat tears rolled down his cheeks. 'Please.'

Oh, God, Trish thought as her heart lurched. What am I doing? To myself and him?

'All right, David. I won't be long.'

The Friends of Dowting's had a shop on

the ground floor and there, in amongst the cards, fruit and flowers she found some individual boxes of fruit juice, with straws attached. She bought six apple-juice packs and took them upstairs. David was lying where she'd left him, eyes closed.

'It's me again,' she said.

He had a quick look to check, then his bruised lips curved slightly. It wasn't much of a smile, but it told Trish more clearly than any words that he hadn't expected her to come back, that he probably didn't expect anything good of any adult.

Whoever the 'she' was who'd sent him across London in the dark, Trish hated her. No one should let a child become so frightened that he reacted like this without provocation. Who could she have been? And what had she been thinking of, to send him after a total stranger in the middle of the night? Fear was the only possible excuse, but fear of what?

Trish picked the straw from its glue on the side of the carton, pushed it into the top and bent it so that David could drink without changing his position. She watched his face as the cool, sweet juice reached his tastebuds and saw that she'd done something good. He didn't want much, spitting out the end of the straw after only a few moments' sucking.

Trish made to relieve him of the carton, but he clung to it, holding it against his chest.

'All right, David,' she said again. 'I just wanted to help. I do want to help, you know, in any way I can. But it would be easier if I knew a little more. Who is it who sent you to me? Is it your mother?'

'I'm not allowed to say.' His hands clutched the juice carton.

'OK. Try not to worry too much. Do you know why she wanted you to come to me?'

' 'If I tell you to go, go straight to Trish Maguire', she said.'

'I know. But why me?'

He looked surprised, as though she should have known. 'I don't know. But she told me your address and how to get there. We used to come and look at where you live. On Sundays. When I was little, she showed me; then I led the way. In case I forgot, she wrote it down and sewed it in my clothes and said if I got lost I must take a taxi and show the address and you'd pay for it. If I got lost. But I didn't. I got hurt.'

'I know. There was a car accident. But you will be all right and it'll stop hurting soon. When did she start teaching you the way to my flat?'

'Since always.' That didn't help much. 'Then yesterday, it happened. She said it: 'Go to Trish like I showed you. I'll come when it's safe. Go now.' She wasn't shouting *then*. She was whispering, but she looked like she did when she was shouting. Cross.' His lips trembled, but he sniffed and wiped his free hand across both his eyes, before gripping his juice box more firmly.

Trish knew he'd been trained not to complain or cry, just as clearly as she knew how frightened he was. Was it because he'd picked up this woman's own fear, or had she brutalised him into it? Who *was* she? And who did she think she was to dump this responsibility on Trish?

'You won't tell, will you?' His voice rose. 'She said I wasn't to tell anyone except you.'

'I must tell the police, David.'

His eyes looked like black holes in his white face. 'No, you mustn't. It's not safe. You mustn't. You mustn't. *You mustn't.*' The whisper was more intense than any scream could have been.

'OK,' Trish said at once. 'It's OK, David. I won't tell and I'll make sure you're safe.'

As his panic receded a little, she thought, What the hell do I do now? 'The nurses are kind to you, aren't they?' she asked aloud, wanting all the reassurance she couldn't give him.

David nodded, then felt with his lips until

he'd got the straw back in his mouth. Noisily sucking up apple juice meant that he couldn't be made to answer any more questions.

'Good. Then you'll be all right here with them until your leg's better. I'm going to have to go now, but I'll come back tomorrow.'

His lips wobbled around the straw, but he didn't protest, just sucked more furiously. Trish had a sudden, almost hallucinatory idea that she'd somehow been time-travelled into the future and was looking down at the child her foetus would have become if she hadn't ill-wished it. She turned away.

'Don't cry,' said a quiet voice in front of her.

A blonde woman in her twenties, holding a grubby toy duck to her chest, gazed at Trish with excoriating sympathy.

'He's going to be all right, I'm sure. He looks so much better than he did last night when they brought him up. I was here then, too. Honestly, I'm sure he'll be fine.'

Trish felt her forehead tightening. She couldn't make herself say anything.

'I'm not surprised you're so shocked,' the woman said kindly. 'It must have been terrible when you heard what had happened. But at least you weren't driving. I can't think of anything worse, can you? For a mother to half-kill her own child, I mean.'

'He's not mine,' Trish said, but it came out as a croak. Suddenly she needed to be on her own, away from even the kindest of strangers. But when she'd pushed her way out of the swing doors and reached the lift, she realised how rude she'd been and rushed back to apologise.

'Don't worry,' said the woman. 'We all go a bit mad when our kids are in here. Mine's doing so well now that I'm functioning again, but it took me at least ten days. Try to get some sleep. You won't do him any good if you give in to it. Better to dope yourself and get some rest than lie worrying all night. I'll probably see you tomorrow, won't I?'

Trish abandoned the effort to explain. She didn't know enough to make it convincing, so she just left the woman believing David was her son and she distraught with anxiety for him.

Walking back to the flat, she was glad to find the streets as unthreatening as usual. Angry with the policeman for putting unnecessary fears into her mind last night, she went upstairs for her usual post-work shower. Even before she'd taken off her clothes, she stared at her face in the bathroom mirror. It was impossible not to see the similarities with David's.

'Who the hell is he?' she asked her reflection.

Getting no answer, she had her shower. Then, with wet hair sleeked back and dressed in floppy shorts and T-shirt, she poured herself a glass of wine and tried to think instead of feel.

The most obvious source of help was Caroline Lyalt, a sergeant in the Met, whose advice was always worth more than most people's. She was also absolutely trustworthy and could be relied on to keep anything Trish said to herself. The two of them had met on a murder case in the past, when Caro had been working with AMIP, and they'd become something more than acquaintances if less than friends. Recently, Caro had been posted to an East London police station, while she worked for her next promotion.

Trish refilled her glass with icy New Zealand Sauvignon and rang Caro's mobile.

'Caroline Lyalt,' said a crisp voice that wasn't actually rude but made it clear that the call had better be important. It was a tone Trish knew well. She used it herself whenever the demands of clients, colleagues and emails got too much.

'Hi, Caro. It's Trish Maguire,' she said very fast, to take up as little time as possible. 'I need to talk to you. Are you very busy, or might we be able to meet?'

'I'm frantic. I'll get back to you as soon as I can. OK? Sorry. Bye.'

Sympathising, Trish took another mouthful of wine, letting the cool sharpness prickle against her tongue and slide down her throat. She thought of David's relaxing as the apple juice eased into his mouth and knew she had to do everything in her power to help. The trouble was that she couldn't think of anything useful to do.

Her mobile was ringing. She hoped it was Caro, but heard her father's voice as soon as she answered it.

'Trish? 'Tis Paddy here. How are you, now?'

'I'm fine,' she lied because they still weren't on the kind of terms that would allow her to tell him about the miscarriage.

She'd pretty much forgiven him now for abandoning her and her mother soon after her seventh birthday, but it had been hard to get over the huge barrier of mistrust. Paddy hadn't even bothered to try to make contact again until she'd established a reputation at the Bar. Then, each time one of her cases figured in the law reports or her name was mentioned in any article about successful women, there would be another letter or phone call from him.

Knowing how he'd thrown all emotional and financial responsibility for her on to his deserted wife, Trish had thought it outrageous that he'd then tried to claim some kind of credit for what she'd become, which was what the timing of his approaches seemed to imply. Everything she'd achieved was thanks to Meg, her mother, who'd fought to make her feel as secure as anyone could. Meg had used her few formal skills to get a job as a doctor's receptionist so that she could be at home when Trish got back from school, even though it had meant going out again to supervise late-evening surgeries. She'd never mentioned Paddy, except to say that he'd loved Trish and had gone only because of his own problems. And she'd encouraged Trish to work and pass every available exam so that she could go anywhere and be anything she wanted.

Grateful for all of it, admiring, devoted and absolutely on Meg's side, Trish had felt it would be disloyal to have anything to do with her father. Only when Meg herself had heard of his approaches and had made it clear that she positively wanted Trish to get to know him, had she felt free to answer one of his letters. Eventually they'd met and slowly found a way to like each other. Then last year, when Paddy had had a heart attack and Trish had been afraid he would die, she'd let herself admit that she loved him.

Trusting him at last, she'd asked why he'd abandoned them, hoping to make sense of the old betrayal and the anger that had propelled her into her career and out of a lot of relationships of her own. He'd told her that he had seen it as the only way of controlling his urge to batter Meg. That second betrayal might not have hurt as much as the first, but the shock of it was with Trish still.

'What about you, Paddy?' she asked, fighting it back as she always did. After all, Meg had forgiven him, even for the time when he'd failed to control his violence and had put her in hospital.

'Fine, too. Now, be a good child and don't ask questions about me heart. 'Tis as good as new. Better than ever since the bypass.'

Child? she thought in a mixture of amusement and irritation. I haven't been your child since you walked out thirty years ago.

'Now, Bella and I were after taking you out to dinner. You will come, won't you? With that fat boyfriend of yours out of the way, I'll bet you're not eating properly, and I don't want my only child starving herself.'

'He's not fat,' she said automatically and without emphasis. She wasn't concentrating on either Paddy or George. Instead, running her fingers over her face, she counted up all the features she shared with David — and with Paddy.

But he's sixty-three, she thought absurdly. Old enough to be David's *grandfather*.

'Trish? Are you there?'

'Yes, I'm here. I was distracted by something. Sorry. Yes, I'd like to have dinner. When?'

'Tonight? We've found a nice little old-fashioned Italian restaurant just round the corner from Cottesmore Court. They still flame things in front of you and there are bottles in straw and Alpine soldiers' boots and hats on the walls. You will come, won't you? Bella's still working, but she said she could get to the restaurant by nine.'

Reeling from the idea that David could be his son — and that she might well have loads of half-siblings she knew nothing about — Trish agreed.

'But why don't you and I meet at half past eight so that we can have a quiet father-and-daughter drink together first?'

'That'd be great, Trish.' He sounded surprised. 'I'll see you there at half eight, then.'

'Right,' she said, before putting down the mobile.

The light on her answering machine was flashing. Even though she knew there wouldn't be one from George — the time difference made that thoroughly unlikely — she played the messages.

There was one from her mother, two from friends just back from holiday and wanting to see her, and one from Anna:

'Trish, are you feeling any better? I felt very guilty after lunch, when I realised quite how much pressure I'd been putting on you when you were feeling frag. I hadn't meant to. Do ring when you've got a minute.'

Trish picked up the phone. An apology from Anna was rare enough to need encouraging. Besides, it would be good to be distracted from Paddy and the idea that he might be responsible for David's existence. Somehow Trish was going to have to find out, and she just couldn't see herself asking him a direct question.

'Anna?' she said when her call was picked up. 'Hi. It's Trish. Thanks for your message. I'm fine. But you're right, I was feeling fragile. I'm sorry I ran out on you.'

'God, I'm glad. I had a sudden ghastly feeling that you might have . . . you know, when I talked about children. Trish, you looked so pale, you hadn't just had a you know . . . Had you?'

70

'What on earth are you talking about, Anna?'

'An abortion. You hadn't just had one, had you?'

'No, Anna. Nothing like that.' Intrusive questions Trish could take, even though she didn't like them. Sympathy would be impossible just now, so she wasn't going to admit to the miscarriage.

'Thank God for that.' Anna's sigh was deep enough to have come from one of the great whales. 'I know I'm tactless, but I'd never have forgiven myself for that. Now, there's a terrific film by a new Polish director on at the NFT next week. I've got a couple of tickets for Wednesday. Would you like to come?'

'Why not? Thank you, Anna. I've got to dash now, so let's talk on Wednesday morning about when to meet. Thanks for ringing. Bye.'

4

The restaurant was all Paddy had promised, with red-and-white gingham cloths and candles stuck in straw-basketed chianti bottles, and packets of grissini criss-crossed between the waterlily-shaped pink napkins. Trish and her father were both drinking Campari-soda to fit in with their surroundings. She liked the fact that he shared the joke so easily. He snapped another breadstick as she asked him when he'd met Bella. It wasn't a very subtle way into the discussion she hoped would lead to information about David's parentage, but it was the best she could do.

'About seven years ago. Why?'

'I just wondered who you were with before that, say nine or ten years ago.' Trish was glad Antony Shelley couldn't hear her clumsy questions. After all her years at the Bar she should have been better at cross-examination than this.

'Why?' Paddy's face was tight with suspicion.

'It was about then that you started trying to get in touch with me,' she said casually.

Oddly enough, it was the truth, although she hadn't been conscious of it until he'd asked his question. Was it a significant connection or a trivial coincidence? His first letters and phone messages had seemed creepy and self-serving at the time. But what if they'd been prompted by his discovery that he was about to have another child? Could that have so shocked him that he'd needed to see how his first had turned out?

'I'm trying to fill in the lost years, get to know you retrospectively,' she said. Paddy was frowning now, but in cynical calculation, Trish thought, not anxiety, so she quickly improvised, adding: 'What were you doing then — for work, I mean?'

'Advising on personal development within corporate structures, just as I am now, but freelance, not as well, and not for nearly as much money. Trish, what is all this?'

'And you had a girlfriend?'

'Sure, and wasn't I the broth of a boy, even if I was in my fifties?'

'Don't go stage Irish on me,' she said, hating the way he used the fake brogue to deflect questions he didn't want to answer. She still wasn't sure whether it was a subconscious response to threat or a deliberately evasive tactic, but then she knew so little about him, in spite of a scary number of shared characteristics.

'So who was she? Or *they*, if you were really such a broth of a boy?'

'You mean you want a list? Leporello, eat your heart out.'

Who the hell's Leporello, Trish wondered, until she remembered an uncomfortable evening at Glyndebourne, helping George with some client entertaining. As senior partner in his firm of solicitors, he had to do a lot of that, and Trish joined in whenever she could.

She wasn't particularly musical, but she'd enjoyed *Don Giovanni* itself. What she'd passionately disliked about the evening was the pomposity of the other guests, the achingly long journey back into London afterwards, and the whole silliness of putting on evening dress at half-past two in the afternoon to flog out to deepest Sussex. If the weather had been good, it might have seemed less absurd as an entertainment for the kind of people who usually gave the impression that they would be too busy to go to their own mother's funeral. In the rain, the whole self-congratulatory pantomime had made her think of Thomas Aquinas' gruesome theory that the pleasure of those in heaven would be greatly increased by the sight of the agony of those in hell.

'I hope your list is fewer than *mille-tre*,' she said, then despised herself for needing to prove she'd picked up his reference. From the glint in his black eyes, he knew exactly what she was doing — and what she felt about it.

'By one or two.' He smashed two grissini at once and sprayed crumbs all over the cloth.

'So, who were they? Come on, Paddy. Stop being so coy.'

'But why do you want to know?'

'I told you. I want to fill in the lost years, get to know you as you were all the time I was being so silly and inventing all sorts of weird, unfair ideas about what kind of man you must be.' That was better. That really might get him talking.

The glint dimmed in his eyes. Disappointment or reassurance? She couldn't tell.

'For God's sake, Trish,' he said, looking at something over her shoulder.

'Please, Paddy. It's very important to me to know the truth about how you lived while I might have known you but didn't.'

'Look, I had only one girlfriend at the time. If I give you her name, will you shut up about it now?'

'So long as you add her address.'

'Why? I warn you, Trish, I will not have you banging on her door, badgering her with questions.'

'D'you really suppose she still lives in the same place after ten years?' Trish said, refusing to offer a direct lie about her intentions. She might not go banging on the door, but she was definitely intending to pursue the woman.

Expecting Paddy to refuse, she was surprised when he took an old envelope out of his pocket and began to write fast and untidily, muttering, 'See to Bella, will you?'

Trish glanced over her shoulder, to see her father's current partner in the doorway of the restaurant, looking around for him. No wonder he'd suddenly turned cooperative. The last thing he'd want would be Bella catching him discussing one of her many predecessors. Happy enough to fulfil her part of the bargain, Trish waited until the head waiter had stopped kissing Bella, then took his place.

Bella looked surprised but pleased, saying when they'd both straightened up, 'You're looking very well, Trish. Paddy was sure you'd be starving yourself into a knitting needle with George away.'

'I may not be nearly such a good cook as George,' Trish said, as she stood between Bella and the table, 'but even I can boil a cauliflower and open a pot of yoghurt. Shall we order your drink while we're here, to save time? They spend so long kissing new arrivals that it takes ages to get them to bring anything to the table.'

Bella turned to the waiter and said she'd like a glass of prosecco, please. Then she and Trish joined Paddy. Trish saw the folded envelope in her place and discreetly put it in her bag while Paddy gave Bella a quite unnecessarily theatrical kiss. Trish wondered whether he was giving her time to get the envelope out of sight or punishing her for digging into his past. She knew her mother wouldn't have minded the evidence of his passion for Bella, but that didn't make it any easier for his daughter to watch.

This business of treating your parents as one adult to another was tough, Trish had found long ago. Ashamed of her truculence, she set out to be entertaining. It was worth the effort. Bella stopped talking to her as though she were a potentially temperamental invalid that night, and they discovered a lot of shared ground. At one moment, Paddy even told them to stop excluding him. They both laughed then, and agreed to order zabaglione all round, even though the menu and the waiter both warned that they'd have to wait twenty minutes for it.

Trish drove home at the end of the long evening understanding both her parents better than she ever had. If a woman like Bella could have spent seven years with Paddy, it was no longer so surprising that Trish's mother, Meg, had once loved him enough to marry him and have a child — and even to make light of his drinking and the violence that had followed it. Meg had always claimed that Paddy had only hit her once, but Trish's professional experience of domestic assaults made that hard to believe.

It was far too late to do anything about contacting his old girlfriend tonight, but Trish couldn't resist seeing where she'd lived. Unfolding the envelope Paddy had given her, she saw that he'd added a note at the bottom. *Don't go stirring up trouble now, Trish.*

She knew she couldn't promise that. If David turned out to be the product of one of Paddy's affairs, bringing the information to light would do a lot more than cause trouble. But she couldn't leave the boy unclaimed in hospital without being sure she'd done everything she could to establish his identity. He'd had her name and address in his fleece, so someone close to him knew all about her. She had to do what she could to find out who he was, however damaging that might be.

To her surprise, Sylvia Bantell was still listed in the phone book above the same address Paddy had known. Trish rang her next morning from chambers. She answered the phone briskly, giving her name rather than her number, which suggested both confidence and recklessness.

'Hello. I'm sorry to disturb you. My name's Trish Maguire. I'm — '

'Not Paddy's famous daughter?' The lightly drawling voice sounded full of amusement.

'You mean he told you about me?'

'Never stopped boasting about you, my dear. Banged on and on for hours and hours about how clever you were, how successful, how beautiful. I used to think you must be the most exasperating brat in the entire world.'

'I'm not surprised.' Beautiful? Trish considered her spiky hair and beaked nose. What was he thinking of? But of course, he didn't know me then. 'I can't imagine why he should have done anything like that. He hadn't seen me for over twenty years.'

'He knew more than enough about you. He could have bored for England on the subject. How is the old bastard anyway?'

'Not bad. He had a heart attack, then a bypass, last year. But he's over both now.'

'Did he ask you to get in touch with me?'

'God no! No, this is private enterprise. I wanted to ask you . . . This is frightfully difficult, you know.' Trish thought that Mrs

Bantell's Kensington idiom must be catching. 'Frightful' wasn't one of her words. 'I wanted to know whether you and he . . . '

'We had a bit of gallop and jump together, if that's what you're asking. But we were both unmarried at the time and well over the age of consent. What's the problem?'

'No problem. Look, I'm sorry, it's a hard thing to say, but you and he never had a child, did you?' She wondered why it seemed so much easier to ask a total stranger than her father.

A chime of musical laughter sounded through the phone.

'Oh, poor Trish. Have you been worrying about losing your status as Paddy's unique and perfect offspring?'

'Not quite that.' Suddenly she was back in the A & E department at Dowting's, looking not at David's mashed-up face, but at the sympathetic nurse who'd told her what to expect after her miscarriage.

'Well, you don't have to worry. If you could see me you wouldn't have had to ask. I'm a year or two older than Paddy and even when we were together I was well past the Change.'

'Oh, I see. I'm so sorry. It's very kind of you to have been so frank. And I'm sorry to have bothered you.'

'That's all right. I find the idea quite funny actually. But you obviously don't. What exactly is it that's bugging you so much? Paddy hasn't been winding you up and telling you I had his infant, has he?'

'Absolutely not. And he doesn't know I'm asking questions. You won't tell him, will you?'

'My dear, I wouldn't dream of it. We haven't been in contact for nine years or more,' Sylvia Bantell said drily. 'But if you see the old bastard, you might tell him I've forgiven him.'

'Forgiven him for what?'

'He'll know,' said Mrs Bantell darkly. After a moment's silence, she added in an unconvincingly casual voice, 'Actually, I booted him out when I found I hadn't acquired exclusive rights to his attention. He was a shocker, you know.'

Now, why are you telling me this, Trish wondered. It sounds like punishment, but you can't still want retribution for the boredom of listening to him talk about my supposed virtues all those years ago. Is it Paddy himself you're after?

She said nothing, assuming there was more to come.

'And, Trish?'

'Yes?'

'You don't actually sound quite as exasperating as I thought you would.'

'I'm glad,' Trish said, still waiting. There were a lot of questions she wanted to ask, but she wasn't going to join in whatever game Sylvia might be playing with her.

'Oh, all right, I'll tell you.' The drawly voice had sharpened. 'You see, one evening he let something slip that made it clear he was seeing someone else. I was so angry I put private detectives on him.'

'Ah, I see. Thank you for telling me.'

'Don't you even want to know who she was?'

'Only if you want to tell me.'

'She was a prostitute called Jeannie Nest, and she lived in a disgusting slum south of the river. When I found out . . . Well, I can tell you I was round to the quack straight away to get checked out.'

This is definitely punishment, thought Trish, torn between an instinct to choke off Sylvia's vindictiveness and a need to know everything. The mention of 'south of the river' seemed too significant to ignore.

'Where exactly did she live?'

'I thought you might ask that,' Sylvia said, sounding satisfied enough to justify Trish's suspicion. 'Hang on and I'll get the report.'

Four minutes later she was back. 'The Mull

Estate, Southwark. Sixty-three, Kingston Buildings specifically. It'll be tough for you if there really was a baby from that relationship. I can't imagine many successful barristers wanting to acknowledge some tart's child from the slums as their half-sibling.'

'I'm surprised you kept a report like that for so long,' Trish said, too angry now to suppress everything she felt. 'What were you planning to do with it? Blackmail him?'

'That's offensive — and ridiculous. If you must know, I assumed he was suffering a temporary bout of *nostalgie de la boue*. Some chaps do. So I waited until he was ready to come back. Then, when I had him at my mercy, I was going to rub his nose in the filth of what he'd been doing.'

'Ah,' Trish said, glad to know she hadn't been unfair to the woman. 'So that you could punish him, you mean?'

'So that I could show him precisely why I would never have anything to do with him ever again. Touch a tart's leavings? Ugh!'

'It must have been very frustrating when he didn't even try to come back.'

'What makes you think he didn't?' Now the Kensington voice was seriously sharp.

Because *I* wouldn't have, Trish thought. We're alike in that, Paddy and I, just as we're alike in our terror of being shut up in a chintzy suburban prison. Aloud she gave the easier answer: 'Because you'd have binned the report by now if he had come back and been made to face it. But I'm glad you kept it, and I'm grateful for the information. Goodbye.'

★ ★ ★

Sylvia Bantell put down the telephone and looked around her immaculate drawing room. It had seemed appallingly dull for the past nine years, in spite of all the new bits and pieces she'd bought for it and the three expensive redecorations she'd lavished on it. Without Paddy Maguire's fiery presence, the room — like her life — had felt empty, however many other people she'd imported to take his place.

Odd to have had the most exciting year of your life at fifty-five, she thought. Paddy had never let her feel secure and so she'd never been bored with him. He'd made her laugh; he'd opened her eyes to life beyond her own little world; and in bed he'd led her into delights that could still make her blush whenever she thought about them.

The edges of the detective's report were digging into her hands. She looked down, rather ashamed of herself. Paddy wasn't ever coming back and it was rather undignified to have betrayed him to his daughter. Sylvia ripped the stiff card covers from the report and wrenched at the tough plastic spiral that bound it. Somewhere in the house was a portable shredder. She'd put the pages through that and forget the whole business: forget that Paddy had once made her feel like a tart herself. And that she'd loved every grubby, painful, thrilling minute of it.

Could his daughter have any idea of what he was really like?

Sylvia didn't think so. With her intelligently attractive voice and the loyalty that had made her reject all implicit criticism of her father, Trish had sounded quite unaware of the truth. Poor Trish.

Later, Sylvia watched each page of the report sliding through the dusty old shredder. It really was over now.

★ ★ ★

Trish reminded herself that she was supposed to be working on Nick Gurles's case, not delving into her father's sexual past. She stuffed the envelope he'd given her into her bag and got back to work, wishing that the nervous-sounding trainee from Sprindlers had managed to track down the missing note. When Trish phoned to chase it up, the assistant said she was still trying to find it.

Two whole lever-arch files were finished by the time one of Trish's fellow tenants looked in to suggest a drink later in El Vino's.

'Not tonight, Bill,' she said, faking regret. He'd never tried to wind her up like Robert Anstey, even though he'd been Antony's preferred junior for the past two years, but she had other things to do. 'I've got to chase up a loose end. But thank you. Have a good time.'

When he'd gone, she packed up her papers. She was pleased she'd made herself work. There were still at least four hours of daylight, which would be plenty to check out Jeannie Nest and still drop in to see David afterwards. Trish looked up the Mull Estate in Southwark and was amazed to see that it was only a little way south of her own warehouse flat on the far side of Borough High Street. It shouldn't take more than ten minutes to walk there.

She shut down her laptop and left chambers to take her usual route home over Blackfriars Bridge, envying all the people who had flats in the Oxo Building. She loved the river and its openness, but when she'd been looking for somewhere to buy, internal space had seemed much more important than any view, however glorious. She'd stretched herself to the limit to buy and convert the huge top floor of an old engineering works and had watched both her earnings and the prices of Southwark lofts climb steadily ever since.

Tempted to go in and change as she passed the iron staircase that led up to her own front door, she resisted, fearing that she might never drive herself out again if she did. Instead she walked on, turning right, left, then right again until she'd reached her destination. It was as though she'd stepped across a frontier. She was facing the most depressing housing estate she'd ever seen.

Built of dirty redbrick, probably between the wars, it looked cramped as well as broken down. Each of the four long blocks was six storeys high, and each storey consisted of a row of front doors ranged along a walkway. Washing hung there and rubbish lay in heaps everywhere she looked.

Trish could see a white metal cube on the top balcony to her left; it looked like a washing machine, or perhaps a fridge. Suddenly the weird statistic that something 'was less likely to kill you than a fridge falling on your head' made sense.

There was no grass anywhere, or trees; only cracked concrete. The area between the blocks was half-filled with rusty cars. Weeds grew in the cracks, and muddy puddles showed how bad the ground drainage must be. A group of small children were throwing stones at the worst of the cars. It had only one tyre left and the windscreen was smashed. Above them a skein of geese flew in arrow-straight formation across the gold-and-blue sky, as though to show the inhabitants of this desolate place just how firmly shackled they were.

Trish found it hard to imagine her father coming here. Even if he'd wanted a prostitute, surely there were more alluring places to find one. Still, if Sylvia Bantell's private detective had been any good, this was the place where Paddy had come on several occasions nine years ago. The lead had to be worth pursuing.

Once she'd double-checked that she had the right address, Trish asked the staring children which block held number 63. One, a blonde girl with gappy teeth and sharp eyes, asked why she wanted to know.

'I'm looking for someone called Jeannie Nest,' she said. 'Do any of you know her?'

'No.' After a second the child's face brightened. 'But I'll show you sixty-three if you give me a pound.'

'Oh, I think that's a bit expensive,' Trish said lightly.

'Then you can fuck off,' said the child, turning and running towards the far side of the concreted space. The others casually went back to dismantling the wing mirror on one of the cars.

Trish blinked, then looked around to get her bearings, before picking her way up a stinking brick staircase to the second floor of the furthest block. Finding number 63 painted beside a peeling, dirty-yellow door, she rang the bell.

There was no sound, so she assumed the bell had been disconnected. She banged on the door. Eventually it was opened by a tall, youngish man wearing black trousers and nothing else. His skin was very white, his hair very black, and he hadn't shaved for days. He said something incomprehensible.

'Could I speak to Jeannie Nest?' Trish said, enunciating carefully.

'Who?'

'Jeannie Nest. Doesn't she live here? She used to.'

The man scratched his bare chest, blinking sleepily, and told her in heavily accented, hesitant English that he'd moved in only a week ago, had never heard of anyone called Nest, didn't know anyone else on the estate, hated it, and wanted to go home. Then he shut the door.

Trish couldn't blame him. But she was here now, and she wasn't leaving until she'd collected some information. She could hear the children in the forecourt yelling at each other; she could hear reggae music beating out from several flats, and people were calling — or shouting — all round her. Someone screamed, but it was a short, unfrightened kind of noise. Trish wasn't sure that she'd have done anything even if it hadn't been, but she was glad she didn't have to worry about it.

She looked along the row of doors for one that gave any sign of welcome. Three down from the flat she'd already tried was a door carefully painted in bright turquoise. The net curtains in the window beside it looked clean. There was even a wrought-iron hook that might once have held a hanging basket. Someone who cared lived there. She tried the bell.

A much older black man opened the door. His back was very straight, and he wore his clothes well. He looked her up and down carefully, before asking what he could do for her. Encouraged, Trish told him she was looking for Jeannie Nest.

'She hasn't lived here for years,' he said.

'But she once did, didn't she?'

'Oh, yes. Number sixty-three.'

'When did she go?'

'Six years ago.'

'Why?'

He didn't answer, and he hardly moved, but the slight backwards pull in his body and the withdrawal in his big toffee-coloured eyes made Trish curious. She asked again.

'I don't want to talk about it. You should understand that,' he said, pointing at her briefcase.

'OK.' Trish wondered if he took her for a social worker. 'It's not really her I'm interested in. It's her child.'

'The boy? Why? What's he done?'

'So, there was a boy?'

'A toddler. He must have been about two when they went. Three maybe.'

'What was his name?'

For a second he looked as though he might answer, then he started to shut the door.

'Please,' Trish said, moving forwards. She didn't jam her foot in the door; it wasn't her style and in any case she had no right.

'I have to go,' said the man, breathing hard.

Surprised, Trish looked along the walkway in both directions. There was nobody there except a watchful-looking white man, very young and much better dressed than the one who inhabited Jeannie Nest's old flat. He caught Trish's eye and smiled pleasantly. He

91

looked as if he'd been running.

'Can I help? You look lost.' His voice had an accent that Professor Higgins might have identified. Trish couldn't.

'Thank you,' she said, smiling back and envying him his almost perfect teeth. 'I'm not lost, but I am looking for someone who once lived here and seems to have disappeared. No one can tell me anything about her.'

'Tough, that. What's the name?'

'Nest. Jeannie Nest. Does it mean anything?'

He rubbed his chin, biting his lower lip at the same time, then shrugged. 'What sort of name's Nest?'

'I don't know. But it's all I've got to go on. Have you lived here long?'

He looked amused, perhaps at the idea that a stranger might think she had the right to ask questions like that. 'Four years.'

'Oh, I see. I think she left here before that.'

'Why d'you want her?'

Trish wasn't going to risk betraying her real interest, even to someone as uninvolved as this. She tried to think of a plausible excuse for her search.

'It's just possible that she might have inherited something from one of our clients.'

'That's nice. I could ask around, if you like. See if anyone's heard of her, knows where she's gone. You got a card? I could phone you.'

'Not on me,' Trish said, uncomfortable and wanting to get out of the place as soon as possible without giving herself away. 'I left them in the office. Don't worry; I'll try the next address my boss gave me.'

'Where's that then?'

'My boss'll have it back at the office. He only gave me this one.' It was a stupid story; she wished she'd prepared something marginally more credible.

The young man was between her and the stairs. Trish told herself to stop overreacting. Just because he lived in this poverty-stricken place, that didn't mean he was either violent or criminal. He'd been exceedingly polite. But she couldn't stop her heart thumping or her throat drying. The handle of her briefcase felt suddenly slippery. She wasn't usually this pathetic.

'What's your boss's firm, then? I'll phone when I've found something out.'

Trish smiled again and told him it didn't matter. Her voice sounded high and tight. She made herself walk firmly towards him. He moved, but into her path rather than leaving her more space.

'I can help you, honest. I know lots of people here. I can talk to them for you.

They'll tell me a lot more than they'd ever tell someone like you.'

'I wouldn't dream of troubling you.' For a sickening moment she thought he was going to stop her, but when she was within touching distance, he stood back and she got past. Finding she was a couple of inches taller than him made her feel better. They were so close that she could smell him.

Peppermint, she thought, and soap or shampoo. Yes, it was shampoo; rather a nice smell, too. She was ashamed of her surprise.

The children were still playing, but they stopped chucking stones at the cars as she came down the stairs. By the time she reached them, they'd formed into a semicircle, waiting for her.

'Gi's a fiver, then,' said the girl who'd wanted a pound earlier. She couldn't have been more than six years old.

'Nah. She's rich,' said one of the bigger boys. 'Look at her. We need a tenner. Or the watch. Look, it's a Rolex. Come on, gi's a tenner.'

The greed in his expression was mixed with hate. Even more uncomfortable, Trish looked at the others and saw them as small, taunting devils in a peculiarly modern kind of hell.

It's never the child's fault, she reminded herself. You've spent your life working for children like these; you can't be frightened of them. Get a move on.

'Come on, slag,' said the eldest, taking a step towards her and showing her the stone he was holding. His dirty hands were much bigger than she'd expected. 'Where's the tenner then? 'S'all we want. Nothing to you. Hand it over.'

Talk about demanding money with menaces, she thought, trying to keep up her courage. It was the clearest example of that particular crime she'd seen since the last batch of baby thugs had come Trick or Treating last November and tried to bully her into giving them something. At least then she'd been on her own ground.

'I'm not going to give any of you any money,' she said as clearly now as she'd said it then, stepping out, straight into a puddle. The children shrieked with laughter, dancing round her, yelling gross insults. There wasn't much that shocked her, but some of the names they shouted were vile. One of the little girls flung a stone at her. It was only a pebble really, but it hit Trish's arm hard. Surprised, she looked back and saw that one of the bigger boys had a broken brick in his hand. He drew back his arm to throw.

'Leave her alone,' said a familiar voice from above her. Trish looked up and saw the shampoo-smelling young man, leaning over the parapet of the walkway above. 'Let the lady go.'

The children scuttled away without protest, letting the bricks and stones drop unobtrusively as they ran. What kind of hold could he have over them, Trish wondered sickly, and how had he got it?

'Thanks,' she said, barely looking at him as she walked fast towards the exit.

'Take care how you go now,' the young man called after her. As she reached the bent concrete bollards that marked the pedestrian route out, she looked over her shoulder. He was still there, watching her, and waved. She had difficulty suppressing a shudder. The children were back, too, staring at her from the shadows beyond the cars, like feral cats. Thoroughly uncomfortable, Trish walked away in the opposite direction from her flat. She wasn't going to lead any of this lot there, if she could help it, even though the diversion meant she wouldn't have time to visit David. She found herself getting deeper and deeper into a hinterland, where nothing looked familiar and every face she saw seemed hostile.

This is not *Bonfire of the Vanities*, she told herself caustically. Get a grip.

Eventually she found her way to the familiar safety of the Leather Market and then Long Lane. Fifteen minutes later she was walking back up Blackfriars Bridge Road towards the river and the comfortable familiarity of her own building.

One of the lofts below hers had just been sold for over seven hundred thousand pounds. Reminding herself of the price seemed to put a bigger distance between the flat and the Mull Estate with its creepy air of violence and the aggressive children. Odd that they'd disappeared at a word from the young man who looked far too expensively dressed to belong anywhere near them. Odd and more sinister than the rest.

The street door clunked shut behind her, and the smell of beeswax polish filled her nostrils. Spicy and invigorating. She'd never really noticed it before, even on the days when her cleaner had been. Now it smelled delectably welcoming.

The wide spaces of polished wooden floor between the big black sofas and the fireplace seemed more luxurious than ever, as did the high white-painted brick walls, which showed off her collection of unframed modern paintings.

It was lucky the marauding children hadn't seen this, she thought as she went to put on the kettle, or they'd have demanded a lot more than ten quid.

5

Mikey watched the tall, dark-haired woman rush away and spat his gum on to the filthy walkway, wondering about her. He didn't think she could be a teacher or a social worker, not with the Rolex the kids had spotted, nor with that haircut, and he knew she wasn't police. Too smart as well as too spooked by a few kids. And anyway he knew most of the filth round here.

But why would anyone come looking for Jeannie Nest here these days? It didn't fit. And that worried him. He liked to know what was going on in even the nastiest corners of the estate. That way he could stamp on any dangerous hints of disloyalty.

He took out another piece of chewing gum and leaned on the parapet, breathing in the menthol, feeling the surge of it freezing up the back of his nose, as he tried to work it all out. The kids came back out after a while, checked to see if he was still there, then started collecting a heap of stones. Every now and then they looked up to see if he'd moved. They were scared of him — all but Kelly, who'd come running to tell him that 'a lady' was asking questions — but they wanted to be like him, which meant they showed him proper respect.

Mikey didn't blame them for trying to get money out of the woman with the Rolex, or for throwing stones at her. He'd probably have done it himself at their age. He wouldn't have bothered to stop them if he hadn't wanted her out of the way fast — and before she could get to anyone who might be mad enough to talk to her.

He looked at his own watch. One day that too would be a Rolex, but for the moment it was the nearest thing he'd found at Argos. It would soon be time for his next call, but he couldn't be early. He needed the clients to wait, worrying about whether he was going to come, sweating just enough to make them want to please him. He always liked seeing the sweat and hearing them stammer as they made their excuses.

'Hey, Kelly!' he called. The draggled six year old picked her feet out of a puddle and looked up, squinting against the light. He beckoned.

'Yes, Mikey?'

'You know that lady?'

'Yes, Mikey.'

'If she comes back again, I want to know, OK? I'll give you another pound if you tell me when you've seen her and what she was doing.'

Her eyes sparkled and her gappy smile grew enormous. 'Yes, Mikey.'

'And don't tell me lies, Kelly. I'll have other people checking, people you don't know. So if they haven't seen her as well, I'll know you're lying. Like always, OK?'

'Yes, Mikey.'

'Good girl.'

She pushed back her matted hair with both hands, beaming up at him. One day she'd be pretty. And useful. But not to him. He wasn't planning to be here in ten years' time, and he had a rule. None of his girls would ever be under sixteen. Too dangerous, and anyway he didn't approve of that sort of thing.

The place was filling up now. People who had day jobs were drifting home, while the others were leaving for the pub or the takeaway. In thirty minutes or so, the crack dealer would drive in, like ice-cream vans in the old days. Unlike the vans, dealers didn't need to play a silly little tune. Everyone who wanted them was always waiting.

A hooded boy slipped out of one of the ground-floor flats and was soon joined by four others. They'd done their main business of the day, nicking mobiles off other schoolkids, but they came out most evenings for whatever else they could pick up. They weren't into jucking yet on this estate, but it'd probably come. Cutting someone's leg — painfully but without risking too much damage — was a passport into several of the gangs that operated in the south of the borough, and it was bound to leak northwards. Even on this estate most of the boys carried knives. Mikey never had, not even in his schooldays. He'd seen how they could get you into trouble more often than out of it, and there were plenty of other ways to make people scared of you.

No one came anywhere near him, which he liked. He didn't mess with the gangs or the dealers, and they didn't mess with him. Their businesses were what you could call complementary, so they respected each other. And none of the older residents would talk to him, but he didn't care. Their silence was like a special suit that stopped the dirt of the place getting anywhere near his skin.

★ ★ ★

Business over, he strolled to the opposite side of the estate and ran easily up to the top floor. Like always, he enjoyed the power his fitness gave him. He worked hard enough at it, too. The hours spent in the gym were sometimes boring, sometimes quite a laugh as he watched the gays preening and saw how the steroid-addicts thought building up huge amounts of muscle was worth the risks they were taking.

When he'd first come back here from his great-aunt's house in the country four years ago, at the age of sixteen, he'd tried to tell one of them about the heart attacks and the 'roid-rage, and the law. He could still remember the pain of his broken collarbone and how the broken ends had grated together when he'd moved. 'I'll give you 'roid rage,' the bloke had said with his foot on Mikey's chest.

He'd stopped trying to help anyone after that. And now the iron-pumpers left him alone, too, unless they needed him. Then they showed all the respect anyone could want. No one dissed him these days, or passed remarks about his size.

He looked back at his sixteen-year-old self in pity. Trying to help this lot of meatheads had been a right waste of time. They didn't even know enough to want to get out of here. All they thought of was making themselves look more powerful, with muscles and pitbulls, instead of getting the real thing.

For himself, he'd be out of here as soon as he'd got control of the business. It shouldn't be long now. He'd been patient and kind, and he'd worked hard. It was starting to look like it'd soon be payback time. Then he'd have the kind of life he deserved, the kind he'd have had years ago if his grandad hadn't been so fucking stupid. And if Jeannie Nest had minded her own business.

Thinking about how they'd wrecked everyone's life between them was the one thing that could really rile Mikey, so he didn't do it often.

'Don't get angry, get even,' he muttered to himself, thinking of the shitty years he'd spent with his great-aunt in Norfolk, bullied by her old man, bored out of his skull, and always cold. Nothing like that was ever going to happen to him again.

When he got to the flat, he opened the door with the key his grandmother had given him when he first came back, calling: 'Nan? You in there? It's me.'

'Make us a cup of tea, will you, love?'

'Sure.' He leaned over his grandmother's plump shoulder and kissed her.

His younger self had despised her for her wrinkles and whiskers, and for being a sad old bag who mumbled round false teeth that didn't fit properly, and who smelled bad and wore too much white slap on her face and too much red lipstick. He knew better now. Now he had more time for her than for anyone else in the world. But he did wish she'd modernise the business like he always told her.

Patience, he told himself as he felt the anger pushing inside his head again. Hang on in there. She'll give in soon.

She looked up from her account books and smiled round the pen she had in her mouth. He knew that sucking pens helped her keep off the fags.

'You're a good boy. You've been doing well, too. The books are looking all right. But I don't like you letting off that pair in Reynolds Tower. They owe us more than seven hundred quid now.'

'They haven't got it, Nan.' He moved into the narrow kitchen to get her tea and called back over the sound of running water. 'And no amount of coming the heavy is going to get it. Not yet, anyway. But she's starting a job next week — office cleaning. I'll wait till she's had her second pay packet and put a bit by, then I'll have a go.'

'What? Get heavy?'

'No. Just the verbal pressure. I know how to make her scared of us without laying a finger on her, Nan. Then I'll make sure she gets used to paying us back, a little bit more each week, till we've had it all. No blood, no mess, just all the interest she owes, then the principal. Right?'

★ ★ ★

Old Lil Handsome eased her back against the chair, and rested one hand over her aching kidney. Nothing could stop that hurting, but it helped knowing her family had produced some brains at last. Mikey was a good boy even if he was impatient. Sometimes she wondered what he was up to when he didn't come back for days at a time, but mostly she could convince herself that he *was* a good boy.

He worked nights for a mini-cab firm, and he did the collections for her, and she was sure he was running a couple of working girls. But just occasionally she thought there could be something else as well, and she couldn't make up her mind whether it was better to know or not. She hoped it wasn't drugs. A bit of thieving she could cope with, but not drugs. Sometimes when he came back to the flat he had a look about him that she didn't like at all. But today he was fine. She put down her pen, waiting till he brought her tea.

It was strong and sweet, like she wanted. She lit another fag; the third of the day. She didn't usually let herself have the third till

105

bedtime, but Mikey's report was worth a celebration. She sucked in the smoke, relaxing as it hit, holding it in her lungs, feeling the power. At last she let it pour out again in a blue sigh. She couldn't think why anyone would want crack or skunk or smack — or whatever the new thing might be. This was the business: a straight fag. And legal, too. Amazing.

'Thanks. But don't wait till the second pay packet, Mikey. By then she'll have spent the first and she won't feel so rich. Get over there the minute she's come home after the first pay day. It'll be more money than she's seen for a long time. She'll be feeling right wealthy till the first time she goes to spend any of it, then it'll seem less straight off. So make sure she spends it paying us back, not buying stuff from mail-order catalogues, nor extra food for the kids. Us.'

He turned it over in his mind, which she liked, then he said quietly, 'OK. Good thinking, Nan.'

She let out the breath she'd been holding, and decided not to give him any more compliments. Too many could make him think he didn't have to try so hard. And she wanted him to try as hard as she'd had to, so he'd value what she was going to give him one day — when she was sure of him.

'Have you thought any more about going to the ones who've already got debts on the catalogues, Nan? Or the druggies?'

Not again, she thought, sucking in the smoke to give her patience. She shook her head, hoping that would be enough to keep him quiet. But he had her stubbornness too.

'I know you don't like going looking for customers, but we could really clean up. I know exactly who owes what. There's one old slapper in Kingston Buildings who ran up over a grand on catalogues last Christmas, buying designer gear for her kids. She's not going to pay that off quickly. I mean, she's on family credit, isn't she? I can offer her and all the rest of them the cash to pay off their debts at one per cent less than the catalogues charge. We'd have a much bigger business in no time. It'd be like the old days you've talked about, Nan, before anyone ever had any catalogues.'

'We don't need a bigger business, Mikey. And I've always waited for them to come to me, like I told you. It's safer that way. As for the addicts, I couldn't trust them to pay any of it back, and I don't like drugs anyway.' There wasn't any point explaining all over again, and his eyes had got the tight look she hated, so she stopped. 'What've you got for me today?'

He unzipped the centre pocket of his leather jacket and took out a neat roll of notes, pinging off the rubber band. Unfolding the list she'd given him that morning, he counted off the fives and tens he'd been collecting all day from this estate and the others all round.

'It's all there, except for the Reynolds Tower two.'

'Good,' she said, checking off the amounts listed against the pile of notes.

Some were torn and dirty, but some were as crisply fresh as if the people who'd handed them over had got them straight from a cash machine. They couldn't have, of course. The people she did business with didn't have access to cash machines because no bank would let them near an account. If they had, the customers wouldn't have come to her in the first place. So these crunchy notes must have been nicked to pay her off with. That didn't worry her. Not her problem, was it?

She hated banks nearly as much as she hated the companies that sent glossy catalogues, enticing people to buy stuff they couldn't afford and threatening to ruin her business. She'd looked at one of the catalogues once and seen all the nonsense they wrote about credit being what they called 'subject to status'. She'd never heard of anyone who'd been refused, however poor they were. So long as they sent up the first payment with a Postal Order when they ordered something, it'd be delivered straight off. Washing machines, designer clothes, toys, furniture; they could get anything, just by posting a letter. Of course, if they didn't complete the payments, they wouldn't get a second chance. Still, it wasn't right.

The smoke caught in her eyes and she swallowed some down the wrong way. A fit of coughing seized her and she had to put down the money and the pen and the fag as she bent over her table, fighting to breathe. Her eyes were streaming and her throat was all scrunched up. After a bit Mikey put his hands on her shoulders and lifted her up.

'Careful, Nan. Careful.' He rubbed her back, good boy that he was, and told her to breathe like she was having a baby or something. Later on he fetched her more tea for when she'd stopped coughing. He'd stubbed out the fag, too, which was a waste.

'Nan?' he said when they were both sitting quiet with their tea and she was breathing again all right.

'Yes?' She hoped he wasn't going to go on about expanding the business.

'There was a woman asking questions, over on the other side. Outside Jeannie Nest's old flat. Said she was looking for her. Does it mean anything to you?'

Lil sat very still. It was the only way she knew to stop the anger eating her up from inside. She'd known since Sunday that trouble was coming, as clearly as if she'd seen the white, blind, nasty look in her old man's face again.

'Police?' she asked.

'No. She said she was a lawyer, but I don't know. Why d'you think she was police?'

Because I've been waiting for them, she thought, but she wasn't going to tell Mikey that. There was enough trouble between him and his uncle as it was.

Her younger son had come to the flat with blood all down his trousers in the middle of Sunday night, and a story of a prostitute he'd hit when she got in his way. It wouldn't have been the first time, but something had made Lil think he was lying.

'Have you seen your uncle this week, Mikey?'

'No. Why, d'you want him?'

'He usually comes round on Tuesdays when he's spent his Giro, wanting money. But he hasn't been in today.'

'Maybe he's sleeping it off.'

'Maybe.' She felt sick as a dog, thinking about Jeannie Nest. Could it have been her blood on Gary's trousers? He'd talked about giving her one often enough. But how would he have found her? 'What did you say to the woman who was asking questions?'

'Nothing. What's the point? I said I didn't know nothing, but I'd ask around for her if she'd leave me a phone number. She legged it then. But I'll hear about it if she comes back.'

'If she wasn't police, Mikey, could she be from the papers? A reporter maybe who's heard your uncle banging on in the pub about how he's going to do Jeannie one of these days.'

He looked like she'd thrown something at him, his head jerking back and shock in his eyes. Maybe he wasn't as sharp as she'd hoped. It was the obvious answer, as far as she could see.

'I never thought of that, Nan. But it'd explain why she went off so quick. She was well scared. The kids helped, of course.' He laughed, showing off his white teeth and his clean pink tongue. 'They started throwing stones at her. Got her on the run, like I said. A reporter. Of course.'

★ ★ ★

Trish was standing under the shower, letting the water stream down over her face, washing off everything she'd seen on the Mull Estate. She couldn't believe that she'd been so scared by a few children under ten. For years she'd argued that anything a child did was forgivable in the context of the way he himself had been treated. She'd ached for even the most violent of them, and blamed their parents for every crime they'd committed.

Now she wondered what it would be like to give birth to a child who stole or bullied or even knifed other children. She didn't think any baby of hers would have grown up vicious, but she couldn't be sure. After all, genes will out; and hers weren't anywhere near perfect. There was her temper for one, which she knew she'd inherited from Paddy, along with a hatred of small, enclosed spaces.

She thought suddenly of George, thrown out of his childhood safety to do battle with boarding school at the age of eight. Was that why he *did* like small, cosy rooms so much and felt threatened by her need for echoing emptiness?

If so, could they ever get it right? She found his kind of safety quite as threatening as he found her need for independence. Was that a product of her genes? Had she inherited her father's inability to stay with anyone for more than a few years? Could she ever be tempted to hit her way out of a failing relationship? Or abandon her child as Paddy had abandoned her? Maybe that was why she'd had the miscarriage. Had her body known she wasn't fit to have a child of her own?

The sound of the ringing phone reached her through the storm of questions and the pounding water. She groped for a towel as she emerged from the shower. The answering machine had long since invited the caller to leave a name, number and any message, and Trish waited to hear who might be trying to get hold of her.

'Trish-love? Are you there? It's your mother. Nothing urgent, but it would be nice to chat.'

Trish reached the receiver before her mother had rung off.

'I was in the shower, sorry,' she said, aware that the last few days had seen her apologising far more often than usual. She had to get a grip soon or she'd fret herself into a frenzy.

'What's the matter?'

'Nothing, Mum. I'm fine.'

Meg, who had often picked up her only child's distress from a hundred miles away, left a silence that stretched to half a minute while Trish tried to think of something cheerful to say.

'You don't have to tell me anything, but I know you're not fine, Trish. I'd like to help, if I could. And you know I won't tell anyone else if it's something confidential. Is it a case?'

'No. A miscarriage. I mean, I — '

'Ah, I'm so sorry.' As Meg talked gently, sensibly, leaving small gaps for Trish to fill if she wanted, she thought how easily anyone else might have misunderstood and assumed she meant a miscarriage of justice — or pretended to assume that. Meg had always been able to interpret ambiguities the right way. Trish hoped she'd been grateful enough for that, and for everything else Meg had always done for her. She was suddenly afraid she might cry.

'So, I'll let you go now,' her mother was saying. 'But would you like to come and stay for a bit? I know how awful it feels after losing a baby, and how it saps all your courage and makes you think that nothing's worth anything, and that you aren't worth anything yourself either. But you are worth a lot, Trish. And the work you do is, too.'

'It's OK, really,' Trish said, even more grateful for the stream of words that had given her time to control herself. She did *not* cry. 'I'll cope better with it if I'm on my own while it's as raw as this. But I'd love to come later.'

'Good. Promise you'll tell me if you need anything, Trish?'

'Yes. Thank you. How's Bernard?'

'Fine. And we've got all sorts of plans. I'm even looking forward to retirement now. See you soon.'

Trish said goodbye, silently blessing her mother for the mixture of protective care and absolute freedom that she'd always offered.

It would have been too easy to take herself to bed and wallow in misery, so Trish put on some particularly well-cut linen trousers and a proper shirt instead of a sloppy T-shirt. Then she went downstairs to cook real food of a kind that would have made even George proud.

After she'd eaten her dinner ceremonially at the table with *Don Giovanni* on the CD player, she phoned Paddy to ask why he hadn't listed Jeannie Nest on the Leporello envelope. He was out, so she left a message discreet enough to avoid dropping him in it if Bella should happen to hear what she'd said but clear enough to show that she was in earnest.

Having settled that for herself, Trish took *The Predators' Ball* by Connie Bruck out of her bookshelf to continue her education in the mysteries of junk-bond financing. That should help her feel more like the high-flying, knowledgeable lawyer she was supposed to be.

Just before she went up to bed, she opened up her laptop and wrote a funny, warm email to George about nothing very much. When she sent it, she saw that he'd sent her another one. It described the trip he'd arranged for his mother to meet some winemakers he knew in Napa Valley, and the extra special wines they'd brought out for her to taste. He added that the winemaking friends all wanted to know what Trish was like and said he must bring her out next time. He hoped her ears weren't burning too hotly after all his boasting about her, and he also hoped that her work for Antony Shelley was going well.

> *Of course, you'll be able to use all your family-law experience in court when you come to explain to the judge exactly how the DOB's directors bullied your client so much that his judgment went wonky. He's probably a typical bullies' victim, isn't he, Trish? In which case you can delve into his childhood and perform your usual miracles of empathy.*

Trish laughed when she saw that and started making a case on those lines, hearing the emotive phrases she might use to describe

116

Nick Gurles's pyschology and that of his tormentors. It was a pity she wouldn't have a jury to persuade this time. Eased by the knowledge that she had George in her life — and that however miserable he might have been as a homesick eight year old, he was securely confident now — she switched off the computer and went to bed.

The sleeping pills were beside her pillow, but she didn't think she'd need one now and settled down with *The Predators' Ball* until the words grew fuzzy and her eyelids were too heavy to hold up.

6

Dave hadn't arrived by the time Trish reached chambers, so she got to her own desk without having to perform her usual dance around his sensibilities. The grey-and-black files above her desk looked invitingly efficient. There were still about thirty-five to be cross-referenced, but within them she knew she had all the facts about Nick Gurles just where she wanted them.

Except the missing note from 13 March, she reminded herself, surprised that it hadn't yet arrived from Sprindlers. She went to the clerks' room to investigate. There were piles of envelopes there, neatly ranged along the table under the tenants' pigeonholes.

'Why hasn't the post been sorted, Kath?' Trish asked the only inhabitant of the room, a temp who'd become something of a fixture over the last few months.

'It's sorted, but Dave doesn't like it being pidged till he's had a look.'

Pidged? thought Trish with all the half-joking outrage of a Bateman cartoon character faced with some appalling solecism. *Pidged*, indeed.

She saw her own pile of envelopes and picked them up.

'Oh, please don't,' said Kath, sounding scared. 'Dave will kill me if he thinks I've let you take it before he's seen it.'

'Me particularly?'

'No. Any of you. He has to see it first, so he knows what's come in and doesn't shout at solicitors for not sending something that one of you's had for weeks and lost.'

That was fair enough, Trish thought, so she smiled at Kath, but went on riffling through the pile until she came to an envelope with the Sprindlers logo in the corner.

'Look, I need this one, so I'll take it now. You don't have to tell Dave — I will.'

'OK. But could you bear to say you took it when I wasn't in here?'

Trish was about to laugh when she thought of all the cases she'd argued that turned on the cruelty of people who used their superior strength or experience to terrorise their victims.

'Sure. Don't worry about it, Kath. I won't let you suffer. Thanks.'

Trish took the envelope back to her desk, ripping it open as she went. It contained a short typed message from Lucy Ranking:

Dear Ms Maguire, I think this 13 March note must be the one you wanted. I'm sorry it's only a photocopy, but I didn't like to send out the original without Peter's approval. I hope that's all right, and I'm sorry it's taken so long.

Smiling at the frightened informality of the covering letter, Trish reached for the relevant file and flipped through until she found the document that had referred to this 13 March note. Then she picked up the photocopy to punch it for filing, unfolded it, and was surprised to see that it was handwritten. She checked to make sure it included the point referred to in her existing files. It did. Then her eye was caught by the final paragraph, and she grabbed the edge of the desk.

Years ago Meg had taken her on a cheap summer holiday in Dorset. Walking along the cliff path between Charmouth and Golden Cap, the nine-year-old Trish had perched on the cliff edge and felt the turf slipping under her feet. Only Meg's hand on the back of her jersey had saved her. She felt exactly the same now as she re-read the note in case she'd made a mistake:

On the other matter, I think it's important not to frighten the horses. Presentation must be as unthreatening as possible. The thing will only work if we get a big enough take-up and so I think the impression to give is of a straightforward savings account, don't you?

Whatever the printed warnings, if we make it look safe and familiar we should be OK.

'Oh, shit, shit and double shit,' Trish said aloud, as she remembered Nick Gurles's cool question about why she herself would have assumed she'd get back her original investment untouched if she'd put money into his MegaPerformance Bond Fund.

'It wasn't a bank account,' he'd said, sounding almost contemptuous.

But this note made it clear that he'd planned to make people like her react exactly as she had done. If the investors' lawyers had a copy of this note, there would be no defence case. And they would have to have a copy. It was a discoverable piece of evidence.

The finger-holes in the base of each file looked like eyes now, full of mockery. Maybe Anna Grayling was right. Maybe Nick Gurles *was* a dishonest bastard behind the smooth charm. If so, it would serve him right if his new employers withdrew their support. The turf began to slip under Trish's feet again as she thought of the implications of that for herself and her career.

Antony was due back on Monday. She couldn't spoil his last few days in Tuscany with news of this discovery, but she'd have to tell him as soon as he was back in chambers.

He might be able to see a way to salvage their case, but just now she couldn't imagine one herself. All she could think of was George's teasing about a case based on Nick Gurles as the bullied victim of his employers.

If you hadn't been so bloody clever, Trish told herself, you'd never have seen this document and Antony could have carried on with the original plan. What she'd done was almost on a par with a naïve pupil asking the client whether he was guilty.

She opened the door and leaned out. Dave's voice echoed down the passage. It sounded as though he was on the phone. This would be a good moment to get out without having to answer any questions. Trish bagged up her laptop, grabbed her jacket and handbag and whipped out of the building as though she was late for the High Court.

It wasn't until she was halfway back across the bridge that she remembered an extra twist to the disaster. She was due to have dinner with Antony and his wife on Monday evening. It was the first time she'd been invited to their house and she'd been looking forward to it. Their parties were famous in the Temple for the glory of the amazing house on the edge of Holland Park, the people they knew, and the astonishing food and wine they provided. Now the idea of going there made her wince.

Tempted to force her way into Nick Gurles's office in the City and demand an explanation, Trish knew she had to resist. Anything she said to Gurles — or anyone else — might cause more trouble.

There was a whole empty day ahead of her. She'd cleared her diary for this, and now there was nothing more she could do until next week. Crawling to Dave would almost certainly produce some poxy little brief that no one else in chambers wanted, but she was far too old and experienced for that. And anyway, she wanted to keep out of sight.

At least it meant that she could do something useful for the other David. She dropped her laptop and briefcase back at the flat, changed, and walked along the south side of the river to Dowting's Hospital.

He looked exactly as he had last time, with his eyes closed and his broken leg strung up with weights. All round him in the colourful children's ward were patients playing with the nurses or visitors, and charging about, some tugging their drips after them. Only David was lying still; and absolutely alone. Trish felt her guts clench, sending bitter fluid into her throat.

His eyelids twitched, as though he had

sensed her presence. But when he looked at her, there was no pleasure or even relief in his expression.

'David, I'm sorry I didn't come yesterday. I was held up until it was too late. How are you?'

'OK,' he whispered. Then he shook his head. He blinked fast, but he couldn't stop the tears.

'I know it's hard, David, and I want to help, but it would be so much easier if you could tell me what your surname is.'

'She said I mustn't.'

'Even though she sent you to me?'

'Yes.'

'If I said her name, very quietly, could you nod if I've got it right or shake your head if I haven't?'

He thought for a moment then nodded. Trish leaned down and breathed into his ear, 'Jeannie Nest?' When she straightened up, she knew she'd wasted yet more time and effort. His face was absolutely blank. It was a nuisance, but there were some consolations, of course. Trish recalled Sylvia Bantell's perceptive comment about the difficulty of acknowledging a prostitute's child as one's half-brother.

'No,' David said, in case she'd been too thick to grasp what he meant. 'Who's she?

I've never heard of her. What's happened to her?'

'I don't think anything has. She was just somebody I heard about who had a boy your age, and there was a reason why she might have wanted me to know him. Or I thought there was.' It was an effort to make herself smile, but Trish managed it.

She hoped she'd get back her usual brains and judgment soon. Otherwise she was going to be washing about in a sea of unnecessary emotion, causing trouble wherever she went. 'But I've obviously been very silly. Look, I've brought you some more apple juice. Would you like it?'

He nodded, so she inserted the straw. While he was drinking, she tried out her father's name and Sylvia Bantell's, too, just in case David reacted to either of them. But he shook his head at both, looking so relieved — and so tired — when Trish stopped whispering questions that she left him alone.

A male nurse outside the bay gave her a relatively reassuring account of David's physical condition. He was still in pain, the nurse said, and it would take weeks before he could walk again, but there was no longer any need to fear internal bleeding or any permanent damage.

'And how far have the police got in identifying him?'

'Nowhere,' said the nurse, surprised. 'All we know is that he had your name and address with him. The police have checked all the agencies that deal with runaways and he doesn't fit any of their records, but then he's a bit young to run away. I heard someone say you thought he might be connected with one of your cases.'

'Yes.' Trish had been so taken up with the idea that David must be her half-brother that she'd almost forgotten the likelier explanation of his search for her. The woman who looked after him had probably got Trish's name from the papers after a child-protection case and found out where she lived. It couldn't be that difficult, whatever Dave had said. There need be no connection with Paddy — or the mysterious Jeannie Nest.

'Before I go,' she asked, noticing how much easier her breathing had become, 'is there anything David needs? I can't help feeling responsible for him. He says he likes apple juice and I assume it's OK to give him that?'

'Fine.' The nurse's face was patterned with lines that made him look much older than his manner suggested, but his lips softened and his voice was warm with compassion as he added, 'But honestly what he needs most is the comfort of regular visits from you. At the moment you seem to be the only person in the world he trusts. When you're here he opens his eyes and communicates a little. When you go he watches till you're out of sight and then shuts down. He barely moves the rest of the time, except occasionally to eat — and that's not nearly often enough. He won't talk to any of us.'

'What about the other children? They all look friendly.'

'They tried, but he won't respond, so now they've given up. I hope the police find his mother, poor little scrap.'

So long as she's not the cause of his terror, Trish thought, saying aloud, 'Or his father.'

'That's less likely, as you must know. He hasn't mentioned any father to you, has he?'

'No. And I haven't asked, but perhaps I should.'

'More important is to get him to eat. Lunch is coming up now. Could you take his tray and see if you can persuade him to have some of it?'

'Sure. I'll do my best anyway.'

David was much too old for the aeroplane games Trish had seen her friends play with their babies to encourage them to eat, but she set about distracting him when the nurse pulled his tray table forwards and put the food on it. She tried Harry Potter, which got them past two forks of pasta, laboriously chewed and swallowed, then Pokémon. But he didn't like Pokémon and had never swapped the cards. She asked if he'd had a scooter, but he hadn't, and so she tried asking about his friends.

His face brightened then, and he started to tell her about Joe, who had red hair and was always getting into trouble at school for fighting. Trish watched a little colour warming David's cheeks and heard his voice quicken. He began to eat more vigorously, talking with his mouth full about Joe's latest exploits.

'What's his other name?' she asked without thinking and watched everything close down.

All the animation in David's eyes died and he stopped talking. He let the fork drop back into the half-empty bowl of food and closed his eyes, letting his head drop back against the pillows. Trish put her hand on his shoulder.

'That was silly of me. I wasn't trying to trap you into giving anything away, I just liked the sound of your friend. I'm really sorry.'

But it didn't help. He did open his eyes, but he stared at her with such bleak, resigned disappointment that she hated herself. She stayed with him, sometimes trying to talk, sometimes letting him pretend to sleep, for another half hour. Realising she wasn't getting anywhere near him, or doing anything to help, she stood up.

'I'm sorry, David,' she said again. 'I'll come back tomorrow, not to ask any questions, just to see how you are and bring you some more apple juice. Is there anything else you'd like? Have you read the latest Harry Potter, or would you like me to get that for you?'

A flicker in his eyes told her he wanted it, but the obstinacy of his lips showed that he wasn't going to ask. She nodded and smiled again.

'I'll bring a copy along with me anyway. Just in case it helps. Bye for now.'

She let her hand rest for a micro-second on his short dark hair and had to force herself to pull back, instead of stroking his head and bending down to kiss it. He looked so small, so lonely, and so brave that she wanted to slay dragons for him.

★　★　★

Back in the flat, she phoned chambers to tell Dave she'd be working at home for the rest of the day and asked whether the police had been in touch with him.

'They took the list of your clients, as I told you, but I haven't heard anything since. Why would I? It's nothing to do with us. You'll be coming in tomorrow, I take it?'

'Probably,' Trish said brightly. 'But you can always get me on my mobile. Bye, Dave.'

There were all sorts of things she should be doing, things there was never time for in the normal maelstrom of her work: seeing the dentist, getting all the clothes that needed mending to the nearest dry cleaners that had a repair service, even persuading the freeholders to organise a building firm prepared to come out to scrape down, fill and repaint her window frames, several of which were showing distinct signs of rot. But none of it held any attraction whatsoever. Still, she had to do something.

Restless but bored, and worried, she moved around her big flat, flying back to the phone when it started to ring. But it was only a nervous-sounding young man in a call centre, wanting to sell her double glazing. She let out some of her frustration on explaining to him why no one with any sense would ever buy double glazing or indeed anything else over the phone and why it was an unconscionable outrage for call centres to disturb total strangers with idiotic interruptions like this in the middle of the working day. The call-centre script obviously didn't include answers to that kind of outburst, so the young man put down the phone without another word, while Trish was still in mid-diatribe.

Feeling guilty — it wasn't his fault, after all, and at least he was working for his living — she made herself collect all the clothes with broken zips, dropped hems, and missing buttons, bundled them up and took them to the cleaners.

She managed to find enough errands to keep her out of the flat until nearly seven o'clock. Her mobile rang at intervals, but none of the calls was important. And all her friends were busy when she rang them. Anna Grayling had time for a five-minute chat, then said she had to go, reminding Trish that they could catch up with everything else when they met at the National Film Theatre next Wednesday.

Eventually there was nothing for it but to go home. At the top of the iron staircase, she realised she could have stayed out longer by going to see a film that evening, too. She hesitated, with the front door open, looking back across the lower roofs all round her. Two men were standing below, pointing up at her. She was too far away to see their faces, but she wasn't going anywhere near them. Turning quickly, she abandoned the idea of the cinema and went inside, double-locking the door.

The red light on the answering machine was flashing. She pressed the play button to hear Caroline Lyalt's voice, saying:

'Trish, I know it's been days, and I'm sorry. Things have been going bananas here, but I'll be at home on Thursday evening from six-thirty if you still want to talk then.'

★　★　★

Lil Handsome was searching the *Evening Standard*, as she'd done every night since her son had come bursting into her flat with blood on his trousers. There should have been something in one of the papers by now. There was one tiny paragraph about a woman's body being found in a flat in West London, but it read like a suicide report, so it didn't count. She lit another fag, the fifth of the day, hoping it would help her think. Her memory was still sharp as a tack, so it wasn't hard to go through everything Gary had said that night. She'd been in bed, woken out of a rare deep sleep by crashing and cursing outside.

At first she thought her old man had got out, so she didn't bother to look at the clock, just grabbed her dressing gown and tied it tightly under her bust. When she opened the bedroom door and saw that the intruder was only Gal, she was glad, even though it was shocking to find he had a key to her place. His dad must've given it to him. She wondered how often he came here when she was out. And what he did then.

'You been on the piss?' she said crossly to hide her fear. 'What're you doing here? And what's that on your trousers?'

He looked down, wiping the palms of his hands down the marks.

'Nothing much, Ma. Gi's some of Dad's clothes, will you?'

'Looks like blood to me,' she said, casual-like. She'd seen plenty of blood in her time and knew what it looked like at all stages of drying and on all surfaces. This looked newish, not sticky any more, but still red not brown. 'You bin fighting?'

'Only a tom, Ma. She come at me out of the dark, like a wildcat.'

She wondered what he'd been reading — or who he'd been talking to. Like a wildcat! Didn't sound like her younger son at all.

'Where was this then, Gary?'

'Wanstead. I'd bin to the pub and come out with me mates. They went off to get their motor; I was going for the van and she come at me like I said. I didn't mean to hurt her. I just give her one and she fell in the gutter. I got the mess on me trousers when I bent down to make sure she was OK. She was breathing fine, so I phoned 999 and waited till the ambulance come. Then I legged it back here. Gi's some of Dad's clothes, Ma. I'll make a cuppa while you're getting them. Mikey here?'

'I haven't heard him come in, so he's probably still out cabbing.' Lil was glad of that. She didn't want them quarrelling, not with Gary in this mood anyway. As it was, she barred the way to the kettle, saying, 'I'll make the tea.'

She wasn't letting him near any boiling water, not if she could help it. She kept her eyes on him all the time she could, except when she was filling the kettle. He'd never hit her yet, but he was so like his dad, she wouldn't be surprised if it happened. She knew well enough that he'd hit plenty of other women, and that he liked doing it.

Could he be telling the truth about the tom? It didn't seem very likely. He was much too wired for one thing, and phoning an ambulance didn't sound like him. Whoever the woman had been, he'd obviously hurt her bad. Lil hoped it really was a stray prostitute, who wouldn't be able to finger him. She didn't want the police around, asking

134

questions. Not now. Not ever again.

The tea made, she emptied the spare boiling water into the sink, so there wouldn't be anything for Gal to throw at her like his father had done. Her hand was stroking her jaw, like it always did when she thought of Ron, even now he was doing life. The hospital had set the jaw straight, but still it ached, even after all these years.

'Come on, Ma. What're you waiting for?' Gal said, taking a step towards her.

She shied; she couldn't help it. It was hard to think of this great hulking brute as the same slippery, bloody little creature that had emerged from between her legs, screaming and rigid forty-five years ago, with the cord like a fat blue-grey worm snaking out between them. She held out a mug of tea, like a shield, giving him the glare that had always made him mind her in the past.

It worked again. He looked at his useless great feet and shuffled a bit. He took the tea. She'd put a lot of milk in it so that even if he threw it, it wouldn't do much harm.

'What're you going to do with the clothes if I give them to you?'

'Change?' he said, making it sound like he was asking her a question. She thought of Mikey's brains, and her own, and asked God for patience.

'And then?'

'Go home.'

'You can't. Not if you hurt this girl as bad as it sounds. Remember last time? You ought to get out of the way for a bit.' Lil looked him up and down and thought of the pesetas she had left after her last holiday. She should've taken them back to the travel agent, but she'd never got round to it. 'Spain. That's where you should go.'

'Spain? Ma, you gotta be joking. I hate all that foreign muck.'

'There's lots of ex-cons living there, so you'll feel right at home, and you can get all the English food you can eat, and cheap booze too. You'll be fine. You got your passport, haven't you?'

'Yeah. But not here.'

No, she thought. Of course not. Nothing so useful. Post Offices used to sell some kind of European travel permit. Could you still get those? Maybe not. Better safe than sorry.

'Go home in the van, park it unobtrusive-like. Get your passport. Don't pack nothing. You don't want the neighbours seeing you carting a case out of there. I'll pack you some of your dad's things, and get you a pair of trousers for now. You can leave them ones with me and I'll burn them for you.'

'I'll need money.'

'I'll give you some.' She might have known he'd ask for that. It was all he'd ever wanted from her. 'Then you can take the van to Dover and get a ferry, like you do for the beer and fags. After that it's a straight drive down through France to Spain. It's not hard. You'll be OK. Go on, go and get your passport. You can come back after a week or two. Take a holiday. Enjoy yourself and keep out of the way till the Old Bill loses interest.'

He shrugged, but she could see he did remember the last time he'd beaten up a working girl, and the nights he'd spent in the police cells and all the interrogations till they'd let him go because they didn't have the evidence. That girl hadn't died in the end, but she'd been too scared to identify him in the line-up. Lil wasn't so sure about this one. This one sounded bad.

★　★　★

The young constable felt as though he was swallowing pints of hot saliva, desperate to stop the nausea. He'd never seen a body that looked like a brown-and-purple shopping bag before. There was blood everywhere, splattered in patterns over the floor and up the white cupboards under the bookshelves. He'd never seen so many books before either,

137

except in a library.

Groping for his radio, he tried to think about the books instead of the body. His fingers slipped and he couldn't work out how to switch the thing on. Then he remembered the woman who'd let him in and who he'd made wait outside. She was a friend of the householder, worried because she hadn't seen her since lunch on Sunday and she should've been at work. They hadn't taken her seriously at the station, which was why they'd sent PC Feather to investigate.

The radio cracked into life so his fingers must have known how to work it even though his mind had forgotten. He muttered into it. They couldn't hear him, so he had to shout and Mrs Mason, the friend, came bursting into the room, looked at the body and collapsed. He stared at her, crumpled into a heap like an old Indian cushion in the middle of her friend's blood.

'Wait there, Feather,' said the radio. 'Don't touch anything. Don't let anyone in. Got that? Feather? Feather?'

7

Chief Inspector Lakeshaw nodded to the pathologist. He slid a scalpel into the dead woman's skin to make the Y-incision that would reveal the flesh of her face and then her internal organs. Lakeshaw dreaded the coils and colours he'd see as soon as the flaps of skin and flesh were parted, and the smell. He should have been used to it all by now, but he wasn't. Every time, he was shocked by the tubes and lumps, brownish-red, purple, grey and orange, still wet, and quivery as soon as anyone touched them. There was something about the way pathologists' dead-looking white-latexed fingers held the plump mobile lumps of dead offal that . . .

Flashes distracted him. The photographer pumped his camera like a machine gun. As the sickening reek rose from the opened cadaver, Lakeshaw was glad of the mask and the drops of lavender water his wife had given him. The smell of bodies, even ones like this that weren't seriously decomposed, was vile. He sometimes thought he'd die with it in his nostrils, however long he lasted after he'd retired.

The saw glittered in the bleak white lights of the morgue as Dr Hardy began to split the ribcage. In a way this performance was hardly necessary. He'd already established that the woman had been strangled with something like a scarf. A few fibres had been collected and would be examined later. It had surprised Lakeshaw, who'd assumed that she'd died from the beating.

Her face looked like a pile of mashed black- and redcurrants, showing crusted maroon breaks in the skin where the blows had got through. One cheekbone was completely smashed and her jaw hung out of alignment. There were broken teeth too. Bruises spread all over her, right down to her slim ankles. They'd all been meticulously measured and photographed for later analysis.

They looked bad enough to have killed anyone, but Hardy was sure the beating had happened after death. There'd been plenty of blood, though. All that stuff about dead bodies not bleeding was so much cock. Lakeshaw thought he might get photographs of this one and the scene for use in some of the elementary training courses.

The spurts of this dead woman's blood had reached at least two feet away from her body as it lay in the centre of the living room. So

Lakeshaw had officers out now, doing house-to-house to find witnesses to a blood-spattered fugitive. And there were others out emptying all the skips and dustbins in the neighbourhood in case the bloke, whoever he was, had been bright enough to get rid of his saturated gear there.

★ ★ ★

Nick Gurles, who'd been checking the time all through the morning, got up and swung his jacket from the back of his chair. Something caught his eye as he looked down, and he saw there was a mark on his tie. He couldn't see it properly, even by squinting, and didn't want to make whatever it was worse by careless scraping. There were mirrors in the bog.

He washed his hands carefully, scraping a minute gob of dirt from under one thumbnail, then dried them, making sure there wasn't the slightest hint of dampness to mark the silk, before picking the ball of fluff off his tie. Some of his colleagues kept spare ties, even spare shirts, in the office, but that had always seemed far too girly. One last check in the mirror and he was ready. He went back to his desk and awaited the Chairman's summons.

They were not going to eat in the directors' dining room, which probably meant that some of the other members of the board disapproved of Gunschwig's decision to underwrite his legal costs. Still, Sir Henry Buxford had all the power needed to keep them quiet.

Nick had always known that if he lost the case he'd be out of a job. That was bad enough, but the nightmare panic he hoped he was still managing to hide was that, if he lost, the civil proceedings might be followed by a criminal charge.

It wasn't likely to happen. He thought criminal trials were usually followed by civil actions, not the other way round. But that didn't stop the nightmares. When they were at their worst, he'd try to distract himself with memories of a story he'd heard once of a bloke arriving at Ford. Reeling from his experiences in the first tough dispersal prison he'd been sent to, this chap had got to Ford and been greeted by an old schoolfriend, delighted to have a replacement for his recently released bridge partner.

But that was just whistling in the dark. The idea of prison — even an open prison — was terrifying. Three times now Nick had woken in the night, screaming. Luckily his girlfriend was away, so there was no one to know how scared he was.

The summons came at last in the form of a phone call from the Chairman's secretary. Nick was to meet him in the lobby.

They didn't say much until they were sitting either side of a table in Brooks's, well away from the City and any eavesdropping journalists. In his own club, with the familiar menu and wine list in front of him, the Chairman looked perfectly at home.

'Well, Nick, how are you feeling?'

'Pretty good, actually, sir.'

'That's the stuff. Case preparation going all right?'

'Yes, I think it is.'

'How d'you get on with Antony's junior, this girl, Trish Maguire? I wasn't at all sure about his choice there, but he thinks the world of her.'

Nick took a gulp of the claret in his glass, wondering whether the old man was trying to loosen him up to make him feel better or get him drunk enough to let out anything he might have wanted to keep secret. Neither of them drank at lunchtime in normal circumstances. Very few bankers did.

'I find her quite aggressive.'

'How, exactly?'

Nick had another go at the claret. It wasn't bad, but it wasn't first growth, which he'd have liked and thought he deserved. 'It's partly how she looks, of course, rather like an eagle: short tufty black hair, ferocious black eyes and a huge great nose jutting out below them. She'll look magnificent as a judge, but it's a bit intimidating on a thirty-something girl. And she's bloody offensive in some of her questions.'

'That's her job. She's giving you a chance to rehearse before the other side get at you. The DOB directors' counsel will be trying to show that any blame lies with you, so you'll be put through the wringer.'

'I know, but it's not just that. I get the feeling that she disapproves of all of us — you know, the whole financial-services industry.'

'That's probably true. She's a pretty left-wing, angsty kind of girl, I gather. Antony and I discussed it right at the start and I know he thinks it could be a positive advantage. She'll be able to draw a lot of fire. What's more, her great speciality is the passion with which she acts for anyone she sees as a victim of bullying.'

Nick achieved a laugh. 'I'm not sure I want to look like a wimpish victim in court.'

'Vanity can be useful, Nick, but it can also make you do damn silly things. Listen to Antony on this one. I've more respect for him than for any man alive. I trust his judgment, as you should. But, apart from Maguire's aggression, how else do you see her?'

'I thought you knew her, sir.'

The Chairman shook his immaculate grey head. 'I shall be meeting her at the Shelleys' next week. That'll give me a chance to find out what she's made of.' He looked friendly suddenly. 'I thought you could give me some pointers, help me ask the right questions.'

'She's clever, no doubt about that. Not attractive really, though she's quite slim and not badly dressed in fact. Too intense for me, though, and doesn't bother much with jewellery or make-up.'

'Gay?'

'Not according to the gossip. I've asked around about her and I hear that she's in the middle of a longstanding affair with the senior partner at Henton, Maltravers. He's said to be pining to marry her. God knows why she won't. He must be worth a good bit by now. On the other hand, she doesn't flirt and that always bothers me.'

'Why?'

Nick laughed. 'Oh, you know, I always mistrust a woman who don't respond when I . . .'

'Chat her up?' The Chairman laughed with him and refilled his glass, just as the white-jacketed waiter brought their pâté.

145

Nick noticed that Sir Henry had barely touched his own wine.

'Yes.'

'I know what you mean, but you were dealing with her in her professional guise, so maybe she was just being grown up. Tuck in. Anything else I ought to know? Anything you've thought of that we didn't discuss originally?'

So that *is* what this lunch is all about, thought Nick. He's wondering whether to go on backing me. What's he heard?

'There's nothing I didn't tell you and Antony Shelley at that first conference we had.'

'Good. I'm glad to hear it.' The Chairman did drink then, but it was the merest sip. He rolled the wine around his mouth. 'Not bad, but not something one would want to risk losing self-control over. How's the pâté?'

'Very good. Thank you.'

'We'll support you all the way, you know, but if the case goes pear-shaped, it will be hard to keep you on at Grunschwig's without upsetting the clients.'

That's a nice, helpful, confidence-boosting thing to tell me now, thought Nick. But he'd known it all along and said so.

'Good man. Eat up. Sleeping all right? You don't want to start getting twitchy and neurotic between now and the opening of the case.'

'Good lord, no. I've never slept better in my life.'

The Chairman raised his glass in a silent toast. 'I knew you'd hack it. You've handled yourself well. Stick with it, Nick, and we'll all be all right.'

Nick knew now what he was being told: it's not only your job on the line, and your whole future in the City. It's also my reputation, so don't screw up by drinking, insomnia, or saying anything careless in court. And if you do screw up, don't expect any mercy from me.

On the surface the man was all charm and kindly support, but beneath it he was as ruthless as any Mafia don. He might not have traitors and enemies killed, but he'd obliterate them professionally without a qualm. Nick knew he'd need his sleeping pills tonight. And he wasn't sure he could face the tournedos he'd ordered now. All that blood.

★　★　★

Trish picked up the phone to ring Caro Lyalt soon after seven, as instructed in the message she'd left on the machine. But then it seemed unfair to interrupt her and her partner, Jess, until they'd at least had a chance to eat together. To take up the time, Trish grilled herself a piece of salmon and ate it with pre-washed baby spinach from a supermarket bag and a slice of olive bread.

She hated the way the spinach dried out her mouth, and squeaked between her teeth, but the hospital had told her she needed iron. George had always thought so. Nothing she'd ever said could convince him that her natural colour was so pale. She shivered as she thought of David's white face and dark eyes and black hair.

It wasn't only those things that linked them. The more she saw of him, the more she recognised the slant of his eyebrows, and the shape of the cheekbones, as well as the way his face tapered around the obstinate mouth to the same pointed chin.

'Oh, stop it,' she said aloud, through a mouthful of half-chewed spinach leaves. 'You're probably trying to turn him into your half-brother to compensate for the miscarriage.'

She opened a bottle of red wine — more iron, lots of flavenoids and all sorts of health-giving properties, and a lot more palatable than raw spinach — and poured herself a glassful. George would have recommended white with fish, but she preferred red and what did it matter anyway? She bit back that thought at once, aware how close she was to the place where nothing mattered at all.

She'd been there before and was determined never to go back. It was a place of permanently sleety winter, inhabited only by large black birds that flapped around her aching head, reeling off lists of her faults and the damage she'd done to other people ever since the day she was born.

Ignoring their shadows, she made herself finish her ration of healthy food, washed up, poured herself another glass of wine and sat down at the laptop to send another email to George.

When she'd finished writing a perky account of nothing much and clicked on 'send', it was nearly half past nine. She decided to give Caro and Jess a few more minutes together, and opened George's latest email, to read that he'd been dreaming about her.

I must have been nearly awake because it felt so real. I could smell your skin, Trish, and feel your bones. Your breath brushed my cheek . . . And then I woke up and you weren't there. I felt cheated

— and deflated. God! I can't wait to get home.

Trish felt her skin prickle at the scene he'd set for her. She knew she'd been right to urge him to fulfil his widowed mother's dream of seeing San Francisco while she was still fit enough to enjoy it, but Trish wanted him back now. At last she reached for the phone.

'Hi, Caro, it's Trish,' she said, recognising her friend's voice. It sounded strained. 'Am I interrupting?'

'No. I'm on my own tonight and there's sod all on TV. Ironic, isn't it? The one night I get to slump and there's nothing to watch. What can I do for you, Trish?'

'It's quite a long story. If you're at a loose end, why not come round? Have a drink and we can talk.'

'What, now?'

'Is it too late?'

'Of course not. And I'd love it, Trish. Give me ten minutes and I'll be with you.'

Trish flung open two of the windows to get rid of the heavy smell of the fish. She couldn't help noticing the rotting window sills again and felt her head tighten at the prospect of the effort it would take to make the freeholder have them repaired. She ground coffee, fetched a bottle of brandy and glasses

150

and a box of Belgian chocolates someone must have brought when they came to dinner. She hadn't opened the box and turned it over to check the sell-by date. There were two months to go. She pulled off the gold string and parted the waxed paper inside the lid. The chocolates looked perfectly edible; there were none of the white spots she'd seen on the contents of other long-forgotten boxes.

A few of the red and purple cushions needed plumping up, and she switched on some of the lamps to make the light softer. It felt strange then to sit quietly on one of the big black sofas and have time to stare around the flat as though with a stranger's eyes. Looking at the Nina Murdoch painting of a road rushing away into the vanishing point under a starkly rendered angular bridge, Trish let herself admit that she was lonely.

Odd that it had taken her so long to understand how much of a space George filled in her life. Odd, too, that she'd insisted on keeping parts of it free of him, especially now that she knew he was not the invulnerable threat he'd occasionally seemed. But even as she contemplated moving into his Fulham house with its valuable antiques, or maybe a bigger version they might buy together, she knew she couldn't do it. Whatever the reason, she needed these lonely, echoing spaces for protection.

Footsteps on the iron staircase outside stopped her worrying about her own selfishness. She resisted the temptation to rush over and open the door, waiting until Caro knocked. But she soon saw that she wasn't the only one in need. Caro, who was never demonstrative, flung her arms round Trish.

Her body felt suprisingly soft for someone who looked so muscular, but her arms were hard as they clung for a second. Trish wondered what Jess was up to, but she knew better than to ask.

'It's great to see you, Trish.' Caro advanced into the room with a jaunty stride that only made her depression more obvious. 'You do have a terrific flat. I couldn't believe it, you know, when you first told me you lived here, a rich brief like you! All I knew about Southwark then was the crime figures. Silly me.'

It wasn't like Caro to chatter either. Maybe it was the streets outside, with their weird loitering figures that had spooked her. Trish patted her on the back and asked if she'd like tea, coffee, wine, brandy or a mixture.

'Wine, please,' she said, sounding more normal. 'You don't look so good either. What's up?'

'Apart from suddenly being made aware that everyone else thinks I live in the middle of some kind of war zone, you mean?' Trish tried to make a joke of it, but the humour didn't come through.

Caro looked surprised. 'Is that why you're so jittery?'

'Not entirely. I . . . '

'Come on, Trish. Are you ill?'

Caro sounded so affectionate and so sensible that Trish found herself talking about the miscarriage and how difficult it was going to be to tell George. Caro's arm was round her shoulders again by the end of the story, but this time it felt like the kindness of a strong friend, not the clinging of a needy supplicant.

'You've got to tell him. And you're right that you can't do it in an email. Wait till he's back.' Caro let her arm drop to her side and swivelled on the sofa so she could examine Trish's face. 'And quite frankly, I don't think he'll be surprised. He'll see that something's wrong the minute he gets here. You look like a ghost.'

'That's encouraging! Now it's your turn. How are you?' Trish hadn't touched her wine. She felt as though she'd had more than enough already.

'I'm fine. It's just that there isn't enough

time for both life and work, and I've got far too much work anyway, but then that's nothing new. I can't stay long, so tell me what else is bothering you. I can't believe it was the miscarriage that made you ring me.'

'No.' Trish walked towards the window overlooking the street. Staring down at the spot where David had been almost killed, she told Caro what had happened there on Sunday night.

'So what's worrying you? That the driver should've been prosecuted? I can't do anything about that.' Hints of the kind of impatience that must have made Caro's junior officers shiver had a different effect on Trish. She controlled her own irritation and spoke as reasonably as she always did when reminding judges of the aspects of the law they seemed to have forgotten.

'No, of course not. I hope they're not going to prosecute her. She wasn't speeding and the child ran out of the dark in front of her. Neither of them had a chance. No, it's the child I'm worried about. Look, Caro, I've probably invented the whole thing because of the state of my post-pregnancy hormones, but listen.' She explained that David had had her name and address sewn into his clothes. 'And that night, the police in Casualty and the medical staff obviously thought he was

154

something to do with me. Since then I've not been able to ignore the likeness, either.'

'Have you ever . . . ?'

'No. I've never been pregnant until this time. I've been lucky.'

'Or careful,' said Caro with a smile. 'You're one of the most sensible women I know. Have you any idea who this boy could be?'

Trish stared down at the street, where she could just see faint black outlines of the old skidmarks.

'My father's always been erratic,' she said at last. 'And although he was in a relationship with a woman who couldn't have had a child at the time David must have been conceived, he was also seeing a prostitute. She lived on an estate not far from here. It occurred to me that David might be her son — and his.'

'It sounds feasible. What have you done about it?'

Trish noticed the warmth of Caro's smile and voice and wondered whether she was being interrogated. She'd once heard Caro explain her favourite technique: 'Make friends with them. Make them like you and feel safe with you. Be patient and kind. You get much more out of people by making them think you like them than by terrifying them or using aggressive body language to suggest you're going to beat them up.'

'I asked the boy if the woman who sent him to me was called Jeannie Nest, but it was clear he'd never heard the name before.'

Caro's face didn't change, but there was something about her that set Trish's antennae quivering.

'What do *you* know about Jeannie Nest, Caro? Have you ever arrested her?'

'I don't think so.' She crossed her legs. 'Honestly, Trish. I can't remember if I've ever had anything to do with her myself, but her name has cropped up recently. Are you *sure* she knew your father?'

'Yes, he . . . used her services nine — ten — years ago. But Caro, how did her name crop up again?'

'Oh, just in a report on something else. Don't worry about it.' Caro's casual voice was not convincing. Trish was about to press her when she hurriedly added, 'Does your father still see her?'

'Apparently not.'

'Good. And you say you think the boy in hospital could be hers?'

'Caro, what is this? You've got your official face on. And voice. What is going on? Where *did* you see her name?'

'You're talking about a lost, unclaimed, eight- or nine-year-old boy who was nearly killed in a road accident, refusing to say who he is and with some connection with a woman who — '

'Who?'

'Who you say worked as a prostitute. Is it any surprise that I'm thinking like a police officer?' Caro's expression gave no clues, but its hardness made it clear she wasn't going to reveal anything else she might know. 'Tell me more about the boy.'

Trish gave up trying to make her talk. Instead, she did her best for David, suppressing all mention of her urgent need to stroke his hair and the other manifestations of frustrated mothering. Even so her breasts ached as she talked and she crossed her arms across her body to hold herself together.

'Why haven't you asked your father about the boy?' Caro asked at the end. She picked up her wineglass and drained it.

'Somehow I couldn't. We're still not on those terms, even after everything we went through when he was ill. In any case, it would be pretty embarrassing for any woman,' Trish said, seeing that Caro was getting ready to go, 'to ask her father if he's been irresponsible enough to spray illegitimate babies around London, don't you think?'

'I wouldn't know. I never met mine.' Caro stood up, kissed Trish again and left the flat with her usual lack of fuss, saying, 'I'll see if I can find anything out for you.'

'Thanks, Caro.'

★ ★ ★

There were no lights on in the flat when Caro got home, and the front door was still deadlocked. More disappointed than surprised, she let herself in, trying to decide what to do about Trish's story of Jeannie Nest.

The name probably wouldn't have meant anything if it hadn't been for a bit of nick gossip about a DC Martin Waylant, which Caro had overheard in the canteen earlier in the day. A couple of visiting Drugs Squad officers had been talking to one of her constables about how the woman who'd just been found beaten to death in Hoxton had had the hots for this Waylant bloke. She'd spent her whole time making up stories of stalkers to get him to come round to her flat so that she could get into his knickers, the poor pillock.

'Lucky him,' Caro's constable had said, laughing. 'Why'd he turn it down if it was on a plate like that?'

'It would've been like screwing your granny,' one of the visitors had said. 'All

158

droopy tits and an arse crawling down the back of her legs.'

Caro had wondered whether to intervene. If it had got much worse, she would have, but she'd fought enough hard battles with canteen-misogynists to know there was no point wading in unless you had to.

'She wasn't that old. Can't have been much more than forty,' the other Drugs Squad officer had said. 'You know who she was, don't you, Paul?'

'No. Who?'

'Jeannie Nest. You know, the woman who gave evidence in the Handsome trial. Maybe you're too young to remember, but she was a bit of a heroine to anyone who was around at the time.'

'How d'you know that?'

'Waylant told me once when he was plastered. At the end of his tether, poor bugger. She was persecuting him by then, and he wanted to be rid of her, but he still thought she was owed for what she'd done for the law. He didn't know what to do. Crying into his beer, he was.'

'Well, he's found out now, hasn't he?' A new speaker had joined in. Caro hadn't recognised the voice. 'D'you think he'll go down for it?'

'That's sick,' the first had said then.

'Bollocks. It's common sense. Sounds as if she'd turned into a stalker herself. Have you talked to the incident room about this?'

'Don't be more stupid than you can help, Smith. You've obviously never met the guy. He's soft as butter. Gave up playing rugger last year after that bloke got his neck broken in the scrum. It wasn't Waylant's fault; wasn't anyone's fault. Just one of those things. But he'd been there in the scrum, right opposite the guy, so he felt responsible. Couldn't bear to risk it happening to anyone else and gave up. It was quite a sacrifice. Rugger had been his life.'

Caro had had her back to them, but it hadn't stopped her listening.

'They're always the worst, though, aren't they?' one of the unfamiliar voices had said, sounding quite serious. 'The soft ones. When they finally snap, they don't know how to stop, so they're more vicious than all the rest put together. I bet it *was* him who knocked her off. Didn't you say the body had been beaten to a pulp, blood and tissue all over the place? You have to phone it in.'

'Look — let's drop it, shall we? They'll know all about it by now. It's none of our business.'

Standing in her dark living room now, Caro wondered whether she could legitimately ignore what she'd overheard, given that she'd had no formal reports of any of it. She'd never met the unfortunate Waylant and she had no idea whether the gossip about him and the dead woman was accurate. She had even less idea whether the victim really had been called Jeannie Nest in another life, or whether she did have any connection with Trish's story. What Caro did know was that if she did pass that on to the incident room, Trish would suffer.

In her normal state Trish was as tough as she was clever, but even when she wasn't white and jittery with the after-effects of a miscarriage, she was seriously screwed up about her father. Getting him involved in the investigation that must be opening up around the dead woman would lead to a lot of hassle Trish could definitely do without.

On the other hand, thought Caro, if there were any real suggestion of this Waylant being suspected of the murder, she would have to pass on Trish's story. No responsible officer could withhold any information that might prevent a colleague coming under unjust suspicion for a crime like that. Caro had no time for the corrupt or the violent, but she'd fight to the death to protect a decent police officer. Increasingly these days, it seemed to be the honest blokes who were taking the rap for the filthy few. If DC Waylant were one of the good ones he'd deserve all her help.

Even at the risk of sacrificing a friend? she asked herself, slipping back into indecision like a hopeless squaddie who couldn't get himself over the wall in an assault-course.

Then the phone rang, releasing her for the moment.

'Hello?'

'I want to order a takeaway,' said a drunken voice. 'Chicken tikka masala, and some poppadums, and — '

'You've got the wrong number,' Caro said, glad it hadn't been a summons to attend yet another brutalised victim. She raised her finger from the talk button and waited for the ringing tone.

The pause had let her complete her own private assault course easily enough. She set about getting herself put through to the incident room.

8

Trish woke to the sound of running footsteps. She couldn't work out whether they were real or part of the dream in which she'd been trying to catch something that mattered. Each time she was nearly there, she'd trip just as her hand reached it, or lose her grip and drop it. She didn't know what it was, a person, an animal, or something inanimate, but its importance was as clear to her as the danger it carried.

Her fear eased as she woke properly. She rubbed her fingers over her face and through her short dark hair, licking her lips to stop them feeling so dry. There was something about the sound of running that seemed nearly as important as the elusive thing of her dream. But she couldn't remember what it was.

She got out of bed to look down into the street. The postman was ambling towards her building, pushing his trolley and as usual shrugging his shoulders to the beat of whatever he was listening to on his Walkman. Trish looked in the other direction and saw the source of the running sound disappearing round the corner at the end of the street. Just an early-morning jogger.

Thirsty, she shambled off to the kitchen to make some tea, pulling the long T-shirt further down her thighs as she passed the windows, in case, as George often said, there might be a balloonist outside trying to look in. Her flat was so high that no other building had windows on the same level, but she could never escape the feeling that someone might see her through the glass.

God, how she missed George! It didn't seem fair that he got to dream of them making love and she had to sweat through creepy nightmares.

Today's T-shirt had blazoned across the front *Boys throw stones at frogs in sport/But the frogs do not die in sport*, which had always struck her as a message that ought to be implanted in the brain of everyone who'd ever been put in charge of a child.

As the domed cordless kettle roared towards boiling point she couldn't help thinking of the absurdity of her flight from chambers on Wednesday. Even though she'd discovered a document that completely screwed up the case she and Antony had planned to make in court, there were still dozens of other pieces of evidence that needed to be cross-referenced. Her brain really was turning to mush in the post-miscarriage flood of hormones, and she couldn't afford that.

Freed from something she didn't want to think about, she made her tea and took it back to bed. She piled up the pillows and got back in. Using her raised knees under the duvet as a desk, she wrote herself a list of everything she had to do today, both for work and for David.

Top of the list was 'Phone Paddy'. Caro was entirely right, she thought. It had been madness to go asking total strangers whether they'd ever had a child with him.

He wasn't likely to leave for work for another hour, but she didn't want to ring too early, so she put that on one side and listed everything she still had to check and sort on Nick Gurles's case. She still hadn't done anything about moving her money, she remembered, and added that to her list, too. It would be hell to work this hard and this painfully until old age, only to discover that all her savings had been swallowed up by hopeless financial advice.

The Internet bank accounts were paying most of the good interest rates at the moment, but she was even less inclined to trust their security against hackers than to believe in the attractive-sounding products of their terrestrial rivals.

It'll be a stocking under the mattress at this rate, she told herself, wondering whether she might have another go at Nick Gurles, using the excuse that she wanted to ask his advice about what she should do with her own money. Grossly unprofessional, she decided. That'll have to wait until after the case.

But she knew she ought to write to her existing financial adviser and tell him she wanted everything liquidated. That would take some time and when it was done, she could decide what to do with the proceeds.

The to-do list was satisfactorily long and made her feel nearly as efficient as if she'd actually accomplished something. She got up to dress, feeling more secure than she had on any morning since she'd lost the baby. The power shower had its usual invigorating effect and she emerged dripping but once more reasonably glad to be alive. She even gave herself time for a bowl of yoghurt and banana for breakfast and remembered to take zinc and Vitamin B.

The streets between her building and Blackfriars Bridge Road seemed unthreatening once more. There were even a few decent cars lined up along the pavements. Not the Porsches and Alfas — they'd be sharing the locked spaces under the railway arches with her soft-top Audi — but a few relatively modern BMWs and even a top-of-the-range Japanese sports car. Years ago someone had pointed out to her that you could always judge the safety of a particular area by the cars that were parked on the street. Clearly things were looking up in this bit of Southwark.

Reflected sunlight glistened on the river as she crossed the bridge, and it lit all the best buildings in the piled skyline to her right, making the gold cross on the top of St Paul's shine. Life would go on, and whatever it did to Trish she could cope. She'd learned that after she'd almost cracked up a few years ago and had had to take a sabbatical. She shouldn't have forgotten it.

Someone was running behind her, panting. She moved out of the way, trying again to remember why running feet seemed so important. A man in a pinstriped suit, with a rolled-up copy of the *Financial Times* in his hand was thundering along the pavement. He gasped a thank-you to Trish as he passed. She wondered what he was late for, and why he was wearing the suit. Even in the stuffiest parts of the City these days hardly anyone wore those any more, or so Nick Gurles had told her.

Watching the man waving his pink newspaper at a taxi, Trish thought she could remember hearing running footsteps on the night David had been half-killed outside her flat. Had there been someone else in the street before it happened — someone who did not want to be questioned about his or her presence? Had someone pushed David under the wheels? This morning, even that thought couldn't spook her. If there had been someone there, running along the road just before the accident, it was much more likely that he'd been in too much of a hurry to stop and get involved in what had happened.

As soon as she reached her desk, Trish added to the bottom of her list a note to ask David how he'd come to fall under the car. That would settle it one way or the other. She couldn't think why she hadn't asked sooner. Then she picked up the phone to talk to her father.

'Trish, I do not have to answer to you for the way I've lived my life,' he said at once. She hadn't realised he had 'caller identification' on his phone and wondered why he bothered. Who was he trying to avoid?

'I'm not asking you to,' she said. 'Are you frantic at the moment, or have you time to talk?'

'It depends what you want to talk about. I

am not going to have a conversation about Jeannie Nest.'

'First I wanted to thank you for dinner on Monday. It was great. And I really liked Bella.'

'That was mutual, thank God,' he said, with a hint of his usual amusement softening the antagonism. 'She said you'd stopped being such a stuck-up judge. Which made me even crosser with your cheeky phone message.'

'It wasn't meant cheekily. It's too important for that.' She couldn't think of any way of dressing up the question that wouldn't be offensive, and so she asked straight out: 'Paddy, I need to know if you ever had another child — after me, I mean.'

'Not that I know of,' he said, sounding so Irish that Trish was instantly suspicious.

'Not even around eight or nine years ago?'

'Trish, will you stop it now! Is this why you wanted to know who I was seeing then?'

'Yes. I'm — '

'Now look here, this is too much,' he said, not sounding at all Irish any more. He was obviously furious. 'Have you been asking Sylvia if I made her pregnant? Is that how you heard about Jeannie?'

'Yes, but — '

'When will you learn to keep your long

nose out of my life?' He sounded really angry.

'Sylvia Bantell didn't mind in the least. In fact, she was very chatty. She said you used to talk about me.'

'So?'

'Even then, before we'd met again?'

'Trish, will you stop this now? It's horrible.'

'OK. Then just explain why you didn't tell me about Jeannie Nest. Was it because you had a child with her? Or was it because she was a prostitute?'

'She was no such thing. Don't be ridiculous. She was a teacher, for God's sake! Who told you she was a prostitute?'

'Sylvia.' This was clearly not the moment to talk about the private detective.

'That's just jealousy and spite. Jeannie was a teacher, and a damn good one. Very beautiful, too. And certainly not pregnant by me.'

'How can you be sure?'

'She'd have had the Child Support Agency on to me like a shot if she had been. Wasn't she all for women's rights now?' The Irish was worryingly back in his voice.

'I went to her flat,' Trish said, 'and I couldn't imagine you there.'

'Sure and 'twas a terrible dump, but she'd some romantic-socialist idea that she'd only learn to understand the kids she taught if she lived like they did, saw them coming and going in their home life. So you don't have to be so embarrassed. Whatever else I did, Trish, I never paid for sex.' He laughed. 'I never had to. And you can tell all your grand friends that, if you're worried about what they're thinking of your miscreant father.'

'Oh, shut up, Paddy.'

'That's better. I was beginning to think there was something wrong wit' you, Trish.'

He'd be calling her a colleen next, which was always the worst sign. 'What happened to her?'

'Jeannie? I've no idea.'

'You just dropped her, you mean? Were you bored, or had you found someone else?'

'Neither, so there's no need to sound so scornful. She refused to leave that sink estate to live with me, or soften any of her high-minded rules to fit in with my life. After I was mugged there one night between her flat and my car, I told her I wasn't going back. They nearly broke me arm, Trish, to get the money from my wallet. 'Twas the last straw, and all Jeannie would say was, 'Fine, if that's the way you want it.' And wasn't I so angry at her not caring about me arm and me wallet, and her prissy virtue and all, that I never spoke to her again?'

'And you've felt guilty about it ever since.'

There was a pause before he said drily, 'Are you asking me or telling me?'

'Neither of us needs to ask the other things like that, Paddy. I know guilt when I hear it. See it, too.'

There was a pause before he said quietly, sounding much more straightforward, 'If it's any help, Trish, it was more than just a fling, what I had with Jeannie. Sylvia, she was just fun. I'd never had a woman with a voice like hers or a house like hers. I'd never been anyone's rough trade before, and I enjoyed every minute of it.'

'I can imagine.'

'And she was a game old trout, too, but I didn't ever love her, and when she kicked me out I never looked back. But Jeannie? Well, she was different. Losing her hurt.' His voice was as English as Trish had ever heard it.

But you walked away from her even so, didn't you? Just as you abandoned my mother and me, she thought. Good women worry you. Like George sometimes worries me. Is it your past that stops me trusting myself enough to live with him?

But she couldn't think about that now. She looked sternly at the phone and said, 'How old was Jeannie when you had your affair?'

'Trish, will you stop this interrogation? Jeannie was part of my life a long time ago.

She's nothing to do with either of us now. Leave it.'

Trish's computer beeped as a new email came through. She said she had to go, and Paddy didn't protest. She read all her messages, then clicked on to Google, which was her favourite search engine, to look for Jeannie Nest. Nothing useful came up, but that didn't mean much. If she had never published anything or posted anything on the Net, there'd be no reason for her to be there. But if she were a teacher, someone should have records.

It didn't take long to get the phone number of the National Union of Teachers, but they said they had no record of anyone of that name. Lots of teachers were leaving the profession, disillusioned by the bashing they got in the media and from the government. Maybe Jeannie Nest was one of them. Or maybe she'd found a man she wanted more than she'd wanted Paddy, married, and taken her husband's name.

Trish looked up the numbers of all the remaining schools in the borough and rang each one, asking to speak to the school secretary. The first two produced nothing, but the third, a pleasant-sounding woman, agreed that she had known Jeannie and her two-year-old son.

'I'm trying to get in touch with her again,' Trish said. 'I wondered if you could help.'

'Of course not.'

'I don't mean I'm expecting you to hand over her address,' Trish said stiffly, wondering whether it had been necessary to be quite so rude. 'After all, I'm a complete stranger. But I did wonder if you'd forward a letter for me.'

'No, of course I can't. Don't you understand? None of us has been allowed any contact with her since she had to move away after the case.'

There was enough bitterness in the announcement to make 'the case' sound serious. Trish wondered what kind of scandal had been involved and who had brought the action.

'What was the case about?'

'Who *are* you?' asked the school secretary, sounding more suspicious with every word.

'I'm a barrister, but that's not why I'm trying to find Jeannie. She was a friend of my father's. He's had a heart attack. I wanted . . . ' Trish let her voice dwindle, hoping to generate enough sympathy to make the woman talk.

'Then I'm really sorry I can't help, but there's nothing I can do. I don't know where Jeannie went, or what she's calling herself now.'

'Then what was the case about? Maybe I can find her that way.'

'It was in all the papers. I don't see how you can have missed it if your father knew her.'

'It's a long story,' Trish said. 'He and I weren't speaking then. I'm trying to make amends now. Please tell me what you know.'

'Oh, I see. Well, I suppose it can't do any harm now. Jeannie was a witness in a murder trial. It was about six years ago now. No one else would testify, even though they must all have seen exactly what she'd seen.'

A lot clicked into place for Trish then. If Jeannie had been the only witness brave enough to have given evidence in a big murder trial, she could have been taken into the witness-protection scheme and given a new identity and family history. And if that had happened, her young son — two years old at the time — might well look blank at the suggestion that his mother was called Jeannie Nest. But it still didn't explain why she might have sent him to Trish.

'How awful. What happened? I mean, what did Jeannie see?'

'It was horrific. A thug from the estate where she lived was beating up a man whose wife owed him money.'

Trish thought of the children on the estate.

Some of them had looked nearly ten, so they must have been around when the killing happened; they might even have seen it for themselves. No wonder they'd reacted so violently to a stranger asking questions.

'He was down on the ground while the thug went at him with a baseball bat. Most people were so scared they locked their doors. His wife was screaming. Jeannie was coming home from the childminder's, with her son David in his buggy, when she saw what was happening. She yelled at the man to stop. He hit her, kind of swatted her out of the way. Luckily the buggy didn't overturn, but she cracked her head against a wall. There was blood everywhere — you know how scalp wounds bleed. But the man ignored her and went back to his victim.'

'She could've been killed,' Trish said, appalled to think of what had happened only ten minutes' walk from her own flat. She hadn't owned it at the time of the murder, but that didn't seem to make much difference. 'I'd never have had the guts to go anywhere near them.'

'Jeannie was always exceptional. And she didn't like letting something go when she felt strongly about it.'

'Even so.'

'I know.' There was much less suspicion in

the woman's voice now. It was as though Trish's genuine admiration had made them friends. 'When she gave evidence, she said that the victim's clothes were already rags and his head and body pulpy under the beating. So she ran, keeping her own blood off David's head as well as she could, to the nearest phone to get the police. Later, when everyone else in the place pretended they didn't know the attacker or the reason for the beating, Jeannie gave evidence against him. She was braver than anyone I've ever met.'

'She sounds it. Thank you for telling me,' Trish said into the phone. 'I'll look up the case. You don't happen to remember the name of the victim or the defendant, do you?'

'Defendant? Oh, you mean the murderer. Hang on a minute. It'll come to me.'

Trish's door opened and Dave looked in, his face so tight with irritation that his glasses were almost bouncing off his nose.

'Don't worry. I'm afraid I have to go. Thank you so much for your help.'

'Handsome,' said the woman, which seemed an odd way of acknowledging gratitude. But with Dave looking like that there was no way of staying to chat. Trish put down her receiver and smiled benignly at him.

'Yes, Dave?'

'I've been trying to get through to you for hours, Miss.' Trish grimaced. She hadn't been 'Miss' to him for a long time. 'I've just had Mr Shelley on the phone from Tuscany and I thought I'd better check that you'll have everything ready for him on Monday morning.'

'Of course I will. I told you that before.' He was good at hiding his doubts behind the wintry severity of his usual expression, but she could tell he was worried this time. That mattered a lot more to her than the chauvinistic jealousy of other juniors like Robert Anstey. Dave knew too much about all his barristers and their strengths and weaknesses. 'Is there anything else?'

'Yes. He won't be needing you while he works on the papers, so I'd like you to take this brief for Maidstone. It's care proceedings on — '

'Not Monday. I have to talk to Antony and go through the paperwork with him.'

'I know that, Miss. This is for Tuesday — right?'

'Yes, fine.' 'Miss' again, she thought. So he's really pissed off. And care proceedings. Can I bear to do something like that just now? I'll have to, if I'm about to be flung off the Nick Gurles case. I'll need Dave on my side if I'm scrabbling for briefs again.

It was a long time since she'd felt as though some extra-terrestrial being was using her in his own private game of Snakes and Ladders, but the sensation came back with shivering familiarity. Bird-shaped shadows flapped in her mind. This morning's euphoria had gone completely.

'Dave,' she said as she took the pink-taped brief from him and put it beside her laptop.

'Yes, Miss?'

'Oh, stop all this Miss nonsense.' Even he looked shocked by the sharpness of her voice. She drove herself to smile. 'Has there been any news — or gossip — about the boy the police were trying to identify?'

'I did hear, *Miss*, that they'd decided to do some DNA tests, but I don't know who they're trying to match him with. However, there have been some runaways among your old clients and their friends, including one of a pair of brothers being fostered by the same people who took in the Brakely lad. You'll remember the case. That was Maidstone, too. Nearly eighteen months ago, wasn't it? It upset you at the time.'

Trish did remember, all too clearly. The boy in that case had been through a torturing time before she'd got him safely away from his mother. Father unknown, she remembered; mother not only a prostitute, but deeply into sado-masochism, and not averse to handing round her six-year-old son to some of her more perverted clients.

'I know.' Dave's voice was as nearly soft as she'd ever heard it. 'That one really got to you, didn't it? Still, you did the business and he's safe now. And you're moving on into nice, clean, big-money commercial work now. So long as you do a good job for Mr Shelley on this case, you'll be fine.'

He looked even less confident, so Trish suppressed all her own doubts and concentrated on the matter in hand.

'But if other children are running away from the foster-parents, that doesn't sound as though they're the ideal home for him either.'

'A lot better than his own mother, poor little bastard. Next Tuesday's case won't be nearly so bad.'

'Is the runaway the right age and colouring for the boy in hospital?' Trish wasn't surprised Dave knew so much about the state of the police investigation into the child's identity. Good clerks knew everything that might adversely affect the reputation of their barristers.

'That's the impression I got,' he said. 'The remaining brother's a bit simple and couldn't answer questions, nor identify the only photograph the police showed him

— touched up, I understand, to make the face look like it must when it isn't mashed up. Another poor little sod.'

'Yes.' Maybe that was the answer, and David was nothing to do with Jeannie Nest or Paddy. It could have been his foster-mother who'd taken the trouble to make him drink apple juice rather than Coke and sent him to Trish.

'Dave? Do you remember a case about six or seven years ago: a very nasty murder in Southwark that turned on evidence given by someone called Jeannie Nest, who's probably been on the witness-protection programme ever since?'

He frowned, pushing his spectacles up his nose, before scratching the left side of his cadaverous face.

'Can't say I do. Not one of yours, was it?'

'No.'

'But Southwark — that's near your flat, isn't it? Are you worried? Someone been stalking you again?'

'No. This is something else. And my place is quite a way from there, only minutes from Tate Modern and well within sight of the London Eye.' That made it seem much safer. Even so she was glad she'd put on the burglar alarm this morning. It had never been one of her routines, which suddenly seemed as stupid as George had always said it was. But until David had come running out of the dark to upset her entire view of her world, she'd had no idea quite how close she lived to the frontier.

'Don't worry. Thanks, Dave.'

Trish swivelled round, reaching for one of the files on Nick Gurles's case. Dave was nodding approvingly when she brought it back to her desk. When he'd gone, Trish tried to think who was likely to have prosecuted the Southwark murder case. It didn't take long to narrow the list down to a few silks. One of them was a friend, so she phoned him.

Like Antony, he was still away sunning himself, but his clerk was surprisingly chatty. His silk hadn't been the leader on the case, but he knew who had and gave Trish the name, one of the toughest of the women who worked in crime. Trish knew her slightly, but they'd never got on particularly well. Trish asked the clerk if he knew who the junior had been. He or she would probably be an easier source of information.

'Come on, Ms Maguire. If it had been one of mine, I'd know, but it wasn't, was it?'

'No, of course not. Thank you.' If Trish wanted more information, she'd have to talk to Selina Mallard QC. The number of her chambers was easily found, and she was there.

Trish explained herself, and heard Mallard say, 'Jeannie Nest? Very brave woman. I couldn't forget her. What d'you want to know?'

'Anything you can tell me.'

'Why? She hasn't cropped up again, has she? I'm sure she went into the witness-protection scheme.'

'I thought she must have. I was hoping . . . I mean, I've heard such a lot about her, I was hoping to track her down, but if she did that I haven't any chance.'

'No.' There was no room for doubt in that firm, contained monosyllable. 'How've you come across her name, if you didn't know about the case?'

'She lived near where I've got a flat, and they still talk about her.' Trish did not want stories of her search whizzing round the Temple. 'I gather she insisted on living in the kind of estate where her trickiest pupils came from. Beyond the call of duty, I'd say.'

'Masochistic. And that's where half the trouble came from. That place was a real hellhole. I'd love to chat, Trish, but I've a lot on. Is there anything else?'

'I'd like to look up the case. Can you remember the defendant's name?'

'Of course. A killing like that isn't something you forget easily. Ron Handsome.'

So that was what the school secretary had been trying to say.

'Thanks, Selina. That's great. I'll see you around.'

'Sure. Oh, somebody was asking about you the other day. Who? Yes, Heather Bonwell. Are you trying for silk this year? She wants you to.'

'Heather's lovely. But I don't think I will. Not yet.' Not if I'm about to screw up Antony Shelley's case. 'Thanks for everything, Selina. Bye.'

With the defendant's name, it was easy to track down the case and read what Jeannie Nest had done and why she'd had to accept the protection of a false name and history for herself and her son.

Lucky that he'd been only two at the time, Trish thought. A bit older than that, but not yet old enough to understand the importance of the new story, witness-protection children were often a danger to themselves and their parents.

★   ★   ★

DCI Lakeshaw and his sergeant were waiting for Ron Handsome in an interview room at the prison. They'd looked at the old photographs of the man he had beaten to death on the Mull Estate and compared them with the pix of Jeannie Nest's body. You couldn't identify a murderer (or even the man who'd organised a murder) by the state of the victim's body, but the effect of the two beatings did look quite similar.

Sue Baker, the sergeant, hadn't had to see the pathologist slicing up the body itself, and Lakeshaw almost resented her freedom from the sights and smells he'd suffered. Still, she wasn't a bad officer and it wasn't her fault he couldn't get the smell out of his nostrils. He ought to think of something else, otherwise he'd be too angry to question Handsome effectively.

The door of the interview room opened and a wizened little man shuffled through ahead of the screw. Lakeshaw looked carefully at the screw. You could learn a lot about an inmate from the way the staff treated him. But this officer was neither afraid of the old man nor respectful. He just looked bored as he handed over the prisoner and left them to it.

The old man coughed, pressing a hand to his chest in a way Lakeshaw recognised from a lot of officers he'd known. Most of them were dead now. Was this tortoise-like thug determined to get his revenge on the woman whose evidence had sent him here before he himself snuffed it? Was that why he'd had her killed now, after all this time? Lakeshaw knew his own face was rocklike from the wary glance Sue Baker shot him. He nodded to her.

'Ron Handsome? My name's Sergeant Baker,' she said in her usual brisk way. The old man didn't smile, but his eyelids flicked upwards and the eyes themselves moved as he stared at her then back at Lakeshaw. He didn't look dangerous. He looked ill and a lot older than the sixty-nine years his records gave him. But then how many of them did look the part once they'd been caught and sent down? Hardly any, in Lakeshaw's experience, which was what gave the do-gooders and the prison reformers all the ammunition they needed to make the middle-class bleeding hearts moan on about making life in prison more comfortable for men like this one.

Lakeshaw wanted to jam photographs of Jeannie Nest's body under the noses of everyone who'd ever complained about police brutality or uncomfortable prisons.

'And this is DCI Lakeshaw,' Sue Baker was saying.

He must concentrate. The rage was getting

worse all the time now and he couldn't let it ride him. Already he'd had to leave the preliminary questioning of DC Martin Waylant to his sergeant. He himself wouldn't have been able to keep his temper for more than a minute if he'd had to listen to the stupid sod making excuses for ignoring a call for help from a woman at risk. What was it he'd told Sue Baker? That it had been a case of crying wolf. The victim had called for help so often when there'd turned out to be no danger at all that it hadn't seemed worth following up this last report, not when the nick was overstretched and undermanned like it was.

Baker nudged him. She was talking. He put the thought of Waylant to the back of his mind and listened.

'As you know, Ron, we've come to ask you some questions about Jeannie Nest.'

The old man pulled the plastic chair on his side of the table nearer him and sat down. Lakeshaw thought of American films he'd seen and even real-life items on the news with killers being taken to and from court and thought this sodding man was damn lucky he'd been convicted in England. In the States he'd probably be chained. Do him good, too.

'Why now?' he asked in a voice as hoarse as coughing could make it without actually

187

silencing him. 'It's been years since I had anything to do with her.'

'Are you sure? Who've you been talking to about her?'

'No one. Why would I? I hate the fucking slag. Always did, even before she grassed me up.' He coughed again, pulling a disgusting handkerchief out of his pocket.

At least he wasn't spitting on the floor, Lakeshaw thought. Not yet anyway.

'Well, someone's been beating her up,' he said, watching Handsome carefully. There was a hint of sly pleasure sliding into the man's eyes.

'Serve her right,' he said, revealing browned teeth as he grinned. 'Why d'you need me?'

'To hear what you know about it.'

'Come on, mate, I've been locked up here for the past six years. How could I know anything?'

'You've got friends on the outside. You keep tabs on what's going on at the Mull Estate, so I hear. Your son Gary reports to you, and so does your young grandson. Have they been keeping tabs on Jeannie Nest for you, too? Or is it someone else?'

'Leave off, will you? I haven't had nothing to do with it. Whoever's done her over, it wasn't me. I hate the fucking slag, like I said, but all I know is that she left the estate soon as she'd grassed me up and hasn't never been back there. That's all my Gal's told me, Mr Lakeshaw.'

'OK. So what about your son himself, then? I'm told he's been talking a lot recently, even more than usual, about seeing Jeannie Nest gets her just deserts. What d'you know about that?'

'Nothing.' Ron Handsome sounded as tired as Lakeshaw felt. He gestured to Sue Baker to carry on. It was just possible that she might get something out of him.

★　★　★

Old Lil was still waiting for news that Gary had done as he was told. He'd wanted her to write down what roads he was supposed to take to get to Spain, but she didn't want any evidence that she'd been aiding and abetting him if he was picked up. Perverting the course of justice, or as her old man would have put it, 'preverting' it — that's what they'd call it. And she didn't want to be involved in any police investigation. Not with the business at stake.

But there was no news of Gal. Just like there was still no news of any tom beaten up, or killed, in Wanstead. There'd been a paragraph in the *Sun* about another dead woman; this one's battered body had been found in a basement flat in Hoxton. The police were interviewing her workmates and all her recent boyfriends, it said, but as soon as Lil had seen that the woman had died some time on Tuesday night she'd stopped worrying about that one. Gal had come with the blood on his trousers on Sunday.

Mikey was due soon with her shopping. He'd be at her about the fags if he smelled the flat like it was, so she opened the windows and emptied the ashtray. Her back was aching and she was afraid it was the kidney again. The hospital had given her a date next year for an appointment with the urologist, but she didn't trust hospitals anyway. Kill you as soon as look at you. And they always made a fuss about the fags.

Worrying about what Gal might have been up to was making her smoke far too much. She'd be out of packets soon and she'd have to go down to the shop herself for more. Mikey wouldn't get them, and she didn't like going out on her own, even now.

She thought of Mikey's news about the woman who'd been asking questions about Jeannie Nest, and she thought about the blood on Gal's trousers. Was it too much of a coincidence? She hated not knowing what was going on and fretting herself to death over it.

Jeannie Nest. Why hadn't she had the sense to keep quiet like everyone else? And why had Ron been so stupid that he'd had to beat a client's husband to death in front of the one person on the whole estate who'd talk to the police?

He'd been bright enough to get out of the way when he heard the sirens, and he'd got rid of the baseball bat somewhere, too, and his bloody clothes, so there was no evidence. The client was so scared she said she'd never seen her husband's killer before and insisted that he'd been wearing a mask so she'd never be able to identify him from photos. All the other neighbours agreed. Only Jeannie Nest came right out with it and gave his name, and identified his photo, and stuck to it all through, in spite of everything.

That was the last any of them had seen of her till they'd come face to face with her in court. And then she'd disappeared, and it wasn't hard to know why, not with Gal telling everyone he was going to make her pay, even if it took him the rest of his life to track her down. Stupid git. Was that what he'd done now? Was it Jeannie's blood?

Lil thought of the night he'd stripped off the trousers and how she'd seen at once that they could give her the protection she'd always needed. They were safely hidden now. She wouldn't use them unless she had to. But there might come a day when she needed to get him out of the way. He knew too much as it was, even if he didn't have the names of her clients or know how much they owed, where she kept her float or what she did with the profits.

No one knew that, except the solicitor who handled everything for her, and he was well paid to keep his mouth shut.

Lil reckoned up her investments sometimes when she was low, and knew she was worth nearly a hundred thousand pounds now, not counting the cottage the solicitor had bought for her. One day soon, when she was sure of Mikey, she'd get rid of the tenants and retire there. No one would know where she'd gone. Then she might be able to relax.

She kept trying to tell herself that her old man couldn't touch her from inside, but she knew how easy it would be. He had plenty of friends left on the outside. None of them would think twice about doing Ron Handsome a favour and teaching his old woman a lesson. She might not have to wait sweating any more for when he came in drunk, wondering if tonight was the night he was going to do her the kind of damage no hospital could put right. But she was still afraid that one day he'd make good his threats to force her to give Gary a share in the business.

Taking the bloody trousers round to the local nick with a tearful account of how she hadn't dared bring them in any sooner should get Gal out of the way for long enough to close everything down and get away. Lil didn't approve of women who turned in their own sons, but she'd do it if she had to.

9

Lakeshaw, red-eyed from staring at his screen for hours, took a break to riffle through the pile of notes and reports on his desk. There was one from a sergeant in one of the East End nicks. He didn't recognise the name, but the message told him that its sender had some anecdotal evidence that might be useful to his investigation. Now that he thought about it, Lakeshaw remembered that the message had surfaced once or twice before. It hadn't sounded urgent so he'd put it back while he dealt with the stuff that was important. But he had a small window now, as he waited for the results of the latest round of interviews in Southwark, so he picked up the phone.

He shouldn't have been surprised to get a woman at the other end of the line, but he was. Luckily she had an easy deepish voice instead of the complaining nasal twang of most of the female officers he'd had to deal with recently. She told him about a boy in hospital and a barrister who thought he might be connected with the murder victim.

'What's he called?' Lakeshaw asked.

'David, but he won't give his surname.'

'I meant the barrister,' he said irritably. 'Not the child.'

'Ah. That's a she: Trish Maguire.'

Lakeshaw stiffened, then reached for the bundle of statements Sue Baker had taken during her interminable interviews with the victim's friends.

'She a friend of yours, Sergeant?' he said into the phone.

'Yes. Do you think there's anything in it, sir?'

'Shouldn't have thought so. It sounds fairly far-fetched to me,' Lakeshaw said, not prepared to trust the discretion of any officer he didn't know. 'But give me the details and I'll get it checked out.'

Sergeant Lyalt dictated them, adding at the end, 'Let me know if you need any more, sir.'

'Will do.' He put down the phone and re-read the statement Baker had taken from one of the victim's workmates. He hadn't been that impressed on first reading it because he was certain the killing had to be the work of the Handsome family. But now that Maguire's name had cropped up twice, he'd have to send someone to look into it.

In the meantime, he also had to decide how to deal with DC Martin Waylant. He'd been telling the truth all right when he'd said the nick had been seriously overstretched the last time the victim had called for help. There'd been a whole spate of break-ins, a death-by-dangerous driving, a drugs bust, and a very nasty rape, as well as all the time-wasting stories of lost kitties and weirdos-gone-walkabout that every London officer had to field.

In the circumstances it wasn't surprising that Waylant hadn't paid proper attention to the poor cow. She'd deserved better, but anyone with half a brain would see that it could have happened just as Waylant claimed. On the other hand, he had admitted that he'd been aware of her real name, and he shouldn't have been.

There was no way a local officer of his rank would have been given that kind of information officially, even if he had been told to keep an eye on her. Lakeshaw would have to establish how he'd found out, but the much more important questions at the moment were who else he'd told, and why, and how much it had earned him.

Lakeshaw's fists were hurting. He looked down at them in surprise and saw they were clenched so tightly on the desk that his knuckles were white. He relaxed his hands, wiping the palms on his trousers, muttering, 'Don't get angry till you have to. There's no evidence Waylant sold Jeannie Nest to the Handsomes. No evidence that anyone did. Not yet anyway.'

Most of the failures in the witness-protection scheme came, as Lakeshaw knew perfectly well, from the witnesses' own inability to stay clear of their old friends, neighbourhood and family. Not many people could separate themselves from their own lives for ever without whispering their secrets to someone. Waylant's guilt mustn't be assumed while there was still a possibility that the victim could have betrayed herself.

★   ★   ★

The smoke was hurting Lil's throat now, but at least that distracted her from the thought of the books behind the boiler and the cash in its hiding places all over the flat, and Gal's bloody trousers. She kept the batty-old-bag smile on her face, squinting at the young copper as though her watery eyes couldn't see very well. She might wish her son dead sometimes, but she wasn't going to hand him over to the police unless there was a clear benefit in doing it.

'You must know what your son's being doing. Gary Handsome,' the sergeant said, in case she was so far gone that she'd forgotten she'd ever had a son. 'Come on, Lil. Give me something here.'

'Mrs Handsome to you,' she answered tartly and saw him exchange a grin with his sidekick. She hated them both. There'd been no sign of them and their like in the days when Ron was regularly putting her in hospital. Couldn't give a stuff about her in them days. Not like now when they wanted something from her.

'He's a grown man. He doesn't live here. Why would I know what he's up to?'

'When did you last see him, then?' asked the sergeant. He wasn't from round here. Some of the officers she'd known since they were kids, but this was a mean-faced bloke with a northern accent and nasty eyes.

Lil dragged on her fag and sniffed, which made her choke so her eyes watered even more. She wiped them with a shaking hand.

'Last week, I think. Or was it the week before? He doesn't come regular. And all the days are the same now. It's hard to know which it was. It was soon after I'd got me pension, that I do know. And I'd had salmon for tea. But if it was last week or the one before . . . ' She shook her head and wiped her eyes again. Ash sprinkled over her clothes. She looked up at the hard-faced sergeant, avoiding the constable's eyes. He knew her and might not be buying all this sad old-age stuff.

Lil let her head droop. There was a mouse turd on the floor near the boiler cupboard. She hoped the little beggars weren't eating the account books. That'd happened once, years ago, and they'd chewed nearly an inch off of the list of debtors. It was a long time before she'd believed Ron when he claimed he hadn't torn off the corner himself. She'd better get Mikey to buy her some poison for them. She didn't want the council's vermin man poking about in the cupboards or under the floorboards and finding anything he shouldn't.

'So you don't know where he was three nights ago, then? Is that what you're saying?'

'Three nights?' she nearly squawked, but luckily saw the sergeant watching her beadily. They must be talking about the woman she'd read about in the *Sun*. She'd been killed three nights ago, when Gal should've been halfway to Spain. Still, what did that matter? Made it easier to lie about him and the blood on his trousers on Sunday night. Not that Lil had ever found lying that hard. Too much practice, with all the stuff she'd had to say to her old man to make life bearable in the old days. 'No. No, I don't think so. Why would I? Who says he was doing anything?'

'OK. Well, never mind. But we'll be back.'

'I'm sure you will. I'll make you a cuppa then, but I haven't got no milk for it now.'

'No, that's all right, Ma. You told us that before.'

'Did I?'

'Don't worry about it. You take care now.'

She waited until they were well away, then got herself to the window to watch them walk to the car. The kidney was hurting again. Sometimes she had to hold her side and bend forwards, hanging down nearly to her toes to make it bearable. It wasn't that bad today, not yet anyway, but bad enough. When they'd driven off, she got the books back from behind the boiler. There weren't any teethmarks. Good. She put on the kettle and waited for Mikey to come back.

'All right, Nan?' he called softly from the door. She jumped. He was getting quieter and quieter these days. She never knew where he was, what he was listening to, or watching.

'I don't know,' she said, trying not to pant. 'Where's your uncle?'

'Haven't seen him. Is that what the Old Bill wanted?'

'Yes,' she said, still trying to keep her voice normal. 'Wanted to know where he'd been three nights since. What's he been up to?'

Mikey stiffened, 'Three nights ago?' he said

at last. He had a smile on him now that she'd never seen before. She didn't like it one bit. It looked pleased and horrible all at the same time. What did it mean?

'How would I know, Nan? He was probably throwing up in a gutter or trying to get a tart to stay with him long enough to get his rocks off. Or shooting his mouth off in a pub somewhere about what he's going to do to Jeannie Nest when he finds her. I've never known him do much else than that. He's a loser, Nan. Here's your milk.'

'You're a good boy, Mikey. If you see Gal, will you . . . ?' She waited a moment, not sure how to ask what she wanted to know. If she kept telling Mikey he was a good boy, they might both believe it. It *had* to be true. And if it wasn't true, then it was even more important that he was convinced she thought it was. She felt shaky suddenly and leaned against the back of her chair, her hand stroking her jaw again.

'Will I what? D'you want me to get him for you, Nan?'

'No. But I do want to know where he is.'

'If I see him, I'll tell him to come.' Mikey thought a bit, then said, 'Or I could take you round to his place now. Would you like that? When you've had your tea. And a bit of a rest.'

It wasn't such a bad idea. The bugger should be in Spain by now, but it wouldn't do any harm to be seen knocking on his door, specially if the police were after him. Judging by the questions today, they were after him for something bad enough to have someone watching his place. If she and Mikey were seen to be looking for Gal, that would show the filth and everyone else that neither of them knew what had been going on.

'Yes, Mikey. That'd be good. Thanks.'

He smiled a much more normal smile, so she breathed easier while he boiled the kettle. She drank her tea as soon as it was cool enough, then she let him help her into his car. With all the cabbing he did, and the two girls he was running, he could've afforded something better than this old banger by now, but it made him fit in with the other mini-cabs, so it was sensible enough. Sitting in the passenger seat, she hoped her stupid son had thought to clean his van of all the blood he must've smeared inside it on Sunday.

If it *was* Jeannie's blood, then she must be dead. If she'd been alive, she'd have had the police round here days ago, with a warrant for Gal's arrest. Unless, of course, she'd been so badly beaten she couldn't speak. That could be what the difference in timing was all about. What if he'd beaten her senseless and speechless on Sunday night, but she hadn't died till Tuesday, so she hadn't been found till then? That would make sense.

'Has that woman you saw been round again? You know, the one who was asking questions about Jeannie?'

'I haven't seen her, Nan.' Mikey ran his tongue across his lips and smoothed back his hair. 'But don't you worry. I've got it under control.'

'What d'you mean?' Her eyes were hurting and she had to lick off a blob of spit in the corner of her mouth as she thought of what he might have been doing. She didn't like nosy-parkers any more than Mikey did, but she didn't want yet another women beaten up — or worse — by any of the men in her family.

'I've got people keeping an eye out for her,' Mikey said kindly. Lil relaxed a bit more. 'If she ever comes back, I'll hear. Then we can decide what to do. If we need to do anything.'

That sounded better. She smiled. 'Good. But don't take risks. With the police all over us, we don't want them to start thinking you're like the others. *I* know you're not, but they won't.'

He nodded, not smiling back, so she said again silently in her head, willing herself to believe it: You're a good boy.

She thought of her husband and their two sons, and the way they all thought violence was the only way of sorting anything. Mikey *was* different. He had to be. He was her only hope. He was talking, but she had other things to think about and didn't listen.

'Nan. *Nan*?'

'What?'

'We're here. Can you manage the walk if I park this far away?'

She nearly laughed. Her impression of a failing old bat must be more convincing than she'd realised. It was only about twenty yards between the entry to this estate and Gal's block. But she took Mikey's arm even so, and hobbled forwards. Anyone watching would've thought she could hardly stand on her own, and that was how it should be. They got up to Gal's floor in a lift that worked in spite of the stink, and knocked on his door.

Straight off she knew someone was in there, even though there was no answer to the bell or Mikey's knocking. Maybe it was a smell, maybe a noise, maybe just a feeling. But she knew.

So he hasn't gone to Spain, she thought. Maybe the police were right and he did do something on Tuesday night. Maybe the excitement of all that blood on Sunday had made him want another go two days later. Or maybe hurting a working girl had made him feel brave enough to carry out his drunken threats to give Jeannie Nest a good seeing-to.

Lil nudged Mikey to one side and pushed up the flap of the letter box. 'Gal, it's your ma. Let me in. Come on, open up.' She was sure it was him in there, even though he didn't answer and there wasn't any more noise. 'D'you want me yelling my questions from out here? Come on, Gal. Let me in. It's only me and Mikey.'

At last the door opened, he stood there, in his vest, unshaven, wearing more filthy trousers, and looking like the stupid mess he'd always been. He had a can of Special Brew in his hand and a fag, dropping ash everywhere. She wasn't surprised Mikey was wrinkling up his nose. He'd always been a clean boy, always cared what he looked like.

'We're coming in.'

Gal gave way, but he didn't like it. Lil was sure that if she hadn't had Mikey with her, she wouldn't have got in. Gal was scared of his nephew. It had surprised her when she'd first seen it because she'd thought he could've smashed Mikey to one side without even breaking a sweat; now that she knew Mikey better, and listened to stories from her neighbours of his exploits in the gym, she understood her son's fear well enough. They followed him to the lounge. She stood in the doorway, coughing.

'Bloody hell, Gal! No wonder you can't get a woman to stay with you for more than two minutes. This is a pigsty and you smell like a pig. You might open the window sometimes.'

'Nan.' Mikey's quiet voice from behind her warned her she was going too far.

'Still, it's your choice,' she said quickly. 'Nothing to do with me. What've you been doing?'

'Nothing, Ma.'

'Don't give me that. I had the police round at my place.' She stared at him, forcing him to look back at her. 'They wanted to know what you were doing *Tuesday* night. I told them I didn't know and I hadn't seen you. I thought you'd be on holiday.'

'Tuesday?' He wasn't as good at lying as she was, and he couldn't manage to look surprised enough. So he had been up to something on Tuesday, had he? She hoped it wasn't the murder in Hoxton. That might get him out of her way for as long as she lived, but it would bring all sorts of trouble with it. She'd never get safely away to her cottage without anyone knowing where she was if there was going to be another murder trial.

Gal's eyes shifted as he looked from her to

Mikey and back again. 'Dunno. I think I was here.' He waved to the piled beer tins all over the room. 'Watching telly. Or wiv me mates in the pub.'

'Likely enough. Well, they'll get here soon, if they haven't already been.' His eyes flickered towards her, then back to his beer can. 'Oh, so they've paid you a call, have they?'

'Searched the place.' He brightened a little. 'That's why it's such a mess, Ma. They threw the stuff around, then they took a lot of me clothes. But there's nothing to find. I ain't done nothing. I've told them that each time they've come.'

'What d'you mean, 'each time'?'

He did look surprised then. 'They come first on Wednesday night, then different ones on Friday, and more over the weekend.'

'Why didn't you tell me?'

'Why would I, Ma? Nothing you can do. Nothing anyone can do because I haven't done nothing. I keep telling them that, but they keep coming back. Still,' he said, cheering up, 'they haven't arrested me, have they? No evidence.'

'Just as well. Why didn't you go on your holidays, like you were supposed to? What happened?'

He looked away, scratching again.

'Lost your money, did you? Or your bottle? It was that, wasn't it? You were scared of finding your way abroad.'

He took a step towards her just as Mikey was saying, 'Nan,' again. But it didn't stop either of them, so Mikey pushed her behind him and stood up to his uncle. 'Don't you lay a finger on her.'

Gal took another step forward. Lil could smell his beery breath even from behind Mikey. But the boy didn't move.

'She's not worth it,' said Gal, turning away. 'The old witch. You may think you'll be quids in if you stick around, running little errands for her, licking her arse for her. But she'll never give you anything. She's a mean old bitch and you'd be better off without her. We all would.'

Lil felt Mikey tense and knew that if he'd been any of the others, he'd have hit his uncle by then. She could feel him fighting it, the urge to lunge and batter. But he was stronger than them. When she felt the fury slinking back in him like a cat that's seen the dog ahead is too big to fight, she said quietly, 'Let's go, Mikey. It won't do any good to stay and argue. Don't come asking for anything more, Gal, because you won't get it. Not now. Not after this. And keep your damn nose clean.'

When they were outside again, Mikey helped her into the lift. 'Grandad phoned today, while you were in the toilet.'

'Did he? Why?'

Mikey shrugged. 'He said he likes to keep in touch with the business, make sure you're treating Gal right. He says you asked for a Visiting Order, Nan. Why? You hardly ever go to see him. What d'you want to do it for now?'

Lil shivered. 'I don't. But your grandad likes to think he runs our business from inside. If I go to the prison once in a while, we can both pretend I'm doing what he tells me.'

'But what'll happen to the business when he gets out if he thinks it's his?'

Lil didn't mind the sharp anxiety in Mikey's voice. She could cope with that. And it was fair enough. He'd been working hard for her for four years now, ever since he'd come back from her sister's after he left school. It was right that he should be thinking about taking over — and without interference from a grandfather he'd rarely seen. She'd always thought of Mikey's twenty-first birthday as the day she'd hand over to him, and it would come in less than two months. Maybe she could retire then and forget all this.

'He's not likely to get out, and if he does,

he'll be too old to bother you.' She patted his cheek, and he let her do it. 'You're a good boy, Mikey.'

They walked by a pair of patrolling police officers, trying to look uninterested in them. Lil recognised one, and nodded to him. Further on they passed a sleekly polished dark-blue car without any markings. A man in a suit got out.

'Afternoon, Mr Smith,' Lil said, making her voice quiver. She clung to Mikey's arm. 'This is my grandson. Mikey, this is Chief Inspector Smith.'

'We've met before,' said the plain-clothes officer, nodding to Mikey. 'Why're you here, Lil?'

'I come to find out what my Gal's been doing,' she said, making her eyes water as she looked up at him. 'Two of your boys come round to my place this morning, asking about him. They wouldn't tell me why. Seems like it must be something big.'

'You could say that.'

'You really think my Gal's capable of something big?'

He knew what she meant; she could see that. But she could see other things, too. This was definitely not about a simple beating. Chief inspectors didn't come out for that. This had to be murder. And the victim was

210

no prostitute. The filth didn't care this much about working girls, even when they were dead.

'Well, we'd best be on our way. Good to see you, Mr Smith.'

★　★　★

Lakeshaw finished reading the reports that had come up from the Southwark team and was glad he'd reserved judgment on Waylant's guilt. Gary Handsome had been seen passing out from drink in a local pub on the night she'd died. According to a whole crowd of witnesses, he couldn't have swatted a fly in the state he'd been in. And the only other feasible Handsome suspect, given that the old woman could hardly walk unaided, was her little mini-cab-driving grandson.

He'd always been a fairly unlikely prospect, and now it seemed that he'd been on shift for most of the relevant night. The cab office had amazingly been able to provide dockets for all his journeys and a Day Book that recorded the money he'd turned in for the trips. He'd covered a lot of ground, even given the empty roads at night.

Now that those two were out of the picture, at least until any new evidence turned up, Lakeshaw would have to spread the net wider. There must have been other men, outside Ron Handsome's own family, who might have been prepared to take on the job of punishing the woman whose evidence had convicted him. They would all have to be identified and interviewed, even though the man himself hadn't given them anything to go on. And, of course, now there was this Maguire character, who couldn't be ignored.

'Sue,' Lakeshaw yelled, without moving from his desk.

She looked round his door a couple of minutes later, her broad, healthy face as keen as ever.

'I'm going to need you to fill me in on this bloke Paddy Maguire, but first find me the SOCOs' list of the contents of the victim's flat, will you? I want to know more about that scrapbook they found, OK?'

10

Trish had another bad night, but she was up and dressing soon after seven on Monday morning. Antony Shelley wasn't likely to get to chambers until nine, or even later, but she wanted to catch him before anyone else did. She ignored breakfast, calling in to Pret à Manger for a large cappuccino on her way to the Temple. She stopped off in the clerks' room to leave a note in Antony's pigeonhole to let him know she needed to see him.

The coffee was halfway down the big cardboard beaker when she heard his voice. Looking up she saw him talking to someone over his shoulder. He was wearing a suit, although he wasn't going anywhere near court today, and he looked well. Towards the end of a long case, his clothes would always be so crumpled that you'd think he had slept in them for a week, and his clenched muscles would have driven his shoulders up under his ears. His nails would be bitten then, and inky, and his skin would have the texture and colour of old mashed potato.

But today, he had the kind of light tan that came from walking around in the heat rather than lying baking by a pool, and his shoulders hung at a comfortable level parallel with the base of his neck. Even his fingers were lying relaxed instead of bent into knotted clumps.

He finished his conversation and came to drop into the client's chair opposite Trish's desk.

'Horrid little room, this,' he said, looking around it. 'I had it for nearly six years myself. You should get a better one, Trish. Especially now.'

'As soon as a decent alternative comes up, I might. But this is fine for the moment, Antony.' She didn't add that she wasn't going to count her chickens too soon.

Robert Anstey had been winding her up again about how she was bound to come a cropper over the case even before it came to court. Thank God he didn't know about the treacherous note she'd persuaded Spindlers to send over.

'How was Tuscany?' she asked breezily, noticing that Antony was staring at her.

'Good.' He nodded as though confirming some tricky point of law, then smiled like a schoolboy. 'And best when we'd got rid of all the guests and could just flop. My wife likes to fill the place with friends and children and children's friends, and then have neighbours in for dinner too, until the whole place is as bad as the Old Bailey on a busy day. But when they've all gone, and it begins to get misty and silver in the mornings and wet in the afternoons and you need a fire in the evenings, it's wonderful.'

'I'm surprised you could bear to come back.'

'Me too. We even thought we might spend Christmas there, which would be a first. But you and I have got Nick Gurles to sort out before I can think about that. How's it been going, Trish?'

She made herself smile slowly. It was fifteen years since she'd been a pupil. Any sign of fear at her age would be grossly undignified.

'Well, there is one problem.'

'Yes?' He didn't look particularly worried.

Trish hadn't felt as tongue-tied as this since her first few days in court. Rather than stumble and stutter and risk looking silly, she shoved her chair back, swivelling as it travelled so that she ended up facing the banks of lever-arch files. Selecting the dangerous one, she laid it open on her desk and began to explain.

'Let me see,' Antony interrupted.

She pushed forward the photocopied document, marked with a scarlet mini Post-it and highlighted at the relevant paragraph.

Antony withdrew from her completely as he concentrated. She'd never known anyone who could shut out every distraction quite as effectively. The first time it had happened, they'd both been reading case papers and she'd become so powerfully aware of absence that for a micro-second she'd wondered if he'd had a heart attack and died.

The atmosphere warmed up as he stopped reading and looked up. 'So?'

'So, we're stymied, Antony. We're all set to claim that we never intended to misrepresent anything, that we were convinced from our mathematical modelling and all the old published studies, that the fund would generate the guaranteed return and no one would lose anything. Now, here's this piece of paper that shows we knew all along that there might be a problem and we were concerned to make sure all the marketing literature disguised that and made potential investors believe we were offering a normal savings account.'

Antony was staring at her as though she was a mute foreigner trying to mime a joke he didn't find funny.

'No, it doesn't. The rest of this note is all about the MegaPerformance Bond Fund, but this paragraph here, the one you've high-lighted, has nothing to do with that. It's about 'the other matter', whatever that was. Not our problem.'

'Oh, come on, Antony. You know it's about our fund.'

'Where does it say that?'

'It's implicit.'

He shrugged. 'I suppose you might argue that, but *I* shouldn't find it very convincing. May I ask what you've done about this?'

'Nothing. I only found it last week and I thought you should see it before I did anything.' She saw an infinitesimal relaxation in the muscles under his eyes. 'But clearly it's discoverable, Antony. We will have to tell the other side.'

'That's debatable. And, as you very well know, we're not allowed to say 'discoverable' any more. It's 'disclosable'.'

Trish was about to ask why he thought they had any option, but a different, more urgent question occurred to her. She tried to find an acceptable way of enquiring whether he'd already known about the document and thought he would get away with hiding it from her as well as from the defence.

'Incidentally, Trish,' he said before she could ask, 'how did you get hold of this?'

'I came on a reference to the main part of the note in one of the other documents, when I was checking the cross-references, realised we were missing this one, and asked Sprindlers for it.'

'Ah, I see. You can't have talked to Peter Loyle, so who sent it to you?'

That pretty much answered the question she'd been too embarrassed to ask. Antony had obviously known all along that this note existed, and so had their instructing solicitor. Why hadn't Antony told her? Was it a test — like tonight's dinner party? And if they were tests, did she want to pass them?

'Peter Loyle was away on holiday. I got a trainee, who was very helpful.'

'I see. Thank you.'

'Antony, what are you going to do about it?'

'Nothing. As I said, it isn't anything to do with our fund. I'm surprised you've worked yourself into such a state about it, but we haven't time to discuss it now. I'll get someone to move the files into my room, and get cracking. And you might as well go home and get some sleep. I've never seen you so peaky. You look as though you haven't had a decent night in weeks.'

'It does feel a bit like that,' Trish admitted.

'Because of this document? What's the matter with you? You usually have a much better sense of proportion.'

'The document and a few other things.

Personal. Nothing to do with chambers.'

'Everything is to do with chambers if it screws up your judgment this badly. Is it anxiety over the police interest in your past cases? Dave was telling me about this boy who was nearly killed outside your flat. Anything I need to know about that?'

'No.'

'Come on, Trish. It's worrying you, isn't it?'

'Of course it is.' She hadn't meant to sound so impatient, so she hurried to explain. 'An eight-year-old child I've never met, apparently coming to find me in the middle of a Sunday night, is run down and nearly killed just outside my flat. Anyone would be worried.'

'Who is he?'

'I don't know yet.' She told him Dave's theory about the foster-home runaway, adding, 'But I'm still not convinced. He keeps saying 'she' sent him to me, which sounds like an adult to me. The police will find out eventually and get him back to wherever he came from, but in the meantime, I do feel responsible.'

'You've talked to him, have you?'

'Yes. I visit him in hospital most days. He's a sweet child. But something's scared him so much that he won't identify himself.'

'My advice is to keep your distance, Trish. It's not a good idea to get involved in this kind of thing.'

'He has no one else.'

'Nevertheless, it's not your problem. Now, Dave tells me you're in Maidstone tomorrow. You can do that sort of case standing on your head, so go home now, rest, and sort yourself out. I need you on top form for Nick Gurles.'

'I'll be fine.'

'So I should hope. But go away and sleep. I'll see you this evening, and we can talk again tomorrow when I've had a chance to review your files.'

Trish didn't like it, but there was nothing she could do except smile and agree that she would see him for dinner. She tidied her room, slung her jacket round her shoulders and went home.

But there was no chance to rest because her cleaner was there, ferociously polishing the floor. The scent of beeswax had flooded the flat, which was fine, but the polisher was heavy and electric and made the most awful screeching noise. Maria switched it off as she saw Trish picking her way carefully over the unpolished bits of the floor on her way to the spiral staircase.

'The man from the company just left,' she said, leaning on the handle of the polisher.

'What man? What company?'

'The man to see the dilapidations, he called them.'

Trish thought about the rotting window sills and frowned. She hadn't got round to phoning the freeholders, or the managing agents. Could one of the other leasees have pre-empted her?

'Which dilapidations?'

'I don't know.'

'Well, where did he look?'

'He didn't. You didn't tell me anyone was coming. He didn't have identification, so I didn't let him in.'

Trish bit back her irritation. Maria couldn't know how worried she'd been about the window sills.

'Thanks. That was sensible. I'll find out what it's about. Will I be in your way?'

'Not if you stay upstairs.' There was an order in that as well as an answer to the question. Trish was tempted to salute, but Maria might have misunderstood.

'Fine.' Trish tried to avoid smearing the new polish as she got to the staircase.

Upstairs, she used the phone by her bed. Neither the managing agents nor the freeholder knew anything about a man coming to look at the building. Fighting a sudden whoosh of panic, Trish reported the rotting window sills and asked them to get someone round as soon as possible.

'Maria?' she called from halfway down the spiral staircase.

'Yes?' She looked irritated as she switched off the machine again.

'What did he look like, the man who came about the dilapidations?'

'I don't know. Fair hair. Tidy. Clean. Respectable.'

'Tall, short, English, foreign, white, black, what?'

'English, I think. Ordinary. Polite. Small. And white, which is why he had fair hair.'

'He could have been a bottle blonde.'

Maria smiled reluctantly. 'No. It was natural. He looked so small and tidy — very clean, too — I nearly let him in. But he had no ID.'

Small, tidy and clean, Trish thought, suddenly remembering the young man who'd called off her infant tormentors on the Mull Estate. She'd been grateful to him for that, but he hadn't been altogether benign. At one moment it had looked as though he might bar her way down from the flat that had once been Jeannie Nest's. And he'd denied all knowledge of Jeannie, even though what she'd done must have been common knowledge around the estate. He might not

222

have lived there at the time of the murder, but it didn't seem possible that he hadn't heard anything about it or the way she'd tried to intervene and then given evidence for the prosecution. So why had he lied? Trish felt as though icy water was trickling down through her spine.

Oh, grow up, she thought. There must be millions of men in the country, hundreds even in Southwark, who are small, fair, clean and tidy.

'Great, thanks,' she said aloud, disobeying Maria's instructions in order to pick up the day's mail from her long desk.

'I try to clean your desk, Trish. But it's impossible. You must tidy it first. How you ever find anything, I don't know.'

'Yes, thank you, Maria. I promise I will sort it. I'll move all the papers one day, so you can swab it down. How are you?'

'I'm fine. I have finished now. I have to go. Thank you for the money.'

While Maria packed up to leave, Trish wished she'd got home earlier. If she'd been here when the man had come knocking on her door, she'd know for certain that he had nothing to do with the one who'd professed ignorance of Jeannie Nest. As it was, she couldn't stop herself inventing all sorts of ludicrous reasons why that man might be coming after her. She put the chain across the door and double-checked the locks on all the windows.

* * *

Lakeshaw was well in control, as he listened to DC Waylant repeating everything he'd already admitted about his dealings with the victim. She'd been paranoid, he said earnestly, always thinking people were following her or threatening her, but each time anyone had been round to her place to check it out, there was a simple explanation.

'After what she'd been through,' Lakeshaw said in a voice so calm he couldn't believe it himself, 'it's hardly surprising that she was nervous.'

'No.' Waylant smiled suddenly, revealing a much less resentful personality. 'But it made life tough for her kid, you know. He wasn't allowed to play with anyone she didn't know or visit friends unless she'd checked them out first. He wasn't allowed out after dark unless she was with him all the time. And when she was scared, she'd scream at him. I could see him sometimes, worrying over what he might have done to annoy her. Poor little bastard. I used to try to get her to ease up a bit, let him live a normal life.'

'That sounds as though you knew them well.'

'Not well, but I was round there quite often.' Waylant's grin looked as if he was trying to seem confident, but it was a poor effort. 'Had to be really, with all her barmy reports of people threatening her.'

'But they were true, weren't they? It's the old story, isn't it? Just because you're paranoid it doesn't mean they're not out to get you.'

Deep garnet-red colour flooded Waylant's cheeks. He looked as though he was about to cry. 'There'd never been anyone there when I checked, sir. Nor any evidence of anyone. I followed it all up, time after time, until that last one when we were so busy.'

'I'll need a full report of every call she made, and everything you did to check. OK?'

'Yes, sir.' Waylant turned to go.

'Not yet,' Lakeshaw said, watching the sag of Waylant's shoulders. He turned back slowly, his face a mixture of sullen obstinacy and fear. 'How did you know who she really was?'

Waylant's face cleared, like a wiped table. 'She told me herself, sir.'

'Why?'

'Because she was lonely?' He let his voice rise at the end of the sentence. 'She said she had to have someone to trust, and she elected me. Because of the job. She knew it would be safe.'

'Did she though? OK, I see. And who did you tell?'

'I've already told you, sir. I never passed on her name or address to anyone. And I never discussed the reasons why she was in the protection scheme. I'm not stupid. Once she'd told me who she was, I knew what a risk she'd taken by testifying.'

Lakeshaw looked at him, wishing there were some physical signs that could tell you when someone was lying. For his money, Waylant was lying about something in all this. The question was, what?

'Sir?'

'Yes?'

'I . . . oh, nothing. I just wish we hadn't been so busy that night, that's all.'

Lakeshaw looked away, concentrating on one of the notes in front of him. If Waylant couldn't come up with something better than that, he was a hopeless liar as well as a professional failure. And if he was that pathetic, he'd soon confess whatever it was that was making him feel so guilty. He'd have to because he'd be longing to be told he wasn't as bad as he feared. The less encouragement he got now, the quicker he'd talk.

11

Trish couldn't obey Antony's instructions to get some sleep. As soon as she closed her eyes, her brain started throwing up lurid pictures of what the small, clean man had wanted in her flat and what he might do now that he'd been frustrated. The only way to stop that was to work, so she got up again to sort out her papers for tomorrow's case in Maidstone. Then she phoned the social worker who would be in court with her. When they'd discussed the few points Trish needed to clarify, she said, 'Sally, I've just heard that a child has run away from the Brakelys in Staplehurst. Do you know if — '

'It's not Gavin, if that's what's worrying you,' the social worker said quickly. 'He's doing really well, Trish.'

'Oh, I am glad. But are you sure he's not at risk there?'

'Absolutely. You know, you're almost the only lawyer I've ever come across who cares enough to remember a client like that after so long.'

'To be honest, I've hardly given him a

thought since the case. But I came across the news in a quite different context, and it reminded me.'

'Ah, right. Well, either way you needn't worry. The boy who ran away is impossible. The Brakelys were saints to take him on, and they did it only because of his younger brother. He's doing all right there, too, but David, the runaway, has real problems. Attention Deficit Disorder and then some. He's utterly uncontrollable and spends whatever time is left after tormenting his brother, in torturing the cat or ripping up Mrs Brakely's clothes. We're doing everything we can to find him — of course we are — but his absence is giving everyone a much-needed break, particularly Gavin, I may say. How did you come across the story?'

'There's a small, dark-haired boy who turned up in London, looking for me, and — '

'Not the one who was half-killed in a road accident? I had no idea you were involved in that.'

'For my sins.'

'Well, whoever he is, he's not our David. Martha Weldon went up to London last Friday to identify him after everyone decided the photographs the police provided were too ambiguous. She said there was no real likeness at all. We're still looking for our runaway.'

And the police didn't bother to tell me? thought Trish. Bastards.

Sally's story made her wonder how many people had come to stare at David while he lay in hospital, and how it must have felt. Like an animal in the zoo probably, or maybe the false Anastasia, who'd been poked and prodded by dozens of Romanov-lovers and -haters as she lay in a Berlin hospital. No wonder he wasn't talking and preferred to lie with his eyes closed, shutting out everything and everyone.

'I hope you find out who he is, Trish,' Sally said comfortably. 'I'm sure you will. Anyway, I'll see you tomorrow. Must go. Bye now.'

Trish ate some cottage cheese and grapes for an early lunch, then fetched her car from under the railway. It was warm enough to have the roof down as she drove to the hospital, and she took her usual childish pleasure in pressing the button on the dashboard and feeling the mechanism lift and fold back the roof.

The hospital friends' shop was just closing when she got there, but she persuaded the volunteer to postpone her own break long enough to sell six individual cartons of apple juice.

Cradling them between her crooked arm and her ribs, Trish waited for the lift with a chattering family group, who were clearly on their way to visit a new baby. She felt the sharp corners of the cardboard digging into her arm and breast and stopped herself thinking of what might have been, shutting her ears to their excited discussion of possible names. She got out at the eighth floor and dropped half the juice cartons.

'Hell!'

'Hello,' said one of the nurses who'd been particularly kind to David. 'You again. Who are you here for this time?'

'David.'

'Didn't they tell you? They've moved him. The police.'

Trish held in the much worse expletive that burst into her mind. Then all irritation disappeared in a wave of fear as she thought again of the small fair-haired man. Had he been here, too? Had she led him to David? Or had he been after David, seen her here and followed her home? Who the hell was he?

She saw the nurse looking curiously at her and quickly said, 'Where have they taken him?'

'I've no idea. It was done all of a hurry this morning, first thing. They should have told you.'

'You're damn right, they should. Could you use this juice for any of the others?'

'I'm sure we could. Thank you.'

Trish left her, seething. Out in the car park, she tried to phone Caro to find out what could be going on, but her mobile was on divert to the message service. Trish dialled the number of Caro's flat, only to be answered by her machine. Trish left a brisk message to say that she needed to talk urgently, then sat in the driving seat in the middle of the car park adding up the scraps of evidence she had and trying to make sense of them.

Suddenly the idea of driving an open car didn't seem such a good one. She switched on the ignition and pressed the button to close the roof. The drive home took less than ten minutes. As she reached the car park, she decided to sweep past the flat to make sure no one was hanging about, waiting for her.

The street was absolutely clear, so she made a U-turn and parked in her expensive space. The great vaulted tunnel echoed to her footsteps. A pigeon burst out from behind a pillar with a noise like a machine gun. The shock made her sweat. Footsteps sounded at the far end of the long tunnel full of expensive cars. She bleeped her locks down and hurried to the entrance. The steps quickened behind her; then she heard

231

another car bleeping and risked a glance over her shoulder. A wholly respectable middle-aged man was opening the door of a large maroon Rover. He raised a hand and nodded. Trish thought he looked vaguely familiar, so she smiled in return, telling herself not to be so sodding paranoid. She'd go mad if she started to hear something sinister every time there was someone running or walking behind her.

Back in the flat, she decided coffee would make her even jumpier, so she boiled the kettle and made some camomile tea. Maybe it would help her get a bit of rest. She knew it was supposed to induce sleep. It tasted of wet hay, but she drank most of it, lying back with the mug balanced against her chest. Her eyes felt heavy. She ought to be using the time to read, but she hadn't the energy to move. The mug wobbled suddenly against her chest and she woke enough to get it safely to the floor before she dropped it.

★ ★ ★

Re-emerging into consciousness felt like pulling herself out of a quicksand. When she was on her feet again, she couldn't believe the clock, which told her that it was already five-thirty. She'd been out for over three hours and she had to be at the Shelleys', ready to charm and sparkle, by eight-fifteen. She phoned to book a mini-cab for seven-thirty. There was no point driving herself to a house where the wines were said to be sublime.

A hard, hot shower helped to drive the sleep out of her mind. Still dripping, she made some coffee. Jumpy or not, she had to wake up properly now. Taking it back upstairs, she picked up the hairdrier and thought about what she was going to wear. Some of the women at Antony's dinners, so she'd heard, came in whatever they'd been wearing at work; others dressed in formal silk and sparkles. She gelled and dried her hair into its usual spiky style, which was the only one that didn't make her look like a bird of prey pretending to be Red Riding Hood's grandmother, and mentally flicked through her wardrobe.

By the time her hair was done, she'd decided on a compromise. There was a longish linen dress in a sludgy green that she'd bought at Monsoon a while ago, which would do. The subdued colour suited her skin, and she still had the kind of firm upper arms that made a sleeveless dress work. She'd add the barbaric necklace George had given her for her last birthday and hope that the mixture wouldn't make her look too out of place, even if all the other women were dressed in suits or strapless silk. The necklace was made of chunks of dull gold and richly dark amber and it suited Trish far better than any of the delicate silver-wire-and-moonstone jewellery currently approved by the fashionistas.

She was not used to this kind of calculation and didn't like having to make it. She was who she was and had never wanted to pretend to be anything else. But the Shelleys' house was unfamiliar territory. To fix herself back into her own, she grabbed some time to plug in her modem and email a brief message to George. His name appeared in her in-box. She checked her watch and saw she had five minutes before the mini-cab was due and opened the message.

You'll be just about off to the Shelleys' for dinner by the time you read this. Or maybe you're already back. It's a real swizz that I'm missing it. People say their food is so devastating you'll never want to eat anywhere else again, and as for the wine . . . Out of this world. Wasted on you, of course. You'd be just as happy with baked beans and supermarket plonk. But do your best to remember it

234

all. *I want all the details. None of that 'all tastes like Ribena to me' crap, Trish. I need the vicarious pleasure of a full account.*

And I may get it sooner than we thought. My mother's beginning to flag, I think. I don't want to shortchange her, so I'm not going to suggest switching the air tickets until she's ready, but I don't think it'll be long. I'll let you know. Love, George.

Trish rarely let herself answer emails the moment she'd read them. The seductive ease of communication meant that you'd click on 'send', only to get ten more messages flooding in. By the time you'd sent your answers to those, the first lot would have written back and want something else. You could lose your mind that way. So she rationed herself. But this one from George had to be answered now, and honestly.

Fantastic news! I miss you so much. I've been wondering recently about the so-called joys of independence . . .

She deleted the last sentence, thinking it sounded far too clingy, then carried on, typing carelessly but fast:

And I wish you were here to come to the dinner tonight. I haven't felt this twitchy for years. Mainly the case, of course. If I bog this . . . well, I can't bog it. That's all there is to it. Sorry. Weedy. Most unlike me. Can't wait to see you. Love, Trish.

She pressed 'send', switched off the computer, set the burglar alarm and was waiting at the bottom of the iron steps as her mini-cab drove up. As she sat in the back of the rattly old car, which smelled of the dressing-up box of her childhood, she tried to psych herself up for the entry into Antony's princely world.

The mini-cab left the harshly lit commercial bustle of Kensington High Street and slowed down as the driver turned to ask Trish the way. Exasperated that he hadn't bothered to look up the address she'd given when she booked the cab, she directed him through the cream-stucco oasis. Ahead of them a black cab going the same way reared up over innumerable speed bumps, like a giant tortoise bent on mating. The houses on either side were huge and the streets wide and quiet.

Checking off the numbers, she told the driver to stop outside the Shelleys'. Double-fronted, the great Victorian villa had a black iron canopy over the front path and black-and-white tiling on what would have been the front gardens. Trish thought it was the kind of house George would have liked. For herself she'd want something either much older or absolutely modern, and a lot less pompous-looking. She rang the bell.

The door was opened by a woman even taller than Trish, with the smoothest glossiest blonde hair Trish had ever seen. She was wearing a beautifully made, classically designed, cream-coloured wool dress. With its perfect neckline, short sleeves and neat waist, it had 'designer-label' written all over it.

She must have to have it dry-cleaned every time she takes it out of the wardrobe, Trish thought in horror.

'Hi, I'm Liz, Antony's wife,' the woman said, standing aside. 'You must be Trish Maguire. I'd recognise that hair anywhere.'

Trish only just managed to stop herself pressing down some of the spikes. She felt about fourteen and clumsier than she'd ever been as she tripped over the threshold.

Inside the house, her first impression was of delicious smells. They came partly from the cooking, she decided, and partly the flowers. There was a huge mixed pink-and-white bowlful on an oak chest to her right. She didn't know much about flowers but recognised lilies, delphiniums, paeonies and roses among the rest. Their scents mixed with the furniture polish and something else teasingly light and hard to identify, which emanated from her hostess.

'D'you want to leave anything?' Liz asked, looking amused. Trish thought she must have been showing too much awe.

'Nothing to leave except this,' she said casually, holding out the small amber-coloured clutch bag in which she kept her keys and money. She dumped it on the chest beside the flowers. 'Who told you about my hair? It's hard to imagine Antony's even noticing it.'

Liz's carefully made-up face creased into a smile that made her look much too young for the expensively formal dress.

'He's not such a misogynist, you know. He's like you — he only pretends. He thinks your hair's a very good disguise, by the way. Even he was taken in for a while and believed in your famous ferocity until he found out how gentle you are. Come on in. We're in the drawing room.'

Gentle? thought Trish. I'm not sodding gentle. And if he thinks I'm going to be a pushover for Nick Gurles, he can think again.

Liz floated ahead down the hall, while Trish stumped along behind, wishing she'd worn jeans and Doc Martens. Then she made herself behave. Tonight she was Antony's guest. Whatever he was up to could be confined to chambers. Liz opened the door into a large drawing room and waved Trish in.

The sparse but perfect furniture, the honey-coloured parquet floors and the ravishing silky rugs made her almost faint with envy. She loved her own echoing, sub-industrial flat, but walking into this glowing mini-palace was like wrapping herself in brightly coloured cashmere. The Old Masters on the walls looked like fakes because they were so familiar. But the thing that surprised her most was the quietness. The doors were so thick and so well-fitted that they muffled all sound, and no hint of traffic or passers-by leaked in.

You could really rest in a place like this, she thought, as her jaw relaxed for the first time in days.

'Come on in, Trish.' Antony's familiar voice, with its edge of slightly malicious amusement, woke her to reality and she moved forwards. He was holding a bottle of champagne. 'You look a lot better for the sleep. Will you have some of this, or something else?'

'That looks great,' she said, looking round

for his wife. 'Thank you.'

'Liz has gone to oversee the kitchen. Come in.'

She followed him into the back half of the drawing room, which overlooked a large garden. There were yet more astonishing paintings, and a blur of cream warmed with dull gold and apricot colours. Later she would notice the patterns of old brocade and faded tapestry beside the admirable simplicity of plain card lampshades and coarse linen covers. Now all she saw was ease and warmth and comfort, and a small crowd of other people, some of whom looked nearly as familiar as the paintings. Antony poured her a glass of champagne and introduced her to Sir Henry Buxford, the Chairman of Grunschwig's.

Surprised to see him there, Trish reminded herself that he was not their client, even though he was underwriting their fees. She wondered whether he was going to grill her about her plans for Nick Gurles or lean on her to collude in the suppression of the disastrous manuscript note, but he was far too sophisticated to do either. He behaved as though he'd never heard of her, but was interested in everything she had to say, offering stories of his own past at the Bar to amuse her.

Watching his bright brown eyes, which she suspected saw far more than he ever let on, and his sensual mouth, she decided she liked him but would have difficulty trusting him without a lot more evidence. She began to let bits of herself show through the careful politeness she'd assumed. By the time they'd both finished their champagne, she thought she knew him well enough to ask whether he ever missed the Bar.

'Why?' he asked, the light in his eyes dimming a little. 'D'you think you would?'

'I know I would. I love what I do, even the painful cases. And all the stories everyone tells suggest you did, too. It must have been a real sacrifice to go on the bench.'

'It certainly wasn't a life that suited me. Unfortunately the one thing you can't do if you stop being a judge is revert to the profession in which you excelled. But I'm interested in your enthusiasm. I'd understood from Antony that you were becoming disillusioned.'

'Not disillusioned exactly,' she said, hardly noticing that Antony was refilling her glass. 'Just keen to work with commercial cases that might let my sore heart mend a little. Sorry, that sounds disgustingly sentimental.'

'Yes. But as expressive a misquotation as I've ever heard.'

She enjoyed the momentary eye-meeting of shared amusement. How interesting that a man like Henry Buxford should know such schmaltzy songs.

'You must beware of caring too much, Trish. I . . . '

'You?' she prompted.

'I was once, long ago, a junior in a big matrimonial-finance case. We were for the wife and it was my big chance to show how sharply I could cross-examine. I really went for the husband, wanting to show my leader — and my clerk — that I could be a man-eating shark, too.' He looked down at his glass, drank, then looked back at Trish. His eyes reminded her of David's for a micro-second. 'The husband hanged himself that night.'

'God, how awful,' she said, putting a hand on his forearm. 'You must have . . . It must have taken you ages to get over that.'

'A while. I . . . '

'Dinner, everyone,' Liz Shelley called from the double doors at the far end of the big room. She opened them, revealing a mass of candles in glass sticks and more flowers, this time scentless, Trish noticed. No wonder, if they took their wine as seriously as George's email had suggested.

'I'm glad to have had this chance to talk to

242

you,' Buxford said. 'I know now that Antony was right all along. My boy Nick is in good hands.'

Oh shit, Trish thought, but she kept a polite smile on her face as they all went into dinner.

★   ★   ★

She didn't get home until nearly one and knew she was lucky to have got a cab so easily. All the way back to Southwark she'd been mentally drafting a mouth watering account of the food and wine to send to George. He'd have appreciated the foie gras in Sauternes much more than she did, but she'd liked the simple, beautifully cooked partridge that came next and the astonishingly fresh-tasting Burgundy. She could happily have stopped there, but the cheeses looked and smelled so amazing that even she couldn't resist, and after that there was a hot apricot tart with crème fraiche.

As she was paying off the black cab, wondering whether she would ever need to eat again, rain started to fall. She shivered as the drops trickled down her bare arms and the cabbie fumbled for her change. Out of the corner of her eye, she saw a man getting out of a beige car that had been parked just ahead of the taxi. The man looked very small. In the

243

glow of the streetlight, his hair looked very fair.

Trish gripped the pound coins she was about to give back to the cabbie, afraid they might slip out of her wet hand.

'Look,' she said, hating her own breathlessness, 'my flat's at the top of those iron stairs there. Could you wait until you've seen me inside the door? Here.' She handed him not only the coins, but also a ten-pound note.

'Sure,' he said, sounding puzzled. He looked around and saw the other man. Hauling on the handbrake, he turned off his ignition then got out of the cab. 'I'll come up with you. Who is he? Boyfriend?'

'Certainly not,' Trish said, glad of the cabbie's broad shoulders and powerful muscles. 'He's probably nothing to do with me, but in a lonely street like this . . . '

'And an area like this. Come on, love.'

Prepared to trust any man who was licensed to drive a black cab around London, Trish let him put a burly arm around her back and usher her up the iron staircase towards her own front door. He waited patiently while she found her keys and unlocked her door. Then he handed her back the ten-pound note.

'Why? I meant you to have it.'

'It's fine. You were right about him. Look.'

Trish looked after his pointing finger and saw the tail-lights of the beige car moving towards the end of the street. There was no bulb over the numberplate. Even so, she could see that there was mud all over the plate, hiding the figures. She shivered.

'Yeah,' said the cabbie. 'Whatever he wanted, he was up to no good. Lock your doors tonight, love.'

'I will. Thank you very much. But look, do take this.' She gave him back the tenner. He raised a finger to his forehead, then pocketed the money, clumping down the iron stairs in the rain.

Late as it was, Trish went round the flat, checking all the window locks even before she did anything about her wet arms and shivering body. But when she was sure there was no way anyone could get in, she stood under a boiling shower for ten minutes. Warm at last, she hoped she'd sleep.

★ ★ ★

Itching with tiredness next morning, she knew she must have big black bruises under her eyes, but she didn't waste time looking at them. Having burned her mouth on a mug of instant coffee, she soothed it with an overripe banana that had been nestling in a bowl of gently rotting apples, then ran to get the car for her trip to Maidstone.

The case was even more painful than she'd expected, but at least it kept her mind from her own troubles. The hopeless mother was a fat, white-faced lump with sparse, greasy hair and ugly clothes, who gave her evidence in a voice that combined a whining edge with blankly obstinate incomprehension. Trish could see her counsel's despair and sympathised. But almost anyone would have been a safer custodian of a child than this woman and so Trish couldn't let sympathy get in her way.

The other barrister was a lot younger than Trish and patently nervous. Going up against her, Trish felt like a fully armed paratrooper exchanging fire with a toddler holding an airgun. But she had a job to do and a child to protect, so she gave the case all the disciplined passion at her disposal. She couldn't bear to watch either the young barrister or the woman she was representing, so she looked alternately at the judge and at Sally, the social worker, who was providing most of the evidence.

When it was all over, and Trish had predictably won, she glanced at her opposing counsel. She was biting her lip and sniffing to hold in tears, while trying to explain to her barely literate client what it was the judge had just told them. Trish wondered whether there was anything she might say in the robing room to console her defeated colleague without sounding as patronising as Robert Anstey.

'Thanks, Trish, you were great,' the social worker said.

'I'm glad you're pleased, Sally. I must say there didn't seem any doubt at all. She couldn't look after one child safely, let alone four.'

'I know. But it doesn't stop it being hard on her. Poor thing. And you know what'll happen?'

'Yup,' Trish said. 'She'll go and have another baby with the next abusive man she finds and, after this, you'll probably have to take it from her the minute they've cut the cord.'

'Probably. It breaks your heart — or it would if there was anything left to break.'

12

The phone was ringing as Trish was making herself yet another mug of coffee the following day. Dumping the coffee jar on the worktop, she grabbed the receiver and recited her number.

'Ah. This is Caroline Lyalt.'

Not 'Caro', Trish noticed, but her name in full. This must be official. So who else was with her?

'Oh, good. You got the message. I need to ask why David was — '

'They said in chambers that you were working at home today,' Caro said, as smooth and obliterating as a steam-roller. 'I'd like to bring someone round to talk to you.'

'About what?'

'We'll explain when we see you. Would twenty minutes' time be OK?'

Trish heard the muffled sound of another voice in the background. Caro must have put her hand over the phone while someone else talked to her.

'Twenty minutes' time would be fine,' Trish said crisply. '*Is* this about David?'

'We'll see you then.'

The phone buzzed in Trish's hand until a recorded voice reminded her to hang up. She tidied up all the papers she'd brought home from chambers, once more pushing Nick Gurles to the back of her mind. By the time she heard a knock on the front door, she was ready.

Caro stood at the top of the iron staircase beside a grim-faced man, whom she introduced as DCI Simon Lakeshaw. Trish nodded to him, then stood aside to let them in. Caro led the way straight to the black sofas and sat down on the one nearest the empty fireplace. Her colleague stood beside her until Trish had taken the other sofa. Then he, too, subsided on to the low, squashy cushions.

Probably about forty, she thought, he had bleak grey eyes, badly pitted skin and a thatch of mousey hair falling into his eyes. He also had a very short neck and an expression that suggested smiling came hard to him. For once Caro wasn't looking much better, quite different from the vulnerable, affectionate friend who had clung to Trish on the doorstep only last Thursday.

'You've spoken to Sergeant Lyalt about a woman called Jeannie Nest,' said DCI Lakeshaw abruptly. 'I understand you've been looking for her. Why?'

'May I know what your interest is?' Trish hoped that Caro still had some boundaries between work and friendship. The thought of everything Trish had told her about Paddy being passed on to this aggressive stranger was awful.

'Don't play games, Ms Maguire. This is important.'

'I'm sure it is, but I want to know what I'm dealing with, and why you're asking me.'

'I understand you believe that the child who was run over outside this building might be her son. I want to know what led you to that idea, and I want the names of everyone to whom you made the suggestion or from whom you have sought information.'

'Where is he now? I tried to visit him yesterday and they told me he's been moved. But no one will tell me where.'

'I must ask again: who did you talk to about Jeannie Nest?'

'*Is* she connected with the boy in hospital?'

'Ms Maguire, this is a very serious matter. I shall answer your questions — if I can — when you have given me the information I need.'

Trish could recognise an obstinacy even greater than her own. Battling with her instinct to avoid answering any police questions blind, she decided that cooperation was probably the only way of getting what she wanted. She told Lakeshaw about her visit to the Mull Estate, the young man who'd denied all knowledge of Jeannie Nest and the scary children; she described her calls to all the local schools, and her discovery of Jeannie's part in the six-year-old murder case, adding that she assumed the case had led to a new name under the witness-protection scheme. She talked slowly and very clearly, as though dictating, which she'd learned long ago soothed the angry police soul.

Lakeshaw didn't react, but Caro leaned forwards as though the five-foot space between the two sofas was too wide to cross with words alone.

'Trish, did any of the people you talked to — and I mean *any* of them — give you any idea of her new name or where she might be living now?'

'Sergeant Lyalt,' Lakeshaw said sharply, as Trish tried to decode the weird stress Caro had put on 'any', 'will you please leave this to me? Now, Ms Maguire, you haven't answered the question of why you believed David might be Jeannie Nest's son.'

Trish wasn't going to drop Paddy in it until she knew more. 'I neither know nor care what name Jeannie Nest took or where she lived. My only concern is the boy. Someone sent

251

him to me, which makes me feel responsible for him. You've moved him from the hospital, which suggests you think he's under threat. Things have been happening round here that suggest that I too may be at risk. So, it's time for you to be frank. What exactly do you know?'

'Jeannie Nest was found murdered last week,' Caro said before Lakeshaw could stop her.

Trish swallowed, the saliva burningly bitter in her throat. She thought of last night's watcher with the blanked-out numberplate. Remembering the lack of reaction from any of her neighbours on the night David had been almost killed in the street, Trish felt the sensation of icy water down her spine again. If it hadn't been for the friendly cabbie last night, she too might have been left for dead in the road. She could have screamed her head off, but no one would have come to help. She gripped her left wrist with her right hand, trying to will calm into her mind.

'Ms Maguire?' Lakeshaw was still looking furious and Caro wary. Trish shook her head, not even having heard what he'd just said.

'*Did* Jeannie Nest have a son aged about eight, called David?' she asked, surprised to hear that her voice sounded steadily confident.

'Yes. He'll be eight next month.'

'Has he been identified positively as the boy in hospital?' If she could keep on asking questions, she might be able to forget the man — or men — who seemed to be watching her.

'I haven't heard. But it seems more than likely that he will be. Now, what I need to know is . . . '

'When will they be telling him his mother's dead?' Trish heard her own voice whipping through the space, effectively shutting Lakeshaw up.

'That'll be taken care of, Trish,' Caro said kindly. 'As soon as he's considered well enough to deal with the news. You don't have to worry about that.'

'I want to be there when he's told.' Do you? asked a small voice in her mind. Wouldn't you rather keep right away now to show the watchers that David's nothing to do with you and that you know nothing about him or his mother?

'Out of the question,' Lakeshaw snapped. 'In any case it may be too late.'

'Sir . . . ' Caro Lyalt began, but Trish didn't need an advocate. She knew what to say. She just hoped she'd have the courage to see this thing through.

'That boy was sent to me by his mother.

253

She had sewn my address into his clothes; she had taught him for as long as he can remember how to find this place. She trusted me to look after him, even though we'd never met. I have to be there when he's told that she's dead. I have to.'

'Sir, he seems to trust Trish. It really might help to have her there.'

'Possibly. But first I need to know who else you've spoken to, Ms Maguire.'

Trish thought she could see a plea for forgiveness in Caro's hesitant smile. She didn't respond to it. 'I talked to a variety of barristers and clerks in my search for the person who prosecuted Ron Handsome when Jeannie Nest testified against him. I can give you their names if necessary. And also my father, who knew her years ago. Now, if there's anything else you need to ask, couldn't we deal with it on the way to wherever David is now? I'm more than willing to tell you anything, but I have to see him.'

It took a bit more persuasion, but eventually Lakeshaw agreed. Trish only just remembered that she was supposed to be meeting Anna Grayling at the National Film Theatre later in the evening. She made the others wait while she phoned and had to leave an uninformative message on Anna's voicemail. The last thing she wanted was Anna getting involved in all this.

'Sorry about that,' she said to Caro, ushering her out of the flat in order to double lock the door.

Caro drove to a hospital in Whitechapel, where David was being cared for in a single room on the fourth floor. There were two uniformed women police officers outside the room, talking to a man in plain clothes. Trish realised that the threat, whatever it was, was considered serious. No hard-pressed police force was going to expend manpower like this without good reason.

One of the officers stepped forward to say, 'He won't talk, sir.'

'Does he know about his mother's death?'

'Yes. Not in detail, of course. He didn't seem surprised and he's hardly cried since. But he still won't say anything.'

'Let me try,' Trish said, surprising the plain-clothes officer, who started to ask a question. They all ignored him as Caro took Lakeshaw on one side and began talking urgently. Trish couldn't hear what they were saying.

'OK, Trish,' Caro said, coming back ahead of Lakeshaw. 'The DCI is prepared to allow you to have a go, on condition that you introduce him to David and try to persuade

255

him to answer questions. OK?'

'So long as Lakeshaw says absolutely nothing until I've had a chance to talk to David myself,' Trish said, hoping she'd made it clear the condition was non-negotiable. Eventually she got Lakeshaw's agreement.

David nearly smiled as he saw Trish walking towards him, then his eyes dilated and his face whitened.

'Don't be afraid,' Trish said. 'He's a police officer, and he's going to make sure you're safe.'

She sat down beside the bed and tried to take David's hand. He balled it into a fist, and not only shut his eyes but creased up his whole face. Maybe he thought if Lakeshaw was invisible, he wouldn't exist.

'David?'

He didn't say anything, clamping his lips together as though she was about to force food into him.

'You're safe now, David. I know that everything that's happened has been very frightening, but the police are here to protect you. You're safe now.'

The boy shuddered.

'This is a chief inspector. He needs to ask you some questions about your mother. I know how hard it is, but we can only help if you talk to us.'

At last David's lips parted. Returning blood warmed the greyish flesh back into its usual plum red.

'She's dead.' His eyes filled, but the tears didn't fall and he didn't sniff.

'I know. He's just told me. I'm more sorry than I can say, and I know how awful it must be to talk about it. But they have to find out who . . . how it happened. Can I ask you some questions?' Trish hoped she was doing the right thing. 'Please, David. It's the only way to make sure that the people who did this to your mother are arrested.'

He looked up at the ceiling. The familiar lengthening of his nostrils and quivering of his lips told her how hard he was fighting not to cry. But he couldn't win.

His hand was still hard and round, but Trish kept hers over it, waiting for the moment when he let himself need something from her.

'David,' said the man behind her.

'Not yet,' she commanded, without looking away from the boy's face.

'I have to. David, can you tell me what happened to make you want to run away from home? Was someone unkind to you?'

'I didn't run away.' He didn't relax completely, but he uncurled his fingers and turned his hand so that he could cling to Trish.

'OK. So, what made you leave home then?'

His mouth shut again and he stared up at the ceiling. His palm was pumping out sweat.

'Chief Inspector, I think you should show him your warrant card.'

He looked surprised, but after a while shrugged and held it out. David peered at it, then looked at Trish for just long enough to show her he had no idea what to do or say.

'David, you must try to tell this man what he needs to know.'

'I can't. She told me never to say,' he whispered. Trish bent forward to hear better. 'She said I mustn't say anything to anyone. Not even you. Whatever happened. I was to come to you and you'd look after me. But I wasn't to answer questions, not from anyone. That's what she said.'

'I know. Don't worry. I'll be back in a minute.' But he clung to her, adding his other hand to hold her back. 'OK, David. I won't go for a while.' She twisted her head so that she could look at Lakeshaw, and was relieved to see some pity softening his bullet-like eyes. 'You must understand.'

'Oh, I do. But we won't be able to leave it like this for long. He's a witness.'

'Only to fear. She made him leave before he saw anything, didn't she, David?' He nodded, tears beginning to slip out from under his lashes. 'I thought so.'

'David?' said Lakeshaw, sounding almost gentle. 'Why did she make you leave?'

He glanced at Trish, who tried to look encouragingly confident.

'She c'llected me from Joe's house and we were walking home,' he said in a voice that was hoarse with effort. 'And she kept looking behind her and hurrying on. We went a different way home, but she didn't stop looking back. Then when we were at home the phone went. I answered it, but when I gave it to her they'd gone. Then later on she opened the back door to let Mrs Tiggywinkle in and she screamed.'

'What did she see?'

'She said it was just another cat, like Mrs Tiggywinkle, and that it'd given her a shock. She said she was sorry. But she put on my fleece and told me to go straight away now to Trish Maguire. So I did. She'd always said that if she ever had to tell me to go, I mustn't ask questions, and I mustn't say anything. I must go straight off, and she'd c'llect me as soon as she could.'

'That's very clear,' Trish said, but Lakeshaw wanted to know whether David had any idea what his mother had seen when she kept looking back in the street.

He took one hand from Trish's so that he could stick his thumb in his mouth.

'And what about in the garden? Did you see anything? Any sign of this other cat?' David's eyes widened and he shook his head, still sucking his thumb.

'What did you say when you answered the phone?'

'Just the number, like she always told me.' He plugged his thumb back in his mouth. Trish and Lakeshaw waited. Eventually, the glistening digit was removed again. 'Then he said: 'David, is that you?' And I said, 'yes.' He said he wanted my mum. Then she took the phone and said, 'hello, hello,' but there wasn't anybody there.'

'What did the man sound like?'

Tears spilled over his eyelashes, making them stick together. 'Angry,' he said as he began to sob, choking as the tears poured out faster and faster. 'Angry like my mum.'

'Get a nurse,' Trish said, trying to stand up. David's stiff, bent body lifted off the bed as he clung to her hand. She sat back, making him lie down again and stroking his dark hair with her free hand. 'It's all right, David, I'm here. I'll stay while you need me. *Get a nurse*, Chief Inspector. Now, David, tell me about

260

Mrs Tiggywinkle. How long had you had her?'

It was a long time before David was calm enough for Trish even to think of leaving him. By then he'd told her all about the cat and how they'd got her as a kitten and how she liked to sit on the garden wall and lick his mother's nose. By that stage, he'd let the nurse hold one of his hands, even though he had his other round Trish's. Lakeshaw urged her to get up and follow him out into the corridor.

'No,' said David, tightening his hand around hers again.

'I won't stay away long.' Trish brushed the hair sideways along his forehead, and felt the wetness of his skin.

She couldn't see how he would ever grow out of this. Whatever else had happened to him might, in time, be eased, but this terror would live with him for ever. Imagining what he was going through made her feel as though she'd been skinned.

'And I won't go further than the corridor. Then I'll be back. I promise.' She smiled but his face was stony.

'She said that, too. My mum. She promised she'd come and c'llect me from your flat.'

'Look, can you see those glass bits in the door?' Trish said.

'Yes.'

'I'll stand so that you can always see my head in one of them. All right?'

He didn't say anything.

'Let me go, David. Just for a bit.' Trish beckoned Caro, who came quickly across the squeaky floor. 'Caro, this is David. You'll be kind to him, won't you?'

'Of course. You told me he liked apple juice. I've brought some.'

Trish should have trusted Caro. She, too, might have no children of her own, but she knew what to do. 'I'll be back in a minute or two and I've promised I'll stay by the glass bits of the doors.'

'Good idea. Budge up, Trish. Now, love, shall I put the straw in the box for you?'

He shook his head and muttered that he wasn't thirsty. Trish had to peel his fingers away from her hand and pull it free.

'Are you all right?' Lakeshaw asked when they got outside. Trish shook her head, unable for the moment to say anything. He produced a clean handkerchief from his pocket and offered it to her.

'Sorry,' she said when she'd blown her nose. 'I don't usually do this. But he's so brave, and he's so lonely. And his mother's dead. It just got to me for a moment.'

'I can see that. You must find your work

hard if you get this involved so quickly with total strangers.' He himself sounded quite detached, only a little curious. Trish wondered how good an actor he was.

'I try not to, but yes, it can be hard.' She buried all thoughts of the child she might have had. 'Now what do you want to ask me?'

'What's made you suddenly so cooperative?'

'The realisation that if David's mother really has been murdered, she can't have been killed the day she sent him to me.'

'What makes you say that?'

'You wouldn't have wanted to know the names of everyone I've talked to about her if she had been. If Jeannie Nest had been killed on the day of the car crash, it would have been irrelevant who I'd talked to about her.'

'Right.'

'So when did she die?'

'Some time on Tuesday night,' he said. 'We think. But, as you must know, timing of death is not an exact science, whatever it may look like on the telly.'

'So are you suggesting that *my* questions might have triggered whatever happened to her?' Trish thought of the Mull Estate and its threatening atmosphere and the frighteningly young baby-thugs playing there. And the blond young man. And her father.

263

Had someone on the estate heard of her questions and found them so threatening he'd had to kill Jeannie Nest? If so, what would he do now to anyone he thought might know too much? And why the hell, after everything that had happened, had Trish forgotten to activate the burglar alarm this evening? She must have been completely barking mad — or suffering some kind of death wish.

For God's sake, stop it, she told herself. The man who came to the flat was probably an opportunist burglar, trying to con his way in past a cleaner who might not have spoken such good English as Maria. The midnight loiterer was probably a drunk who'd been peeing in the gutter and scarpered out of embarrassment. If you fantasise like this you'll turn into one of those neurotic victims who're too scared to leave their own front doors. Brace up.

'Is that what all this is about, Chief Inspector?' she asked in an impressively firm voice. 'You think *I* caused this woman's death by asking the wrong questions?'

'It seems possible.'

Oh, God. Please no, she thought. It was hard to sound calm as she started to speak again, but she managed it. 'Even though she was so scared on the Sunday that she sent

264

David away? Isn't it much more likely that whoever had been frightening her came back to kill her later? A boyfriend — or someone connected with the Handsome case who's been looking for revenge ever since she testified?'

'It's possible, but I'm not convinced. I do think your questions triggered the violence.'

'Well, I don't believe it. There has to be more to this. What did Jeannie Nest say when she reported the harassment?'

'What harassment?'

'All that stalking stuff David described. His mother sounds completely terrified. I don't believe anyone in the witness-protection programme would keep quiet about what happened. She'd have reported it straight away. So what *exactly* did she say?'

'Very little,' he said, giving no sign that he'd been trying to resist the suggestion that the victim had made a report.

'I don't believe you. If she was frightened enough to send David to me, she must have asked for protection.' Trish waited, but Lakeshaw didn't comment. 'What happened when she rang in? Or wasn't there anyone there to take her call?'

'Of course there was. It was logged and investigated,' he said stiffly.

'And?'

'And nothing. No action was considered necessary. All the panic buttons in her house were checked and found to be working. There was one in every room and beside the front and back doors. She was considered to be safe.'

'Ah, I see. No wonder you want to blame me and my questions for what happened then,' Trish said, trying not to sound as relieved as she felt. For a minute she'd believed she might have been responsible for what had happened to Jeannie Nest. 'It must be awful to realise that a woman died because no one took the trouble to listen properly.'

The flash of bitterness in Lakeshaw's eyes made her add, 'Or are you afraid one of your officers actually sold her new name and address to the Handsomes? If they're moneylenders, they'd be able to afford a pretty crunchy bribe. Is that it?'

Lakeshaw moved a little way down the corridor as a nurse came towards the door of David's room with a stainless-steel bowl in her hand. Trish stood her ground. 'I'm not leaving the window here. I promised David.'

'I think it's about time you came clean about your father and his connection with Jeannie Nest, don't you?' Lakeshaw didn't seem to be even trying to avoid sounding offensive.

So Caro doesn't have any boundaries, Trish thought, battling with a sense of betrayal. She must have passed it all on.

'It's the most likely reason I've come up with to explain why I was chosen for David's refuge,' Trish said at last, deciding that anything less than the truth would only cause trouble. 'My father was in a relationship of sorts with Jeannie Nest at about the time David must have been conceived. But he can be of no interest to you over this because he hasn't seen her since, and he had no idea she'd had a child.'

'How can you be sure of that?'

'Because he told me so,' Trish said coldly. 'There may be no evidence, but I have no reason not to believe him.'

'I see.'

'And I can assure you that he would not have taken my interest as a spur to go and beat the poor woman to death.'

'Beat her to death? Who says . . . ?'

'It was a figure of speech,' Trish said, sighing. 'Because I know that's how Ron Handsome killed his victim six years ago. Surely his family must be your likeliest candidates for Jeannie's murder.'

'Possibly.'

Trish could feel her eyebrows pulling together, setting up the usual headache as she thought of the few streets that divided her own expensive building from the murderous estate.

'What's the matter? You're shivering.'

Bleakly she repeated what she'd already told him about the man who'd tried to get past Maria and the one who might or might not have been intending to molest her on her way back from the Shelleys'. Lakeshaw didn't seem very interested but he politely made a note and said he'd look into it.

'Right. Well, I think that's all we need from you now.'

Trish blinked at the dismissal. 'Are you intending to interview my father?'

'Of course.'

'I'd like to be present when you talk to him.'

'Why?' Lakeshaw said.

'Because he's had a heart attack and a recent bypass. I don't want him worried.'

'Or risk giving himself away? It's that, isn't it? You lawyers are all the same.'

Turning away from his contempt, Trish realised that she'd broken her promise to David. She and Lakeshaw were nearly parallel with the staircase now, yards from the glass panel in the doorway. She moved back at once and waved at David through the glass. He'd been watching for her, obviously fretting, but he waved back.

'I want to be there as my father's daughter, not as his brief,' she said, turning to face Lakeshaw again. 'Any woman would.'

'OK,' he said. 'I'm going to Kensington now. I can give you a lift.'

Thinking that it was lucky Antony was now doing the bulk of the work on Nick Gurles's case, Trish went back to David's bedside to explain, stroking his head as she tried to comfort him. She left with the memory of his head filling her hollowed hand.

13

'Trish, will you get the fuck out of here?'
Paddy spat out the words, but she didn't
mind that nearly as much as the hatred in his
eyes. His chin was shaking and his lips were
so harshly compressed that they made a thin
line across his face.

Her throat tightened. She had to make a
huge effort to speak at all and when she
forced her voice it sounded as harsh as his.

'This is DCI Lakeshaw. He needs — '

'I know who he is. Will you get out of here?
Now!' Paddy's face was the colour of borscht
as the blood pounded in his veins. A muscle
was beating under his left eye. Trish felt her
knees weaken as the implications of his fury
hit her. She gripped her hands behind her
back and tried to fight off the ideas she
couldn't bear.

'How do you know him?' she asked.

'None of your business. Now go.'

'I only want to give you the kind of legal
protection any — '

'Bollocks! You've been sniffing around
since last week, asking questions about
Jeannie. And now you've joined this bunch of

manipulative jokers who've been making my life hell. I won't have it, Trish. Get out.'

The injustice of it hit her like a heavyweight's fist. 'But, I — '

'So, may I take it, Mr Maguire,' Lakeshaw interrupted, sounding almost oily in his satisfaction, 'that you waive your right to legal representation?'

'You may take it that I have absolutely no intention of answering any questions about my past girlfriends with my daughter present. If I want legal help, I'll call my solicitor.'

'Ms Maguire, you have your answer.' Lakeshaw was holding open the front door of Paddy's flat, with the uniformed WPC who'd driven them from the hospital beside him as back-up. Trish hesitated.

'I'm an adult of sound mind,' her father said, sounding marginally calmer. 'I do not have to answer to you. Do as you're told for once in your life.'

'Dad, Jeannie Nest is dead,' Trish said, making herself look at him. His eyes bulged. 'If this man charges you or cautions you, will you promise to phone your solicitor before you say anything whatsoever? You don't have to have me, but you must have someone with you. It's very important.'

'I know she's dead. Now get out.'

Trish went. Not until she'd reached the

271

tube station and bought her ticket did she realise she must have left him thinking she was convinced he was a killer. There was no evidence for that; only Lakeshaw's suspicions. Trish wouldn't believe them — couldn't — without hard and irrefutable evidence. Paddy had to know that now or they'd never have a chance to rebuild even the relationship they had had, let alone a better one. She stuffed the ticket in her pocket and trudged back to his flat.

The achingly slow lift took far too long. She ran up the eight flights of stairs, so that she was sweating and breathless as she put her finger on the bell.

The WPC opened the door. Seeing Trish, she shook her head.

'I have to see him for one minute. Your boss can be there all the time. Come on. You know you've no right to stop me.'

The WPC stood aside at once. Trish walked past her to the living room, where Paddy was sitting with his head in his hands, staring at the floor between his knees. Lakeshaw looked almost happy.

'Dad?'

He raised his head. His eyes looked dead, exactly like those of a man she'd once prosecuted for the vicious and calculated murder of his wife.

That doesn't mean anything, she told herself.

'What now?' He sounded as though he couldn't bear her. She stiffened herself.

'I just came back to say I know you didn't do it. I didn't say so before, and it's important that you know I'm absolutely certain of your innocence.'

She thought she heard a half-stifled snort from DCI Lakeshaw, but she wasn't going to look away from her father to check on anyone else. He glared at her for a moment more, then twisted his lips into a small, chilly smile that did nothing to reassure her. His eyes did not change.

'Thank you. That should make it possible to drink with you again.'

'Mr Maguire, we haven't finished yet,' Lakeshaw said.

'May I stay, Dad?' Trish asked, needing to see the warmth in his eyes again. 'Not because I think you're in any danger of incriminating yourself, but just in case I can help. Please? And then we could have that drink.'

'No.' The monosyllable sounded less hostile, but still not very friendly. 'I don't want you involved in this nonsense. But it won't be long now. Why don't you wait in the kitchen while I finish with Lakeshaw?'

'All right.' She shut the door carefully behind her and crossed the narrow hall to his small grey-and-white kitchen.

It was pristine, apart from a mug that had obviously held coffee standing upright on the draining board. She washed it up, dried it as though his innocence depended on her leaving no moisture at all, then opened all the cupboards until she found the one that held the rest of the set. The only sign of any kind of untidiness was an old-fashioned spike on top of the fridge, where she knew he kept his credit card receipts until he'd checked them off against the monthly statement. It had always amused her that a man like Paddy should be so meticulous. Now she realised it could come in useful.

A moment later, she walked into the living room with three receipts from an Indian takeaway restaurant in her hand.

'When was Jeannie Nest killed?' she asked Lakeshaw, ignoring her father.

'The time of death has not been precisely established. As you should know, it's not an exact science.'

'But it was one night last week, wasn't it? On Monday, my father was dining with me and one other person in an Italian restaurant. On Tuesday, he had a delivery from the local Indian restaurant, and on Wednesday . . . '

'Ms Maguire, this is another charming display of daughterly loyalty, but these receipts merely establish your father's whereabouts in the early part of each of those evenings. They are not relevant. And we know about them in any case. We're finished now, for the moment. Thank you for your cooperation, Mr Maguire.'

Something in his expression made Trish turn to glance at her father. She was surprised to see gratitude in the way he was looking up at the tall police officer. When Lakeshaw had gone, she said, 'What was all that about?'

'What?'

'That sycophantic little smile I wasn't supposed to see.'

'Sycophantic? Are you not getting a little over-imaginative now, Trish?' The Irish jocularity sounded even more ludicrous than usual.

'No.' And even if I were afraid my suspicions were imaginary, she added to herself, your accent would have alerted me. What the hell is going on here? 'Why does Lakeshaw think you're involved? You told me you hadn't seen Jeannie Nest since you quarrelled over her refusal to leave Southwark. Wasn't that true?'

'Stop this, Trish.' There was no hint of a

brogue now. 'I've had it up to here with the police and I'm damned if I'll put up with an interrogation from my own daughter.'

'Just tell me that one thing, then I'll leave you in peace. You must know that I'll find out from the police if you've told them. *Have* you ever seen her since?' As he glared at her, Trish felt like a skewer that had been lying on the hob until it was red hot. Dangerous, yet unnaturally pliable. 'You have seen her, haven't you? When was it?'

'It probably wasn't her at all, Trish,' he said, with a kind of spurious ease that made her feel as though she were back on the edge of the slipping cliff. 'The hair colour and spectacles were quite different, but when I heard her speak, I had a feeling it was Jeannie.'

'When was this?'

'Oh, about two months ago at that conference when I was speaking about the effects of stress in the workplace. I was mingling with the delegates, like you have to while they have coffee midway through the morning, when I heard her voice. I looked round and didn't recognise her until I saw the way she tossed her head when she got into an argument with someone. Then I knew . . . short dark hair and big specs or not, it was Jeannie.'

'Did she see you?'

His eyes flashed, just as she knew hers did when she was particularly angry. She could hardly bear it. He'd tried to hide his connection with Jeannie Nest from the beginning. Now here he was being shifty about their most recent encounter.

'I've no idea. Someone came up to talk to me, and when I looked for her later, she wasn't there. When I asked to see the list of delegates, her name wasn't on it.'

Oh God! Trish thought. He *has* been trying to find her. Is this all that Lakeshaw has, or is there more?

'Of course not,' she said aloud, watching him carefully. 'She went into the witness-protection scheme after the Handsome case. You must have known that would involve a new name.'

'Why would I? It's the sort of thing you'd know. But it's not my world.'

Trish just looked at him. His eyes were as hard as Lakeshaw's and they didn't shift.

'But you must have known about the trial, and the evidence she gave. You'd known her well; you must at least have been curious enough to follow the reports.'

'Of course I did. I read every word in the paper, and I thought it was typical of her. Brave and right and so pigheaded you could turn her into sausages as soon as look at her.'

Trish stared at him, appalled to think he could be so flippant about a woman who'd just been beaten to death, a woman he'd once loved.

'Don't look at me like that,' he said, his voice ripping through the air between them. 'We were history by then. What she did then was nothing to do with me. And this is nothing to do with me either.'

'But — '

'Trish, I tell you, I won't have it. I'm sorry the woman's dead, of course I am. But that's as far as it goes. Now I need a drink. Will you have some whiskey with me or am I still under suspicion?'

'Don't be ridiculous.' It had been a very long day, and she didn't like Irish whiskey, but she couldn't leave him like this. 'Of course I'll drink with you. But have you got any crisps or anything to have with it? I'm starving. I haven't had anything to eat since a bowl of yoghurt and muesli for breakfast.'

'Olives, that's all. They're in a jar in the fridge. Bring the glasses when you come back, will you?'

She went to fetch them, feeling as though she had lead weights dragging at her ankles. It couldn't have been as much as four hours since Caro and Lakeshaw had come to the flat, but it seemed like four days. She ached for George and for sleep and for certainty.

* * *

Next morning all her joints were stiff, as though she'd run the marathon instead of merely battling with her ideas about her father. The hot shower helped loosen her muscles, and so did the familiar walk across the river to the Temple. Antony hadn't arrived in chambers by the time she got there. She tried to phone Caro for news, but she wasn't answering. Trish left a message for her and dialled the number of Lakeshaw's incident room. She had to leave a message there, too.

'Trish, how are you this morning?'

She put down the phone and looked at Robert Anstey. He seemed revoltingly cheerful.

'I gather you've already run into storms with Antony. Quicker even than I expected. How are you bearing up?'

'I'm fine, thanks,' she said, smiling sweetly. 'He's been great. Isn't his house fantastic? I'd never been to dinner there before Monday.'

Robert scowled and turned away. It was a small victory and it did nothing to ease Trish's mood. She wished Antony would hurry up and come into chambers and tell her what he wanted her to do about Nick Gurles. She wondered who had told Robert that there was a problem on the case and hoped it hadn't been Antony himself.

'So, Trish,' he said as he walked into her room at last. It was just after half-past twelve. 'I gather you did your usual effective job in Maidstone.'

'Thank you. And thank you very much for dinner on Monday. I had a great time.' It amazed her to remember it was only about thirty-six hours since she'd left his house.

'Good. But now we need to talk seriously about Nick Gurles. I thought we might do it over lunch. Are you ready?'

'Well, yes. OK. I mean, fine. I'll just get my bag.'

'You won't need it,' he said.

He walked exceedingly fast as they left Plough Court and headed towards Smith-field. Trish had to hurry to keep up, in spite of her long legs, but he wasn't even breathless as he said casually, 'What did you make of Henry Buxford?'

'I liked him,' she said truthfully, forcing her mind to ignore Paddy and the dead woman and her son. This was her own life and she had to concentrate on it. 'And I could see both why he'd done so well at the Bar and why he'd detested being a judge.'

Antony laughed. 'We all warned him at the time, but he thought it was his duty. He'd made more than anyone sane could spend in a lifetime and was bullied into believing he had a duty to do it. What a waste! Here we are.'

She knew there was a negotiation to come, but was not sure of the form it would take. She wished she were in better mental shape for it. When the waiter had brought menus and left them alone again, she thought of asking what he planned to discuss, then decided that would only underline her junior status. Instead, she read the menu carefully and chose a green-bean salad followed by calves' liver.

'You still look like hell, Trish. Haven't you stopped tearing yourself apart over Nick's note yet?'

'Of course I have, although I'm not comfortable with the thought that you're not going to disclose it. If it's nothing to worry about, then there's no reason not to let the rest of them have it.'

She tasted the wine the waiter had just poured into her glass, which meant she didn't have to catch Antony's eye. The scent was intriguingly grassy, nothing like as rich or subtle as the Burgundy he'd given his guests on Monday, but pleasant.

'Trish?' The malicious edge had softened, and his voice sounded real and kind. She looked up in surprise and saw something like compassion in his gentle eyes. Then they sharpened enough to alert her to what he was doing.

'No wonder you're so good in court,' she said, laughing to protect herself. The pale-blue eyes sharpened like needles as his face settled back into its familiar sardonic lines.

'Now we've got that out of the way,' he said, reassuringly caustic once more, 'let's have it. What's the real problem? If it's not the police interest in your old cases, and it's not the document, what's up?'

'I . . . ' Would it be worse to explain that she was afraid her father was about to be arrested for murder or to admit to the miscarriage and what Antony would undoubtedly see as the irresponsibility of getting pregnant just before a big case? He had some very entrenched views about women who assumed a right to more privileges than their male colleagues simply because they were the ones who gave birth.

'When I left for Tuscany, you were tough, witty, in control, and apparently serene. Now you're all over the place. Jumpy as hell. Your eyes are twice their normal size, you're as pale

282

as a piece of celery, and you look nearly as awful as you did when you had to take that sabbatical in ninety-six. You're not going to crack up on me, are you, Trish?'

'I had a miscarriage,' she said lightly, banishing as many memories as she could. 'They tend to leave one looking washed-out and a bit quivery. It's been nearly two weeks now though, so I should be over the worst. But it was unexpectedly flattening.'

'Ah.' His face cleared. 'That explains it. Although my doubts about your judgment obviously weren't so far off-beam. What on earth were you thinking of? And why on earth didn't you tell me on Monday?'

'It was a mistake.' She heard her voice crack and tried to divert him by asking what Henry Buxford had been like as a pupil master.

'Never mind that now. I hope this pregnancy wasn't a Freudian kind of mistake, to give you an excuse to get out of a case you're afraid you can't handle.'

'Certainly not.' Robert Anstey's taunting face filled her mind and gave her all the determination she could possibly want. 'I find the case absolutely fascinating and I'm looking forward to sitting behind you for however long it takes.'

'Good. That sounds more like you. So, tell

me how you're going to feel about defending Nick Gurles now that you've convinced yourself he did deliberately misrepresent his fund?'

'You sound like all those people at dinner parties,' Trish said, putting on a simpering little voice to parrot the all-too familiar question: ' 'How on *earth* can you bring yourself to defend someone you know is guilty?' Whatever I may think about him, I'll give him my best shot. Of course I will. I always do. Everyone, whatever they're like, deserves to have their case put as well as it can be. You must know that I don't have any problems with that.'

The waiter brought their food, giving her a chance to organise her ideas while he fiddled about laying the plates in front of them and refilling their glasses.

What she'd said was true enough, even though there were some clients she had always gone out of her way to avoid, cab-rank rule or no cab-rank rule. Parents who'd neglected or killed their children and expected counsel to use the cut-throat defence to get them off were high on her list of clients she'd do anything to avoid.

'The junior on this case has got to be impregnable,' Antony said as soon as the waiter had gone. 'Convince me that can

284

still be true of you.'

'Impregnable. Hm. A Freudian choice of words, maybe, Antony?' Trish said to punish him. His eyes brightened.

'That's the first sign of normality I've seen in you since I got back. It's encouraging, but I'll need more if we're to go on with the case together.'

She watched him as he carefully removed the spine of his Dover sole, spreading the Colbert butter all over the big, white plate. Thoughts spread through her mind with similar profligacy. Jeannie Nest had risked her life to stand up for what she knew was right, and ultimately lost it. Trish would be risking only reputation and fees. Were career advantage and money enough of a reason to fall so very far short of the standard Jeannie had set?

How much money could you possibly want? Trish asked herself.

She was already earning five or six times what most teachers like Jeannie were paid, and she didn't even have a child to keep. But it was nothing like the fortune that funded Antony's life and possessions.

On Monday night he'd given her a vision of what she might one day have, if she turned herself into another version of him. Could it be worth it? She had no evidence to suggest that she could ever rival his brains or achieve his mastery of the court — or his own emotions — but she could get a lot nearer if she were prepared to make a few sacrifices. And even if money like that couldn't guarantee safety, it would help provide a certain amount of insulation from the rougher side of life.

In retrospect his invitation to dinner in Holland Park looked a little like Lucifer's showing off the Cities of the Plain. This was temptation in all its naked glorious awfulness. She opened her mouth to announce her resistance, but he wouldn't let her.

'Not yet, Trish. Not here. Despite the welcome hints of returning normality, I don't think you're yet in a fit state to decide something as important as this. I want you to think about it seriously, decide where you want your practice to go and what you want out of life, and then commit yourself, one way or the other.'

'There isn't time for that sort of luxury. If I were to stand down, which I'm not saying I am, you'd need someone else to start now. Otherwise he'd never get up to speed.'

Antony looked up from his surgery on the fish. The entire backbone, undamaged and springy, rosily flushed along the spine itself, hung from the tines of his fork, dripping butter on to the neat fillets below. A faint, satisfied smile lifted one side of his mouth. She was curious to see how thin his lips were. She'd never noticed that before.

'In the circumstances, I'll risk it. We both want you on the case, so long as you're prepared to give it your all. I have confidence that you'll see your way to the right decision, once you've considered all the options.'

'We? Both?'

'Me and Henry Buxford.'

'So, Monday night *was* a test,' she said with a drop of acid in her voice, noticing how he'd put the personal pronoun first — and used the wrong one.

'No, not intentionally. It was supposed to be a pre-case celebration, but once Henry and I knew there might be a problem, he wanted to meet you. To see what you were made of.'

'And what was his verdict?' she asked, aware now of all kinds of probing in the cheery questions he'd asked under cover of the stories he'd told about his own early career at the Bar.

Antony's half smile turned into something harder. 'That you'd be better on the team than off, but that if you were going to cause trouble we needed to know now — in time to get someone else as good as you could be, if you chose. Think about it very carefully, Trish.'

She felt the familiar tug between her eyebrows as she took in everything he was threatening with such careful understatement. She picked up her glass, hoping the taste of the wine might clear her thoughts. It didn't.

'Your liver's getting cold. Eat up.'

He ate in silence — very fast — and it was only once the plates had been cleared and he'd ordered coffee that Trish said, 'Why did you pick me for the case in the first place?'

'Why d'you think?' he asked with some of the old malicious amusement making him look a lot more familiar.

'Someone suggested it must have been my experience with abused children,' she said hopefully. 'Which would allow us to suggest we were bullied by the DOB directors into doing things we'd otherwise have resisted.'

'Nice thought. And we might even use it.'

'But that wasn't why, was it?'

'No.' His smile looked positively evil for a second before it relaxed into ordinary mockery. 'You're an excellent advocate and, as we've seen, meticulous in case preparation.'

'So are all the others in chambers, or they wouldn't still be here,' she said and heard the famous Shelley laugh, which could make the strongest squirm.

'Yes. But they don't all have your talent for bringing everything down to the personal. After the last two cases with Bill, I've decided that's what I need. I tend to dryness, as does he, and even the brightest of judges can switch off without a bit of light relief. We won't overdo it, of course, or turn it into an episode of *The Archers*, but a bit of the personal might just swing this one for us. We'll see, anyway.'

It might not have been flattering, but it made sense of a sort. And in a world that increasingly seemed mad as well as terrifying, there was comfort in that. For as long as it took them to drink their coffee and get the bill, Trish even believed it. But once they were walking back to chambers and she caught several quizzical glances from people who knew them both, she was back to wondering what his real motives were. Did he *want* to lose the case? Had Henry Buxford perhaps got some reason to want Nick Gurles to go down? Was there something more about Nick that Trish hadn't yet discovered? Was Henry Buxford hoping Gurles would give him an excuse for . . . ?

Have you gone completely mad? she asked herself in silent fury. It's a ludicrous idea.

14

Caro sat with her hands clenched in her lap, waiting in barely controlled impatience. She had about a million things to do in her own nick, but here she was helping Lakeshaw again — and wishing that she had never picked up the phone to his incident room in the first place.

'Just exactly how well do you know this Trish Maguire, Sergeant?'

Caro's mind crackled in response to his mood. Tendons in his short neck were quivering like overwound springs. She tried to slow down her own reactions — and voice — to stop the two of them exploding against each other and to make sure she didn't say anything ambiguous. Trish had enough to deal with as it was.

'Before last week, I'd have believed we weren't much more than acquaintances,' Caro said carefully. 'We'd encountered each other on a couple of cases, and my partner and I have occasionally seen her socially. Drinks, the odd meal. You know how it goes.'

'What happened last week?'

'We talked to each other like friends, sir.

Real friends. I don't think you can ever go back after that.' She caught his expression and added firmly, 'Don't get me wrong, sir. Friendship doesn't mean I'd protect her from anything I thought she'd done. But it means that I know enough about her to trust her. And it was after that meeting that I phoned your incident room.'

'Good. How much did she tell you about her father's background?' He shoved the words out of his mouth, as though they tasted disgusting.

Caro shook her head. 'Nothing.'

'Concentrate. This is important.'

'I am concentrating and I'm sure she said nothing.' Caro made her voice even slower and forced herself to forget all the other problems waiting on her desk — and at home. 'She's talked a bit about him before — how he left her and her mother when she was seven or eight, I can't remember exactly, how he started trying to get in touch with her about nine years ago once she started doing well at the Bar, and how she resisted for ages. She was surprised, I think, to discover she liked him and could recognise aspects of herself in him.'

'Poor woman.'

'Sir?'

'Never mind. Get on with it. What did she

tell you about his violence?'

Caro felt as though someone had hit her under the chin. Her head jerked up and she was gripped by the sudden paroxysm of nausea that comes from constriction of the jugular.

'Violence, sir? What violence?'

'Jeannie Nest had to take out an injunction against him, nine years ago. He slammed her against the wall, knocked her out. She was concussed for days. That stopped him contacting her then, but . . . '

The nausea was getting worse. Caro hoped she wasn't going to throw up. This news could destroy Trish. 'Why did he do it, sir?'

'That we don't know. He's not saying anything and obviously Jeannie Nest can't. But it could have been the pregnancy. Maybe she refused to have an abortion, or asked him for money. Whatever it was, he lost his temper and lashed out.'

'But that was nine years ago. You've no reason to believe he'd do the same today?'

'We have our reasons. Sergeant Lyalt, I think you ought to look at some of the photographs of the body.'

'It's all right, sir. I've seen enough scenes of crime in my time to know what it'll look like. But what evidence have you to make you suspect Paddy Maguire now?'

'I doubt you've seen many like this body.' Lakeshaw spread a sheaf of glossy colour prints in front of her, fanning them out like the bloody duck breasts Jess always ordered in their favourite restaurant. In a dry unemotional voice that somehow still expressed satisfaction, Lakeshaw went on: 'He strangled her first — with a ligature, so we've got only fibres as evidence — then beat her dead body with a chair until it broke. After that he used one of its legs. As you'll see here, and here, the blows have not only ripped her clothes to shreds, but also flayed the skin off her.'

Caro pushed away all consideration of Trish, her friend, and flicked the switch that gave her the impermeable membrane she used to keep herself sane in the face of all the brutality she saw every day.

'These suggest that the perpetrator must have been covered in blood, even though the wounds were inflicted post-mortem.' That sounded very cool, she thought. Good. 'They also seem very similar to those I've read about in the case in which she testified against Ron Handsome. His victim was beaten in almost exactly the same way. Why aren't you concentrating on him and his family?'

'We did. It was the obvious answer,

particularly as his son Gareth has an even stronger history of violence than Paddy Maguire. Unfortunately Gareth Handsome has an alibi, too. He was making a nuisance of himself in the local pub on Tuesday night until he passed out, drunk, and had to be carted home by some friends and the bouncer, who's known him for years. Coupled with the fact that he's thick as pigshit and couldn't have found out Jeannie Nest's new name and address to save his life, that makes him an unlikely suspect.'

'But I thought you still hadn't pinpointed the time of death to Tuesday night.'

'True. The pathologist thought it was the likeliest time but is now looking into other possibilities.'

'OK. But why is Gareth Handsome your only suspect from the original case?'

'He's not. The old man, Ron, who's still serving his sentence, has contact with plenty of old mates who still live in the area. Several of them are capable of this sort of thing. They're all being interviewed, but so far none of them look half as promising as Paddy Maguire.'

'But why?'

'Then there's Ron Handsome's grandson,' Lakeshaw went on as though she hadn't interrupted. She realised he wasn't going to tell her anything about Trish's father, so she tried to concentrate on what he was prepared to say. 'The grandson would've been a possibility, except that he was out cabbing for most of Tuesday night and there are dockets at the cab office and records of all his takings. He had a full shift. No, at the moment, unless the pathologist revises his likely time of death, Maguire's our best prospect.'

'I assume you've searched his flat.' Surely he'd answer a question as easy as that, she thought.

'And his car, and his lock-up garage,' Lakeshaw said impatiently. 'Of course we have. But there wasn't anything there. Or at his girlfriend's place. But we haven't searched his daughter's. Yet. She keeps leaving messages on my phone, which suggests she's worried, and I want her to sweat a little longer. I need to know more about her, too. How honest is she — in your estimation?'

'She's a barrister.' Caro didn't add that Trish kept leaving messages for her, too.

'That's what I mean,' said Lakeshaw bitterly.

'She would never cover up a murder.'

'Even for her father?'

'Especially for her father. Sir, believe me, she doesn't trust him. She may have forgiven him for abandoning her, but she's still

295

obsessed about it. Most of the time she struggles to feel any warmth towards him at all. She wants to, but she's still suspicious of him. You couldn't accuse her of being an accessory without looking stupid.'

'OK, don't get so excited. You know her; I don't. I'm only asking.'

'Will you warn her about her father's past?'

'Don't be ridiculous.'

'But if he did this, I mean, if there's even the slightest chance that he could be this violent . . . ' Caro pushed away the photographs. 'Trish could be in real danger if he suspects she's helping us.'

'I'm glad you used the word 'us'. I was beginning to think you'd gone over to the other side. Once we've collected the evidence against him, you can talk to her. Not till then. Sue, where the hell are those reports?' he bellowed through the open door.

Caro watched as a woman about five years older than she was, and two stone heavier, put a pile of witness statement forms on his desk.

'Sergeant Baker, this is Sergeant Lyalt. Will you tell her everything you now know of Paddy Maguire, so that she understands just what we're dealing with here. I don't think she's quite got the picture yet.'

296

Lil had got soaking wet going down to the shop to buy more cigarettes, and she was very puffed as well as worried. Mikey hadn't spent any time with her for days. She'd sometimes heard him coming in late at night or leaving before she was up, and once she'd heard him mutter, 'I'll kill the fucking bitch.'

Lil would have given a lot to know which bitch he was talking about. And she'd have given even more to have proof that he was just saying it, like all the other people who said things like 'I could've killed him' without meaning a word of it. So far she was still managing to believe he was a good boy, but there were times when it was hard.

She reminded herself that he'd been leaving her lots of little notes to ask if she wanted any shopping done. Once she'd scribbled a reply on the note, asking for more milk and another Battenburg, and it had been waiting for her in the kitchen next morning. She'd felt better as soon as she saw it, but she still wanted to know where he was all the time he was out of the flat and who it was who was pissing him off so badly.

She had to make her own tea again today. Just as she was sitting down to it, someone started banging on her door. She couldn't think who'd do that instead of ringing the bell and looked very carefully through the spy hole. There didn't seem to be anyone there, but the banging went on. It sounded as though it came from about the level of her own waist. Bending down, she looked through the letter box and saw an angelic little girl's face peering back at her. The child revealed gappy red gums as she smiled.

Lil stood up to unchain the door and open it.

'You're Mikey's nan, aren't you?' said the grinning child, scratching her bum.

'That's right. But he's not here.'

The child's face fell. She raised the grubby hand to scratch her head. Nits, thought Lil, keeping well away. It had always been she who'd had to comb Mikey's head in the old days because his slag of a mother couldn't be bothered, and she never wanted to have to do that again.

'Can I come in then an' tell *you*?'

'Tell me what?' Lil asked, letting her in. The child pranced ahead of her towards the sun that came blinding into the lounge, where Lil had everything ready to record the week's takings after her tea.

'What's these?' asked the child, leaning over the big account book. 'It looks like sums.'

'It is,' said Lil, approving of her curiosity even though she didn't intend to encourage it.

'I like sums.'

'You go to school, do you?' That made a change on this estate.

'Of course. Mikey said.'

'What did he say?' Lil asked quickly. It was the first she'd known of her grandson having any real contact with the kids on the estate. This grimy scrap couldn't be the 'she' Mikey wanted to kill, could she?

'That school's the only way to get out of here. If you find a teacher who likes you she'll change your life. It was on the way to school today I saw the lady Mikey wanted again.'

Lil breathed deeply to slow down her heart and all the ideas banging at her brain. 'Mikey told you he wanted a lady?'

The scruffy blonde head nodded. 'The lady who came asking for Jeannie Nest. We threw stones at her when she wouldn't give us money.'

'What did Mikey say to you then?'

'He chose me,' the child said proudly, 'out of all the others, an' he said he wanted to know if she ever came back. Well, she didn't come back, but I see her sometimes on the way to school. It's always at the big white place near the old factory. The one with the

299

black stairs — you know. Near the railway.'

'Yes,' Lil said, thinking about the streets she hardly ever saw these days. 'Yes, I know the one. Does she live there?'

'I dunno. But it's always there I see her, on the stairs, an' she's got a key.'

'Well, I'll tell Mikey.' Lil smiled at the little girl. 'What else does he tell you?'

The child screwed up her forehead and her nose, trying to think and looking like an evil little pixie.

'He says you shouldn't never wish for something 'cos you never know when you're going to get it.'

Lil couldn't help smiling at that piece of nonsense. She felt a lot better for hearing it, too. 'D'you know what he means?'

'No, but he often says it. Like he says I got to go to school.'

At least it sounded as though most of the advice was wholesome, if muddled. Lil bent towards the child, hoping to get to know her better, find out more. 'Would you like some cake?'

'Nah. I just want my pound.' She held out her scratching hand, with the fingers already bent to grab a coin.

'What pound?'

'Mikey gives me a pound when I see the lady,' the child wailed. 'Always.'

'But he's not here. I'll tell him when he comes back and he can find you,' Lil said, not prepared to hand over money to settle debts that might never have been incurred. This one wasn't big, but principles were principles.

The child ran at her and kicked her leg, hard, screaming, 'I want my money! I want my money! Mikey said I could have my money.'

Lil took her by the shoulders and drove her to the front door. There she turned her captive round, keeping her own sore shins well out of kicking range.

'Oh, my God! If you do that again, I'll make sure you never get any money. But if you behave and don't make any more noise now, I'll get Mikey to find you and give you whatever he's promised as soon as he's back. Understand?'

'I hate you, you slaggy old witch,' cried the girl as she pulled herself out of Lil's hands, spat and ran down the walkway.

Lil watched her go, wiping the spit off her trousers and thinking she'd be glad if she never saw the filthy little creature again. Mikey would have to deal with her. Lil went back in to write him a note in case she was already in bed again when he came back.

But she heard his step outside before she'd finished the note and soon felt his hand on her back and his cool breath on her neck as he bent to kiss her head.

'Hello, Nan. Sorry I've been out such a lot. One of my girls is playing up. I've done the collection and it's all here.'

'Thanks, Mikey.' Her breathing eased. Even the kidney felt better. If it was one of his working girls making him so angry, that wasn't too bad. They asked for it, those girls, after all. 'I was writing you a note.'

'So I see. Anything important?'

'A little girl's just been in to tell you that she's seen the lady who came round here asking questions.' His hands were suddenly so tight on her shoulders that she was frightened, but he took them off after a minute and she heard him laugh.

'That must be Kelly. She's a good little thing.'

'She's a nasty, greedy piece of work,' Lil said sharply before telling him about the demand for money and the spitting. Mikey laughed again, a bit more natural-sounding this time.

'She's a bright kid, Nan. Don't you worry about her. I'll find her and pay her off.'

'She only went a minute or two before you got here. I'm surprised you missed her.'

'I'll go and find her now.'

'But . . .'

'It's important, Nan.' He was halfway out of the door when he glanced back at her.

Lil saw the tight white look on his face and pressed herself back into her chair. Now she thought she knew just why Gal was scared of him.

'We need to be sure who was asking questions about Jeannie Nest — and why, Nan. Don't look so worried. I can sort it out.'

'Mikey, what . . . ?' Lil said, but he'd already gone. She reminded herself that he was a good boy, and not quite twenty-one, but the words seemed to have lost some of their power. She cut herself another slice of Battenburg, but the crumbs caught in her throat and sent her choking to the sink.

★　★　★

Trish was halfway across the bridge, planning to ring Anna as soon as she got home to make a new date to meet, when the rain came down like a cavalry charge, thundering and drumming as it hit anything solid. She was soaked through before she'd reached the end of the bridge, which seemed appropriate enough after the day she'd had. She'd flogged over to Whitechapel to see David on her way into chambers, only to find he'd been moved again. Neither Lakeshaw nor Caro would return her calls, so she had no idea what was happening. Robert Anstey had been peculiarly vile at the monthly chambers meeting this evening and Antony had watched her defend herself without showing the slightest support for her or dislike of what the bastard was doing. The one comfort in the whole miserable day was that Antony had come up to her afterwards and told her lightly that he'd always known she'd be able to wipe the floor with Robert if it came to a fight. She'd tried to talk to Antony about Nick Gurles, but he wouldn't, telling her they'd talk after the deadline he'd already given her.

Now she could see water spurting back up from the handrails at the edge of the bridge and her shoes were squelching at every step. The smell of warm damp dust was wonderful, but it couldn't make up for the discomfort of the abrasively wet denim of her jeans, rubbing against her legs. And of course every taxi in sight was occupied. She put her head down against the deluge and walked as quickly as she could under the railway bridges towards her flat.

She was concentrating so hard on her feet that she didn't see George's Volvo until she was almost past it. Then she risked a quick glance upwards. Lights shimmered through the rain that filled her eyes and blocked her vision. Rushing up the iron stairs, barking her shin on the top step as she misjudged the distance, she fumbled in her pocket for her keys.

Two minutes later, she was plastered to George's front, feeling the water trickling down her face and his lips clinging to hers.

The spiral staircase was too narrow to take them both side by side, so she went up first, feeling his hands on her hips. He slid his fingers down so that he could run them along the extra-sensitive strip at the back of her thighs. She wished she wasn't wearing jeans. The thick wet denim got in the way. At the top of the staircase she turned. Five steps below her, George's head was level with her breasts. He leaned forwards. His lips were very warm against her chilled skin above the T-shirt. She bent down to kiss him, and felt his hands on her zip.

By the time she'd got rid of all her clinging wet clothes, George was lying back against the white sheets in her huge bed. The San Francisco sun had turned his usual London pallor pale gold, which made his eyes even bluer than usual. She wanted to tell him how fantastic he looked, how much she'd missed him. But as he pulled her down beside him, she lost the urge to talk.

Sharing the shower later, half-drowning again as they kissed under the pounding jets, then swallowing even more water when the effort to soap each other without falling over had made them laugh too much to breathe sensibly. Trish got water in her ears and soap in her eyes and she leaned against George's hot, slippery body as he held them both up against the cold ceramic tiles. He said something, but she couldn't hear with the water roaring in her ears. He turned the water off. In the steamy silence, he rubbed the soapy water from her face and told her he loved her.

'Me, too.' She backed against the door of the shower, pushing it open. Colder air played over her back. Shuddering in the contrast, she reached for three hot red towels and handed him one. She wrapped a small one around her hair so that it wouldn't drip any more and tucked a big bathsheet around her breasts. 'What about a cup of tea in bed? Or a drink?'

'In a minute,' he said, more serious than he'd yet been. 'Trish, what's been happening? Now I can see you properly, you look . . . worn to the bone.'

'Nonsense,' she said, rubbing a clear space

in the condensation on the nearest mirror. She made a face at her reflection. 'I look sleek and plumply loved. Now.'

'Liar. Tell me, Trish.'

So she told him the easy bits, about Nick Gurles and the case, about David being nearly killed outside the flat, and about her probably neurotic fear of the man or men who might or might not have been trying to get at her or the flat.

'You see, it's nothing more than an idea in my mind. They were probably three quite different small young men with fair hair, and I'm not at any kind of risk.'

George grabbed her again, clinging as tightly as she'd clung to him downstairs. 'Trish, if something had happened to you while I was away, I'd . . . '

She tipped back her head so that she could see his face. The surprising vulnerability he'd revealed in his emails was written all over it.

'But it didn't, George. I'm fine.'

'No, you're not. You're scared.' He rubbed a finger over each of her eyebrows in turn, then frowned and scooped a little water from under her eyes. 'And there's more, isn't there? Something else you haven't told me.'

Trish didn't want him to hear about the miscarriage now, when he was so peeled, so unprotected.

'What is it, my love? Are you ill? Have you found a lump?'

'No. Nothing like that,' she said as quickly as she could.

She didn't want him worrying about cancer or worse. But she didn't know how to lead into the enormous subject of their child in a way that wouldn't hurt, and she couldn't bear him to be hurt now.

'Trish, this kind of suspense is worse than any bad news. What's happened?'

In the end she just told him about the miscarriage directly, forcing herself to keep looking at him as she explained everything that had happened.

'You look even more scared now than when you were telling me about Jeannie Nest's killer and the man who might have been coming after you. You didn't really think I'd shout and rage at you because of this, did you?'

'No, of course not. But I thought you'd be hurt, distressed, upset. I mean, it was *our* child.' Frustration made her tongue feel twice its usual size. 'None of those words is quite right. But . . . don't you know what I mean?'

'Yes, I do. And if I sat down and started to think about dead children, I'd be all those things. More. But this isn't about a dead child, Trish. This was only a potential human being, only a short stage further on from an egg unfertilised or a wasted sperm. It didn't work out this time, but there's no reason to suspect it never will. And if it won't, it won't. There's more to life than reproducing; there really is.'

She felt as though someone had lifted a great heavy slab off her body, noticing its weight only as it left her. But as the blood rushed back, it set up new pain.

'Oh, George.'

'What?'

'You're so . . . I don't deserve you.'

'I know,' he said, laughing. 'I'm perfect.' She squinted at him, trying to think up some suitable retaliation, but she was too grateful to tease him now.

She put on some loose cotton trousers and a clean coral T-shirt and went down the spiral staircase to find something they could eat. There she saw that the table was already laid with candles waiting to be lit in the glass candlesticks. She hadn't noticed either in the excitement of finding him here. Now, she became aware of spices in the air and garlic.

'You'd been cooking. You must have been back for ages,' she called over her shoulder.

'I wanted you to have a celebration,' he said, rolling up the sleeves of his oldest, softest blue shirt. 'But there's nothing that won't keep if you'd rather go out.'

'No. I'd love to have this.'

As they ate a lamb tagine with couscous, she told him that his email about her management of Nick Gurles's case had been prophetic. Knowing that George was absolutely trustworthy, she also told him in detail about the incriminating document she'd found and the choice Antony had given her.

'Tricky,' George said, and from the heaviness in his voice she knew he'd seen all the implications at once. 'Have you decided what you're going to do?'

Trish put her elbows on the table and started to peel an orange. The smell of spurting zest mixed with the hot wax from the candles made her feel like a child at Christmas.

'Almost, but not quite. Every time I think of going along with the non-disclosure, I remember Jeannie Nest and what she risked in order to stand up for what was right. And then I start thinking that Nick Gurles and everyone else involved at the DOB are not better than the loan sharks she testified against.'

'Aren't you exaggerating a bit, Trish?'

'They're all taking money from the needy — or greedy — for their own profit.'

'There is one fairly big difference,' he said

with a laugh somewhere in his voice, 'in that the Handsomes' operation was illegal.'

'Oh, I know. And once you add in the physical violence, there's no real comparison, but still . . . '

'Don't look so worried, darling,' he said as she put down her fork. 'You'll come to the right answer if you don't scrape away at yourself like this. Antony's right: give it time. Now, would you like coffee? Or some miraculous, truly sublime home-made vanilla ice cream?'

'What?'

'Come on, do have some. I spent hours picking the seeds out of vanilla pods, and then even more hours stirring the custard just so that you could have your favourite pudding. They also serve who only stand and stir, you know.'

He was so clearly trying to keep her from worrying that she said yes, please, she'd love some ice cream and meekly ate it with a crisp almond biscuit. He'd made those too.

When they'd done the washing up, she asked if he'd mind very much if she made one call to Caro Lyalt. He kissed her and said he ought to read his own office emails anyway, and if she wouldn't mind his using her laptop and the second line, he'd be happy as a sandboy, whoever she wanted to phone.

Several of her friends had to cajole and negotiate for time alone when they were at home with their partners, but George had always been able to leave her free to work whenever she wanted. He would listen and do anything he could to help when she needed support, and he could even disagree in silence if she was in one of the moods when overt critcism roused her to fury. She hoped she did as much for him.

She checked the number of Caro's mobile and punched it in. The phone rang for a long time, but it didn't divert to the message service. Trish didn't count the rings, but they went on and on before she heard Caro's voice.

'Yes?'

'It's me, Trish. Is this a good time to talk?'

There was a pause. Then Trish heard a sigh. 'There aren't any good times. But I'm not in a meeting, if that's what you mean.'

'Caro, what's happening? I need to know.'

'What do you need to know?'

'First, where David is. I tried to see him in Whitechapel this morning on my way into chambers, only to find he's been moved again. Second, why you've gone cold on me. Third, why Lakeshaw won't return my calls either. Fourth, what progress he's making with the murder.'

'You know I can't answer any of those. I've no information about his work or his ability to return calls. My own work is completely separate from his. Similarly I have no idea of your protégé's whereabouts. All I do know is that there was good reason to think he might be in danger, and so he was moved. Social services were fully involved and quite happy with everything that was done. There's no scandal here, no police brutality.'

'Then why won't you talk to me?'

'Trish, don't push me on this. You have your professional etiquette, I have mine. You know I can't discuss cases that are under investigation. Oh, except that I can tell you the driver has been completely cleared of all suspicion that she deliberately drove over David. And that neither she nor anyone else heard the running footsteps you reported; nor did anyone see any evidence of another person at the scene.'

'I'm not asking you to betray official secrets, Caro,' Trish said, mentally filing the news about Sarah Middlewich and the crash. 'I'm asking you, as a friend, to explain what you think I've done — or might do — that's causing you such a problem.'

The other woman said nothing, so Trish had to try again. 'Caro, when I think of that evening we spent here, when I told you about

313

my miscarriage and you were so kind to me, I can't believe it's you stonewalling like this.'

'That's emotional blackmail.'

'No, it's not. It's a reminder that we're *friends*. Aren't we?'

There was another sigh. Then Caro said very fast, as though she'd only get it out if she didn't give herself much time, 'Did you know that your father has a history of violence against women?'

Trish felt as though she'd fallen from the cliff edge now and was whirling in space, waiting to hit the ground. 'Yes, but I don't know how you've got on to it.'

'And obviously I can't tell you.' Caro did not click off her phone, so Trish knew there was more. She tried to talk but her tongue felt as though it was frozen solid. She forced it to move.

'Are you suggesting he really might be implicated in the death of David's mother?'

George looked up. Trish couldn't explain anything then, so she shook her head. He nodded and turned away to give her privacy. She knew he would wait until she was ready to tell him about this.

'I'm not suggesting anything. It is not, thank God, my case.'

'Or that *I'm* in some way involved? Is that it, Caro? You, or Lakeshaw, have decided that

I was round at the Mull Estate, trying to find out Jeannie Nest's new identity and address for my father. Is that really it?'

'Don't be stupid. Of course it's not.' There was a pause, which Trish did not feel inclined to fill. 'If you had been, you'd never have gone to the estate, you'd have used your legal contacts. And you'd certainly never have said anything to me about her. But, let's face it, you could make a case for that story, couldn't you?'

'I could make a case for almost anything.' Even Nick Gurles's innocence. 'But not this. Caro, you should've told me straight away, not made me ferret around for it.'

'I shouldn't have talked to you at all. When DCI Lakeshaw comes back to you . . . '

'I won't drop you in it.' Trish wondered if she sounded as bitter as she felt. It surprised her to find Caro so cowardly.

A little energy returned with the robust response, 'That wasn't what I was going to say. I was warning *you* to be careful. Don't let that temper of yours make you say more than you mean. Lakeshaw can be highly provocative. And I'll deny ever having said that.'

'Then you shouldn't be using a mobile. Someone's bound to be listening. Bye.' Trish was ashamed of hanging up so abruptly.

She knew she ought to phone her father,

but she had no idea what she'd say to him. She couldn't believe that he was capable of killing anyone, but there was a despicable little worm of reassurance that was tunnelling through her brain. If Paddy *had* murdered Jeannie Nest, then Trish could forget about the small blond man — or men — who'd seemed so threatening.

'That's sick,' she said aloud, making George look round from his emails again. She wanted to tell him everything Caro had hinted, but she needed to get it straight for herself first.

She tried to believe that she would have noticed something frightening in Paddy if he'd been able to commit a crime as terrible as this. But then she'd never seen anything in him to warn her that he'd ever hit her mother. It had taken his confession to make her see that capacity in him. The worm of reassurance had metamorphosed into something monstrous. Now that she'd had time to think, she knew that she would infinitely rather be beaten up in the street than discover she had a killer for a father.

★ ★ ★

Caro was fighting her conscience on two fronts. She took out the sheaf of photographs

DCI Lakeshaw had insisted on leaving with her. The body was in worse shape than any she'd ever seen. She wished Lakeshaw had given her some idea of the evidence that made him so sure Paddy Maguire had been the perpetrator. Either he didn't have enough yet or he didn't trust her not to pass it on. If Maguire was guilty, Caro wanted him charged, convicted and locked up as soon as possible, but she hadn't been able to bear the thought of what Trish would go through if it happened without warning.

At least asking the question about his violence meant that Trish would be aware of what was going on, and that might in itself be enough to make her watch out for herself. If Paddy Maguire were capable of doing this to an old lover, what would he do to his daughter if he thought she were in league with the police?

15

Lil Handsome sat opposite her husband at one of the tea-stained grey tables in the visitors' room. His wizened face and scrawny neck made him look ill, and much older than her, even though they were only two years apart and he never had to do a hand's turn in here. He was coughing too, and spitting brown phlegm into his handkerchief, in a way that made her feel downright ill. If anything could make her give up the fags, it'd be this.

'How's business?' he asked breathlessly when he'd wiped his mouth.

'Not good.'

'Why? Have you been slacking off?'

'I've told you before,' she said with as much patience as she could find for him, 'it's the mail-order catalogues. People can buy anything they want from them. And they're not like banks. They give credit to nearly anyone, whatever they put in the small print. I've known women run up a thousand pounds on toys and stuff just to give their kids a good Christmas. Oh, my God, it's disgusting.'

'They can't buy food from catalogues,

though, can they, Lil? Nor pay the electric. When the Giro's run out, they've either got to sit in the dark or come to us. You should do well enough out of that at the interest *you* charge.'

'It's small stuff.'

'Then why aren't you using Gal to get more men as customers, like I told you?'

'He's no good at it, Ron. Listen . . . '

But he wouldn't listen. He never had. Now he was jabbing a finger towards her, only just holding himself from shouting like he used to do.

'He says you've shut him right out, in spite of everything I told you — you and the boy.'

So that's why he keeps phoning Mikey, Lil thought. *And* why Mikey's fretting about who'll get the business in the end. Maybe it's that making him so angry. But if so, why's he muttering about killing 'the bitch'? Who is she?

'I'm warning you, Lil.'

Hating him, she reminded herself that there wasn't a thing he could do to either her or Mikey from in here.

'Leave off, Ron. The boy's helpful now I can't get about like I did. Brings my shopping and that. And he's much better with the customers than Gal ever was. More honest too.'

Her husband's eyes went all cold and thin, while the rest of him got very still, just like the first time he'd hit her. Lil hadn't had any idea then what was coming. Later she'd learned to read the signs, of course, but not that time. She'd been talking happily while she made him his tea. Pregnant, she'd been feeling sick, and the food she was cooking made it worse, but she'd been brought up to give a man a hot meal when he came in from work, so she was doing her best. But throwing up earlier had made her late.

He'd told her to stop chattering and get his bloody food on the table. She'd said it wouldn't be long. He'd looked at her then like this, all cold and narrow and still, and asked her what she'd said. Thinking he must have wax in his ears, she'd said it again, louder, and then she'd felt his hand crashing into the side of her face.

That time the boiling water had been a mistake, she was sure. But it'd given him ideas and he'd used it on her again later. Thank God, he couldn't touch her any more, however much he jabbed his finger and effed and blinded.

'I won't fucking well have it,' he said, still quiet and dangerous. 'Letting your own son go hungry and giving everything to a boy like that. It's not right, Lil. A man of Gal's age deserves respect. See to it, or . . . '

It was good that there was the table between them and the officer on his little platform checking them all.

'Or *what*, Ron?' she said, letting herself sound more powerful than she'd ever done in the days when she'd tried so hard not to make him angry. She could feel how much he wanted to hit her now, but she wouldn't look away from him. In here she was safe.

'Or I'll send round some of my mates to make you do it. I'm serious, Lil.'

He probably would, too. She saw a way to find out what she'd come for.

'How d'you know they'd do it for you? A washed-up has-been like you.'

He didn't answer, but he looked more than happy; she could tell he was pleased with himself about something.

'Have you been sending them round to someone else, Ron? Jeannie Nest, maybe? There's a lot of talk that something's happened to her. Was that your doing?'

'Of course not,' he said, but he still looked pleased with himself. 'I'm glad she's got what she deserved, but I didn't do it.'

'How d'you know she has?'

'I c'n read, can't I? We get the papers in here.'

'There hasn't been anything about Jeannie

in the papers. Did you get it from Gal?'

'Don't be daft! Why would Gal know anything? He hasn't never had anything to do with that slag.'

'Then who did tell you?'

Ron shrugged. 'Had the police in, didn't I? Asking the same like what you've just asked. But it's nothing to do with any of us. She was a nosy-parkering bitch and women like that don't change. She'll have pissed off lots more than us. Any of them could've gone after her. Interfering like she does is what gets women into trouble. Always.'

No, it isn't, Lil thought. Taking up with men like you and Gary is what gets women into trouble.

'D'you swear you don't know anything about what happened to her?'

'Oh, stop nagging, woman.' Ron coughed again, then couldn't stop, and was soon almost heaving his guts up.

He wouldn't be seventy for another year. Sometimes when she saw famous people on the television, she couldn't believe how old they were supposed to be. They looked years younger than her and Ron. Of course, they didn't have her worries.

When he was quiet again, his forehead was shiny with sweat. 'You're killing me, like you always did. Get out of here. And no more playing favourites with the business or you'll find yourself in trouble. I mean it.'

I've got trouble whatever I do, she thought. 'I'd best be off then to get the bus. Is there anything you need?'

'Phonecards and fags, for Christ's sake. You should know that by now.'

'I've already given them to the screw.' She pushed back her chair and levered herself to her feet, feeling the pain in her knees and her back and her jaw. Oh my God! I hate him, she thought.

'I'm going for a scan next week,' he said suddenly.

'Why? What for?'

'Me lungs. See why I've got this cough.'

She picked up the shopping bag and, nodding to the officer, walked out.

'You're leaving early, Lil,' said the officer on the gate.

'No point staying. I've handed in his fags. He's told me he's going to hospital. Nothing more to be said.'

She walked painfully down the long pavement towards the bus stop and the phone box, wondering how she'd feel if he was really ill or if he died. It would make life a lot easier, but she still didn't like the idea. She hoped Mikey would be at the flat when she got home. She didn't want to be on her own today, not with all the memories Ron had stirred up.

★ ★ ★

'And so, Antony,' Robert Anstey said, recrossing his long legs, 'you must see that it would be in Trish's own best interest to relieve her of this case before it makes her ill.'

'Are you sure there's not just a smidgeon of self-interest in this unprecedented concern for her?'

'God no!' Robert said virtuously. He leaned forwards to underline his sincerity, gazing at Antony with the Olympian kindliness of a consultant surgeon pronouncing a death sentence.

Marshall Hall eat your heart out, Antony thought, hiding his amusement behind his usual polite detachment.

'It's just that I haven't seen her as white and twitchy as this since she had to take her sabbatical. And you know how worried we all were then.'

'Indeed, but she sorted herself out well enough to write an important book during her months away from chambers. And she's done superb work since.' Antony was even more amused to see Robert's full lips pouting like a Victorian courtesan's. Clown! he thought.

'Only in family law and she knows her way round that like the back of her hand. Nick Gurles's case is different. It's clearly putting her under much too much strain. Haven't you noticed that she's hardly been in chambers at all since you got back? She's clearly terrified of your finding out how inadequate she is. It'll be ghastly for her if she cracks up in the middle, embarrassing for chambers, and disastrous for poor Nick Gurles.'

Antony sat in his comfortable leather chair, saying nothing. He'd never liked Robert Anstey, and had in fact voted against him in the year he completed his pupillage, but there was no denying his competence. And he was far from stupid. In fact, occasionally he saw rather further than Antony would have liked.

'You must see that you're doing her no favours by putting her under this kind of stress. It's really not fair, Antony. She's a lot more fragile than she or anyone else has realised.'

Antony thought of Trish's eagle nose and spiky hair and the ferocious determination that had kept her fighting through every case she'd ever had, however unattractive her client. She might care a little too much, but to him that was preferable to Robert's heavily blunted antennae.

'You really can't take the risk, Antony.'

He stood up, surprising Robert, who twitched like an electrocuted sheep before standing up and trying to look nonchalant as he leaned on the back of the chair he'd just vacated.

'You do yourself no good by this kind of intervention, Robert. I have absolute faith in Trish, and I won't be dictated to by any junior in my chambers. Now, I've got work to do, so you'll have to excuse me.'

Robert flushed, but he was not stupid enough to protest. At the door he turned back. His face was controlled again and a familiar, rather unpleasant little smile was tweaking at the muscles either side of his full mouth.

'I hope — for your sake as well as Nick's — that you won't be disappointed this time.'

Antony merely smiled and waited for him to leave.

★ ★ ★

Mikey must've seen Lil from the windows because he had the kettle on by the time she got to the top floor. He mashed the tea, and she saw he'd got a new Battenburg for her. It made a change to have someone to notice what you liked and get it for you. She shouldn't have been so worried about what he was up to. He *was* a good boy, after all.

She peeled off the yellow outside and broke open the neat little squares of pink and yellow sponge. She always ate both pink ones first before touching the yellow bits.

'Why d'you always leave the outside, Nan?'

'I don't like the almond.'

'I could buy you ordinary cake then.'

She shook her head. 'It's this I like. You're a good boy.'

'Did Grandad say anything?'

'Not much. Only the same stuff about giving Gal a share of the business.'

Mikey flashed a dangerous look at her, then calmed down as he saw her smile.

'Don't worry about it, Mikey,' she said quickly. 'You know I won't. And your grandad's not well. It's his lungs.'

'I'm not surprised, the amount he smokes, stupid git. What did he tell you about Jeannie Nest?'

'Nothing, except that he hadn't had anything to do with it. But I don't know if he was lying. I thought I'd be able to tell.' Lil picked up the last yellow square and ate it carefully, making it last. There was a crumb left on the plate, so she licked her finger and picked it up. 'But I couldn't.'

'Nan?' Mikey said, after a long pause.

'Yes?'

'You know what Uncle Gal said to you, the other day when we were round at his place?'

'That you're only here for what you can get out of me?'

'Yeah. You didn't believe it, did you?'

'No.' Old Lil considered her grandson, handsome as his name and healthy and helpful. And a lot less angry now than he'd been the last few days. Maybe now was the time for the final test. It would be good to know for sure that she could trust him so that she could get out of this place and leave off all her worries. 'And you didn't believe him when he said you'd never get the business, did you, Mikey?'

Slowly he shook his neat head. 'No. I think you'll retire when you're good and ready, and if Grandad isn't out by then, I think you will want me to take over.'

'You're right there. And I'm nearly ready to do it now.'

His nice white teeth showed as he smiled. 'Don't rush for my sake, Nan. I've got enough to do with my girls and the cabbing. Like I said, the girls have been playing up. It's hard enough to fit in sorting them with the collecting, let alone all the planning and accounting you do. I can wait, you know.'

Patting his hand, she said, 'I know. And you're a good boy. Help me up, Mikey.'

When she was balanced on her feet, she took him through to her bedroom and then on to the kitchen, showing him the false cupboard backs and all the other hiding places for the cash boxes with the float and the account books. She saw the brown-paper package with Gal's bloody trousers in it, but she didn't explain and Mikey didn't ask. She made him laugh with her story of the mouse's teethmarks on the debtors' list.

'I'm going out tomorrow for most of the day,' she said as she covered the last hiding place again.

He did look startled then. 'Where? What d'you mean?'

'I've got things to see to if I'm about to retire. I'll be back in time for tea. Will you be here?'

'I'll do my best, Nan, but I can't promise.'

★ ★ ★

In all her years in court, standing up to hostile judges or cross-examining obstructive witnesses, even standing alone in a cell with a client who'd been accused of appalling crimes, Trish had never felt so uncomfortable.

She rang the bell of her father's flat in Cottesmore Court, just south of Kensington High Street.

'Trish! Come in,' he said, nearly smiling. Then his eyes hardened, perhaps in response to her stiffness. 'Unless you're planning to ask more questions about Jeannie Nest. If you are, you can bugger off now.'

'Paddy, I have to know why the police suspect you. It isn't just that you once had an affair with her, I know that. There has to be more. But they won't tell me what it is.'

'I should hope not.'

'Please let me come in and talk.'

'Trish, it's ancient history. And I don't want to discuss it.'

'Not any more, it isn't. She's been murdered, and they think I was only asking questions about her because — '

'You don't have to tell me that,' he said. 'I've had them round here, saying it to my face, over and over again. But I thought you said you were certain I couldn't have had anything to do with it.'

'Yes, I did.' She had to hang on to that. The alternative was unthinkable — even though she couldn't always stop herself thinking about it. 'I mean I am. But I've heard something I have to ask you about.'

He didn't give her any help, just stood

between the door and the jamb, barring her way in.

'Paddy, you told me once that you hit my mother. Did you ever . . . were you ever violent with Jeannie Nest?' He still said nothing, but Trish thought she read guilt in his face. 'Oh, God! Tell me it wasn't serious.'

'Of course it wasn't, but I told you, Jeannie was all for women's rights and all that crap, and she took out an injunction to stop me coming anywhere near her, but it was nearly nine years ago.'

'She *what?*' No wonder Lakeshaw had added him to the list of suspects, even if it had been years. 'What on *earth* did you do to her?' Trish heard the lift whining behind her and quickly said, 'Look, let me come in. We can't talk about this out here.'

'I've got Bella in the flat.'

'Does she know about the police and what they think?'

'Of course she does, and isn't she hopping mad about them?'

'And about me?'

'How would I know?'

'Then let me come in, Paddy.'

'No. I'm not going to talk about it any more.'

'Who is it?' called Bella's voice.

'Only Trish,' he shouted over his shoulder.

'But she's not staying. I'll be back in a jiffy.'

'All right,' Trish hissed. 'So tell me out here. What did you do to Jeannie Nest to make her go to a lawyer?'

Paddy Maguire sighed and rubbed the sweat off his ruddy face with the back of one wrist. There were long black hairs poking out of his shirt cuff.

'We had a row when I said I couldn't bear her living in that slum and that I wanted her to come away and share my flat — the one I used to have in Battersea. And she wouldn't. She got all sanctimonious and blathered some prissy nonsense about her pupils. She got right under my skin, so I took her by the shoulders and shook her.'

'That's all?'

'Well, the wall was nearer than I'd thought, so she hit her head.'

Trish felt her muscles sag and she breathed more easily. She was about to ask how bad the injury had been, but Paddy was talking.

'It was a mistake, Trish, an accident. The shaking? Yes, I plead guilty to that. I always did. But the head injury was accidental.'

Trish almost pitied him. Almost. 'How serious was it? Was she knocked out?'

'For a few minutes. And when she came round, didn't I cart her off to casualty to get her checked out? She was fine. They did all the scans, and there was no problem except a small concussion. But she said she never wanted to see me again. And when I went round the next day with flowers, to make sure she was all right, she said she'd set the lawyers on me, and so she did. That's how it was, and why I didn't give you her name in the first place. Now will you go and leave me to make my peace with Bella?'

She counts for more than I do, does she? Trish thought. Well, I suppose that's fair. She's the one at risk here, not me.

'Sure. But next time tell me what's going on. You made me think all sorts of stuff with all this shilly-shallying. One thing more: did you see her again after the conference?'

'No, I did not.'

'And did you ever work out which of the unfamiliar names of the delegates might have belonged to her?'

He took a step back. Trish thought once more of shoving her foot between the door and the architrave.

'I didn't even think about it,' he said very quietly, then just as quietly he shut the door in Trish's face.

Questions were screaming through her mind. Why didn't you think to look? Is this another lie? Have you been trying to track her down? Is it too much of a coincidence that she was attending that particular conference? Why would she have gone anywhere near it when it was to include a seminar led by Paddy Maguire?

Trish put her finger on the bell again.

'I told you to bugger off, Trish.'

'Just one more question: were you named on the programme for the course, the one when you saw her?'

'Sure I was.'

'So if it was Jeannie, she must have wanted to get in touch with you. When was it, exactly?'

'I told you — a couple of months ago.'

Had Jeannie been trying to decide whether Paddy had reformed enough to know he had a son?

'Have the DNA results come through yet?'

'Not that I know of.' Once more he shut the door.

Down in the street, Trish's mobile started tinkling like one of the carillons that had so surprised her during a weekend she'd spent with George in Amsterdam. She pressed the button and heard Lakeshaw's voice, sounding almost tentative.

'Ms Maguire? I wonder if you can help us.'

'That rather depends on what you want.' She didn't feel like helping anyone just then.

'The boy won't talk to us, and we know there's more to come. Will you see what you can do?'

'Why should I, after all the obstructions you've put in my way and everything you've done to my father?'

'Because you care. Or so you told me.'

When she didn't say anything, he tried a different inducement. 'And because getting the truth from David may be the only way we're ever going to be able to charge anyone. If you refuse to help us, I can only suppose it's because you're afraid his information will incriminate your father.'

'Don't be ridiculous. You're right, though — I do care. I'll come now, if you'll tell me exactly why you had to move him.'

'I can't go into that. But there was a perceived risk, on which we had to act.'

'You mean someone was asking questions? Who?'

'I've told you, I can't go into it.'

'You'll have to tell me where he is, if you want me there.'

'If you'll meet me at Kensington High Street tube station, I'll take you there. Where are you now?'

Trish wasn't going to admit that she'd been at her father's flat, so she simply said that she could be at Kensington High Street tube

within ten minutes and agreed to meet
Lakeshaw there, outside the station, by the
newspaper stand.

★ ★ ★

The small private nursing home at the far end
of Hornton Street was done up like a country
cottage, with white-painted furniture and
cheerful chintz curtains. Trish thought it
seemed far too expensive for any witness-
protection budget, but maybe they'd picked it
as the least likely place for anyone to look for
David. He was in a private room watching
television, with a uniformed PC sitting
outside. When the boy looked at Trish, his
eyes were so dull, and his face so immobile,
that she was afraid they must have sedated
him.

She dragged a chair across the pink carpet.
The legs bounced and scraped as they caught
in the dense pile. This time she didn't try to
take his hand.

'They've only just let me come back,
David. They were afraid for you and wanted
to check me out to make sure I was safe.' His
face didn't change. 'This looks much more
comfortable than the other hospital, and
you've got your own telly.'

Now there's a subtle remark, Trish, she told

herself with all the derision she usually kept for ineffectually deceitful witnesses. No wonder he won't respond. 'I've brought you some apple juice.'

'They give me lots,' he said, pointing his chin at the bleached-pine chest of drawers between the windows. A neat pyramid of untouched individual juice-cartons was stacked there.

'Oh, good. David.' She let her voice lose all its cheery brightness. 'Mr Lakeshaw has said that you won't tell them anything. I understand that your mother told you that you mustn't let anyone know who you are and who she was, but everything's changed now. No one else can hurt her ever again. And the police can only help to make you safe if they have all the facts. Please try to help.'

He rolled his head on the pillow in the familiar way, and she saw tired tolerance in his black eyes. One more adult playing games with me, was the message she read in them. One more adult I can't trust.

To her horror, she felt a tear in her left eye and brushed it away. But that only produced another, then more. David's dull eyes sharpened a little. Trish fumbled for a handkerchief. There was a box of Kleenex beside the apple juice. She pulled out a handful and wiped her eyes with her back to him.

'Sorry,' she said, coming back to sit beside him.

'Did you know her?' he asked, wary but possibly less angry.

'No, but I wish I had. I've been talking to one or two people who knew her, and they all say wonderful things about her. But that wasn't why I was crying.' All her experience told her that he was at the age when direct, truthful explanation was the only acceptable kind. 'I . . . I lost my father — in a different way — when I was only a little younger than you. And I can remember so well what it felt like and how for years afterwards I didn't want to know anyone else or trust anyone else ever again. And that made me understand a little how you must be feeling. So I cried.'

'Did he die?'

'No. He just went away. For a long time I thought it was because he hated me. Or I'd been too bad to bear.'

David blinked. Just once. But it was enough. Although they'd told him his mother was dead, the child must still believe at some level that she'd sent him away because he hadn't been good enough.

Trish knew then that, whatever happened in the police investigation, whatever was

338

proved about his parentage, she would feel a responsibility towards him for the rest of her life.

'It was the eyes that scared her,' David said suddenly.

'Eyes? What eyes?'

'She said it was a cat, but they were too high up. And if it had been on the wall, they'd have been too low. I saw them. And they were people's eyes; they didn't have fur and whiskers round them.'

'What else did you see, David?'

'It was dark.'

'Were they men's eyes or women's?'

'A man's.'

'What did you do when you saw them?'

'She was cross.'

'Was she? Why?'

'I asked who the man was. She said there wasn't any man, just another cat like Mrs Tiggywinkle that had made her jump. And I said it was a man, that I'd seen him. And she told me to stop making up stories. And she shouted at me.'

'What did she shout?'

'For once in my life will I do what I'm told, and go straight off to Trish Maguire, like she'd always told me.' His lips trembled. 'She was cross. And she didn't come, and she said she would. She *promised*.'

'David, she couldn't come because she was dead.'

'I know!' he shouted. 'I'm not stupid!'

Trish smiled steadily at him. 'And I think she was frightened when she was shouting at you. That makes people seem cross sometimes. I think she was frightened of the man whose eyes you saw. That's why she sent you to me, to make sure that you were safe, whatever happened. And that's why I — and the police — want to help find him so that you can go on being safe.'

She waited for him to talk, but nothing came.

'He could have been the man who rang her up before. Can you remember any more about his voice on the phone? Did it have any kind of accent?'

He shook his head.

'Can you remember anything else at all?'

'No. Only that he was cross, like her.'

Trish got to her feet.

'I've tried,' he said, grabbing her hand. 'But I can't. I can't. Don't go.'

'It's all right, David. I'm not cross, and I'm not going away. I just have to talk to Mr Lakeshaw for a minute.' She could see his face through the wired glass panel in the door. He nodded to her. 'Then I'm coming back. All right?'

Reluctantly, David let go her hand. She went out to tell Lakeshaw the little she'd learned, before returning to the child's bedside. He was flicking through the television channels, pausing for a while on Discovery, then restlessly moving on. Trish sat, waiting for him to stop or to ask her for something. At last he put down the zapper.

'Did you watch much telly at home?' she asked.

'No. My mum only let me have forty minutes a day.' His bottom lip trembled again, and a trail of mucus slid out of his nose as his eyes filled with tears.

'And what about at Joe's house?'

'Yeah, sometimes.' David sniffed. 'His mum didn't mind how much we saw.'

'Would you like to see Joe?'

His face brightened so much that Trish felt a qualm. But even Lakeshaw couldn't refuse to let the child's best friend visit him for ever. 'And what about your relations?'

'I haven't got any.'

'You must have. Everyone has cousins, uncles, aunts.'

'I asked my mum once and she said they were all awful, they'd be boring, and we were better off without them.'

Were they afraid of retaliation from the Handsomes? Or had they disapproved of

341

Jeannie's way of life and her apparently fatherless son?

'What did you do at Christmas-time?'

'Mum and I used to go to Joe's house for Christmas lunch sometimes. And sometimes to Frankie's.'

'Who's Frankie?'

'She's a friend of Mum's. She lives with Richard. They work with Mum at the teacher-training.'

'What's their surname?'

'Frankie's is Mason and Richard's is Platter.'

'Right. And did your mum have a boyfriend?'

'I don't know.' He was frowning. 'There used to be Martin, but he stopped coming.'

'What was he like?'

He smiled. 'We played football.'

'So he was kind to you?'

'Yes. But when he wouldn't come any more that made Mum cross.'

I'll bet it did, thought Trish, but it doesn't sound as though he could've been the one who terrorized and killed her. 'What about Paddy? Did you ever see him? Or hear her talk about Paddy, or Patrick? Or even Pat?'

'No. I don't know them. There was just always Martin till he stopped coming. I don't know his other name.'

'OK. Don't worry about it. That's great, David. Thank you. Will you be all right if I go out for a bit? I've got to do some . . . some shopping.'

'When will you be back?'

'As soon as Mr Lakeshaw lets me come, when he's sure you're safe.' Trish kissed David's forehead, then waved at him from the door.

'That looked very cosy for a pair of total strangers,' remarked Lakeshaw unpleasantly. 'What else did you get?'

'Nothing useful to you,' Trish said, 'except the fact that he never saw or heard of anyone called Patrick, Pat or Paddy and that his mother had some friends.' She repeated all the names she'd got from David, surprised to see him flinch at Martin's.

'What does that tell you?'

'Nothing. It took you a very long time to get that much.'

'It was more than you'd got with all your experts, wasn't it? I take it I can come back and visit David?'

'I can't stop you coming to the building. But the constable may not admit you to his room. It depends.'

'On my cooperation?' she said, intending to be provocative.

'On our analysis of the risks you may bring to David.'

And what about the risks to me? she thought, less scared now that George was back and staying in her flat most nights. Even the sound of footsteps creeping up behind her didn't spook her as much as they had. And she hadn't seen any small blond men hanging around her flat for days.

16

Mikey saw Trish Maguire come out of the nursing home and wait on the corner of the street. She didn't look half as rich and superior these days, which was something. The kids on the estate might have scared her a little that first day, but even they hadn't made her look like this. She was pale and there were great grey bags under her eyes. Her expensive hair was a mess and she was wearing crumpled jeans. But she still didn't look behind her, stupid cow.

A black cab came up with its light on. The driver stopped for her and she said something through the window, asking if he'd take her to Southwark probably. It just showed how even rich lawyers didn't know all the law. Black cabs had to take you wherever you wanted to go. Not like mini-cabs. They could choose, which was how Mikey liked it. He wasn't ever going to have drunks sicking up in the back of *his* car.

When she'd got into the cab, Mikey switched on his own engine and followed them till he was sure they were going home.

Then he took his own private shortcut back to Southwark.

He phoned her number at the flat to make sure there was no one else there, then he waited in the phone box until her cab drove up. He didn't usually let her see him, even though he liked to remember the night when he'd made her so scared she'd had to pay her cabbie to walk her up the stairs to her flat.

So far that was the closest he'd let her get to him after that first meeting on the estate. Considering she had no real routine that was a miracle. He'd followed her for long enough to know who her friends were and what sort of work she did and where she bought her food and parked her Audi, and how she lived. But he *still* couldn't work out why she was so interested in Jeannie Nest. Nor why she'd come to the estate for information in the first place.

Everything else was going so well, what with his nan almost ready to retire and his hopeless uncle making such a fool of himself that he was no rival any more. Mikey couldn't let this nagging worry about what Trish Maguire wanted and how much she knew spoil everything.

There'd been one bad day when he'd seen her rush out to work without putting on her burglar alarm. It wasn't the day her cleaner came, so he'd thought he'd get a chance at last to go through her place and find out who she really was and what was driving her. He'd followed her across the river to make sure she was going to stay at work for once, then he'd come back here. But just as he was about to try to force the locks, he'd heard someone else on the iron stairs behind him. Turning, casual as you please, he'd seen a tall fat man, whose face was all over suspicion.

'Mr Rogers?' Mikey had said, cool as cool. The big bloke had looked surprised. 'There's a mini-cab been ordered for Rogers. That you?'

The bloke had said there was no one called Rogers at that address, so Mikey had just said, 'Cheers, mate.' Then he'd left without running. He'd got back in his car and pretended to be calling control on the radio so he had time to see the fat man take out a key and let himself in. Up till then, Mikey had thought Trish Maguire lived on her own. It'd been a nasty shock to find she had a bloke.

★   ★   ★

Trish stepped across the post on the doormat and shut the door. It had always been one of George's bugbears that she'd bend down to pick up her letters in full view of everyone, a target for any nutter in the street, with her door open and her flat exposed. These days she shut and double-locked the door every time she came home.

Most of today's envelopes were bills or circulars, but there was a card from her mother with a wonderful Dot cartoon that made her laugh out loud. She read the note inside as she walked to the kitchen. Her hand was already on the kettle lid when she read: *Don't be afraid, Trish. I know that some of Paddy's past can seem worryingly high-coloured, but he's not a bad man. Whatever the circumstances may suggest, or the police try to insinuate, he couldn't have killed this woman. I lived with him for ten years. I know that.*

So the police had been questioning his ex-wife as well as everyone else, Trish thought.

She should have felt reassured, but she didn't. There had been plenty of women who'd lived with killers and trusted them, having no idea what they did when they left the house. And there'd been mothers, too, who'd been emotionally destroyed when they discovered that their apparently charming, normal sons had cellars-full of body parts. No one could be certain that her husband or lover or child was innocent, never really know for sure, however much she might long to believe.

Needing to talk to someone else who would understand all that, Trish rang Caro.

'Trish, I've told you, I cannot — '

'I'm not asking you to. It's not that, Caro. I'm worried about the boy, David. Lakeshaw let me see him today, but he suggested . . . no, he threatened that I wouldn't get to see him again unless I cooperated. But I've nothing to cooperate with. It's like being tortured for information you don't have. Please help. I know you could, if you chose.'

'Talk to Lakeshaw, Trish, it's not my case. I'm really sympathetic. Really. But I can't do anything.' Caro's voice was strained rather than angry, so Trish took a chance.

'Then just tell me this: why doesn't Lakeshaw trust me?'

There was a sigh, then Caro began to speak very fast. 'He doesn't believe your story of why you went looking for Jeannie Nest. And he doesn't believe that you didn't know anything about David before. He hasn't confided in me, but my guess is he thinks you knew them both already. What did he want you to ask David today?'

'More of the same. Who, why, or what so

frightened his mother that she . . . ' Trish broke off, wondering why she'd been so slow. 'You mean he only wanted to see me and David together again to assess how familiar we were with each other?'

'Probably, but I could be wrong.'

Oh shit, Trish thought. Why didn't I work it out in time to stop myself kissing the poor child? 'Are you busy tonight, or would you like to come and have some supper? George is back.' Trish could hear the smile in her own voice. She was beginning to get used to the depth of her need for him. And she didn't mind it nearly so much now that she'd seen the gaps in his emotional armour. 'So you'd get something much better than with only me.'

There was a pause, during which Trish heard only Caro's breathing and her own. 'Oh Trish, I'd love it, but I can't. Not till this case is over. But I'm glad you've got George back with you now.'

Putting down the phone, Trish wondered what more doubts — or suspicions — could be making Caro so hesitant. She had to know, so she rang Lakeshaw, but he wouldn't speak to her.

★ ★ ★

350

Lil had had a good day. Her Essex solicitor had taken her to see the cottage, explaining that he'd already told the tenants they'd have to go at the end of the month. Luckily they weren't making difficulties about it. They and the ones before them had only ever been allowed to rent it by the month. Then she'd gone back to the solicitor's office and he'd taken her through the accounts. It seemed she'd have about three hundred pounds a week to live on after tax, the solicitor's bill, and the outgoings on the cottage, which would be plenty on top of her pension and whatever Mikey paid her.

She'd told the solicitor that all things being equal, she'd move into the cottage in two months' time and that she'd like him to go on working for her without telling anyone who she was or where she came from. The story would be just that she was the new tenant of the cottage. He'd agreed and as usual asked no questions, which was why she'd always been happy to pay his bill.

By the time she got back to the estate that night she was so tired she felt like a rag that's been caught in the mangle. It was years since she'd walked through the place alone in the dusk and she didn't like it at all. Passing the spot where her husband had beaten a man to death, she saw three boys with hoods over their heads, shadowing their faces so much she couldn't even see if they were blackies or not. But they didn't come after her and nor did anyone else. She got to her block safely, then she saw Mikey's little girl, kicking pebbles into a puddle.

'I told you Mikey said I could have a pound,' she said when she saw Lil.

'I know. He told me, too. Has he given it to you?'

'Course he has,' the child said, proudly digging in the pocket of her draggled dress. When she opened her fist, Lil saw three pound coins lying in the damp palm.

'Three? What else did you do for him?' she said, worried to death all over again.

The gap teeth showed again as the child grinned. 'I told you — every time I see the lady, Mikey gives me a pound. He said to save the money, so I haven't spent it. You tell him I haven't spent none of it. See? There's still three pounds here.'

'Yes. That's good. I'll tell him. What's your name?'

'Kelly.'

'You're a good girl, Kelly, but you shouldn't be out on your own late like this.'

'My mum sent me. She's busy. She'll call when I can come in again.' Kelly kicked more pebbles into the muddy water, deliberately slopping it over the edge of her shoes.

Lil was furious with the child's mother, but it wasn't her responsibility and she needed to sit down. The lift wouldn't work, so she had to climb all those flights up to her flat. In the end, she was pulling herself up with her hands, clawing three steps higher than her feet. The bag over her wrist bumped at every step, and her knees were killing her.

There was no light on in the flat, so Mikey must be out again. She wished he was there. She didn't think she'd have the strength to find her keys. Leaning against the wall by her door, she waited till her breathing was more normal again. Then she tried to get at the keys, but it was hard to see, and her hands hurt.

Hard-edged metal dug into one finger and she forced the rest of the stuff out of the way and got the bunch out. Her hands were shaking though and she couldn't fit the right key into the lock. Men were coming up the stairs, several of them, not talking. She thought of Ron's threats, pushed the key into the lock at last and turned it, leaning against the door to open it.

'Mrs Handsome?'

She was inside and pushing the chain into its socket, but she wasn't quick enough. He pushed the door further open.

'Mrs Handsome? Nothing to be afraid of. It's me — Chief Inspector Smith.'

She'd never thought she'd be that pleased to see the police. A minute later, she was on the settee with her head between her knees, his hand on her back and his voice saying, 'There now. You'll be all right in a minute. My WPC's making you a cup of tea. Come over all faint, didn't you?'

'I thought you was after my pension. Leave me be and I'll be all right.'

He let her sit up. 'And I thought you weren't scared of anything now that your old man's safely locked away, and you've got your grandson with you. Where is he?'

'Out with his cab, I should think. Ouf. Thanks.' She smiled at him, remembering to make her chin wobble and therefore her voice. 'What can I do for you, Mr Smith?'

'It's Gary again.'

'Oh, my God. What's he done now?'

'You know how he's always telling his mates in the pub that he'll give Jeannie Nest a right seeing-to?'

'That's just his talk. He's always been all mouth and no trousers.' She bit her lip as she thought of the bloody trousers in their hiding place. Was it time to use them yet? No. Not until she knew more. 'You know that. Has something happened to her, then?'

'You know it has. Don't you remember when my boys came to talk to you and Mikey and after that you went along to see your Gary?'

Lil couldn't bear it. Not now. Not tonight when she was so tired. She didn't want to have to think and plan and work out what he knew and what he wanted and how to protect herself and her business and her grandson.

'When did it happen?'

'Why d'you ask that, Lil? Why when? Why not, what's happened? Or how bad is it?'

'All right, then. How bad is it?'

'She's dead.'

'Jeannie? Oh my God. Why? Why now? It's been years since . . . '

'That's what we want to know.'

'Well, I can't help you, Mr Smith. I would if I could, you know that.' She grabbed his arm, clinging. 'I liked her. And I owe her. She had my old man put away and I got a chance to stop living in fear all the time.'

'OK, Lil. Steady on.'

'But why hasn't it been in the papers, Mr Smith? I've been looking every day, in case I could see why you were all so keen to talk to my Gary.'

'There was a para or two with a report of a woman found dead in a flat in Hoxton, but there weren't any details as far as I know.'

355

So that was Jeannie, she thought. But why Tuesday night? Why not Sunday? What had Gary been doing on Tuesday?

'Now, Lil, come on and tell me what your Gary was doing up here last Sunday night.' His voice was quite kind, but it changed when he snapped out: 'Not now.'

Lil couldn't think what he meant, barking at her like an angry dog, then she saw his uniformed girl with a tea tray in her hands. 'What's she doing in my kitchen?'

'Making tea, like I said.'

Careful, Lil, she told herself. Or they'll start searching. And there's the books and the money as well as the trousers. 'Then get her back. I could do with a cup. Just what I need after that dizzy spell.'

He called for the girl. She came back all right, but her tea was washy, so it didn't give Lil back any of her strength. She lit a fag instead.

'OK. Now tell me: what was Gary doing here on Sunday night?'

'It wasn't Sunday you wanted to know about last time, was it?' she said, making herself feel vague.

'He was seen, Lil. Coming out of your flat at four in the morning last Sunday — or Monday it would've been by then — muttering to himself. Looking dangerous, they say.'

'Some people can't keep themselves to themselves, can they? What d'you think he was doing? He came for money.'

'D'you give him any?'

'Yes. Everything I had left of my pension, and the last bit of my last lot of holiday money I never changed back into pounds.' They might have found the pesetas when they searched his place, so it was just as well to have a story to account for them. 'Mikey wasn't here, so I had to give him money. I didn't dare not, Mr Smith. Gal's a big lad — you know it as well as I do.'

'That why you keep Mikey living here, is it, Lil? Like a bodyguard, kind of?'

'Mikey makes me feel safer when Gal's drunk.' She wasn't going to let them get away with putting that word 'bodyguard' into her mouth like that. Concentrating on everything Smith was saying behind his words was making her feel dizzy again. Or maybe that was the fag. She stubbed it out and drank some more washy tea. It was still filthy. 'How did Jeannie die? And when? Was it that Sunday?'

'Was Gary drunk that night?'

'He seemed like it. Talking ever so wild, he was. Tell me what happened to Jeannie.'

'I don't have any details. What was Gary saying that night?'

'I can't remember as such. But he wanted tea, and I was afraid he was going to throw the kettle at me. I've still got the scars on my chest from when his dad did that, and I couldn't think of anything else. I had to make the tea, but I put lots of milk in his mug and I threw away the rest of the boiling water so he couldn't do me a mischief.'

'That's tough, Lil.' Smith looked as if he meant it. 'But I want you to try to remember what he said.'

'It was just 'gi's some money, Ma.' I think. And then, you know, all that 'hurry up or I'll do you' kind of thing. What does he say about it?'

'Nothing. We can't find him.'

She kept her eyes down, afraid of letting him see her relief. Could it be that her stupid, brutish son had finally done something useful? Had they scared him enough when they questioned him to make him do what he was told and go to Spain?

'He didn't say nothing about going away when Mikey and I went round to his place. And I'd have thought there were enough of your boys hanging around to see everything he did after that.'

He grinned at her. 'They were only there for that one day.'

'Why? Did they discover evidence to show

he couldn't have killed Jeannie?'

'You'd like that, would you?'

'Of course I would. He's my son.'

'You're a good old thing. Mikey about?'

'No. I told you. He's prob'ly cabbing. It's his shift in the evening.'

'OK. Thanks, Lil. If you remember anything more, let me know, won't you? Constable! We're off.'

The girl came out of the kitchen, looking smug. Lil wondered what she'd found.

'You've got mice, you know, Mrs Handsome. You should get the council round. It's not healthy having them in your kitchen like that. And you shouldn't leave cake out; that's what brings them. You get your grandson to buy you a tin for that cake.'

So she hadn't found the false cupboard back, the cheeky cow. Good. Lil wanted them gone, so she could check whether Mikey'd been at it while she was away with her solicitor.

17

'Paddy enjoyed living on the edge — and making other people join him there.'

Trish looked at Sylvia Bantell's still-handsome face and wondered quite what sort of edge she meant.

'But he'd never have hurt anyone. Not seriously, I mean.' Sylvia tucked her perfectly smooth silver hair behind her ear. The gesture revealed a large drop pearl earring, hanging from a discreet diamond stud. 'What on earth has brought on all this panic, Trish?'

'I'm not panicking.' That wasn't a word or a state of mind Trish allowed herself, but an insidious idea was crawling into her mind like some particularly revolting reptile: what if Paddy had met up again with Jeannie Nest after the conference two months ago, tried to persuade her on to whatever edge Sylvia had meant, and then been frustrated when Jeannie refused? Trish knew all about his temper, but could it ever have been bad enough to push him into the kind of violence that ended with a dead body?

'Panic is the only thing that could possibly excuse such an aberration. He's your father, for heaven's sake.'

'Oh, God, I know.'

'Come on, Trish! This is idiotic. Are you sure you're not making up the whole story as an excuse to come and see what kind of old bat Paddy once knew?'

Amusement surfaced through Trish's angst for a second, like a spring breaking through rock. 'No, although it's great to get such obvious confirmation of his good taste.'

'So you've inherited his blarney, have you?'

And his propensity for violence? Trish asked herself as the spring dried up abruptly. Aloud, she said, 'I meant it. But what I really came for was the report you said you'd kept on Paddy's visits to Jeannie Nest in Southwark.'

'Now why would you want that?' Sylvia asked, leaning against the softly padded back of the pale-yellow sofa and crossing her legs. Her pleated Prada skirt lifted over her knee cap as she moved, catching briefly on the clinging Lycra tights. A waft of cloying tuberose scent teased Trish's nostrils. She'd always disliked that particular smell. 'It was compiled nine years ago. Nothing in it could give you any clues to his activities now.'

Trish had had trouble imagining her father in search of romance at the Mull Estate in Southwark, but she couldn't see him here either. Her own perfectly tidy jeans and linen jacket made her feel clumsy and out of place amid the silk lampshades, and the cool blue-and-yellow femininity of the room. Everywhere she looked there was a highly polished antique table covered with gleaming silver bits and pieces and little porcelain boxes or plants in highly decorated, gilded cache-pots.

Lakeshaw had given her a brutal description of the state of Jeannie Nest's body. Surely no one capable of that kind of frenzy could hide all signs of it for so long. How could a man capable of beating a dead woman like that ever have fitted into a room like this? Or made love with a woman like Sylvia Bantell? Or been the occasionally exasperating but often funny and sometimes lovable father Trish knew?

'I'd never been anybody's rough trade before,' Paddy had said. Had it been his fake brogue, his hairy wrists and hints of physical aggression that had excited Mrs Bantell? Was her rich, breakable, Kensington lifestyle so boring that she'd had to import some danger? Had Paddy ever threatened *her*?

'It might help, even after so long.' Trish heard her voice hoarsen as her throat tensed. 'And I can't think of anything else that could. I'm . . . desperate, you know.'

362

'I can't see how my detective's report could possibly soothe your fears.'

'It might give a reason for what happened between him and Jeannie Nest, and so make it clear that their relationship could not have ended with his killing her.'

Distaste blew across Sylvia's face like litter across a velvety lawn. 'My dear girl, I've already given you the reason. He went to her for the kind of sleazy paid sex that would allow him to indulge himself without having to bother about the other person's feelings.'

'But she was a teacher,' Trish protested. 'Not a prostitute.'

'So the story went. But you know how badly paid teachers are.'

'Are you suggesting she supplemented her income generally? I mean, did the report mention other men?' That would help, Trish thought, and bring in lots more possible suspects.

'Leave it, Trish. It's old history. It's also rather unpleasant to think of Paddy's beloved daughter picking through his sex life like this.'

'You said you'd kept the report.' Trish was determined to drive through the distaste to whatever facts there were. 'That doesn't sound like such very old history.'

A faint blush warmed the lifted skin over

Sylvia's perfect cheekbones. 'If you must know, I shredded it after your first telephone call.'

'Oh shit,' Trish said. Seeing the distaste ruffling Sylvia's calm again, she apologised, but her mind was spinning.

Could the report, perhaps re-read for the first time in years after she'd phoned, have contained something dangerous to Paddy after all? Or had it served its purpose as punishment, if not of Paddy himself then of someone who cared about him? Or maybe the report made no suggestion that Jeannie was a prostitute and did not show him in such a bad light after all. Maybe Sylvia had destroyed it as a way of preserving her picture of his supposed failings.

And maybe, Trish told herself with savage sarcasm, all really is for the best in the best of all possible worlds.

'Now, given that there's really nothing I can do to help . . . ' Sylvia let her voice drift into silence as she glanced down at the delicate watch that hung loosely around her fragile wrist.

Trish obeyed the signals and got to her feet. 'Thank you for seeing me.'

★ ★ ★

364

So that was the perfect Trish, Sylvia thought as she carried the coffee tray back to the kitchen. Not much like Paddy — except in the scruffiness. She could have been quite a pretty girl if she'd let her hair grow and dressed in something more becoming. Although that nose might have looked even more ferocious in a more feminine setting. What was her mother thinking of, to let her grow up without having it corrected?

Running hot water into the delicate Worcester cups, Sylvia wondered if the Paddy Maguire she had known could really have whacked a woman to death. It didn't seem very likely. On the other hand, he had always had a shocking temper. And if the wretched Jeannie had had a child — perhaps put the Child Support Agency on to him after all these years — it wasn't impossible that her whining might have triggered a thrashing. And if that had got out of hand . . . Perhaps one ought to talk to the police, just in case.

★ ★ ★

Outside Sylvia's house, Trish stood on the top step of the pillared portico, breathing in warm air. After the pot-pourri and tuberose scent, the dust and petrol fumes came as a relief. Trish walked down the three broad steps and out on the pavement.

Once she felt herself right off Sylvia's territory, Trish phoned Lakeshaw and had to leave a message, as usual. A sudden gust of wind blew dust into her face and she turned her back, while still talking into her phone. Through her sore, bleary eyes, she thought she saw a face staring at her and blinked to clear her vision. By the time she'd got rid of the grit, everyone around her looked quite uninterested, but she was sure there had been someone watching her. Searching for the familiar slight, blond young man, all she could see were strangers. Could one of them be working for Lakeshaw, hoping to catch her giving away something that would incriminate her father? Or was it Jeannie Nest's killer, tracking her to find out what she knew?

Trish felt as she sometimes did in nightmares, with her brain screaming at her to run and her limbs refusing to obey the order. Breathe, she told herself. Breathe and move.

It worked. Still feeling unsafe but once more with some control over herself, she walked on towards Hornton Street. She'd left her car in the car park there, but she thought she'd take an extra half hour to drop into the nursing home to see David. As she caught sight of Waterstone's on the opposite side of the road, she remembered her promise to buy him the latest Harry Potter. She waited at the crossing for the lights to change.

There was a man walking down Allen Street, pausing to look in the bookshop's window. His backview looked extraordinarily like Nick Gurles's. He had the same confident, almost swaggering, walk, and the same beautifully cut suit.

It couldn't possibly be Nick, Trish thought. Not on a weekday morning. Unless Henry Buxford had already sacked him. But in that case, Antony would have told her; let her off the hook.

Tomorrow was the deadline he'd set for her to give him her decision about her whole future in chambers. In the old days, if she'd been faced with a dilemma like this, she'd have been flogging her mind up and down and all round every important question, but for some time now she'd had enough confidence in herself to wait for the right answer to emerge from her subconscious. So far, this time, nothing had happened. But she was still hoping.

The lights changed and she crossed the road. The man who looked like Nick had disappeared, so she walked on into Waterstone's. There was a tall pile of copies of the new Harry Potter near the till. She grabbed one and flipped her credit card on to the glossy jacket as she joined the queue to pay.

Holding the book against herself like a breastplate, she went to see David. But when she gave her name to the nursing home's receptionist over the intercom, she was told that he'd been moved yet again.

'Oh, sod it. And sod Lakeshaw, too,' she said aloud. The intercom crackled as though the receptionist had only just stifled some kind of protest. Trish couldn't be certain that she'd been told the truth, but it was obvious that she wasn't going to get through the door.

She retreated to the pavement, wishing she had something urgent to do. Antony had said he didn't want her in chambers until tomorrow and she couldn't do anything for David if he kept being whisked away from her. Caro had made it clear she didn't want any contact until Jeannie Nest's killer had been arrested, Lakeshaw wouldn't answer calls, and Paddy didn't want her either. George would be hard at work catching up with the backlog that had accumulated while he was in the States, and the last thing she wanted to do was dump yet more of her angst on him.

Anna Grayling had left another message on her mobile yesterday, suggesting lunch, but Trish didn't feel strong enough for that yet.

She wanted to do something useful, and the only thing left was to follow up David's information about his mother's friends from the teacher-training college. Trish wasn't sure what they'd be able to tell her, but something useful might come of it. She picked about in her memory until it produced one of the names David had given her, then set about finding out where in North London there were teacher-training colleges. It didn't take long to find the one that employed Frances Mason.

The switchboard operator asked if she'd like to be put through, but Trish didn't want to be rejected before she'd even started to ask questions, so she said she merely had a letter to send and needed the full address and postcode. Equipped with those, she went to collect her car from the gloomy concrete car park under the public library.

She had her usual moment of doubt about the level on which she'd left the car, but found it without too much difficulty and bleeped up the locks from twenty yards away. Nothing happened, no electronic squeak and no flash from the indicators. She pressed the button again, checking that the tiny red light flashed. So the battery was working. Her hand was already on the door when she saw the mess on the back seat.

Some bastard had broken in through the back quarter light and found the briefcase that had been well hidden in the shadows under the seat. Now it was lying open, with all the papers strewn around it.

'Oh, fucking hell!' Trish's voice boomed and echoed from pillar to pillar.

Luckily there was no one around to respond. When she'd got her temper under control, she pulled the driver's seat forward and bent to collect all the papers between her hands. It took nearly ten minutes to sort them out on the car's soft roof, and clip the various bits and pieces together. As far as she could remember, everything was still here, and none of it was particularly confidential. There'd been no money in the briefcase or credit cards. But there had been her own private photocopy of Nick Gurles's treacherous note.

With her head buzzing and her insides lurching as though she was on some appalling fairground ride, she scrabbled through the piles of paper, searching for the copy. One bundle slipped off the edge of the roof and landed in a patch of oil.

'Oh, shit,' she muttered. She could feel her mind revving up even more, and her heart was bouncing.

She bent to pick up the papers, cleaned the tacky oil off them as well as she could with an old tissue from her pocket, then put them back with the rest of their heap and stacked each neat pile back in the briefcase. As she reached the last, a clutch of bills she had yet to pay, she saw a greyish corner of photocopy paper peeking out.

'Oh, thank God,' she breathed, parting the bills to see Nick's note. She leaned against the car, trying not to feel sick with relief.

I must have been mad, she thought. What on earth would Antony have said if I'd let it get out like this?

She ripped the copy into tiny pieces, determined to feed them down the nearest drain.

Her head felt thick and soupy, as though she might be about to get a cold. Or worse. She could almost see the black birds flapping in the sleet. Refusing to give in to them, she finished tidying the papers, snapped them back into the briefcase, and drove out of the car park, taking extra care not to brush any of the inconveniently sited concrete pillars. She'd once been in such a bad temper that she'd reversed smartly into one, denting the boot of her first decent car. Never again.

It took her nearly forty minutes to drive to Frankie Mason's college, but twenty of those were spent stuck in the almost stationary traffic along Kensington High Street. After that, once she'd left the streets she knew well, she had to stop twice to check her route on the map.

There was no one in the hall of the big redbrick building when she reached it, and no one to ask her business as she walked past the empty reception desk. The first person she saw was a woman in her twenties, dressed in jeans and T-shirt, coming down the wide staircase. She smiled at Trish as they passed in the hall, their shoes clattering on the old encaustic tiles.

'Hi,' Trish said before she lost the opportunity.

'Hi?' said the younger woman, coming to a halt.

'My name's Trish Maguire. I'm looking for Frankie Mason. Is she in today, or is she still recovering . . . ?'

'Isn't it ghastly?'

'Awful,' Trish said, glad of the opening. She might not have to betray her ignorance of the name under which Jeannie Nest had been living. 'And they're no nearer finding who did it, I gather.'

'No. The police have been round here, asking millions of questions, but we were all gobsmacked. I mean, everyone admired her. Loved her, too. She's . . . ' The woman's eyes were filling, rather as David's had done. 'She was just the best, you know. I wish she'd told us about the stalker and how scared she was. She could have. Anyone would have given her and David a refuge while the police dealt with it.'

'I know,' Trish said soothingly. 'But I really need to talk to Frankie now. D'you know where I could find her?'

'In her office, I think. It's the first door on the right as you get to the top of the stairs. But I don't know whether she's . . . '

'Thanks,' Trish said, already halfway up the first flight.

She knocked on the door at the top of the stairs, and a weary voice invited her to come in. Pushing open the plain door, made even heavier than the Shelleys' by the fire-protecting spring closure, Trish saw a small woman dressed in long, droopy plum-coloured cotton with an acid-pink Indian shawl around her shoulders. She had untidy dark-red hair, almost covering long gilded earings, and a face that had been a battleground between warmth and cynicism for a long, long time.

'Yes?'

'Frankie Mason?'

'Yes.' Suspicion was tightening every muscle in her face, making her look like a shrivelled old cat. 'Who are you?'

'Thank heavens I've found you,' Trish said, surprised to hear her voice shaking. 'My name's Trish Maguire.'

Frankie's amber-coloured eyes widened just enough to tell Trish a lot of what she needed to know. She hurried on.

'I'm so sorry to bother you, but you're my only hope now. I need to know more about David. And *why* she sent him to me. No one else can — or will — tell me anything. I know you were her friend. Please help.'

'Do the police know you're here?'

'No. It's private enterprise.'

'So how did you find me?'

'David told me your name. I worked out the rest. It wasn't that difficult.'

Frankie got up. Trish saw she was lame, pivoting on her left leg while she swung the whole of her right hip, as though she had to kick the whole world along with every step. Was this why Jeannie hadn't thought her capable of looking after David?

'I tried to get her to talk to you herself years ago,' Frankie said, pulling herself along the long window sill so that she could remove a pile of books from the only spare chair. 'Have a seat. I told her it was mad not to get in touch with you. But she said she couldn't. She said she knew you'd protect David in an emergency, but she didn't want to have anything to do with you herself.'

Frankie looked embarrassedly around her room, as though trying to think of something that might soften the rudeness. 'Would you like a cup of tea?'

Trish nodded and thanked her. Boiling the kettle took a while, but eventually they were both sitting holding thick white mugs, waiting for the tea to cool enough for drinking.

'But I don't understand,' Trish said, having burned her tongue, 'why she was prepared to trust me with David if she felt like that about meeting me herself.'

'All she'd ever say was that she knew your father wouldn't harm *you*, and therefore David would be safe with you. There wasn't anyone else who'd be able to guarantee that.'

'What?' Trish felt the chair sway beneath her. 'Are you telling me she thought my father might have done something to David?'

'That's what she said, and it was hard enough to get even that much out of her. She was far too terrified of him to say any more.'

'She couldn't have been. Not recently. They hadn't had any contact for years; not since before David was born. My father didn't even know David existed.'

Frankie Mason looked at her in pity. Pretend it's a brief, Trish instructed herself as she fought to hold on to reality. There has to be something in all this that makes sense.

'Did she actually tell you in so many words that she was terrified of Paddy Maguire?'

'Of course. As I said, it wasn't at all easy to get it out of her. She was too scared to volunteer anything. But, you see, I knew something was terribly wrong. Her migraines were getting worse and worse, and she was losing more weight every week. It got so that she was scared of her own shadow; any sudden noise would make her sweat. And she couldn't bear strangers. I told her I had to know what the problem was if she was to go on working here. Eventually, she poured out the whole story.'

'Look, how much did she tell you about the trial?'

Frankie had the bunched-up end of her pink scarf pressed against her mouth. Over the bright cloth, her eyes looked blank.

'What trial?' she asked, letting the scarf fall. 'There wasn't ever a trial. Your father wasn't prosecuted. You can get an injunction without that, thank God.'

'This wasn't anything to do with my father. She was the chief prosecution witness in a murder trial just before she moved up here.'

'No, you've got that wrong. She never said anything about that. And she would have told me. I'm sorry.'

In Frankie's patent sincerity, Trish began to see a different story, and one that might make sense. Breathing more easily than she had for days, and therefore feeling less stiff with every moment, she checked it through for gaps and flaws. As far as she could tell, it held up.

In this version, Jeannie Nest would have obeyed all the rules of the witness-protection programme, and kept to herself everything about the Handsomes and the danger they might be to her and her son. But, needing a story to satisfy this woman, who'd seen her fear and wouldn't stop asking questions about it, Jeannie had used Paddy as a decoy. That way, she'd have been able to tell one kind of truth, talk frankly about an assailant and how frightened she'd been, and get back all the warmth and support she must have longed for, without ever risking the real secret.

'Did she say anything to you about what happened this time to make her so much more scared than usual?' Trish asked. 'I mean, she'd never sent David to me before. There had to be something new — different — to make her do it.'

Frankie bit her lip, then bent down to put her mug on the floor beside her chair.

'She only admitted any of it that once. I tried to find out more, but she got almost hysterical and said the questions made her migraines worse. I knew it wasn't the questions doing the damage but her own fear.' Frankie's eyes were full of misery. 'I had to tell her so, but it made her very angry. I explained that the migraines were a psycho-somatic manifestation of her anxiety and until she faced it and worked out a rational way of dealing with it, and one which did not involve the ludicrous risk of teaching David the way to your place weekend after weekend, the migraines would go on getting worse. They were bad enough as it was, with projectile vomiting and days of blinding headaches. Something had to change, but she wouldn't even try.'

'So you quarrelled,' Trish suggested as her mind span off into a whole new story with new lead characters and a new dénouement.

'No. There wasn't an actual falling-out, but she never confided in me again.'

'And yet it was you who found her, wasn't it?'

As a deep shudder ran through Frankie's body and she retched, Trish tried to speak gently. 'Why did you go looking if you were no longer such close friends?'

Frankie found a tissue to wipe her mouth and then her eyes. 'She hadn't appeared in college for three days, and she always rang if she was ill or had a migraine. This time there'd been nothing. I kept trying her phone, and all I got was the answering machine. By Wednesday morning, I was sure something was wrong. The police wouldn't believe me, but I made such a fuss they sent a constable with me to break into the flat on Thursday, and we found . . . ' The scarf was back against Frankie's lips.

'And it was then, was it, that you told them about Jeannie's terror of my father?' Trish's whole world looked different as she awaited confirmation of the source of Lakeshaw's suspicions.

She couldn't believe he'd been so credulous. This woman had had no reason to reject the story she'd been given, but Lakeshaw should have known better. He'd had access to all the facts about Jeannie's real identity and therefore the true reason for her fears. It was monstrous that he'd come after Paddy.

'I think so,' Frankie said, squinting at Trish. 'But I can't remember exactly. I had so many interviews with Sergeant Baker, and . . . '

'Who? Haven't you been seeing DCI Lakeshaw?'

'No. She was only a sergeant, and her name was Baker.'

Trish realised she'd been so hung up on Lakeshaw's pursuit of her father that she'd forgotten there must be several lines of enquiry and probably dozens of officers working on the case. She'd touched only the edge of it.

'But it doesn't matter,' Frankie went on. 'I mean, the police knew all about it all along. She always told Martin Waylant every time she was scared, all about the people who followed her and the silent phone calls and the rest of it.'

Trish drank some tea at last. It was tepid now, and had far too much milk in it for her taste. But she didn't care.

'Was Martin Waylant her boyfriend? David said there was one called Martin.'

'He was the nearest thing she had to that. You see, your father ruined every chance she might have had of a proper adult relationship with a man of her own age. Martin wasn't much more than a boy when it started, and he's a police officer. That made her feel safe for a while, which was good for David.'

'Why? Wasn't she a good mother the rest of the time?'

Frankie looked away, fiddling with the scarf again. 'Mostly. But when the migraines were bad, she could be so snappy that she'd terrify him. And sometimes, I'd see him trying to get through to her, to wake the old fun and affection, and she'd just shut him out. It was fear that made her do it . . . understandable fear, but it damaged him.' Her voice strengthened as she looked directly at Trish's face again. 'That's your father's fault, too.'

'And yet David cries for her in hospital.'

'You must know how that works,' Frankie said, impatience making her spiky again, 'after all your experience. He had no one else, so he had to make his mother into a good person, in his mind at least.'

'What do you know about my experience?' Trish asked.

'She told me all about you, when I was trying to stop her taking David to your flat. She'd kept a scrapbook full of cuttings of your cases, which she showed me then. It was her way of proving to herself, I think, that you weren't like your father. She really admired the work you were doing — and the fact that you lived there in Southwark in amongst all that crime and poverty.'

Trish thought of her huge, art-filled loft and blushed. Then she thought about the scrapbook and wondered how long Jeannie's murderer had spent in the flat and whether he'd found it, too. Had it been he who'd been following her today and broken into her car?

Fear was very odd, she thought, struggling for detachment. It made your mouth taste of metal and your brain feel mushy.

'You will look after David now, won't you?'

381

Frankie said. 'She was so sure she could trust you. I couldn't bear it if . . . '

Trish wasn't going to make any promises she might not be able to keep, even to a stranger she would probably never see again.

'I've taken up enough of your time,' she said, standing up and ignoring the disappointment on the small cat-like face. 'Thank you.'

As she left the building, she rang Paddy on her mobile. He was hiding behind his office voicemail and his home answering machine, but Bella answered her own mobile.

'Hi, it's Trish.'

'Ah. Yes. What can I do for you?' Bella said, as coldly as if she was speaking to a stranger.

'I've been trying to get in touch with Paddy, and I can't find him.'

'Can't you leave him alone? Haven't you caused enough trouble already?'

That hurt. 'Bella, don't. As it happens, it wasn't me who put the police on to him. I've just found out who it was, and now I know why they suspected him. It's all a mistake. That's what I wanted to tell him. It's only coincidence that I was also asking questions about the woman they think he killed.'

'I've never believed in coincidence, and there have been far too many in this case.'

Trish thought about passing on everything

she'd learned today and explaining how the only real coincidence in the whole miserable business was that she had bought a converted warehouse flat so near the grim estate where her father had once had a girlfriend. Sylvia Bantell might be sure Jeannie had been moonlighting as a prostitute, but on this one Trish was inclined to believe her father. Still, until she had filled in the last missing parts of the story — such as who really had murdered Jeannie — there was not much point trying to explain anything.

'D'you know where he is? I mean, they haven't arrested him yet, have they?'

' 'Yet'? What d'you mean, 'yet', Trish? No, they haven't — because he didn't do it. But he's staying out of everyone's way just now. He's had enough.'

'Has he told you about David?'

There was a gasp. Then Bella said, 'Yes, but how did you know? Have the police broken their promise of confidentiality already?'

'What do you mean? Has the DNA test come through?'

'I thought that's why you were phoning,' Bella said, sounding as though she was in the middle of a fog. 'The results came yesterday. David is his. Which is why he's keeping out of the way. He doesn't know how to deal with it himself yet, and the last thing he wants to do is answer questions from anyone else. If the news does leak, he wishes to be well out of reach.'

'What's he going to do about the boy — his son?'

'Trish, be reasonable. What can he do? He's a man in his sixties, not in good health, with a triple bypass. He can't start looking after a strange child just because once, years ago, a woman he was seeing got careless. Even if . . . ' The fog had closed in on her, cutting her off from Trish, who thought, Even if what? Even if he doesn't go to prison for life?

Pretending she hadn't thought it, and Bella had never even hinted at it, Trish asked mildly whether her father was intending David to be brought up in care.

'Presumably,' Bella said. Then her asperity loosened into a plea that sounded as though she was begging for something quite different from the words she used. 'But Trish, it wouldn't be all that different from the life this boy must have lived in both Southwark and Hoxton. And he'll be safe. He won't have this terrible threat hanging over him. He'll be fine. You must harden your buttery heart sometimes.'

'He's not just 'this boy', you know.' Trish thought of David's fingers, white with stress as they clutched her wrist, and of the moment when he'd melted into relief when she first gave him her name. Her father might be able to see that child go into care; she couldn't.

'Maybe not, but Paddy can't be expected to look after him. That woman caused him no end of trouble at the time, and he's been in hell these past two weeks since she died. Hell. Trish, you have no idea how offensive the police have been as they've dug through his past and cross-examined us both about the way he treats women.'

Then they must have something else, Trish thought. Lakeshaw is elusive, rude and unreasonable, but he wouldn't have wasted so much expensive police time on the unsubstantiated word of Frankie Mason. Would he?

'Look, Bella, I thought he had an alibi. Didn't you say over the phone last week that you'd told Lakeshaw he was with you all of Tuesday night?'

'Yes, of course I did. And he was.' There was an energy in Bella's voice now that didn't ring true, and some odd stresses, like a singer who just manages to hit top A but has to strain for it, spoiling the sound, turning it into a scream.

'Then have they changed their minds about the time of death? Or were you . . . ?' Lying seemed too offensive a word. 'Fibbing?'

'No. I thought it was true. Hoped it was.' Bella's voice was taut now and the anguish was all too audible. 'But I'd been sleeping so badly the last few nights before then that I took a pill that night. I probably wouldn't have known if a herd of elephants had charged through the room.'

'You mean, he might have gone out that night?' Trish felt cold down her back again. And this time it was spreading through her entire body.

'Something's convinced Lakeshaw that he did. He keeps coming round badgering Paddy to admit that he got up and left the house in the middle of the night.'

'What evidence has he got?' Trish heard her voice snap like a trap.

'He won't say, but it's clear there's something. I've tried to ask Paddy if he went out just for a few minutes for some innocent reason. But it just makes him furious with me, so I can't go on. I'm sure if he did go out, there's a simple explanation. But he won't give it. You know how stubborn he is, and he's sworn all along that he was in bed with me. I'm so worried, Trish. If there is some evidence that he went out, all this denial makes him look . . . makes it look as though it could have been him who killed that poor woman. I know he couldn't have, but oh,

Trish, *why* won't he say what he was doing?'

Trish slammed her fist backwards into the car door. Her hand hurt so much that she stood back to look at the damage. There was only a faint red mark on the skin, which explained the throbbing, but there was an oval depression, about nine inches long and four high, in the side of the car.

She wished she could concentrate on the dead woman, or David, or even Paddy himself, but all she could think of now was the question thudding through her brain: is he going to take my career away from me just as he took my childhood?

So far she'd managed to avoid saying anything to anyone in chambers about the murder or Lakeshaw's suspicions of her father, but if it came to an arrest she'd have to warn Antony. And there was no way he'd want her as his junior on a big commercial case if her father were charged with murder. The publicity would be unavoidable — and damaging.

'Trish? Are you still there?'

'Sorry, Bella. I've got to go.' As Trish shoved her phone back in her bag, she realised that her subconscious had made the decision on her future, just as she'd hoped.

In a world where nothing was certain, where emotion could drive people to fierce cruelty, women could be beaten up and killed, and children could be abandoned by their own parents, a successful career was the only safety worth having. If she wanted the kind of unassailable security Antony Shelley had, she'd have to do the kind of work he did and in the way he did it.

She phoned his direct line in chambers, willing cool confidence into her voice. When he answered, she told him of her decision and asked to be allowed to go on working with him on Nick Gurles's case.

'Good,' Antony said without any particular emphasis. 'I'm glad. And Henry Buxford will be, too. He was impressed with you. Now, Nick Gurles and Peter Loyle are coming in for a con. tomorrow afternoon. I want you there, and I'd like you to come in at twelve so that we can go through all the evidence first.'

'Of course, I'll be there. Thank you, Antony.'

'See you tomorrow.'

18

Mikey Handsome was having a lie-in. He'd been late last night, partly on purpose to give his grandmother plenty of time to check all her hideyholes for evidence that he hadn't touched her money, and partly because one of the girls' punters tried to get away without paying and had to be sorted out. And after that, Celeste, as she called herself now, needed reassuring. Mikey didn't much like going where all the punters had been before him, but sometimes it was necessary. And there were condoms, after all.

When she'd made him his coffee and they were drinking it together, she said, all coy but breathless, too, 'I thought you'd have had a go at me, Mikey.'

'What?'

'When that old bloke wouldn't pay, I thought you'd say it was my fault and, well, you know . . . '

'Beat you black and blue with a coathanger?' he suggested and heard from her frightened giggle that was exactly what she'd thought.

'Have I ever laid a finger on you or Barbie? Have I?'

She shook her head, looking even more scared. So she should. He was angry now. Now it mattered more than ever that everyone should know — and admit — that he wasn't like the rest of the family, that *he*, like his grandmother, had too many brains to indulge in stupid violence.

'Come on, Celeste. Have I ever fucking-well threatened to lay a finger on either of you, let alone actually done it?'

'No, Mikey,' she whispered. 'Don't. Please.'

'OK. So don't fucking-well accuse me of it, right?'

'No, Mikey.'

'Makes me angry, that kind of thing.' He shot his cuffs and settled his shoulders. 'I don't expect aggro from you when I come here, Celeste. I want peace and quiet. And I don't like it. So don't do it again.'

'No, Mikey.' She looked like she was about to cry and she was pushing herself back against the wall, tightening her silly, feathery robe round her. He'd never liked it, but she said the punters did.

'And get that thing washed. It's filthy. Beginning to smell, too. Remember what I told you?'

'Keep clean, keep honest, and don't tell no

lies. I ain't forgotten, Mikey. I've never told you no lies. I promise.'

'Great. Where's the takings then?'

She scrambled off the bed, letting him see too much doughy, dimpled thigh. She ought to lose weight as well as get cleaned up, but he couldn't be bothered with the hassle of making her do it. If she started losing customers, which she soon would, he could let her go and find a replacement. But if everything went as well as it should and his nan gave him his due, he might not have to go on with all this for much longer.

It was no wonder he'd needed a lie-in with all that aggro. Now, sitting up in bed, wondering whether to get himself some breakfast here, or go out and have it cooked for him in the café, he tried to assess how much longer he'd have to wait for the business. His grandmother must know by now that he wasn't going to beat her up. He knew she'd been afraid of that at the beginning, and for a long while after he'd come back, but he'd done everything he could to reassure her, and it had worked — until this last mess over his stupid uncle.

He didn't mind that his nan had been scared at first; it showed how sensible she was. But she must know it was safe to trust him by now. And she must know he'd sussed all her hiding places long ago. After all, *he* wasn't stupid, and the flat was no bigger than a dog's bowl, not like Trish Maguire's.

He'd monitored the hiding places ever since he'd first found them, knowing exactly when she'd taken money out, how much she gave his uncle (the stupid waster), how much she took for herself, and how big a float she liked to have in the flat. What he didn't know was what she did with the cash when she did take it, but that was OK. He could've found out if he'd wanted to. She'd worked hard for it; and it was hers. Or it had been. Now it was time for him to take control before his grandfather got out and wrecked his life again — or forced her into handing everything over to his uncle.

The bloody trousers were lying where she'd first put them. He still wasn't sure why she'd kept them in the first place, but he assumed it was for insurance. That's what he'd have done and usually they thought about things in the same way. He'd always liked that.

Lying back in his clean bed, Mikey thought about how he would run things when she'd retired. He'd take custom back from the catalogues and expand the operation into something worth having, and he'd start funding some of the drug addicts. He wouldn't deal with all of them. She was right that most were too unreliable. But there were some who'd pay up. He'd go for them, a little at a time, as an experiment.

And he'd move off the estate as soon as he could afford it. He'd decided that long ago, but it had taken a while before he'd worked out what kind of place he wanted. Now he knew. He wanted a loft like Trish Maguire's, and a gym of his own.

Soon he'd have other people running round doing all the work, and he'd pull the strings and make the decisions and give the advice. And his nan? Well, she'd be tucked up somewhere, safe and warm, and with plenty of Battenburg cakes to keep her happy. Mikey would see to that. He'd see her right in every way. Give her her cut whenever it was due, just like he collected her pension for her now. He wasn't going to rip her off.

'Mikey? You in there?'

'Yes, Nan. D'you need something?' He got off the bed and pulled on his sweats.

'I've got the kettle on. D'you want some breakfast?'

'No, thanks. I'm going to go to the gym. I'll have something after. Shall I bring you anything when I come back?'

'I need more fags,' she said, which was a first. She knew what he felt about them. Was this another test? He put on his trainers and went out to see.

He ran the long way round to the gym so that he could pass Trish Maguire's building. It took him seven minutes longer, but it was worth it to monitor her comings and goings. And he liked being at the point where the borough started to get rich. You stepped from one world into the next just crossing a single road. It showed him how easy it was going to be for him to get away from all the failures on the estate and have the life he should've had all along.

All Trish Maguire's windows were shut today, which told him she'd already gone out. She wasn't usually off so early. He wondered what was happening and where her fat boyfriend was.

★　★　★

Antony had drilled Trish backwards and forwards through the evidence, finding connections she'd never even guessed at. Almost able to forget about her father and Jeannie Nest, she'd been exhilarated by the process and full of more admiration for Antony than she'd have confessed to anyone. As he'd asked her questions, she'd watched him untwist the ropes of fact and straighten every strand, before whipping them together again in unrecognisable forms.

At the end, he put his hands behind his back and stretched so that the tendons in his neck cracked.

'Good. Well, I think we're ready for Nick now.' He looked at his shabby old watch. 'Where are they?'

'In the waiting room, I imagine,' Trish said, laughing as she got to her feet. She felt released from some of the last weeks' angst. This was her world. She was OK here.

Nick came in with such a broad smile she felt as though he'd flung his arms around her.

'Trish! I'm so glad you haven't abandoned me.'

'Of course not. You look well.'

'Thank you. I wish I could return the compliment, but I have to say you look exhausted. I hope it's not because you've been toiling over my wretched case.'

'You should be glad she has, Nick,' said Antony. 'She's done a very good job. Sit down, Trish, and let's get going.'

She exchanged tightly polite smiles with the Sprindlers partner, whose trainee had sent her the treacherous note. He didn't look half as pleased to see her as Nick was.

'Now, Nick, we need to run through one or two things, so that I have everything clear in my mind,' Antony said. 'Just tell me in your own words how you came to design the MegaPerformance Bond Fund.'

As he obeyed, explaining every stage of his plans, Nick kept up the boyish enthusiasm with which he'd greeted them. It was quite unlike the smoothness he'd originally shown Trish, and she liked it better.

'Right,' Antony said as Nick finished describing the drafting of the documents for the fund. 'Is anyone putting pressure on you by this stage?'

'Good lord! Of course they are. It's been made abundantly clear that if I don't come up with something pronto, I'll be out on my ear.'

'And does that distress you?'

'Absolutely terrifies me.'

'Even though, when you do decide to leave, you pick up a good job back in the City at a greatly enhanced salary?'

'Even so. You've no idea what the atmosphere at the DOB is like. Was like. It may have changed. Margins were so tight, and the shareholders so angry, and the board so desperate, that they spent the whole time sniping. Panic turns people into bullies, you know.'

Antony nodded. He didn't even glance at Trish, but she could feel his awareness of her and his determination that she should understand the message he wanted her to take from Gurles's account.

'Was the MegaPerformance Bond Fund the first product you'd taken to them after the launch of the Big-Day Booster Account was so successful?'

'Lord no! I'd been battering my head against the brick wall of their negativity for months. They nagged me to produce stuff, then wouldn't let me do anything with it. Every idea I came up with — and some of them were damn good — was turned down. Sometimes I thought they might be using me as a weapon against the shareholders — you know, to prove they were trying. After a while I was sure they were planning to offer my head at the AGM.'

Trish kept her face blank, but she was intrigued by the story Antony was drawing out of their client. She wondered whether someone had briefed Nick to rearrange it, or whether he'd refrained from telling it this way in the first place because he hadn't wanted to look like a wimp in front of a woman. She could see how the facts and documents she'd so carefully amassed might support it, but it wasn't quite what he'd told her earlier in the year. On the other hand, it was something they could use more easily.

Clever old George, she thought with a private smile.

'Right,' Antony said sharply, bringing her back into focus. She nodded to him to prove that she was awake. 'But then suddenly they did want you to put one of your ideas into practice. Is that what happened?'

'Yes. They remembered the MegaPerformance Bond Fund and asked for all the papers again. I provided them. They suddenly got all over-excited and said they must have it up and running within a month. It was the most incredible scramble to get everything done and all the documents drafted, but we worked twenty-hour days and just made it.'

'Right. I see. And did you yourself have any doubts about it?'

'Well, of course I did. Who wouldn't? I mean, all investments carry risk. I didn't have any idea it would go belly up so fast or so spectacularly. I'd never have presented it to the board in the first place, if I had.'

'And did you express your reservations?'

'Absolutely. But face to face. I never wrote to anyone about them, so there's no documentary evidence. Unfortunately.'

'Yes. Now we come to this memo here.' Antony pointed to the note that had caused Trish such problems. 'The one that includes a paragraph about 'the other matter'. Can you

398

tell me why you didn't email it? I think all your other communications with your head of department were emails. Why wasn't this?'

'I can't imagine.' Gurles uncrossed his legs and leaned forwards. 'But there must have been a reason at the time. Occasionally we had server problems. It could've been that the screens were down that day, and I didn't want to wait. But it's not relevant to this, you know. It had nothing to do with the MegaPerformance Bond. It was about a savings account we were thinking of setting up for students, which never went anywhere.'

'Right. Well, the state of the server shouldn't be impossible to check,' Antony said. Trish looked at Gurles, but couldn't see any anxiety. Maybe it was even true that the server had been down. She still wasn't convinced of the genuine otherness of 'the other matter', but she'd just heard Gurles claim it, unprompted, and so she could — just — keep her doubts to herself.

'Good. Then I think that's all I need.' Antony's eyes twinkled. He looked like everybody's favourite uncle. Trish didn't believe in the expression for a moment, and she knew exactly what he'd been doing. When he turned to her, the twinkle was doused. 'Trish, is there anything else you'd like to ask Nick while he's here?'

'Yes, one or two things.'

'Fire away,' Nick said, swivelling in his chair so that he was facing her. He looked strong and serious, but affectionate with it. More and more she got the feeling he'd been coached. But she had enough faith to know it wouldn't have been Antony who'd done it.

'You've read the depositors' statements about the losses they incurred on the fund?'

'Yes. A lot of very sad stories, aren't they?'

'In the light of those, can you still say that the marketing of the fund and the terms and conditions were clear enough to protect the naïve investor?' Her tone was deliberately provocative and it duly provoked him.

'Come on, Trish. This bond was paying five per cent over the odds. Everyone knows you get increased risk with increased rewards. If they were greedy enough to want so much more than they'd have got in any of the DOB's entirely safe accounts, or in gilts, then they deserved to lose it.'

Trish sat back in her chair and looked at Antony, all her body language saying, 'I rest my case,' like an American attorney.

'As I've explained before,' Gurles went on, decoding the gestures without too much difficulty, 'no bank is in business to protect investors. It's in business to make money for its shareholders, not its depositors.'

'Fine,' Antony said. 'Now that we've got all that emotion out of the way, we must press on with the facts of the case.'

Trish wanted to get up and walk out, but she'd committed herself now. Nothing Gurles had actually said surprised her; it was the venom with which he'd talked about his investors' greed that had given her the shock.

Later, when he and the Sprindlers partner had gone, Antony said quietly, 'So, Trish: better or worse?'

'Both.'

'And you wish we were for the depositors?'

'Of course. But then I've always preferred being for victims.'

'Nick Gurles is one of those.'

'Only just.'

'But enough for you to do your best?'

'I'd do that anyway, as you very well know. But yes, I think he is. Just.'

'And you're sanguine about the document?'

'I have to be. Nick claimed that 'the other matter' had nothing to do with the bond fund, so I have to accept it.' She hesitated, then said, 'Do you ever feel, Antony, as though you're counting — '

'Angels on a pinhead? Of course. That's part of the job. And one of the most entertaining parts. But you know that, Trish.

You're bloody good at it yourself. One of the tough guys in spite of your white face and your scruples. Ouf, it's been a long day. What about a drink? I don't have to be home for another forty minutes.'

'I'd love to, but I have to get back. I've got this business of the boy from the car crash to sort out still.' And I've got to find out whether my father's been arrested for murder yet. She opened her mouth to tell Antony about it, then shut it fast. It couldn't happen. Paddy *had* to be innocent. Therefore there couldn't be any evidence against him. Therefore the police would never arrest him.

'Is the boy giving you problems?'

'Nothing I can't handle. It's all just a bit emotional.'

'Ah. Well, I'm sure you'll sort it out. You're good at emotion,' he said, talking so fast he was almost gabbling. He couldn't have made his intentions clearer if he'd written them out on a hoarding: *Do not try to embroil me in your personal life.*

He was right, too. It wasn't his problem. But it might be George's. And it was time now to talk about it. Walking home towards the bridge, Trish hardly noticed her favourite view of the piled, pinkish-white buildings, topped by the great grey dome of St Paul's, or the fact that a strip of sunlight was lying

402

along the Thames like a gold sword. She was sure now that she would have to take David to live with her, whatever happened to Paddy.

As Frankie Mason had pointed out, David's mother had trusted Trish to look after him. And she was his half-sister. But there would inevitably be problems, and she wasn't at all sure that George would welcome them. If it came to a choice between the two, what would she do?

It couldn't come to a choice. There wasn't one to be made. She couldn't abandon her brother to the care system, and she couldn't face life without George. Treacherous thoughts sneaked into her mind about how much easier solitude was than dealing with other people. But she was long past that stage. George had taken her into a world where being open to someone else was not only possible but essential. She couldn't go back.

There were windows open in the flat, which meant he'd let himself in and was probably cooking something nutritious in the hope of tempting her to eat again. She realised she was hungry for the first time in weeks.

The door opened while she was still four steps from the top and he stood there, holding out his arms, with the glorious scent of his own version of bouillabaisse floating all round him.

'Hello, Shorty,' he said, kissing the top of her head. She tipped it back on her neck, feeling the tendons crunch, to kiss him properly. Then her lips stiffened.

'What, Trish?' George sounded as though his patience was held on a short leash. 'What is it now?'

'I've just thought of something. I must make a phone call.'

'No! Unless someone's in danger of life and limb, Trish, you must have your soup first.'

'I'm fine, George. I had lunch — a sandwich. I'm fine.'

'Well, I'm not. I've spent the past two hours making this soup and I'm not having it thrown in my face. *Is* anyone in danger of life and limb?'

There was enough reality mixed with his mocking voice to make her stop. She smiled, and completed the kiss before putting her arm round his waist and sweeping him into the flat.

'Sorry. I got carried away. The soup smells wonderful. Let's have it, while I tell you what I've just realised.'

He grinned and tapped her cheek with one saffron-coloured finger. 'OK. Pour the wine.

I'll just fry the croutons and then we're there.'

The soup poured from his ladle into warm white bowls like rosy cream with chunks of white fish in it. He sprinkled cheese on top, then spread even more vibrantly coloured *rouille* on to his newly fried rounds of mini-baguette, before floating them like votive coracles across the surface of the soup.

Trish picked up her spoon and tasted it. Like almost everything George cooked, it was ambrosial. She gave it, and him, the compliment of silent eating until she was halfway down the bowl. Then she drank some of the sharp, cold wine, sat back, and said, 'You've been very patient with all this hassle about my father. Not asking qustions and all that.'

A sardonic smile twisted his face. 'You were in that mood where questions only make you miserable — or angry. I didn't fancy dealing with either and I knew you'd tell me in the end. You always do. More soup before you start?'

She shook her head, admiring the way he managed his feelings so neatly, with so little waste of spirit. She'd learned a lot from him, but she still hadn't got the trick of this. 'No. I'll finish this while I tell you, then we can have hot seconds while you point out where the gaps in the argument are. You always see those far better than I do.'

He blew her a kiss, then picked up his own spoon again.

She told him again about the night David crashed into her life, her gradual realisation of who he must be, and Bella's recent confirmation that he was, indeed, her half-brother. Trish waited there in case George wanted to say anything, but he just nodded and reached a big hand for more croutons, which he spread with great delicacy, handing her one.

The physical softness of the orange emulsion lying between her tongue and palate made the fiery taste even more shocking. But it was the kind of shock she enjoyed. In a way it seemed rather like George himself. Apparently gentle, domesticated, almost as *padded* as his well-covered bones, he packed a real punch. He was full of the kind of acerbic intelligence anyone else would have paraded at every possible opportunity. Not George. It was there for anyone who bothered to find it, but he'd never use it for aggrandisement — or aggression.

He'd never have made it at the Bar, she thought with a hidden spurt of laughter as she considered the mix of self-importance and histrionics so many of her colleagues felt was essential to their calling.

Swallowing the laughter and the crouton, she went on to tell him the story from the other end. She repeated everything she'd heard from Frankie, from David himself, and from Lakeshaw's hints and evasions.

'And it's David's comment about the eyes, you see. He knew they weren't a cat's because they were too high, though if the cat had been sitting on the wall they'd have been too low.'

'So?'

'So, my father once told me that Jeannie Nest was my height or a little taller. David also said that Mrs Tiggywinkle liked to sit on the wall and lick his mother's nose. Now that sounds as though Mrs Tiggywinkle's eyes would have been about on a level with Jeannie Nest's. Which suggests that the person whose eyes scared David so much was shorter than his mother.'

'This is all very speculative, Trish,' he said, as usual not letting her get away with any sloppy thinking. 'You're about to tell me that it couldn't have been your father because he's taller than you and would therefore have had eyes easily as high as the wall. Am I right?'

'Absolutely bang on.'

'I'm far more convinced by your story of Jeannie Nest having to talk about her fear but having to conceal the truth of it and using your father and her history with him as a

407

blind. Have you run that theory by Lakeshaw?'

'I might have, but he won't speak to me. And I didn't think it was fair to use Caro as a messenger. And then again . . . ' she paused and waited for George to fill in the gap.

'Just in case it's not the truth, and your father is arrested, you want to keep this for the defence to use to get him off,' he said.

'Exactly. It would be irresponsible to hand it over now and waste it.'

'You'd do that, Trish, even if you thought he was guilty?'

'I don't know.'

'Of course you would. You'd have to. It's your job to do your best for your clients.'

And yet I got so prissy about the thought of one ambiguous handwritten document that I was prepared to throw everything away, she told herself. Moral standards don't count when you apply them randomly. You have to be consistent. Jeannie was.

Yes, said a rather different voice in her mind, and look where it got her. And her son. What ultimate good did she do at such an appalling cost? Apart from getting one murderous thug put away for life, of course.

'Stop frowning, Trish. There's no need for all this torment. It makes perfect sense to me, and whatever your nightmares tell you, I do not believe your father is a killer.'

She grabbed another crouton, smothered it with rouille and ate it in one bite, wishing as she tried to chew that she, like snakes, could dislocate her jaw to deal with the enormous mouthful. George was laughing at her by the time she got it under control, then leaned across the table to kiss her.

'And now the rest. Have you got a suspect for these eyes that are too near the ground to be your father's?'

'No. But I do wonder if it's the person who's been following me.' She tried to sound scientifically detached, but she knew her voice had quivered.

George's face hardened. 'Trish, for God's sake! Why didn't you tell me?'

'I suppose because I kept trying to persuade myself I was making it up.' She manufactured a smile, hoping to see George relax. 'I did tell Lakeshaw early on, but he wasn't very impressed. And nothing ever happened, you see. It was just a feeling I had that someone was watching me. To have talked about it would have made it seem as though I was giving in to neurotic fantasy. But now I think he could've been real all along.'

'Who is he?'

'I don't know, that's the trouble. To start

with, I thought he was the young man who answered my questions on the Mull Estate when I first went there. I told you about him when you first got back from San Francisco. I've been thinking a lot about how he pretended he knew nothing about anyone called Jeannie Nest. I don't see how anyone could've been living there for four years and not have heard the story. Could they?'

'I shouldn't have thought so.' George's face was changing as his concentration turned inwards, away from her. 'You're not talking about a slight chap with fair hair, by any chance? And very clean clothes and an engaging smile?'

'You've seen him, too, have you?' Trish said as her spine started to prickle.

'Yes, one day when I was coming here to cook. I had bags of food and I was concentrating on getting them out of the car so I didn't look up till I got to the bottom of the steps; then I saw him, up at the top by your front door. I challenged him, and he said he was a cab driver, called out by someone whose name I can't remember. I said he'd got the wrong address and saw him go back to his car and get straight on the radio. It all seemed so plausible that I never thought to tell you about it.'

'I bet it's him. And I bet he is the one who

tried to get past Maria with stories about coming from the freeholder to inspect my dilapidations. George, you do see why I *have* to call Lakeshaw, don't you?'

'Yes. And then we must sort out what we're going to do about David.' The 'we' that sat between them was comforting. 'I can see the temptation of taking him in, Trish. Believe me.'

Now beside the 'we' was an unspoken 'but', digging holes in the reassurance. She waited again.

'He sounds thoroughly engaging, and I know he's your half-brother. But, Trish, think about everything you know from your work. It's hard enough to bring up a child who hasn't been damaged, especially when both parents work as hard as we do.'

'We don't know that David's been damaged.'

'Oh, come on. Of course we do. He's lived in fear almost all his life. He witnessed the killing of a man, and his own mother being beaten up, when he was two. He felt her blood dripping on him and even if he doesn't remember that, he'll remember her fear. He's going to find trust even harder than you do.'

Trish flinched and thought about explaining that it was herself she didn't trust, not George — or David. 'And he may have inherited a tendency to violent temper, if not actual physical violence. You've forgotten to remind me of that family failing, George, along with my inability to believe in other people.'

He looked as if the last of his patience was fast disappearing. She knew he loathed what he called 'drama', which usually meant her expressing strong feelings too vigorously.

'Sorry,' she said abruptly, not wanting to hear the reprimand again. 'I need a pee.'

She fled up the spiral staircase, not sure whether she was saving George from the irritation of her presence or getting out of the way before she yelled at him. In the bathroom she stared at her reflection in the big mirror over the basin. Antony Shelley had once told her not to look so anguished. Now she knew what he'd meant. She looked ill, too.

Was it just delayed after-effects of the miscarriage and anxiety over Paddy, or was she really in danger of cracking up again? As she stared, her reflection shimmered and changed and in the place of the cool, slightly funky woman with the spiky hair was a witch with hollow cheeks and eyes like hot black charcoal and a mean red slash of a mouth.

George's reflection in the mirror behind her made her face return to normal and the feeling of his arms round her and the resilient solidity of his body behind hers, pulling her back into his strength, made her feel as though she might get through this after all.

'It'll be all right, Trish. The right answer will emerge. It always does if you're patient enough.'

'I don't know that it will. Neither you nor I are the same as we were, and my father may be going to prison for murder. Even if he doesn't, he's not going to take on David. George, I cannot let that child be abandoned to the care system.'

'Even though you've fought nearly all your professional life to get children away from hopeless or wicked parents for exactly that?'

She felt as though he'd stabbed her, even though he'd only put into words everything she'd been facing for days. She struggled to be fair.

'I know. Which is why I've said I'll go along with Antony and Sprindlers and give Nick Gurles's case everything I've got. If I can earn enough to give David a truly happy, productive, safe childhood, I'll have done something useful, probably more useful than arguing children into a care system that even when it doesn't actively fail them hardly seems to equip them for successful adulthood.'

'Trish . . . '

'I have to, George. I felt abandoned because of what Paddy did to me and the residue of that has often nearly screwed up you and me. But at least I had my mother. David hasn't anyone now.'

'Calm down, Trish. It doesn't have to be so dramatic.'

'It's pretty dramatic for David.'

'True,' George said, after giving the proposition some thought. 'But what if his early experiences mean that he turns out to be psychotic? Or sociopathic.'

'Then I'd just have to deal with it.'

'And what, Trish, if we do manage to have our own child? Will David be able to bear that? And would we ever feel that ours would be safe with him in the house, too?'

Talk about anguish, Trish thought. She turned to face George. This was too important to be said to his reflection. 'David has lived with this appalling threat and been told all his life that if the worst happened, he must go to Trish Maguire. Well, it has, and Trish Maguire can't fail him. Her father and his might, but she *has* to look after him. George, you must understand.'

'I suppose I'd better have a look at him.'

She said nothing, still not sure what he was going to decide. In that icy moment she knew

414

that she needed him if she were ever to be whole.

'If he's going to be my son — or even my half-brother-in-law — I need to get to know him first.' His arms tightened for a second before he let her go. 'And you'd better phone Lakeshaw to tell him about the height of the man in Jeannie's garden.'

19

Mikey felt his muscles tugging as he jogged back from the gym. It had been a good workout and he felt almost right with himself again. Each time his feet hit the pavement in the new trainers he felt the good bounce they and his own strength gave him. He came round the corner, dodged the wrecked bollard and the big puddle beside it and saw the police van at the bottom of his building, and stopped.

'Mikey! Mikey!'

He forced himself to stop looking at the van and saw Kelly flying towards him over the smashed-up concrete.

'Mikey, they've been beating up your nan.'

'What? Who — the police?'

'No. The men. The ambulance came and took her, and the p'lice are in the flat now.'

'Christ, Kelly. I gotta go. Is she . . . ? Was she . . . ? D'you know how bad it was?'

'She wasn't dead, Mikey. I promise.'

That's something, he thought, sprinting towards the building. All his life everything he'd really wanted had been taken away from him. He couldn't bear it if he was going to lose his nan, too. Not now when everything was working so well. It wasn't fair. He didn't bother to try the lift, but ran upstairs until he saw them outside her flat.

'Hey!' he called. 'What's happened? One of the kids said my nan's been taken to hospital.'

'Is that Mikey?' said a familiar voice.

'Mr Smith,' he said, recognising the police officer. 'Is she OK? What happened?'

'One of your neighbours heard her calling for help and phoned us, which is a pretty good miracle for this place.'

Except that if it was Margery from next door she'd have known she'd never be able to put enough money on her electric key if it wasn't for Nan.

'Thank God. But did you catch them before they — ?'

'No. By the time we got here, they'd gone. But I expect she'll be OK, Mikey. She's a tough old bird. It looked like broken ribs to me, and some bad bruising to her face and maybe back.'

'Her kidney,' he said. 'If they've been kicking her back again she's in trouble. The last time she was pissing blood, the doctor said . . . ' He choked.

Smith put a hand on his shoulder. 'That'll be for the hospital to say. They were taking her to Dowting's. You'll be able to see her there later. But do you know who it could've been, beating her up?'

Mikey was thinking fast. Was this the time to drop his Uncle Gal in it? But how could he get at the trousers without letting the police into the other hiding places? And what would his grandmother do if she decided it had been the wrong time to use them? Could she go back on her almost-promise to give him the business?

'I know she was scared of my uncle,' he said, and saw greedy pleasure make Smith's eyes glisten. 'You know we went round to his place after you were here that time?'

'Yes.'

'Well, I had to put her behind my back because I thought he was going to hit her then. I . . . I shouldn't have ever left her, but I thought she'd be OK. She said she would.'

'As a matter of fact, where've you been this morning?'

'I went to the gym like I always do at seven. They must've known that, whoever it was. I always go. Anyone here could've seen me jogging off. Same time, same route usually, same clothes.'

'That could be it. OK. We'll be off now, but we'll take your grandmother's statement as soon as the doctors give us the all-clear. She may be able to tell us more.'

So, he thought, they've already talked to the neighbours, old Margery probably and some others and knew he hadn't been there. That was good. It would be typical of the filth to suspect the wrong man for something like this.

'We've taken prints, but there's nothing else we can do here. We'll need yours for elimination. You can come down to the station later and give them. But you'll be all right now?'

'Sure.' Mikey wasn't certain if it was rage or worry that was making his head feel so bad. 'I'll get the place cleaned up first for when she can come back. And then I'll have to see if she's OK. You'll talk to my uncle, won't you?'

'Of course.'

'Great.'

Mikey watched them go, then had a shower. The water pressure was weak here, but he never fancied showering in the gym, not with that lot around, watching him. Dry, dressed, and certain that the Old Bill had gone, he cleared out all the hiding places. He took the books and the money, still not sure where he'd be able to put it all safely but certain he had to get it out of the way before they thought of making a real search. Then he fetched her shabby old blue suitcase, laying

419

the business stuff at the bottom, then filling the rest with her nightclothes and brush and washbag. He'd take it to her in hospital, then if he was stopped on the way, he should be able to talk his way out of it. And then, when he was back and clearing up he could 'find' the trousers. And that should settle it all. Or it would so long as he could think up a good enough story about why they were in the flat and why his grandmother hadn't done anything with them before.

Terrified of what Gal would do to her, was the best story. Yes, he'd come, forced her to hide them, then told her if she let anyone know about them he'd come back and kill her. Yes, that could work.

But it might be better to do it now. He could take the case and leave it in the back of his car, go into the nick to give them his prints and show them the trousers, saying he'd found them under his nan's nightclothes when he was packing her stuff for the hospital.

★   ★   ★

Trish was drinking coffee while George ate his bacon and eggs. They'd got to the stage of agreeing that if they were to take on David, they would have to employ a nanny.

420

'There isn't room to keep her here, if David has the spare room,' Trish said, sitting with her elbows on the table and her big coffee cup between her hands. 'So I'd better start looking for something to rent nearby.'

'So you're expecting us to carry on as we always have?' George said. 'With a boy with a blood claim on you living here with you, and me having only visiting rights?'

'George, I thought we'd agreed . . .'

'In principle, but not in detail.' He put down his knife and fork and smiled at her. She couldn't smile back. Already she could feel the walls of a budgie's cage pressing around her.

'Trish, I'm not trying to bully you, or force you to live with me, so you don't have to look like that.'

A smile, rather shaky, seemed possible then and she watched his eyes soften in response.

'I just want to be sure that we've faced all the implications before this is irrevocable.'

'Would it be?' She drank too big a mouthful of coffee and had to fight to swallow it.

'Yes, it would. I know you like to keep all your options open. Christ! I'm not stupid. I know that's why you've insisted on our keeping our separate houses, and it's fine, it's suited me, too — but with a child you can't.

If you take him on, you can't hand him back if it gets too difficult. This is crunch time, Trish.'

First Antony Shelley and now you, she thought. 'Are you saying that I always hedge my bets?' The answer to that was easy once she'd put herself to the question. Of course she did.

'It's only me I can't trust,' she said at last and saw all the tenderness she'd ever wanted in his eyes.

'I know. I've always known that. But, Trish, surely by now you know you're not going to turn into . . . '

'My father? Do I? I might feel safer if I even knew what he is.'

The phone rang. Trish reached for it, hoping it would be Lakeshaw, who'd played his usual game last night. She'd left as detailed a message as she could, and that might have persuaded him she was worth talking to.

'Trish Maguire.'

'They've arrested Paddy,' Bella said, sounding on the edge of hysteria.

The news hit Trish like a punch in the stomach. But with the breathlessness came enough adrenaline to keep her upright.

'Trish, you must help. You must get him out. You will come now, won't you? Trish?

Trish, are you there?'

She couldn't let herself feel anything now. Now, if ever, was the time to behave like a detached professional.

'Hold on, Bella,' she said, clamping down hard on her own instinct to scream. 'We'll do whatever has to be done, but calm down. Has he been charged?'

'He's been arrested, I told you.'

'There's a difference. Has he got a solicitor with him?'

'Yes.'

'Good. That's good. Then they won't be able to trap him into confessing to something he hasn't done.'

Trish felt George's hand on her shoulder and she leaned back, knowing he would be there, supporting her. His arms hugged her and she felt his chin on her head.

'I'll go there at once, but Bella, just tell me: what grounds did they have for an arrest?'

'He was seen leaving the flat that night, when I was zonked out on the sleeping pills. He got into the car and he won't say why or where he went. But they've said something about seeing the car on lots of different CCTV cameras, going towards the victim's flat.'

'Oh, shit!' Deal with it later, Trish, she told

herself. 'Look, don't worry too much. I'll get over there now.'

'But Trish, what about your work?'

'It's fine. I'm not in court today. I've got time. I'll go over there and I'll let you know what happens.'

★   ★   ★

Lakeshaw was re-reading the scientific evidence, waiting for Sergeant Baker to report the result of her first formal interview with Paddy Maguire. He'd asked her to start because she was good at getting suspects to trust her and talk. He'd go in later, if they needed a heavy mob, but for now all he could do was wait.

He wished Jeannie Nest's killer had been less skilled and allowed her to fight back just long enough to scratch the bastard. There was nothing useful under her nails, and the pathologist had said the killer had never touched her with his hands. He'd looped the fabric ligature round her neck from behind and twisted it with some implement, which he'd probably taken away with him. It might have been a long spoon; there was one missing from the set in the kitchen. Then he'd beaten her with the chair that used to stand in front of her desk. It had broken under the assault, and he'd ended up using one of the legs. He'd never touched her himself, and so there were no fluids, prints, or anything else to prove who he'd been.

The only evidence the pathologist hoped would come in useful were the few fibres they'd collected. There were some from Frances Mason's long cerise cotton skirt and some from the plod's uniform, obviously deposited when they'd found the body and Mason had fainted. But among the rest were some brown polyester fibres, which had no counterpart in anything either had been wearing, or in anything else in the flat.

The killer had brushed against the body as he left, the forensic boys thought, and some fibres from his trousers had stuck to the bloody mess he'd made of her face. It was a pity that nothing they'd found in Paddy Maguire's wardrobe or flat had produced fibres that were anything like these. But of course he could've got rid of whatever he'd been wearing at the time. It was exasperating, if not surprising, that nothing had emerged from the search of bins and skips in the vicinity.

'It'll be in the river, probably,' Lakeshaw muttered.

A moment's doubt about Maguire's guilt was soothed by his memory of Frances

Mason's description of the victim's terror of her old boyfriend, and of the CCTV footage of Maguire's car speeding through the empty streets towards Hoxton.

'I wasn't going anywhere special,' Maguire had said when Lakeshaw had confronted him with news of the footage and forced him to admit that the sparklingly clear film did indeed show him in the driving seat. 'I was just moseying about. I couldn't sleep and I didn't want to disturb my companion, who was very tired after several bad nights, so I got up and went for a drive. I can't even remember where I went.'

He'd been lying. Lakeshaw was certain of that. He'd gone somewhere deliberately and felt guilty about it. It was a bugger that the CCTV cameras had only tracked him driving towards Hoxton, then given out before they could have nailed him at the scene of the crime.

One day, thought Lakeshaw, there'd be cameras at every junction — and film in the lot of them — so that anyone and everyone could be tracked from the beginning of every journey to the end, but it hadn't happened yet. They'd caught Paddy Maguire on two garage forecourt cameras, a speed camera that had flashed as he'd bombed past it at fifty-five miles an hour, and that was it, until he'd been filmed driving back towards Kensington an hour later and even faster.

'Sir?'

Lakeshaw looked up and saw DC Martin Waylant looking like a man on his way to the result of an AIDS test. He'd been cleared now of all suspicion that he'd sold Jeannie Nest's new name and address to the Handsome family, but there was no doubting the fact that he'd let her die because he hadn't taken her fears seriously enough. And the gossip that Sergeant Lyalt had belatedly seen fit to pass on might explain why. Waylant already knew how guilty he was, but Lakeshaw had it in mind to rub it in hard enough to leave a permanent reminder so that he would never do anything so fucking irresponsible ever again.

'You sent for me, sir.'

Lakeshaw wondered if he had the strength to keep control of his temper. He nodded, but he wasn't going to ask Waylant to sit down, or shut the door.

'May I sit down?'

'No. I want to know if it's true that you'd been having a sexual relationship with the victim.'

Waylant stumbled and stuttered, flushed the colour of a rotten tomato, then eventually mumbled out an account of an affair that had started in pity, turned into something that mattered to him for a while, then become difficult, and finally made him itch to get away.

'Which is why I thought her last call was a ploy, sir,' he ended up.

'She was old enough to be your mother. What the hell were you thinking of?' As he spoke, Lakeshaw saw a whole new picture of what might have happened to Jeannie Nest, with Waylant himself battering her dead body with a broken chair. The picture grew in his mind, like an email photograph downloading pixel by pixel. Then it shrank back as he reminded himself that Waylant had been on duty on the night of her death, and the records showed exactly where he'd been throughout, and who'd been with him. He hadn't had enough time alone to get to her flat, let alone kill her and mash her body to a pulp.

'Sir, I don't know. It kind of just happened.' Waylant's jaw clenched under the tension. 'So when I heard she was demanding to see me, I thought it was a way of getting me to go back there to the flat so that she could get me into bed again. I . . . ' Now the red in his smooth cheeks was turning grey. 'I didn't know there really was someone after her. You have to believe me.'

'Take me through it from the beginning. She called round, didn't she, the night before she died?'

'Yes, sir. The desk sergeant sent for me and I took her into an interview room. I listened for a bit to her stories about this bloke following her and phoning at all hours. I didn't take notes or put on the tape because, like I said, I was sure it was just a ploy. But I did tell her I'd be round to check out the flat and the places where she was sure she'd seen him, as soon as I could. But I was busy and . . . '

'Embarrassed by her? You've got a real problem here,' Lakeshaw began as the phone rang. He grabbed it, hoping Baker had broken through to Maguire and got something useful.

'Sir? DS Watkins from the front desk, sir. I've a Trish Maguire here, sir. She's very anxious to speak to you, says she has essential information about your case.'

'Tell her you couldn't get hold of me.'

'She says it's really urgent, sir.'

'Take a message. Tell her to go home; I'll get back to her when I can. And if she starts bellowing about her father's rights, remind her he has a solicitor with him.'

Lakeshaw crashed down the phone and looked at Waylant, who was still standing obediently in front of him. Now he looked like a schoolboy awaiting a beating.

'Oh, for Christ's sake, sit down. Right. Now, do something useful for a change and tell me anything you can that will help us nail this bloke.'

'But there isn't anything. Otherwise, I'd have — '

'There must be. Why exactly did you ignore her?'

'Because I'd heard it all before and because after a bit she started to say things like: 'I'm desperate, Martin. I don't know what I'll do if you won't take me seriously. I can't go on like this. It would be easier to be dead. I tell you, I'm desperate.' And I could see she *was* desperate, but I thought it was for . . . '

'Sex, I suppose, you being such an irresistible stud.'

'No, sir.' Waylant looked and sounded defeated. 'Nothing like that, but because she'd clung and cried and told me she couldn't live without me often enough, and sounded just like this. If it hadn't been for all that, we might still have been . . . OK.'

'And she might still be alive,' Lakeshaw said sourly, disliking everything he'd heard.

'D'you think I don't know that? D'you think I'll ever forget it, as long as I live?'

'I hope not.' Lakeshaw wondered when

430

Sergeant Lyalt had first heard of the affair. She'd probably known for weeks. If so, he'd have her guts for garters. It was a crucial piece of evidence that could have saved them days and days of unproductive time.

'So what exactly did the poor cow say that night? Before she started to show her desperation?'

'That's what I've been trying to remember. I've been going over and over it ever since. I think it went like this: 'Martin, he's back. I know it's him. I keep seeing him in the garden now, as well as the street, waiting for when I open the back door to put the cat out. I know he's going to do something soon. I have to put the cat out through the window now, so that he can't force his way past me. Even when I can't see him, I know he's waiting out there somewhere. Please, Martin. I can't go on like this. I know he's going to hurt me soon. Please help. You must. There's no one else.'

'I knew it was nonsense, sir, but she was in such a state that I promised to go round as soon as we had a free moment here. Then when I said she'd have to go home and wait for me, she flung herself at me, clinging and crying about how Michael Handsome was going to kill her and no one cared.'

'Who?' Lakeshaw was on his feet, his hands

bunched into fists again.

Waylant stood, his jaw hanging open, making him look like an idiot. Lakeshaw fought his hands back to his sides.

'Who did she say was going to kill her?'

'Handsome. The bloke she was so scared of. Sir, what is this?'

Lakeshaw watched Waylant's face get even more blank and wondered which of them had lost it.

'She actually told you it was one of the Handsomes?' Waylant nodded. 'Not Paddy Maguire?'

'Who?'

'Paddy Maguire. The man she told Frances Mason all about, who'd beaten her up when she was pregnant, and against whom she'd taken out an injunction.'

'She never said anything about anyone called Maguire, sir. It was always the Handsomes.'

'She *must* have told you about Maguire. According to this Mrs Mason, she was shit scared of him because he'd put her in hospital years ago and was now stalking her.'

'She never said anything to me about any Maguire. She hated mentioning names. But it was the Handsomes she was so scared of. Everyone knows that.'

Lakeshaw felt dizzy with rage that this idiot

hadn't had the guts to come clean in the beginning. 'You're absolutely sure, Waylant, that she never said anything to you about anyone called Maguire?'

'Of course.' Waylant had stopped looking scared; now he was all injured innocence, the little shit. 'I'd have told you that at once if you'd let me speak to you. I've been trying to talk to you for days.'

The phone rang. Lakeshaw picked it up and barked his name into it.

'John Smith here, from Southwark. I think we might have your man for you, Lakeshaw. A pair of brown polyester trousers has come to light with a lot of blood on them.'

'Thank God for that. Where?'

'Well, they belong to Gary Handsome, but they've been found in his mother's flat. He forced her to hide them for him in case we searched his place, as of course we did. I know it'll screw up your time-of-death because he's got that alibi for Tuesday night. But we all know pathologists make mistakes sometimes. He was probably sober enough to have gone round there in the early hours of Wednesday morning.'

'Ah.' Lakeshaw was looking across the desk at Waylant, but seeing only his own mistake.

He was trying to remember if the name of the man who'd terrified Jeannie Nest had ever been mentioned in any of his conversations with Waylant. He was sure it hadn't. He'd never have ignored that. They'd talked about the Handsomes, of course, but only because he'd been trying to get Waylant to confess that he'd taken their money to betray Jeannie Nest.

Once it was clear that he hadn't, Lakeshaw hadn't bothered any more with Waylant, fobbed him off on to Sergeant Baker every time he tried to talk. Then had come the Handsomes' alibis and Frankie Mason's information about Paddy Maguire. Then the CCTV films showing Maguire roaring towards Jeannie Nest's flat, which proved he'd been lying ... Shit! All that wasted time.

'That poor woman,' Smith was saying down the phone into Lakeshaw's half-attending ear. 'She's been so badly beaten and bullied first by her husband then her son until she'd do anything either of them told her. Even hide incriminating evidence for them. Though why she didn't burn the trousers I don't know.'

'Maybe the worm's turned — or been thinking of turning — and she hung on to them to use against him.'

'Maybe.' Smith didn't sound convinced. 'But you'll need to get the lab on to the bloodstains. Will you send someone for the trousers?'

'Straight away. Have you picked up Handsome yet?'

'No. We didn't want to bugger up your plans. D'you want us to arrest him for you? We easily could. We've checked and he's back from wherever he's been hiding.'

'Who knows about the trousers?'

'His nephew, young Michael, who found them and brought them straight in, his mother obviously, but she's in hospital, and three officers.'

Something sprang open in Lakeshaw's mind and he clamped a hand over the phone.

'Waylant, did you say just now that it was *Michael* Handsome who so spooked the victim?'

'Yes, sir.'

Lakeshaw thought of the mummy's boy he'd seen when he'd been round to suss out the Handsome family with one of the local plods. Looking much younger than his almost twenty-one years, little and blond and rubbing his old granny's back. Could he ever have been capable of doing what had been done to Jeannie Nest? Lakeshaw was determined not to let another stupid mistake make itself around him, so he kept his cool.

'That's more than enough,' he said into the

phone. 'Yes, you'd better pick him up right away, and the nephew too, but don't ask any questions yourselves. We don't want the clock running before I've got them here.'

'The nephew's at the hospital, seeing to poor old Lil, who was badly beaten up this morning.'

'He's what?'

'He was collecting stuff for her when he found the trousers, brought them straight round. He's a good lad, and told us all about his uncle and how he'd threatened the old girl. Mikey looks after her, you know.'

Lakeshaw put down the phone without another word and ran, bellowing for Sergeant Baker as he went. He caught sight of Trish Maguire in the front hall, arguing with the desk sergeant, and took a moment to tell them both that she could see her father.

'Where are you going?' she asked.

'I can't stop to explain. Talk to your father. I'll sort out the formalities later.'

★　★　★

Mikey was sitting by his nan's bed with the case under his feet. It had all gone well at the police station. They'd taken the trousers and practically wet themselves in gratitude. He knew they'd soon find that there was blood from two women on them, but that wouldn't matter. It might even help the story. Gal's Wanstead victim had probably reported the assault — or at least gone to hospital to get herself patched up — so once they really started looking they'd track her down. And unlike Miss Nest, she was still alive to identify her attacker. It would all fit. Gal had done her two days before the murder. They'd think it'd just got him feeling excited and brave enough to do what he'd always talked about: have his revenge on the woman who'd put his old man inside.

Mikey'd had to waste quite a bit of time 'explaining' how he'd found the trousers, but he was here now. And not before time, he could see. His nan was white as paper and her face was kind of sunk in, so that she looked even older than she was. Her eyes were closed and her mouth looked crumpled. Her body was all tied up to machines and there was a bag hanging beside the bed. He knew from the red in it that they had got her kidney. And he knew what that meant.

The doctor had taken him on one side and warned him months ago that any more punishment and it'd give out. At first Mikey couldn't think what he was talking about when he said that Mrs Handsome ought to stop riding the motorbike now and playing rugby. But eventually it had dawned on him that the bloke was making a feeble joke. Once that was out of the way, they'd had a serious talk about how dangerous it would be for her to risk any more damage to the kidney. It could be as little as a bad fall on her back, say, downstairs. If that was true, it meant that a kicking like this might be fatal.

It didn't need the nurses being so kind and telling him they'd made sure she wasn't in pain, or keeping away from them to give him time alone with her, to tell him she was dying. He'd known that if her remaining kidney went she was done for.

'Be careful what you ask for; you may get it,' Miss Nest always used to say when they were talking after school. 'You could do anything and go anywhere and be anyone, Michael, but be careful what you ask for; you may get it.'

Well, he'd got the money now, and his uncle wouldn't be troubling him for a long, long time. He could go anywhere, do anything, be anyone, just like she'd always said. But just like she'd said, he might not want it when he'd got it. With his nan dead he'd have lost everyone he'd ever cared about. A tear trickled down his face, like a fly walking down it. He pushed it off, but then another came and another.

He wished his grandmother's eyes would open. He picked up her hand and stroked it, but there was no movement from her. He wanted to hear her say, 'You're a good boy, Mikey,' like she always did. But today her lips were lying thin and slack against her teeth. It was odd seeing her without her red lipstick. Her mouth looked pale purple, as though she was dead already, but he could hear her rattly breathing and see her chest rising under the thin blankets.

'Nan . . .'

She didn't answer.

'Nan.' Nothing moved except for the rhythmic lifting and collapsing of the bedclothes over her chest. 'I only wanted to talk to her.'

It didn't seem fair. Miss Nest had been the one person who'd believed in him in the days before his nan even knew who he was. His slag of a mother couldn't be bothered with him and his dad just clouted him whenever he was out of prison, and all the boys at school had picked on him because he was small and pretty. But his teacher had listened to him and liked him, encouraged him to work and taught him how to protect himself from the bullies. And then she'd gone and given evidence against his grandad.

Like Gal and his grandad, he'd hated her

for grassing them up, but he'd hated her much more for running away and leaving him to the useless teachers he'd had after her. They'd all known who he was and what his family was, and they'd treated him as though he was like the rest, good for nothing, which was why his nan had eventually sent him to her sister in the fucking country. Older now, and a lot more sensible, Mikey could put the blame squarely on his grandad, but at the time it had felt as though everything was Miss Nest's fault. If she'd kept her mouth shut, they'd all have been OK. And she'd have stayed at the school and seen him through to the kind of life he'd deserved all along.

He hadn't believed it when he'd seen her in the street, only minutes from the estate one Sunday when he'd been coming back from an all-night cabbing shift. He'd known her at once, in spite of her short dyed hair and spectacles, and he'd been amazed at the excitement he felt. He wanted to talk to her, to tell her that he was going to be someone after all, to hear her talk to him again like she used to do. There'd been a small boy with her, and Mikey had followed them back to Hoxton.

He looked down at his nan's unresponsive face. Her wild grey hair offended him, just like it would've offended her. He smoothed it back around her head. She didn't wake. Another tear crawled down his skin.

'That's better, Nan,' he said, wiping it off. 'It was the way Miss Nest tossed her head back that I recognised first. But I watched her for a while to make sure. And when I was sure, I went to say hi. But she wouldn't talk to me. She pretended she didn't know who I was, and every time she'd push past me without saying anything. That was at first. Later, when I phoned up to explain I only wanted to talk, she swore at me. D'you know, she once told me to fuck off?'

The tears were falling faster now. He borrowed the corner of the bedsheet to wipe his face.

He wanted to tell his nan how it happened. She'd have understood, he knew that. He hadn't told her before because it wouldn't have been fair. She had enough on her plate what with Gal and everything without having to worry about her beloved Mikey maybe being arrested. But now she was dying it was different.

He'd gone round the back of Miss Nest's new garden flat because he knew that door would be easier, than the front and he'd broken in, all quiet like because he knew now she'd never let him in herself. He'd soon realised she must be in her lounge because of the music. He'd taken off his shoes by the back door so as not to bring in any dirt and bent down to lay them quietly on the mat.

★　★　★

She was lying on the floor in the lounge, on her back with her hands under her head and all the music pouring over her. Mikey watched for a while, liking the look on her face. He liked seeing all the books she'd always had in her old place, too, and the Mexican guitar hanging on the wall with its bright strap.

'Hello, Miss,' he said at last and saw her face gathering up into a knot of hate.

She was on her feet quicker than anyone her age should've been able to move, and he could see she was going for the panic button. It looked huge and red as he judged the distance between it and her hand. He had to stop her pressing it, so that he'd have time to make her understand that he only wanted to talk. He grabbed for her dress and missed it, but he got her scarf, both ends of it to hold her back from the panic button. She was shouting by then, so he wound it tighter and tighter round her neck until she was quiet and still. He hadn't meant her to die. He'd only wanted to talk.

442

The CD stopped eventually and the flat was very quiet. Then the cat came in and started crying. And cars passed and a noisy empty lorry, banging as it bounced over a bump in the road. He had to get some more noise going in here before one of the neighbours suspected something. He was still wearing the surgical gloves he'd used when he was breaking in so he just picked up another CD, the nearest one, and put it on while he thought about what to do next.

The idea came as he stood there, looking at her swollen face and trying not to move in case he left any evidence on the carpet or on her body. He'd seen the films and he knew how they could work out who'd been at a scene of crime just from fibres. So he'd backed away, as careful as the howling cat, and shut the back door.

★   ★   ★

It hadn't been hard to fake enough mini-cab jobs to cover the time it took to get back to Southwark — everyone was always faking dockets and accounts anyway for the tax and all that — and get his uncle's trousers from their hiding place. He'd kept them in their brown paper till he was back at Jeannie's place. Then he'd put them on, still wearing

443

his gloves, and picked up her chair and smashed at her body till the chair broke and then smashed again with just the legs, making sure that the blood spurted all over the trousers and that he wiped both legs of the trousers against the body.

'And it didn't hurt her, Nan,' he said, the tears trickling back down his face. 'She couldn't feel it, so it didn't matter. It was the only way.'

The door opened and a young nurse looked in, and smiled.

'Don't worry so much,' she said, handing him a bunch of Kleenex from the box on his nan's table. 'It looks much worse than it is.'

'What?'

'She'll be fine in a few days. The doctors have given her some very strong painkillers because it was such a bad beating. At her age they don't want her suffering. But she'll be up and about again in no time. You'll see.'

'But her kidney. There's all that blood in her urine.' He pointed down at the bag, swinging gently from the metal frame of the bed.

'I know. And that's what was worrying them most. But they think it'll be all right. She won't need the catheter once she's up and about again.' The nurse smiled. 'She's tough, your grandmother. We'll be putting her back in the main ward later on today. And any minute now she'll wake up and eat her dinner. You'll see. She's got a good appetite, hasn't she?'

Mikey looked back at his nan in horror and saw her eyelids twitch and the eyeballs beneath them move wildly from side to side. He didn't think they did that when you were unconscious.

'Thanks,' he whispered to the nurse, not looking away from his nan's face.

'That's OK. I'll look in again in about half an hour. She'll be ready for her dinner by then.'

He waited until the nurse was well out of sight, then he said strongly, 'Nan! Nan, I know you can hear me.'

'You're a *good* boy, Mikey, to come and see me like this,' she whispered. 'I didn't know you was here.'

'Oh, yes you did. And you heard it all, didn't you?'

'Heard what?' she said, licking her lips and trying to look puzzled. But he'd seen her with the police. He knew she could turn it on whenever she wanted. He'd seen the future now and he couldn't go back, even if he could've trusted her. That would've been way too dangerous. He smiled and said he'd better rearrange her pillows. She didn't look comfortable at all.

'I'm fine,' she said, her eyes getting bigger and her breaths shorter. 'I'm fine. Mikey, leave me be. The nurses can do anything that needs doing. Don't you fret about me.'

'I'm not fretting, Nan. It'll be easy, you'll see,' he said. He didn't have a choice, not now. He moved round the bed so he had his back to the glass bit in the door, pulled out two pillows from behind her messy grey head. Her shaking hand was reaching out, just like Jeannie Nest's, towards the bell. He pulled it clear and laid her arm neatly down by her side before he pressed the pillows over her face.

She started to thrash about, making far too much noise. He leaned harder. The plastic tube from her arm slapped his hand and he nearly hit her. Then something else touched him and he heard a voice say, 'Now, now. Let her go, son.'

Someone pulled him off and took the pillows from his nan's face. It wasn't papery now; it was bright red and she was coughing and gasping.

'You little shit.' She spat out the words between heaving coughs. 'You're worse than all the others.'

'Michael Handsome,' said a man's voice

446

behind him, 'I'm arresting you on suspicion of . . . '

He didn't hear the rest, staring at his nan's face. Now she hated him, too. There were tears streaming down his face. It wasn't fair.

Epilogue

Trish breathed carefully and settled her gown more elegantly across her shoulders, thin as a coathanger now because she hadn't been eating much the past few days. George was getting worried again, but he knew how she hated him pushing food at her just before a case, so he'd let her alone.

'I'm ready.'

'Fine. And it's agreed, is it, that I'll deal with all the financial cross-examination, and you'll tackle the personal stuff?'

'You're not really asking me, Antony, are you?'

'No.' He laughed. 'But an order always seems so much more civilised when it's phrased as a question. Feeling all right, Trish?'

'Never better. I slept fantastically well last night.' She saw the derisive glint in his eye that said 'liar'. 'Ah, good, there's Nick. D'you want to go and say hello?'

'No, Trish, you'll do it much better. Think of him as one of your damaged children and be nice to him.'

'Yes, maestro,' she said drily and enjoyed

his laugh. Maybe this would be all right. She moved across the lobby towards Nick Gurles, who was standing beside Peter Loyle, looking like a model of calm confidence. 'Nick! Good to see you.'

'Trish, you're looking gorgeous.' He bent and kissed her cheek, whispering, 'What happens if I throw up in court?'

'Try very hard not to,' she said seriously. 'It'll be fine, Nick. Really. Antony knows what he's doing. None better.' She nodded to Peter Loyle, whom she hadn't yet forgiven for keeping the memo from her in the first place, and went back to find Antony exchanging witticisms about skiing with the plaintiffs' silk, Henry Falkowski.

The doors to the court opened and an usher stood there.

'We're off,' Antony said. They walked side by side into court, not equals — they would probably never be that — but on the same side and with the same intentions at last.

Nick wasn't sick and there was very little for Trish to do. Once the judge rose for the day, Antony led his small team back to chambers for a combination of post mortem and planning. When they'd settled everything, and Peter Loyle had left with the client, Antony invited Trish to have a drink with him.

'On any other night, I'd love it,' she said, 'but my brother's moving in this evening, so I have to get back.'

'I didn't know you had a brother. What does he do?'

'He's going to be eight the day after tomorrow. He's a new acquisition.'

'The number of stories you keep behind that white face of yours would rival Scheherezade's. I look forward to hearing this one in due course. Anyway, I'm glad my hunch about you and your capacities was right. See you tomorrow.'

Trish rushed back across the bridge, determined to check everything one last time before David arrived. His bedroom was all ready, with the books whose titles Lakeshaw had given her from a quick study of the scene-of-crime photographs, and a few others, some that she'd loved as a child and some that thoughtful friends who were also parents had advised her to get for him. There was apple juice in the fridge and biscuits and all the things she thought he might like.

'Nervous?' George said.

'Aren't you?'

'Terrified,' he said, but he laughed and seemed infinitely more confident than she was. But then there was nothing new in that.

'George, you won't let David make any

450

difference to us, will you?'

'Not to the core of us, Trish. But you know as well as I do that his presence in our lives will change things.'

The phone rang before she could say anything. It was Caro, returning Trish's call. Trish explained what she and George had decided to do about David, adding at the end, 'So Caro, we were wondering whether you and Jess would be his godmothers.'

'Are you sure? It's a huge honour. Hang on and I'll have a quick word with Jess.'

Trish turned to report to George, who was pretending to read the paper. He folded up the sports section and sat waiting.

'She'd love it, Trish. We've both got goddaughters, but no godsons. This will be a treat as well as an honour. She's longing to meet him, and I'd love to see him again. He's a sweet child. And he's come through so much.'

'Great,' Trish said, encouraged. 'We'll fix a time for you to meet, once he and George have got to know each other a bit better.'

'Where are you all going to live?'

Trish didn't flinch, although it was still a difficult subject. 'We're going to start off here, with George keeping Fulham, then, once we've seen how things are going and David's had a chance to settle, we'll look for somewhere for the three of us.'

She felt George's hands on her waist and leaned back a little. His lips brushed her bare neck, just below the hairline.

'Caro, I've got to go now. They'll be here any minute, and there are things to do.' George's hands tightened around her waist.

'Before you go, Trish, what about your father?'

'It's going to be a long time before he's forgiven any of us. He even seems bitterly angry with David, just for existing. That's probably only guilt coming out as rage, but David's too young to understand it, so I'm keeping them separate for the moment.'

'I'm sorry for my part in it all. You know that, don't you, Trish?'

'Of course. Otherwise, I'd never have wanted you as David's godmother. And it wasn't you, after all, who arrested Paddy. That was sodding Lakeshaw.'

'If it's any consolation, Trish, he hasn't done himself any favours either. Rather too many influential people have heard about the cock-up he made over the interviews with DC Waylant. But I don't suppose even Lakeshaw would've arrested your father if it hadn't been for the CCTV films of him driving that night.'

'I know,' Trish said. 'Paddy played his own

452

part in what happened to him. He knows that, too. We'll get it all sorted in the end. Bella will help. She's so saintly that she's forgiven him his nocturnal wanderings — did I tell you he'd been off bonking someone else? — and she doesn't seem to mind the idea of David, so she may be able to effect a rapprochement. I hope so.'

George's hands were moving now and his lips setting up a trail of tingling around the back of Trish's neck and shoulders.

'Caro, I really have to go. Give my love to Jess.'

George turned her round as she clicked off the phone and dropped it on the sofa.

'We haven't much time,' Trish said.

'We'll always have time,' George said, stroking the tops of her thighs again. 'You shouldn't worry so much, Trish. All will be well. You'll see.'

We do hope that you have enjoyed reading this large print book.

Did you know that all of our titles are available for purchase?

We publish a wide range of high quality large print books including:
Romances, Mysteries, Classics
General Fiction
Non Fiction and Westerns

Special interest titles available in large print are:
The Little Oxford Dictionary
Music Book
Song Book
Hymn Book
Service Book

Also available from us courtesy of Oxford University Press:
Young Readers' Dictionary
(large print edition)
Young Readers' Thesaurus
(large print edition)

For further information or a free brochure, please contact us at:
Ulverscroft Large Print Books Ltd.,
The Green, Bradgate Road, Anstey,
Leicester, LE7 7FU, England.
Tel: (00 44) 0116 236 4325
Fax: (00 44) 0116 234 0205

PLAIN DEALER

William Ardin

Antique dealing has its own equivalent to 'insider trading', as Charles Ramsay finds out to his cost. Offered the purchase of a lifetime, he sees all his ambitions realised in an antique jade cup, known as the 'Loot'. But as soon as the deal is irrevocably struck he finds himself stuck with it like an albatross around his neck — unable to export it without a licence, unable to sell it at home, and in a paralysing no man's land where nobody has sufficient capital to take it off his hands . . .

NO TIME LIKE THE PRESENT

June Barraclough

Daphne Berridge, who has never married, has retired to the small Yorkshire village of Heckcliff where she grew up, intending to write the biography of an eighteenth-century woman poet. Two younger women are interested in her project: Cressida, Daphne's niece, who lives in London, and is uncertain about the direction of her life; and Judith, who keeps a shop in Heckcliff, and is a divorcee. When an old friend of Daphne falls in love with Judith, the question — as for Cressida — is marriage or independence. Then Daphne also receives a surprise proposal.

SEARCH FOR A SHADOW

Kay Christopher

On the last day of her holiday Rosemary Roberts met an intriguing American in the foyer of her London hotel. By some extraordinary coincidence, Larry Madison-Jones was due to visit the tiny Welsh village where Rosemary lived. But how much of a coincidence was Larry's erratic presence there? The moment Rosemary returned home, her life took on a subtle, though sinister edge — Larry had a secret he was not willing to share. As Rosemary was drawn deeper into a web of mysterious and suspicious occurrences, she found herself wondering if Larry really loved her — or was trying to drive her mad . . .

THREE WISHES

Barbara Delinsky

Slipping and sliding in the snow as she walks home from the restaurant where she's worked for fourteen years, Bree Miller barely has time to notice the out-of-control lorry, headed straight for her. All Bree remembers of that fateful night is a bright light, and a voice granting her three wishes. Are they real or imagined? And who is the man standing over her bedside when finally she wakes up? Soon Bree finds herself the recipient of precisely those things she'd most wanted in life — even that which had seemed beyond all reasonable hope.

WEB OF WAR

Hilary Grenville

Claire Grant, a radar operator in the WAAF, still mourning the death of her parents and brother in an air raid, finds coming on leave to her grandmother's home difficult to face. Martin, a friend from her school days, now a pilot in the RAF, helps her to come to terms with her grief and encourages the flimsy rapport between Claire and her grandmother. War rules their lives and it is some time before they meet again. Claire is in love, but there are many quirks of fate yet to be faced.

SUSAN IN AMERICA

Jane Aiken Hodge

Susan has high hopes of her American trip. Shy and studious at Oxford, she felt herself always on the outside of things there. Surely everything will be different at Radcliffe College, where she has a year's fellowship. But in New England she is lonelier than ever. Her tutorials with glamorous Professor Winter soon become the high points of her week, but when their intellectual cut and thrust leads on to passion, she finds herself in uncharted waters, risking shipwreck among the strict conventions of 1930s Boston society.